FLIGHT THROUGH INFINITY

D. R. HILL

Dedication

To my dad,
Thank you for always being my biggest supporter and greatest fan.

This is for you.

CONTENTS

ONE

The Nomad was alone. The universe in its entire enormity stretched endlessly beyond comprehension. But the infinity was empty. Pinpricks of existence dotted the eternal infinitude, yet the vast distances between the isolated systems were nothing but darkness and oblivion; the silence of the infinite void was absolute and unending. The Universe was cold. The Universe was dark. The Universe was silent. The Nomad was alone.

The Nomad stirred suddenly as the silence was broken. He roused from terrifying slumber, but no nightmares had plagued his sleep; so long had passed since he had dreamt that now the very concept of dreaming seemed abstract. The Nomad yearned for nightmares, for any fleeting image, no matter how insignificant, to come to him in his sleep. Instead, his sleep was haunted by the silence of existence, something infinitely more harrowing. Within that silence, he feared he might cease to exist altogether. Perhaps he already had; what his life had become was hardly existence.

The Nomad wearily shook the darkness from his thoughts and gazed about the cockpit, at the surrounding assortment of dials and readouts. The high-pitched beeping that had awoken him continued to sound. He had heard it hundreds, possibly thousands of times before, but his mind was still whirring in the haze of hypnagogia; he glanced dazedly around at the myriad of buttons and controls blinking beneath the glow of a holographic interface, finally turning his attention to the correct switch. Flicking it, he silenced the alarm. The power cells were charged.

The Nomad fumbled for his canteen floating in the footwell. Unscrewing the seal from the canister, he took a sip of fluid before lulling his head back against the headrest. He gazed out of the cockpit, into the infinity through which he was drifting. Millions of stars and galaxies shimmered faintly in twisting constellations; they shone sapphire, silver, amber, and crimson, immense clouds of dust diffusing their light in murky hues of bronze and umber. It was beautiful. It was daunting. And it was terrifying.

Flicking another switch on the dashboard, the Nomad initiated collapse of the solar panels. He peered out the canopy at the mirror-like cells, the panels glimmering with reflected starlight as they began to smoothly contract and fold inwards. Within moments, the photovoltaic modules had fully retracted, concealed now within the wings of the Fighter. The Nomad turned his attention to the main interface of the instruments panel, booting up the core systems. A momentary lag in the worn circuitry delayed the powering up, but within a few seconds, the cockpit lit up with a cacophony of read-outs. Sifting through the flight computer with lazy swipes of his hand, the Nomad navigated to the system scanners, initiating every option available within the menus.

He sat and watched the displays tick over, an array of instruments and scanners powering up each in turn, beginning to survey the solar system in immense complexity. The scans, as they always did, took hours to run. The Nomad drifted back into sleep for a time, awakening now and then to grimace at the dwindling energy readouts from the Fighter's power cells. The scans had always been power-intensive, but the power cells were worn, holding only a fraction of the charge that they once had; they were coming to the end of their lifespan, and it had been far too long since the Nomad had been able to replace any of them.

When the scans were finally complete and the last of the scientific instruments had powered down, the Nomad begrudgingly reopened the Fighter's solar panels to top up on charge. Turning his attention to the results of the scans, he rapidly scrolled over the complex data, sifting with efficient and well-trained acuity through the hundreds of figures and graphs. He was disappointed, such as he always was; in all the time he had lived this way, he had still not yet been able to rid himself of the disease of expectant optimism. The data was congruent with his long-range scans, yet in spite of this he had hoped that the system would be more promising. But it did not matter. It never did. His situation was still the same, and so was his routine.

The Nomad rapidly tapped a brief sequence of buttons, before throwing a series of switches. Carrying out his pre-flight checks, he examined the needles on an array of dials and analysed all the information projecting across the digital holograms. Folding away the solar cells for a second time, he primed the pulsejets and engaged the antimatter fuel tanks. Taking hold of the flightstick, the Nomad deftly rotated the Fighter, the arcjets of the reaction control system firing in a staccato of puffs to swivel the ship around its central axis. The nose of the Fighter pivoted gently, the stars blurring across the outside of the canopy as its pilot adjusted both pitch and yaw.

The glare of a distant class K yellow sun reacted with the photochromic glass of the canopy as it swung into view, polarising it to a dark tint. With a short burn of the arcjets, the Nomad neutralised the Fighter's spin, stabilising the ship. Gently, he palmed the thruster and the pulsejets engaged. Equal quantities of antimatter and matter flooded the combustion chamber, colliding to annihilate one another in perfect symmetry, producing vast quantities of energy, channelled and expelled through the nozzles of the pulsejets.

The Nomad sank back in his seat as impetus took hold. His weight doubled, then quadrupled, and finally octupled under the intense acceleration. His breathing rasped as his chest collapsed, and his vision faded and darkened, all the while his fingers remained locked around the thrust lever. He held on, bracing against the staggering forces exerting on his body, finally drawing back his arm with dwindling strength, easing off the thruster. The weight gradually lifted from behind his eyes, and air flowed once more into his lungs. The pulsejets disengaged and his body returned to weightlessness. The Fighter glided rapidly, but almost imperceptibly, through the vacuum of space, towards the heart of the solar system.

Hours passed as the Fighter continued to streak a line through the blackness. The Nomad watched numbers tick over on his displays as the astronomical units to his destination slowly dwindled. He powered down the majority of the ship's systems to conserve power, even going so far as to disengage the autopilot. He sat watching the burning orb of yellow plasma steadily swell, every so often nudging and rotating the joystick to correct his pitch and yaw. Each correction was followed by a short burst from his pulsejets, but the alterations to his flight path were minute; for the most part, the Nomad stared steadily ahead through the tinted glass at an almost indiscernibly changing scene.

The Nomad had come to accept boredom for

what it was long ago. Now he welcomed it. Boredom meant familiarity. Familiarity meant routine. Routine meant little complication. The Nomad lived for routine. Routine was all he had, and as monotonous as it had become, it meant he was still alive. Change was the unknown. The unknown was dangerous.

Eventually, a point of light emerged out of the glare of the star's corona, progressively enlarging to a crescent of reflected starlight. The Nomad adjusted yaw, centring the planet in his tracking as he systematically booted up the various flight systems onboard the Fighter. A last burst from his pulsejets set him on final course as he watched the navigation computer calculate an approach vector for orbital insertion.

A mauve gas giant loomed large ahead. Surrounding the planet, a scattering of small frozen satellites shimmered in the light of the yellow sun. The Nomad pulled back on his joystick and the arcjets swivelled the Fighter back a full one-eighty degrees. He shifted the stick swiftly forwards to cancel out the revolution. Now facing away from the rapidly approaching planetary system, the Nomad shoved the thruster, initiating the pulsejets for a hard burn. Antimatter and matter reacted again, the exhausts expelling a white jet of energy that translated directly into force. The Nomad was pressed powerfully backward into his chair once more. His chest tightened and his vision tunnelled in the immense prolonged deceleration. When his relative speed fell to within approach parameters, he killed the thrusters and was jolted suddenly back into buoyancy. Deftly pivoting the Fighter back round, the curved horizons of the giant planetary body filled the window of the canopy.

The Nomad rolled the Fighter, dropped pitch, and the planet scudded overhead. Delivering a short series of bursts from the pulsejets, the Nomad lined up for his final approach. A singular last kick of acceleration ensnared him within the gas giant's powerful gravitational field, perpetually dragging the Fighter over the horizon as it was captured in orbit. As the Nomad was carried around to the sunward-facing hemisphere, he gazed up at the swirling bands of cloud effervescing throughout the soupy atmosphere.

Checking the decay of his orbit, the Nomad powered down nonessential systems and briefly studied the planet's magnetic field readings. His scanners indicated moderate levels of antimatter captured by the powerful magnetosphere, channelled by the field lines into the gas giant's inner radiation belt. The Nomad engaged a series of switches and began deployment of the antimatter collection coils. The mechanical groan of hydraulics sounded throughout the cockpit as four magnetically charged coils rose from beneath covered ports in the Fighter's hull, telescopically extending outwards from the fuselage. The familiar clicking of the electromagnets powering up sounded, and as the coils extended to full length, the noise was replaced by a gentle hum.

The conductors were energy intensive, taxing the reserves of the power cells, but in this case, the rapid depletion in charge was a price worth paying; as the power cells' energy levels began to plummet, the needle of the fuel gauge steadily climbed. Antimatter ensnared in the planet's radiation belt was drawn inwards by the magnetic field of the collection coils, funnelled towards the craft, and fed into the Fighter's fuel tank as the miniscule ship sailed around the planet in orbit.

As the Fighter steadily refuelled, floating silently across the daylit hemisphere, the Nomad reclined and watched the upper atmosphere of the gas giant drift below him. In a matter of moments, his orbit had carried the Fighter over the terminator, across the thin line of twilight, to the dark side of the planet beyond. In the shadow of night, the tempestuous skies flashed with silent streaks of lightning, momentarily illuminating the gargantuan cyclones of gas. Before long, the eternal freefall of orbit had swung the Fighter back around to the daytime side of the strange world, delivering him thereafter back to night in a perpetual rapid diurnal cycle, all the while, the gas giant slowly revolved on its own axis. After several scores of orbits and a half turn of the planet, a diode above the fuel gauge illuminated; the tanks were full.

The Nomad reverted a half dozen switches

and the electromagnets' low drone subsided to the sound of retracting hydraulics. The collection coils stowed themselves and the port covers locked shut. The Nomad brought up the flight computer interface once again and one by one examined the satellites encircling the gas giant. Carefully studying their orbits, rotation, mass, density, and predicted elemental compositions each in turn, he selected what seemed the most prosperous candidate, and instructed the flight computer to plot a course to insert the Fighter within the tiny moon's orbit. The computer clicked and jarred into its calculations before producing a series of potential results. Choosing the flight path that best balanced time and fuel-efficiency, the Nomad adjusted the Fighter's pitch and rotation and initiated a short burn of the pulsejets. The small spurt of acceleration seemed at first to barely alter the Fighter's orbit, yet as the ship drifted around to the darkened face of the gas giant, the planet was receding from view.

Still hooked within the immense gravity well, the Fighter yielded to the forces manipulating its freefall, rapidly slowing in its drift away from the planet, coming to a brief moment of inertia before the inevitable tug of the gas giant began to draw the tiny ship inwards again. The Fighter accelerated as it plummeted towards the crescent of sunlight on the planet's far horizon and picked up speed as it slingshotted around to the daytime hemisphere. Hurtling across the mauve sunlit face of the gas world, the Fighter was flung outwards again on the precipice of orbital escape, thrown on its trajectory even further away from the gas giant in a vast sweeping arc. Still beholden however to the tug of the colossal gaseous sphere below, the craft slowed again at the peak of its parabola and began to drop for a third and final pass, this time swooping so close to the gas giant that it tore through the thin veil of the thermosphere. The Nomad's ship juddered as wisps of air ripped across the fuselage, but in seconds, the gas planet was receding again. The Fighter launched outwards, nearly attaining escape velocity altogether as it soared away into a far-flung orbit.

The Nomad gazed ahead as his craft sailed distantly above the gas giant, sighting a mote of light as it emerged faintly from out of the dark. The miniscule glimmer swelled across the canopy, revealing itself to be an aspherical satellite of ice and dust. The irregular-shaped moon tumbled slowly end over end, hanging suspended in distant orbit, swept up by the tidal forces of the behemoth world below. Closing in fast, the Nomad swivelled the ship backwards and fired the pulsejets to decelerate. The Fighter slowed, and with a tilt of the flightstick, the Nomad spun back to face the moon's scarred and pitted surface.

Craters sat within craters, jagged bluffs and mesas rose vertically out of smooth plains, and canyons carved through the ice and rock, snaking in great fissures across the glinting lunar surface. Each feature spoke of a violent past: an asteroid captured by the inescapable grip of the gas giant's gravity well, locked now eternally in a cold and distant orbit around its remote adoptive world. A wispy tail of gas and dust trailed behind the moon's orbit, shed from the satellite, as each time it emerged from the shadow of its celestial parent, its surface heated and sublimated under sun exposure. The Fighter drifted into the shimmering tail and a gentle crackling sounded throughout the cockpit, millions of microscopic flecks of dust and ice clattering against the glass of the canopy.

The crackling faded, the Fighter drifting out the far side of the tail to the outer circumference of the moon's orbit. As he drew closer to the tumbling ice ball, the Nomad glimpsed down at the silvery surface. A speck of shadow swept rapidly over the hills and valleys below, growing ever larger as the Fighter descended towards the ground. Inverting the ship upside down, the Nomad lifted up on the joystick, firing all the arcjets on the underside of the craft. The gentle nudge of thrust propelled the Fighter downwards and the ship began to slowly decrease in altitude, approaching the moon's surface.

Pivoting the Fighter back upright, the Nomad made several adjustments to the controls, orientating the craft for the impending touchdown. Drawing a stiff lever downward, he listened to the whirr of hydraulics as the Fighter's landing gear deployed from the undercarriage. Cautiously tweaking the flightstick, his other hand firmly clasping the thruster, the Nomad deftly guided the Fighter lower. The ship hung aloft, remaining suspended by intermittent bursts from the arcjets as the Nomad scoured the landscape below from his cockpit in search of a suitable landing zone.

Finally, the Nomad steered the Fighter down toward a smooth crater basin. A long gentle burn slowed the craft as it eased down into a plume of dust. The landing skids contacted the silver regolith and the dampeners softened the touch down.

The Nomad powered down the reaction control system and arcjets, and as the dust settled, he took a long moment to gaze about the alien landscape surrounding him. The black star-speckled sky cut a stark line of contrast across the horizon, rising against the white shimmering terrain below. Potholes and boulders seen from above now took form in their true scales, standing as vast ravines and sheer mountains carved from the barren lunar surface. As the minute moon continued to tumble in its orbit, the gargantuan orb of the mauve gas giant emerged steadily over the onward horizon, rising upwards from behind the rim of the crater.

The Nomad reached beneath his legs and pulled his helmet from under the seat. Placing it over his head, he locked it into his collar bearing, sealing his extravehicular activity suit. He toggled a button on the helmet and a gold-coated solar visor slid down across his face. Checking his EVA suit's power supplies, the Nomad powered on the rig, watching as the internal heads-up-display projected onto the inner visor. Turning his attention to the control panel before him, the Nomad rotated a safety valve and depressed a series of buttons, initiating decompression of the cockpit.

A claxon buzzed throughout the cockpit, swiftly accompanied by the loud hissing of evacuating air, but as the pressure dropped, the tumult diminished to the eerie quietude of a vacuum, until all the Nomad could hear was his own rasping breath inside the confines of his helmet. The Nomad lifted a final handle on the control panel and the Fighter's canopy rose smoothly and silently, retracting from the cockpit, exposing the Nomad to the raw emptiness of space. Unclipping the harness across his chest, the Nomad climbed cautiously out of his seat and stood. Taking several moments to familiarise himself with his weight in the microgravity environment, he kicked off from the floor of his cockpit, rising upwards in a controlled but high-soaring bound. The red and white battle-scarred Fighter receded beneath him as he sailed along the upward arc of his trajectory, before finally, several metres above the cockpit, the weak tug of the moon began his leisurely fall. His boots connected with the silver regolith and a cloud of dirt kicked up around him as he landed gently beside his Fighter. Waiting a prolonged moment for the dust to finally settle, the Nomad strode a bobbing circumference around his ship as he visually inspected the fuselage.

The half dozen laser burns were continuing to fade from radiation exposure, along with the Fighter's colouration itself. The nose of the Fighter was looking worse than ever, stripped of all its paint by millions of micrometeorite impacts. The warped front skid of his landing gear was still going strong; so long as he was careful, the damage shouldn't get any worse. The recent weld on the starboard wing was holding up well, and ducking beneath the undercarriage, the Nomad examined the array of scientific equipment and scanners he had outfitted to the Fighter. All were still in good operational condition and remained firmly attached to the hull by their makeshift housing and brackets.

Finally, the Nomad turned his attention to the antimatter tank expansion and its accompanying shielding jury-rigged to the aft end of the undercarriage. Several new dimples, no doubt micrometeorite collisions, had appeared since the last inspection, yet overall, the plating and electromagnetic shielding coils were still serviceably protecting the canisters from the perils of spaceflight. Irrespective, the integrity of the tank expansion did little to reassure the Nomad. He wasn't happy with the modification; he never had been. Even after all this time with no incident, he felt little reassurance by the simple fact that they had held out to date.

Expanding the volume of the antimatter tanks beyond the outer hull, outside of the ship's armoured fuselage and electromagnetic shielding field, was an act of insanity. It was an accident waiting to happen. One that would inevitably spell disaster, if not instant and utter oblivion. But the Nomad had had no choice; or so he had convinced himself. It was the only conceivable way of effectively extending the ship's range. Without doing so, he would have died of old age long before he ever reached his destination. Even still, and even with all of the precautions he had taken to safeguard the tanks, the Nomad felt uneasy whenever he thought about them.

The tanks housed the most volatile and destructive substance in the universe, annihilating regular matter instantly on contact. The resulting reaction was the direct conversion of mass into energy at an exponential rate. The products: high energy gamma rays and a stream of exotic particles. When controlled and directed, they provided the immense thrust necessary for the near relativistic speeds achieved in spaceflight. When uncontrolled but still directed, the reaction produced devastating weapons of war. If both uncontrolled and undirected, the end result was only ever disaster. Even so much as a microscopic rupture in the antimatter tanks would see both the Nomad, the Fighter, and anything else within a suitably vast radius, utterly and entirely annihilated. This simple truth haunted the Nomad. He had fought so long and so hard for his continued existence; the notion of that existence balancing so precariously on the integrity of a few millimetres of alloy seemed like a cruel vindictive mockery. But, as the Nomad reminded himself: he had had no choice.

TWO

The Nomad ducked beneath the portside wing of his Fighter and manually unfastened the cargo pod clamps. In such low gravity, there was no need to operate the lowering hydraulics; the pod weighed so little, that with nothing more than his own strength, he was able to lower the cargo capsule softly to the ground. As it descended gently from the wing, the Nomad delivered a sharp horizontal tug to the pod, in this instance its mass mattering, heaving it out from underneath the wing during its slow fall. The metallic capsule ejected another billowing cloud of dust from the moon's surface as it touched down on the crater floor. Once the regolith resettled, the Nomad depressed the access panel and awaited its gentle spring-loaded retraction.

Peering into the cylindrical vessel, the Nomad moved aside several toolboxes and spare component canisters until he came across the container he was looking for. Clicking it out of the fixture rails of the cargo pod, he removed the canister and laid it on the astrobleme floor. Opening the round case, the Nomad withdrew a collapsible tripod, erecting it several metres away from his landing site. Returning to the container, he then cautiously pulled out a small microwave unit. Fixing the microwave emitter atop the tripod and unfolding the unit's solar cells, the Nomad left the device to charge, returning back to the cargo pod, this time to retrieve a collapsible cold trap. Taking a mallet from the toolbox, the Nomad made his way back over to the microwave emitter, hammering the spike of the cold trap into the regolith. The Nomad continued this back and forth for several minutes, systematically unloading various devices from the cargo pod and setting up an array of equipment around the perimeter of the landing zone.

Next in the sequence was a solar-powered refrigerator unit; attaching it to the cold trap, the Nomad powered up both devices. The umbrella-like canopy of the cold trap unfurled in a wide dome, suspended above the ground by the prop driven into the regolith; meanwhile, the motor of the heat pump silently whirred into action, injecting refrigerant throughout the canopy, rapidly chilling the hood. As the underside of the cold trap steadily dropped in temperature, the Nomad returned to the microwave emitter and primed the device. The Nomad stepped clear of the emissions zone; detecting its operator was at a safe distance, the device began to blast pulses of microwaves into the permafrost below.

Dielectrically excited by the rays of electromagnetic radiation beaming into the ground, the frozen water molecules that had been held captive in the subsurface ice for millennia began to heat through agitation. Unable to form water in the vacuum of space, the thawing ice instantly sublimated, escaping from the rock and dust as vapour. Much of the evaporated water was lost to space as it jettisoned from the permafrost, but that which rose beneath the cold trap snap froze on contact, condensing immediately to ice across the underside of the canopy. After a matter of minutes, a substantial ice sheet crusted the umbrella of the cold trap.

Throughout the process, the Nomad had taken the time to set up a secondary microwave device; insulated inside a mesh cage, this one served as an oven, dedicated to melting ice into water. Alongside the microwave oven, the Nomad prepped an electrolyser designed for the separation of water into its constituent elements: hydrogen and oxygen.

Once these two devices were ready, the Nomad returned to the cold trap. Holding a button for several seconds, the Nomad activated the heating filaments within the canopy. The filaments briefly rose the temperature of the umbrella above melting point, just long enough to thaw the ice's outer layer and separate it from the underside of the canopy. No longer fixed beneath the umbrella, the sheets of ice, now beholden only to gravity, drifted downwards in slow motion, finally coming to rest on the ground.

Collecting up the ice sheets, the Nomad fed them each in turn into the microwave melting unit before sealing it shut and initiating its cycle. The magnetron inside the oven powered up, bombarding the ice with pulses of microwaves, changing its state again, the ice this time able to melt into water inside the pressurised unit. As water formed, it was filtered and drained into the device's collection tank. With the first batch gathered, freshly extracted from beneath the lunar surface, the Nomad linked the water collection tank via a hose to a port on the Fighter, refilling the ship's reserves. All the while, a second crust of ice began to condense across the umbrella of the cold trap.

After several cycles of ice formation, followed by its subsequent melting, the ship's water reserve tank, for the most part serving as the Nomad's drinking supply, was full. With the Fighter topped out, the Nomad switched tact, feeding all subsequently produced water directly into the electrolyser he'd set up. Inside the electrolysis chamber, the water was broken down into hydrogen and oxygen gas; both products thereafter were cooled and compressed, resulting in liquefaction, and then fed, once more via a system of hoses, into the Fighter. The two elements were housed in separate pressurised tanks, serving respectively as cryogenic fuel and oxidiser for the ship's atmospheric chemical propellant thrusters. Finally, with the Fighter fully refuelled, the surplus of oxygen produced in the subsequent rounds of electrolysis was then compressed and used to replenish both the Fighter and the Nomad's respiratory oxygen supply.

Several hours after the Nomad had first touched down, the process of resupplying and refuelling was finally complete. The Nomad collapsed down and stowed all of his equipment, the majority of which he had salvaged at one time or another during his endless journey across the stars. With everything packed methodically back into the cargo pod, the Nomad sealed it shut and rolled it into position below the wing. Activating the hydraulic clamps, he watched the retractable arm affix to the pod, lifting it back into position beneath the wing.

Breathing heavily inside his helmet, the Nomad panned his gaze back and forth across the crater in one final sweep, ensuring again he had left nothing behind. The only evidence of his brief visit to the perpetually tumbling moon were his footprints. With no wind or active geological processes to erode the marks his boots had made, his footsteps were stamped eternally into the reflective dust of the astrobleme.

With the mauve behemoth gas giant hanging directly above in the dark skies, the Nomad turned back towards the open cockpit of his Fighter. With a well-judged bound, he leapt up from the low-gravity surface, landing atop the nose of the ship. The Nomad lowered himself lazily into the pilot's chair, closing the canopy with a pull of a lever, sealing the cockpit as he buckled his harness. Reverting several switches, the Nomad began repressurisation. A crescendo of hissing air, punctuated by the knell of a claxon growing in volume, reverberated throughout the cockpit. Once the process was complete, the Nomad raised his visor, powering down his rig, before removing his helmet completely, stowing it securely under his seat.

Glancing one final time across the silver moonscape, the Nomad powered up the necessary systems for take-off. A long burn of chemical propellant from the lift-off engines suspended the Fighter on a cushion of thrust and carried the small craft swiftly away from the lunar surface, inserting the ship back into a high orbit around the gas giant. Consulting the results of the system scans once more, the Nomad selected the coordinates of a small terrestrial world on the fringes of the star system's habitable zone and plugged them into the flight computer. The jarring circuitry processed the data and calculated a flight path.

Rotating and twisting the Fighter with the ship's arcjets, the Nomad aimed the nose of the vessel towards the horizon of the gas giant. Pushing the thrust lever forwards, the Nomad sank heavily back in his chair as the pulsejets ignited, rapidly accelerating the Fighter towards the curvature of the gas giant's horizon. The tiny spacecraft cut through the veil of the planet's upper atmosphere as it hurtled past the immense world, claiming a boost in speed from the gravity assist. Finally achieving escape velocity, and still accelerating, the ship was flung clear of the gas giant's orbit and was sent careering off towards the centre of the solar system.

THREE

White plasma erupted from the Fighter's pulse engines, glaring as a geyser of luminous discharge throughout the black void. The prolonged burn slowed the ship to approach velocity. Precise firing from the reaction control system arc jets swivelled the Fighter back on its axis, and as the Nomad was spun back to face his destination, a crimson world loomed into view through his canopy. Little more than a cold dust ball on the very fringes of the star's habitable region, from orbit, the world appeared anything but habitable. The yellow sun's light refracted through the hazy atmosphere encircling the ball of rock, and as the Nomad gazed down on its incarnadine surface, through the hundreds of whirling dust storms, he looked out across a world scarred with canyons and desiccated riverbeds. The world had once been far more than the ubiquitous desert it had decayed into, that much was clear, but it had likely been millennia since water had trickled across its surface. Now, from orbit, the planet appeared dead: a carcass adrift in a decaying universe. But as the Nomad well knew, carcasses were still often ripe for scavenging; all he required was a few morsels, a few scraps of rotten flesh left clinging to the carrion.

With a few short burns from the pulse engines, the Nomad manoeuvred into a high orbit around the scarlet globe, positioning the Fighter so that the array of scientific instruments fitted to the undercarriage aligned with the atmosphere. Booting up an assortment of scanners, the Nomad selected a few compositional scans and allowed them to run their course as he sat watching the celestial body revolve slowly beneath him. After a number of orbits, the scans had run their course. Now left with a packet of unprocessed data to sift through, the Nomad wasted little time in finding what he was after. The atmospheric readings were promising enough to warrant investigation of the world, and the more he studied the figures before him, the greater his certainty became. What he was looking for existed on this forsaken ball of rock, but more importantly, he knew exactly where to search for it.

The Nomad fed the coordinates into the flight computer and allowed it to whir away as it plotted various trajectories for atmospheric insertion. Powering down the scanners and flight computer, the Nomad adjusted his pitch and roll, waiting for the approaching window on his final planetary loop. Briefly firing the Fighter's pulsejets in a deorbital burn around the nightside of the planet, the Nomad pressed back into his seat as his speed bled away. Killing the pulsejets, he pitched the Fighter back towards its travel vector, lifting the nose above the curvature of the horizon. The Nomad sat patiently as his orbit began to decay, and before long, losing altitude, the Fighter dipped into the thermosphere, skimming the very outer reaches of the terrestrial world's sky. The Fighter began to shudder as it sank deeper into the veil of gas enveloping the world, and as the ship plunged into the mesosphere, the vibrations inside the cockpit intensified. Amber plasma began to glow across the underside of the Fighter as the gasses beneath it were compacted into a shockwave of intense heat. The searing flames licked up across the hull, flickering across the canopy, growing ever hotter as the Fighter speared deeper into the atmosphere. Tearing now into the stratosphere, the ship quaked fiercer and fiercer as the lower atmosphere rapidly approached, the friction of gasses syphoning speed from the Fighter as it continued to plummet.

The Nomad heaved left on the joystick. Elevons on the wings angled against the air, causing the Fighter to bank. The projected landing zone swerved violently away from the approach vector across the head-up display. The Nomad veered right in correction, banking the opposite way, the Fighter's nose still pitched upwards. The landing site recentred in the approach path, then veered wide off course in the opposite direction. Intentionally overshooting the turn, the Nomad curved his flightpath right of the landing zone; banking out of the arc, he swerve left again. He continued this weaving line of descent, serpentine left and right, rapidly shedding both altitude and velocity until the fiery plasma enveloping the Fighter died away.

Straightening his descent, the Nomad finally dropped the Fighter's angle of attack, granting him a view of the approaching landing site dead ahead. Now on target, the Nomad flicked various switches, locking the elevons and slats on the wings and tailfins into an airbrake. The forces of deceleration strained at the Nomad's harness as he lurched forwards in his seat. The Fighter was now deep in the troposphere, the ground rapidly approaching.

The Nomad watched the figures tick over on his HUD. His flight instruments made recommendations for slight alterations to his approach; for the most part the Nomad ignored them. The Fighter was a part of him, an extension of his own body; he could feel the wind beneath his wings, the density of the atmosphere. The currents of air spoke to him through the feedback in the Fighter's controls. The shuddering and jerking of the craft came almost as a comfort; he didn't fight against the tide, he didn't wrestle against the controls, instead he followed the rivers of airflow, anticipating, reacting, embracing the wind. He was always in control. There was no need to bluntly carve a path through the air, instead he navigated the flowing streams of wind, knowing that they would guide him to where he needed to be.

The landing point was approaching fast. The Nomad disengaged the airbrake and switched thrusters from the arcjets over to the chemical vertical-take-off-and-landing engines. Pitching the Fighter back, the Nomad engaged the VTOL thrusters and allowed the chemical jets to brake, shedding away the last of the Fighter's speed. The craft hung suspended above the surface of the alien world on a cushion of lift. The Nomad deployed the landing gear and slowly reduced thrust, allowing the Fighter to gradually descend the last few metres. Red dust swept up in the vortex of exhaust plumed around the Fighter. Engulfed by the crimson cloud of sand, the Fighter's landing skids touched down on the surface of the alien world.

Grit rained down across the landing site, crackling as it showered the Fighter's canopy. Powering down the chemical engines, the Nomad examined the readouts before him: a mostly nitrogen and carbon dioxide based atmosphere, with traces of argon and various sulphates; far from breathable, yet fairly innocuous under the protection of the Nomad's EVA suit. But amongst the otherwise inert cocktail of gasses existed a small percentage of oxygen; a reliable though not conclusive biomarker, atmospheric oxygen regularly indicated the existence of life. Life was what the Nomad was searching for.

He didn't expect to find anything exceptionally complex; he doubted this planet could even sustain anything much more intricate than single cellular bacteria. Yet the oxygen levels in the atmosphere suggested that there was a biomass of some significance somewhere to be found, and if his orbital scans had any indication, the valley he had just touched down in was the best place to search: the site of richest oxygen concentration on the entire planet.

Donning his helmet, the Nomad purged the cockpit of air, preventing the loss of any of his own precious atmosphere to the alien world. All fell silent as the Nomad was plunged into a vacuum; with the last vestiges of air evacuated from the cockpit, he initiated retraction of the canopy. The instant the cockpit seal was breached, a torrent of air gushed into the Fighter and sound returned. Readings of pressure and gaseous composition flashed up across the inside of the Nomad's visor. When the canopy had fully retracted, the Nomad unclipped his harness and rose to his feet, taking a moment to familiarise himself with the world's gravity.

The downward tug of the desert planet was several orders of magnitude higher than the tiny ice moon he had just left, but even still, it was a relatively low gravity world. The Nomad sat himself down on the rim of the cockpit and swung his legs over the side. Dropping gently into the alien dust, he gazed about at the barren hillsides of the foreign valley. He took his first few steps; his gait was light and bounding, but his feet more or less remained in constant contact with the ground as he strode a circumference around the Fighter. Once again, he carried out a series of post-landing checks.

Little had changed since the last inspection: the front landing skid was still slightly warped, the weld in the wing was holding perfectly, and none of the scientific equipment on the undercarriage had shaken loose during atmospheric entry or landing. With a sense of dread and unease, the Nomad looked over the antimatter tank. All was as it had been: the ship was still holding together and functioning as the Nomad needed it to, serving as a lifeboat adrift alone in a never-ending sea of stars.

Ducking beneath the starboard wing, the Nomad lowered the second cargo pod via the hydraulics and disengaged the clamps. Dragging the pod through the red silt of the dried-up lakebed, the Nomad pulled the container clear of the Fighter and retracted the access panel. From out of the pod, he lifted a cumbersome dodecahedron, hoisting it out by a pair of handles. Straining against the device's weight, even in low gravity, the Nomad lowered the machine onto the shingle and dragged it further still from the Fighter. When he had a suitable berth, the Nomad activated the device via a single button located between the two grips. A small diode blinked, and once the Nomad had stepped clear, the machine unfolded.

The solar panels encasing the device unfurled, splaying out across the ground in a polyhedral net of reflective photovoltaic cells. Centred in the flattened external structure of the machine was a pyramidal device, gradually charging in the yellow sun's rays. It was perhaps the singular most important and valuable piece of technology the Nomad had ever salvaged: a biomatter recombinator. In the long time since his rations had run out, this had been his only safe source of nutrition.

Whilst the device's cells recharged, the Nomad returned to the cargo pod and gathered a number of empty airtight canisters, clipping each of them to the belt of his EVA rig. Glancing out across the long-dried-up lake, the Nomad activated his suit's short burst scanners. His HUD flashed to life as various rocks, crags, and distant slopes showed augmented reality data readouts. But the Nomad turned a blind eye to all nonessential information. There was only one thing he was searching for, and when a possible detection sprung up several kilometres in the distance, he minimised all other information across the inside of his visor.

With his rangefinder locked on to a milky-tinged slope just over three thousand metres away, the Nomad began his hike over to the far side of the alien basin. His feet sank into the crusty lakebed, the mud clumping between the treads of his boots like clay; there was more moisture in the ground than the Nomad had first thought. Soon, a long trail of footprints extended to his rear, leading all the way back to the Fighter, the small spacecraft continuing to recede in the distance with each further step he took. On the Nomad trekked, alone across the expansive wastes, the digits on his visor gradually ticking down. Finally, the Nomad drew near the slopes. He could now see for himself that the milky hue tinging the otherwise crimson landscape was indeed the very thing he was looking for: organic matter.

Swathes of feathery cream moss carpeted the hillside in dense clumps. As the Nomad closed to within the final few hundred metres, he realised the alien flora swept down into a bowl sunken into the plain of the lakebed, where the growth was at its richest. Fine filaments of silver stamens coiled upwards from the mossy growth, quivering in the gentle breeze swilling about the basin.

Arriving at the rim of the hollow, the Nomad stepped down and knelt aside the nearest patch of moss, allowing his suit's limited scientific equipment to run a preliminary analysis. The data readouts projected onto the Nomad's visor, bringing a sense of relief to the weary traveller. The growth was both plant-like and fungal in cellular structure; though highly toxic to the Nomad's biology in its current form, it was constituted from a spectrum of amino acids and carbohydrates that were somewhat akin to the Nomad's. The growth appeared both photo and chemosynthetic, drawing energy from both the yellow sun's light and from the rich source of minerals deposited in the long dried-up lakebed. Assuming the average conversion rate, there was easily enough biomass here to supply the Nomad with provisions for the near future.

The Nomad unclipped the various canisters from his belt and arranged them on the ground. Next, he drew a spatula-like implement from a slot in his belt. Unscrewing the cap of the first container, the Nomad proceeded to use the flat tool to scrape up some of the moss; the whitish growth separated from the soil without too much effort. The Nomad spooned the sample into the capsule and repeated the process, methodically harvesting tufts of alien flora until all of the containers were filled and sealed. Reclipping each of the canisters to his belt, the Nomad rose back to his feet and began the long return march towards the Fighter.

Retracing his own footsteps, the Nomad finally arrived back at the landing zone. The biomatter recombinator had long ago reached full charge and was primed and awaiting the Nomad. Approaching the device, the Nomad unclipped the first canister from his belt and inserted it into a circular recess on the pyramidal unit. The machine's holographic display flickered to life as the recombinator awoke from standby and began analysing the organic matter. Whilst the machine constructed a detailed digital model of the molecular composition of the alien flora, the Nomad loaded the rest of the canisters into the remaining slots on the recombinator. Waiting for the device to complete its analysis, the Nomad took the time to fill his water canteen from the Fighter's drinking reserves, ensuring the recombinator's own water levels were topped up.

By this point, the biomatter recombinator had built up a full digital structure of the alien moss. Ready to go, it prompted its user that it was primed. Without hesitation, the Nomad triggered the next phase of the cycle and made his way over to the Fighter. Sitting on the ground, leaning against the landing gear of his ship, the Nomad made himself comfortable for the long wait. The recombinator had begun the complex process of deconstructing the moss via millions of intricate chemical reactions into its constituent organic molecules. Once this process was complete, the device would sort and separate the cocktail of chemicals, removing those intrinsically toxic to the Nomad's own biology, whilst retaining those that were compatible with it. Then, the recombinator would begin the final stage of the process, reassembling the various organic molecules deemed safe to consume, into more complex proteins and carbohydrates capable of offering the Nomad sustenance and nutrition. It was complex, time consuming, and highly inefficient, but it was about the only way the Nomad could feed himself without being poisoned.

In the hours that followed, the Nomad slipped into slumber. He awoke sometime later to the faint beeping of the recombinator. The alien landscape was twilit, the yellow star soon to disappear beneath the horizon. Judging from the planet's rotatory period, he had likely been asleep for quite some time; but time was relative to the Nomad. If there was one thing he did have, it was time.

Rising groggily to his feet, the Nomad made his way over to the recombinator and opened the dispenser tray. He looked down in muted disappointment at the vacuum-packed nutrition bars the machine had formed from the moss; there were fewer than he had hoped, but more than he had feared. Either way, he knew he would have to repeat the whole process a number of times to ensure he had enough food to survive until whenever next he came across a viable source of organic matter. But he wouldn't do so immediately. He'd forgotten how long it had been since he had last eaten, but he knew it had been too long; if he didn't eat something now, he might not have the energy to complete the journey to the moss colony and back a second time.

The Nomad stowed the nutrition bars in his pouch and opened the excreta tray of the recombinator. It was brimming with grey powder. Far greater in quantity than the consumable food produced, the waste products of the reaction had been sapped of every ounce of nutrition and water. Taking the refuse a short distance away, the Nomad inverted the tray, emptying the toxic by-products out across the ground. The Nomad returned to the biomatter recombinator, restowing the excreta tray before removing the various collection canisters, hooking each in turn back onto his belt. Powering down the device into standby, the Nomad returned to his ship. Depressing a covering panel on the hull, the Nomad exposed a twist lever. Activating it saw a series of flat ladder rungs extend from beneath the Fighter's hull, allowing the Nomad to climb back into the cockpit. The rungs retracted as the Nomad seated himself in the pilot seat and closed the canopy.

Venting the alien atmosphere from the Fighter, the Nomad was plunged momentarily back into a vacuum, before repressurisation flooded the cockpit with his own air supply. The Nomad removed his helmet and wiped the sweat from his brow. He took a swig of water from his canteen and unwrapped one of the nutrient bars. He sunk his teeth into the dry, bland mass of protein and carbohydrates, packed with whatever nutrients and minerals that the biomatter recombinator had managed to extract from the toxic alien flora. The meal was utterly unsatisfying and conjured a horrid thirst. The Nomad forced down the remainder of the bar with several large gulps from his canteen. There was no enjoyment to be had from it, but irrespective, it sufficed. It was no different from any other meal the Nomad had experienced in recent memory. At this stage, the very notion of taking pleasure from eating seemed like an abstract concept to the Nomad. Pleasure was a luxury that had been absent from his life so long he had almost forgotten it. Eating served one singular purpose: survival.

FOUR

Finished with his lacklustre meal, the Nomad once more purged the air from his cockpit and drew back the canopy, allowing the rush of alien atmosphere to surge around him. Dropping down into the rusty sediment of the valley, the Nomad set out on his second expedition across the lakebed. The sun had long since faded from amber to scarlet, minutes ago having sunk beyond the horizon entirely. This time, the journey would be in the dark. The stars shimmered through the hazy skies, casting a dim glow across the lonely dust world. Guided by the torch on his helmet, the Nomad followed the crisp beam of luminance, plodding slowly but determinedly across the breadth of the valley.

Finally, he neared the hollow, the moss glinting faintly with bioluminescence, guiding him in, like a silver beacon in the dark. Drawing the gear from his belt, he began his second harvest. Once each container was filled to the brim, sealed, and fastened to his EVA rig, the Nomad set off again, starting the return journey to the biomatter recombinator. Loading the containers into the device on arrival, he initiated the cycle of molecular deconstruction, sortation, and recombination.

Lying supine on the slopes of the valley whilst the process took place, the Nomad watched the foreign sky glimmer through a veil of dusty atmosphere. Meteors streaked in constant crisscrossing trails of vaporised rock, whilst a nearby red flare star periodically intensified in radiance, burning bright for a score of minutes, before fading back to a dimmer glow as the cycle repeated again.

Once the process of recombination had finished, the Nomad collected the dispensed nutrition bars, stowing them in his food hold in the footlocker beneath his pilot's seat. He emptied the recombinator excreta tray and reorganised the canisters on his harness, venturing out across the valley on his third expedition. The walk seemed shorter this time, the familiar always seeming quicker when compared to the novel, and before long, the Nomad was scraping more of the milky flora from the valley basin. The return journey had the illusion of being quicker still, yet the wait for the recombinator to carry out its complex chemistry never seemed to diminish. During the fourth harvest, the sun rose, transforming the dim nightscape back to one of hazy rust. By the time the fifth harvest was complete, the yellow star was approaching its zenith. During the seventh harvest, the Nomad took a few moments to eat and drink once again, finally setting out one last time to gather what little remnants of the alien moss were left.

When all was said and done, the very last

scraps of alien moss scrubbed from the valley and processed, the Nomad powered down the biomatter recombinator and allowed the solar panels to fold away, collapsing the device into its original dodecahedral shape. The Nomad hauled the cumbersome machine carefully back into the starboard-side cargo pod, before dragging the storage unit across the red sand into position beneath the wing. Locking the cargo pod back into place, the Nomad activated the hydraulics and clambered up into the cockpit. He closed the canopy, purged the alien air, repressurised, doffed his helmet, clipped himself into the seat's harness, and lulled his head back into the seat for a brief moment of respite.

Powering up the flight computer, the Nomad performed his routine of pre-flight checks and primed the VTOL jets. The chemical engines started to hum at low frequency as they warmed up, ascending in tone to a high pitch howl as the hydrogen and oxygen mixed and ignited. Fire and steam erupted from the exhaust nozzles in a torrent of force. Dust blasted into the air and swirled in a blinding cyclone as the Nomad steadily increased thrust. Slowly but surely, the landing skids lifted from the ground as the pillar of updraft took hold of the Fighter. The craft continued to rise steadily until it hovered over thirty metres from the floor of the basin.

The Nomad raised the landing gear lever back into its upwards position and the hydraulic tripod and skids folded away into the undercarriage of the

Fighter. Tilting back on the flightstick, the Nomad lifted the ship's nose, aiming the Fighter towards the heavens. Checking various readings across the control panel, the Nomad toggled the rear thrusters from pulsejets over to the singular rocket engine. Pressing forwards on the thruster, the Nomad felt the delayed surge of power as the chemical propellant ignited and a torrent of fire erupted from the aft of the Fighter.

The archaic method of propulsion was ideal for atmospheric take off, allowing enough thrust to propel a ship to orbit, without accelerating the craft to speeds that proved dangerous when in opposition to a wall of air resistance. Antimatter pulsejets on the other hand, would rapidly accelerate the Fighter to velocities that would crumple the craft in the resistance of the alien atmosphere; in addition, antimatter was incredibly rare, only accumulating naturally in significant quantities when captured in powerful magnetic fields. Hydrogen however, the fuel which burned within the rocket thruster, was the singular most abundant element in the universe.

As the velocity of the Fighter increased, the ship's wings carved through the thick soup of gasses of the lower atmosphere, generating lift. Now held aloft by aerodynamics alone, the Nomad powered down the VTOL thrusters, switching control back over to the reaction control system arcjets. Pulling further back on the joystick, the elevons pressed against the airflow over the wings, increasing uplift.

The nose of the Fighter pitched into a greater angle of attack and the ship began to shudder amidst the deafening roar of the rocket engines. Punching out of the thick troposphere, the Fighter pierced the stratosphere. The atmosphere thinned further, the Fighter continuing to climb faster and faster. The sky dimmed to black and the first stars shimmered against the heavens. The vibrations diminished and the roaring faded as the atmospheric pressure dwindled, all the while, the Fighter continued to accelerate.

Soaring rapidly out the mesosphere and into the thermosphere, the Fighter reached orbit. The Nomad eased off the thruster and the rocket engine cut out, the fiery exhaust trail extinguishing in an instant. With the chemical thruster disengaged, the Nomad switched control over to the antimatter pulsejets. Priming the interplanetary engines, he once again nudged the thruster forwards. Antimatter and matter collided, and an immense kick of acceleration shot from the rear of the Fighter, propelling it almost immediately to escape velocity. The Nomad shut his eyes, enduring the strain exerted by the forces on his body, easing off the thruster when he was free from the terrestrial world's gravitational grasp.

Drifting swiftly away from the crimson world, the Nomad opened the flight computer's holographic display, prepping the machine for faster-than-light jump calculations. The computer clicked and groaned under the strain of the complex quantum relativity equations, finally churning out a number of possible jump paths. The Nomad sifted through the array of potential destinations, eventually settling on a blue giant, eighty-seven light-years away. Selecting the star, the augmented reality navigation trajectory flashed up across the Fighter's HUD. An elongated parabola slung the Fighter on a close pass to the yellow sun.

Barely needing to alter his current orbital path, the Nomad adjusted the yaw and pitch of the Fighter and initiated a burn of the pulsejets. The enormous forces of acceleration took hold of the Nomad once more, wrenching him back into his seat as he hurtled furiously in towards the heart of the solar system. His breathing rasped and his limbs turned to lead, the Fighter careening ever faster towards the star. After a number of minutes, his constant acceleration had delivered him up to a tiny fraction of lightspeed, and the enormous ball of burning gas expanded across the Fighter's canopy. The photochromatic glass tinged to an almost opaque black, polarising out the dazzling light and heat that would otherwise have blinded the Nomad in an instant. The face of the sun contrasted into focus, its glare so highly filtered that the fiery details of the surface were unveiled. Black chasms the size of planets boiled and effervesced in an infernal sea of searing plasma. Flares licked outwards in great burning tongues from the blazing corona, a constant wind of ionised particles tearing away in every direction.

Even with the canopy tinted to near opaque, the glare was too much to withstand; the Nomad squinted, straining to lift the immense weight of his hand to shield his eyes, all the while he hurtled swiftly around the circumference of the immeasurable sphere of glowing plasma. The pull of the star's gravity couldn't contain him now, but it was enough to offer the Fighter one last gravity assist, accelerating the ship up the forever rising energy exponential towards lightspeed. The Nomad kept the pulsejets engaged as the star receded rapidly behind him, but his rate of acceleration was declining. Approaching relativistic speeds, the Fighter was steadily increasing in mass, demanding ever greater quantities of energy to accelerate further. Though he was still several orders of magnitude away from lightspeed, on pulsejets alone he would never achieve it.

Straining to extend a hand forwards, the Nomad reached for the protective casing on the control panel before him. Lowering the cover exposed a horizontal lever handle, slantingly striped in black and yellow, labelled with over a dozen warnings. Taking hold, the Nomad pulled it firmly upwards and engaged the ship's superluminal drive.

Inside the warp core, a hundred lasers focussed on a floating mass of superfluid exotic matter. As the lasers fired, the substance rapidly shed heat, cooling in an instant to absolute zero. Upon reaching zero-point energy, a second array of lasers focussed on the exotic matter, countering the spin of the particles. The mass of the exotic matter began to decrease, falling towards zero, before, through some quirk in quantum relativity, continuing further into negativity. As the excitation continued, the negative mass of the exotic matter rose steadily, causing distortions to the very weave of spacetime. The warp drive channelled this negative energy, lowering the mass of both the Fighter and its pilot to near negligible values, peaking waves in the fabric of the universe, creating both negative kinetic energy and a repulsive force of gravity.

The Nomad's vision of the stars distorted as if he were viewing the way ahead through a magnification lens. With the superluminal drive engaged, the limiter imposed on the antimatter pulsejets was lifted. The Nomad punched the thruster up to its maximum and the antimatter tanks began to rapidly flood the annihilation chamber. The expulsion of energy from the Fighter's engines intensified, and even in his low mass state, the Nomad could feel the unfathomable forces of acceleration seize hold of him, flattening him into the upholstery of his chair. The Fighter was free to accelerate at its maximum potential, no longer inhibited by the Nomad's biological limitations, his body's mass now near insignificant. Likewise, the Fighter was no longer inhibited by its own mass, now able to climb into the steeper regions of the mass-energy exponential curve that otherwise forbid approach of lightspeed due to the bizarre laws of relativity. The Fighter began to accelerate at an unprecedented rate, steadily climbing the vertical section of the momentum curve, rapidly speeding towards superluminal velocities.

Several metres in front of the Fighter's nose, an ethereal blue haze steadily began to radiate. Spacetime ahead of the ship had contracted, and to the rear of the craft, it was rapidly elongating. The blue luminosity before the craft was electromagnetic radiation, emitted as the velocity of the Fighter started to exceed the speed of light in a vacuum. The sapphire glow intensified as the Fighter, contained within the bubble of warped spacetime, shot clean past the light barrier.

The yellow sun and the rest of its solar system were now long gone. The Nomad had left the star system and was tearing through the interstellar medium. Both lightyears and decades receded in the Nomad's wake as the passage of time distorted and slowed. As the distance between stars yielded to the Nomad, he knew all too well that so did time. For him, mere seconds were passing, yet he knew that outside of the warp bubble formed by his FTL drive, hours were racing by in the blink of an eye.

Relatively speaking, the Fighter itself was not exceeding lightspeed, yet due to the contraction of space before it and its expansion to the rear, from an onlooker's perspective, the Fighter was measurably surpassing it by several magnitudes. Likewise, by the quirks of physics, his ship would also be invisible on approach to any onlooker, appearing only after having passed the observer, and perhaps more confusingly, as two separate images departing in opposite directions. These implications had once fascinated the Nomad, but now they were merely facts of his day-to-day existence. He had lost count of the number of times he had travelled these speeds and distances; but the number was tiny when compared to the amount of FTL jumps left ahead of him. It was all just routine.

FIVE

Warp core still engaged, the Nomad flipped the Fighter via the arcjets. With the ship spun rearward, the effects of the superluminal drive, namely the polarity of the spacetime distortions, were likewise inverted, acting now against the vessel's velocity. The blue glow of Cherenkov radiation subsided. Spacetime ahead of the Fighter's direction of travel, past the ship's tail, elongated. Behind, in front of the ship's nose, it contracted. With the reversal of the warp field, the Fighter dropped to a subluminal velocity. But even without the warping of spacetime, mass close to zero, careening backwards through interstellar space, the Fighter was still travelling at near lightspeed.

Lurching the thruster to full throttle, the Nomad fired a prolonged decelerating burn. Even with his mass near zero, the force of the deceleration pinned him crushingly back into his seat. The Fighter plummeted down the energy exponential, shedding momentum at a phenomenal rate as the Nomad's destination raced swiftly closer. Dropping to non-relativistic speeds, the Nomad finally reached approach velocity for orbital insertion, the target celestial body: a class B blue giant star.

As the Fighter's antimatter reserves began to dwindle, the Nomad killed thrust to the engines and pivoted the Fighter front-facing once more. Reraising the yellow and black striped lever, he disengaged the FTL drive. The stretched and contorted bubble of space surrounding the Fighter snapped back to normal, the lens effect smearing the stars ahead into focus.

Dead centre to the canopy, a piercing azure pinpoint of light twinkled, the brightest star in an otherwise unending sea of constellations. Though now at but a miniscule fraction of lightspeed, the Nomad was still hurtling towards the heart of the approaching stellar system with unfathomable speed. Even still, the distances of infinity were so vast that the Nomad sat for hours, watching in silence as the tiny mote of sapphire swelled across the canopy, growing from little more than a speck of light, to an orb of fiery indigo raging against the night.

Spearing through the star's heliopause, the Fighter tore out of the interstellar medium, piercing a bubble of solar wind and sailing deep into the domain of the blue giant. Upturning the Fighter, the Nomad pitched backwards, issuing a final decelerating burn from the pulsejets, slowing the ship enough for gravitational ensnarement, locking the vessel in a remote and distant orbit around the blue sun.

Adrift on the far-flung fringes of the solar

system, the Nomad powered down the pulsejets and reaction control system, before finally lowering the protective safety casing over the warp core lever. With the ship floating silently in the dark, the Nomad flicked a switch on the dashboard and watched as the Fighter's solar panels began to unfurl from the wings, expanding to a reflective array. The mirror-like cells shimmered dimly as they began to soak up the sun's cobalt rays, feeding energy back into the Fighter's power cells.

Leaning back in his chair, the Nomad glimpsed at the current charge level. His heart quailed with a spike of terror in his chest; the cells were close to dead. Another few lightyears further and the Fighter would have hit zero. With charge completely depleted, the superluminal drive would have cut out, followed immediately by the ship's life support systems, and all other forms of electronics and controls. He would have been stranded in interstellar space, strapped inside a metal coffin, locked hurtling along an unalterable path at deadly speed, no way of recharging so far from the nearest source of light, with only a few minutes of breathable air inside the bubble of the canopy.

Before making the interstellar jump, the Nomad had figured the distance was approaching the limits of the ship's range, but until now, he had not fully appreciated just how degraded the power cells had become. He had been reckless. Careless. Greedy. He should have picked a closer destination.

He should have ensured the cells were at maximum charge before making the jump. He should have kept a closer eye on his instruments.

For whatever reason, the low charge alert hadn't sounded during warp. Had the cells not lasted as long as they did, it would have spelled the end. The terrifying reality was that the Nomad had almost condemned himself to death. He had been lucky. Very lucky. The near brush with death was too close for comfort. He needed stricter protocol: more stringent routine. Routine was what had kept him alive so far, but was it enough? Each jump took its toll on his aging ship. He could make repairs, but sometimes parts needed replacing entirely, parts he simply did not have.

The Nomad had fought so long and hard for his survival; he couldn't fail now. If nothing else, that was his reason for continuing. Because, if he did not, then all of the hardship that he had endured until this point had been for nothing. Continuation was the sole purpose of his existence. He continued because that was all he knew how to do. The other motives and desires that had once guided him had now faded into nothingness. Despair, emptiness, loneliness, these were all merely remnants of things he had lost; and as terrible as they were, they were better than feeling nothing at all.

And so, he continued on. He rested. He waited. He stared out at the infinite universe as the photovoltaic cells absorbed the steady wind of photons. When the alarm sounded to signal the cells were at full capacity, he muted the alert. The Nomad prepped the vast array of scientific instruments and carried out his system scans. Once again, he recharged the power cells. Booting up the reaction control system, he reached for the flightstick. A jerk on the controls engaged the RCS arc jets, rotating the Fighter. Neutralising his spin and coming to rest, the Nomad primed the pulsejets.

Piloting the ship in towards the core of the system, he manoeuvred into orbit around a bronze gas giant. The Nomad raised the antimatter collection coils. He waited. The tanks filled. He lowered the coils.

Guiding the Fighter to a nearby comet, he landed on its icy surface. He inspected the ship. He set up his water collection equipment. He refilled the tanks, replenished his oxygen, and refuelled his chemical propellant. He packed everything away.

Climbing back into the cockpit, he carried out his pre-flight checks. He took off. He scanned for organic life. None to be found. He recharged the cells. He powered up the navigation computer, calculating his next FTL jump. Engaging the pulsejets, he slingshotted past the blue sun. He engaged the warp core. He jumped.

Arriving in the next star system, a pair of binary red dwarfs in tight orbit, he began the routine once more. He had taken a shorter jump, leaving more breathing room as far as charge went, yet the cells were still becoming ever less efficient. He recharged. He refilled the antimatter tanks from a gas giant's magnetosphere, replenishing his water, oxygen, and hydrogen from an icy moon in its orbit.

Whilst landed on the lunar surface, the Nomad removed the panelling from his dashboard and thoroughly inspected the tangle of jury-rigged wiring and circuitry. Eventually, he located the short circuit responsible for the low power alert failing to sound. He patched the wiring and ran a series of diagnostic tests, only to discover another half dozen gremlins buried deep in the electronics. Unsurprised, the Nomad worked his way through the list of faults in the complex motherboard, until one by one, he had repaired each problem.

In the time it took the Nomad to complete the repairs, the gas giant above him completed a full rotation on its axis. When they were done, he took the time to chew through a bland nutrient bar, sipping at the water from his canteen to make it more palatable. Carrying out the requisite pre-flight checks, he took off from the dusty ice-crusted moon. Performing a close flyby of the gas giant, the Nomad launched the Fighter towards the inner reaches of the star system, running further scans for any suggestion of life. There were a handful of terrestrial worlds bathed in the dim crimson glow of the two red dwarfs, yet all bar one lacked anything more than a trace atmosphere, and the one which did was engulfed in a dense smothering veil of toxic gasses, intense heat, and crushing pressure. Any life that existed on that hostile world would be little more than extremophile bacteria.

The Nomad deployed the Fighter's solar array, bringing the degrading cells back up to full charge before carrying out FTL calculations. A white main sequence star lay sixty-two lightyears away. It was unlikely to harbour any life; such stars rarely did due to their relative youth. But the Nomad still had enough rations to last him a couple more jumps, and this star was a decent halfway point towards a binary system of two yellow main sequence stars. He plotted his course, blasting the Fighter down a close approach trajectory to the larger of the red dwarfs. He engaged the FTL core, accelerated to lightspeed, and watched as the view of the galaxy before him warped out of shape behind the blue haze of Cherenkov radiation ahead.

As the Nomad had predicted, the class A main sequence star harboured no life. The blinding sun burned hot and young, still having not yet condensed the last of its accretion disc into planets. The system was in a state of chaos and flux. Planetary orbits unstably crisscrossed one another. Small protoplanets and planetesimals collided, showering the larger bodies in violent bombardments. Further out, in the colder regions of the juvenile solar system, gas giants and ice giants were taking shape, waging immense gravitational wars as they vied for stable orbits. As they wrestled for permanence, they threatened to send each other flying off, either into interstellar space, or on catapulting trajectories inward towards the sun. But, even in this infantile and tumultuous system, the Nomad managed to recharge his cells, refuel his antimatter tanks, collect the water and oxygen he needed, and plot a jump away from the maelstrom of cosmic dust and colliding rock.

Dropping out of FTL and slowing to approach velocity, the Nomad gazed on at a pair of yellow suns. Separated by just under a hundred astronomical units, they were far enough apart that each had its own isolated system of planets, yet close enough together that every planet experienced two separate daily sunrises, one of their parent sun, and the other of a much fainter star just bright enough to be visible during the daylight.

The Nomad carried out his usual routine: deploying his solar array to charge the Fighter's power cells, running detailed analysis of the two systems via the ship's scientific equipment, locating a planet with a powerful magnetosphere, and collecting enough antimatter to refuel the pulsejet tanks. He touched down on an icy asteroid and collected enough water and oxygen to get him to the next system. Then, he analysed the planetary data, searching for possible life signs across the binary system.

The smaller of the two suns was sorely lacking in terrestrial worlds, likely due to the gas giant in close proximity to the sun; it would have disrupted the orbits of any rocky planets during the migratory phase of the system's formation. The second of the two stars had a host of small terrestrials; one positioned in the very heart of the system's habitable zone.

Studying the potential golden world further, the Nomad grew suddenly excited, noting the presence of an atmosphere. His excitement quickly tapered off as he delved deeper into the data, looking at the breakdown of its gaseous composition. It was mostly nitrogenous, with high levels of carbon dioxide and monoxide, laced with small quantities of methane. Only traces of oxygen; not a true golden world. The atmosphere was primordial in nature. There were high levels of water vapour present, and though slightly on the more tropical end of the spectrum, the surface temperatures were very favourable. There could indeed be life on this remote ball of rock; there was almost certainly surface water, maybe even enough to form an ocean. The Nomad had found life before in far harsher conditions, and this planet had all the starting ingredients required for its genesis.

Minimising the results from the scanners with a lazy gesture, the Nomad swivelled the Fighter around and punched the thruster into a quick burn. The vessel hurtled sun-bound, racing towards the smaller of the two class K suns in a gravity slingshot.

Streaking across the glowing corona, the Fighter's canopy blackened almost to total obscurity. Curving out passed the colossal sphere of plasma, the Nomad sat patiently as his momentum flung him into a distant orbit.

In the space of a few hours, the gravitational catapult manoeuvre had delivered him into the bounds of the star's celestial brethren, slotting him neatly into orbit around the second sun, on target to intercept the terrestrial world in question. The Nomad watched in anticipation as the glowing speck expanded gradually in his view. With the Fighter sailing ever closer, the world took form as a thin crescent of reflected light, but as the Nomad crossed inside the planet's orbit, the daylit hemisphere of the world revolved quickly into full view.

The planet was a grey and murky marble, pocked and scarred with infernal pits and fissures. Black and silver clouds swirled in raging tempests, flashing with lightning as great tendrils of electricity surged through the storms. Down below, volcanoes churned out torrents of smoke and ash, spewing rivers of larva that fed into lakes of fire. A good third of the southern hemisphere seemed to be ablaze with volcanic eruptions, but north of the equator, the world seemed comparatively tranquil.

Sulphuric rains fell into muddy valleys and collected into a million runlets and rivers. Great lakes had taken form, gathering in the many basins and ravines riven across the planet's surface. In the millennia that followed, the lakes would coalesce into seas and oceans. No doubt one day this world would become a paradise of biodiversity, provided no cataclysmic event destroyed the budding ecosystem beforehand. The planet was the perfect cocktail of chemicals, conditions, and circumstance to birth an abundance of life; its potential seemed boundless, but the Nomad cared little for potential.

On average it took several billion years from initial biogenesis to the formation of complex life. By that point, even with the time dilation experience during superluminal travel, the Nomad would be long dead. The fact that this planet held the potential to one day become a rich jungle world was irrelevant; what mattered was the here and now. The planet was still primordial. It was the perfect crucible for biogenesis. The big question was, had that biogenesis already taken place? Was there life to be found on this young and primitive world?

From orbit, the Fighter's instruments would offer little insight. Eager to save on fuel and time, the Nomad forwent orbital insertion; with a slight adjustment to his pitch and trajectory, he poised the Fighter for direct atmospheric entry. The primordial world loomed larger and larger in the final minutes of the Nomad's approach. There would be no deorbital burn, no skimming the atmosphere to shed his momentum. His approach was a direct vector. Like a meteor, his only form of deceleration before impact was the resistance of the atmosphere. But unlike a meteor, the Fighter had the benefit of fixed wings; the Nomad would have control over his lift, pitch, yaw, and roll throughout the descent. With some clever and calculated piloting, he could prevent the landing from becoming a crash, even with his current intercept speeds.

The Fighter hit the atmosphere hot. The moment the gasses enveloping the world became dense enough to push back against the plummeting Fighter, the ship's heat shields flared red. The Nomad steeply pitched up the Fighter's angle of attack as it collided with the wall of air. The whole craft vibrated and groaned under the stresses and temperatures of the atmospheric bow wave beneath him, but the violence of the descent, the heat, the shuddering, the thundering tumult of rupturing air, all were products of the speed being shed from the Fighter: momentum syphoned off into alternate forms of energy as the ship ploughed deeper and deeper into the dense ocean of atmosphere.

Once the Fighter had expelled enough velocity, the Nomad pivoted the vessel on its yaw and rotary axes, banking the craft heavily against the air. The Fighter plunged into a helix, corkscrewing downward, continually yielding speed to the resistance of the atmosphere. The ground was fast approaching, but as the air thickened, the vessel was decelerating ever quicker. Down and down the ship spiralled, the Nomad slowly canting his pitch lower, until finally the ground beneath the Fighter rose into view throughout the cockpit's canopy.

The Nomad deployed the airbrake and switched over to chemical propellant, peeling out of the corkscrew, allowing the wind to provide lift beneath the Fighter's wings. Storm clouds plumed into black anvils, cyclones twisting bleak and grey below. The shuddering ceased and the heatshields cooled, as held aloft on the wind, the Fighter glided serenely across the cloud tops.

Slowly losing altitude, the Fighter sank through the cloud ceiling. The light across the canopy dimmed, the surrounding mist transitioning quickly from foamy white to foggy grey. Rain beaded across the glass, the droplets growing to thick splatters that swiftly congealed into a gushing film flowing over the entire hull of the Fighter. Lightning glared through the darkling storm and turbulent winds began to buffet the dainty ship.

The in-atmosphere flight instruments were going haywire. Needles revolved in disquieting loops around their dials. Numerous warnings flashed up across the holographic interface. Several buzzers and alarms were sounding throughout the cockpit. The Fighter was shaking, rattling as it shot through the storm, plummeting and lurching upwards as it dropped in and out of pockets of turbulence.

The Nomad slowed his breathing and muted the alarms, gripping his joystick loosely as he rode the violent weather steadily down. Suddenly, he cleared the giant cumulonimbus all together, emerging out beneath the cloud floor, swooping into a stream of yellow sunrays. The Fighter stabilized in the airflow, settling once more into a smooth glide. Peering out across the alien world, the Nomad gazed on in awe at the brutal and rugged landscape unfolding beneath him. Jagged escarpments and doming mountains rose upwards from the black lava fields. Rivers and streams gushed and bubbled down from the slopes, converging in freshly sculpted valleys, collecting into hundreds of reflective lakes glinting silver in the sullen light.

Even from this vantage the Nomad could not yet answer his question. There appeared to be everything required. All the correct building blocks of life were present. But was it too early in this planet's history for the ubiquitous organic particles of nature to have coalesced into the intricate chemical structures and processes that constituted organic life? He could see no evidence as of yet, but he had barely caught a first glimpse of the world. The Nomad pulled back on his joystick and pitched the Fighter parallel to the ground, maintaining altitude as he continued to glide out across the extensive plains.

Thousands of square kilometres drifted slowly beneath the Nomad as he navigated updrafts and air currents to stay aloft, all the while he surveyed the vast new world below. There was a strange sensation that accompanied being the first ever to lay eyes on something; undoubtedly no one else had ever seen these valleys and lakes before, nor even visited this planet in any respect. It was a sentiment of both great privilege and impossible loneliness; one with which the Nomad was all too well acquainted.

Wherever the Nomad went, he was the first. Everywhere he travelled he was the first to discover it. Each valley, each mountaintop, each plain, every continent, every ocean, every world, all the asteroids, all the planets, all the stars, each and every single place he visited, everything he saw, he was the first, and he was the only. No one else had seen the things he had seen. And no one else ever would.

Yet with each new planet he visited, as different as they were from the others, they all seemed to be mere variations of the same theme. The universe was infinite, and therefore by its very nature it had to be repetitive. Every world was unique, the variation limitless, yet the laws of existence were in themselves limiting. How could each planet truly be different if each must be confined to a few basic guiding principles?

True, the planet the Nomad was soaring over now was different from any other in the universe, but what were those differences? Most life bearing worlds existed once as analogues to this planet; their mountains were in different places, as were their rivers; maybe their atmospheric compositions varied marginally, likewise the overall chemical make-up of the rocks. Perhaps they were different masses and sizes to this world, positioned at different distances away from another classification of star. But at what level does that variation become perceptible to the observer? If the mountains were arranged somehow differently across the horizon, would the emotional impact be changed in some way? If the rivers meandered down alternate courses, would that somehow make any distinction? What if the hue of the stone were a different shade, or even the sky an altered tinge? Would the overall experience of gazing out across this foreign terrain be any different, even if every aspect were changed beyond recognition?

The Nomad had been the very first to gaze out across innumerable landscapes. Though at first each had appeared novel and unique, with every new planet the Nomad visited, the differences diminished, steadily seeming more and more contrived. As the years had passed, the marvel of exploration and discovery had faded into monotony. Now, gliding high above the sullen primordial world, this upsetting realisation dawned poignantly on the Nomad. He suddenly felt ashamed. Defeated. He had become desensitised to the beauty of the universe. What was the point in exploration if you were numb to everything you discovered? Was it all just routine?

SIX

Soaring high over the rugged juvenile landscape, the Nomad surveyed the valleys and waterways for any signs of life. So far, the world appeared sterile: a stack of tinder and kindling yet to receive a spark, all the promise of life, but as of yet, no flames.

The Nomad had accumulated a debt of resources to approach so close to the planet's surface. He had spent little in the way of fuel to enter the atmosphere, relying on gravity, air resistance, and lift up until this point; the currency with which he'd paid his fare was gravitational potential energy. Now, in order to leave the clutches of this world, he would need to expend large quantities of chemical propellant in order to regain the energy he'd forfeited and reach escape velocity. If the Nomad did not find anything of use on this world, those resources now committed to him leaving would be entirely wasted. And so, with ever growing determination, the Nomad continued to scour the geography as he glided over thousands of square kilometres of primordial scenery, hunting, searching, looking for any evidence or hint of organic material scattered across the lifeless surface.

Drawing back on the joystick, the Nomad tilted the nose of the Fighter upwards as a jagged sierra drew in from over the horizon. Clearing the craggy peaks, the ship climbed back into the clouds, the view of the world below vanishing through the gloom. The Nomad dipped the Fighter's pitch, sinking back out of the cloud ceiling. The ground below clarified once more into focus, and a tinge of green suddenly caught his eye.

Between the foothills below, a lake pooled in a valley basin, the glinting waters pluming with verdant swirls. The emerald mere blurred beneath the Nomad as the Fighter raced over, but before he could lose sight of it, he tilted the flightstick, banking the ship back around to circle the lake.

The Fighter began descending in a great looping helix as the Nomad continued to study the vibrant blooms streaking the lake. The colouration could have merely been minerals spewing into the water from submerged volcanic vents. But as the Fighter descended, the Nomad became more and more optimistic of a second possibility. As he drew closer, he convinced himself he was gazing down at an algal bloom.

Bringing the Fighter downwards in an ever-tightening circumference, the Nomad continued to study the emerald plumes, searching for any final clue that could affirm his hopes. Swooping across the lake's surface in one final surveying pass, he saw it. Clinging to the shore, deposited across the grey sand by the lapping waves, a thick film of residue congealed along the waterline. It was unmistakably organic.

The Fighter pitched back, the VTOL thrusters angling towards the ground, and rode a cushion of hot exhaust downwards. A pillar of dust enveloped the craft, and the landing skids touched down, sinking into the volcanic sand of the new-born world. The Nomad donned his helmet, purged the cockpit of his precious breathable air, and raised the canopy, allowing primordial gasses to flood into the craft. Rising, he familiarised himself with the gravity of the new world. He was on the heavy side, but his weight was still mostly favourable; he wouldn't want to trek very far, but fortunately he had touched down barely fifty metres from the lakeside. Extending the steps from the side of the Fighter's hull, the Nomad clambered down onto the unweathered rock. Registering that the ground beneath his feet was barely a few thousand years old, he took a moment to gaze about the alien terrain.

Carrying out his post-landing inspection of the Fighter, the Nomad lowered the starboard cargo pod. He lifted the now especially weighty biomatter recombinator from out of the container and positioned it clear of the ship. He initiated the machine's start up procedure and watched as the pentagonal solar cells unfolded to expose the internal pyramid. Leaving the device to charge, the Nomad descended the steep shingly slope towards the water to inspect the algal growth closer.

The jade lake lapped glutinously against the rocky shore. Just above the waterline, a thick algal layer coagulated in the sun. The bloom was more concentrated than the Nomad had thought from altitude. Fertile and rich with life, there was more than enough biomass contained in the lake to replenish his rations and then some. Whether or not the algae's biology was even vaguely compatible with his own, and how he would go about harvesting it, were separate matters all together.

The Nomad knelt by the water's edge and initiated his suit's scanners. A reel of data swiftly transcribed itself across the HUD of his visor. The algal growth was a eukaryotic colony consisting of a range of specialised cell types. Though primarily photosynthetic, there appeared to be a subtype of organisms within the colony that were heterotrophic: animalistic cells that obtained their energy by swallowing and digesting various other types of microorganisms within the biological soup that the isolated lake had become. Though fascinating in and of itself, that was not what he was scanning for; instead, the Nomad turned his attention to the molecular analysis of the organisms.

In its unprocessed state, the alien bloom would be highly poisonous to the Nomad. Fortunately, the algae shared a number of basic building blocks common in the Nomad's evolved diet. If these initial readings were accurate, the Nomad could expect a much higher yield from the biomatter recombinator than he was used to. The only question now; how could he harvest the algae?

Seating himself on the shoreline, he watched the viscous green waters slosh over the beach in gentle rhythms. The tempest loomed overhead as the break in the storm began to collapse. The skies darkened. Lightning sparked in white arcs through the murk. Splotches of rain started to patter against the Nomad's visor, before finally, the heavens gave out in full and a deluge of acidic precipitation lashed downwards. Glancing back up the slope, the Nomad remotely triggered the closure of the Fighter's canopy from a control on his wrist.

The verdant lake danced viscously as a chaotic upheaval of ripples scattered across its surface. Watching the rain streak across his visor, the Nomad felt suddenly thirsty. Sipping from the overly filtered water from his suit's dispenser, the Nomad swilled the tasteless fluid around his mouth as an idea took hold. The solution was simple.

Rising to his feet, the Nomad clambered up the muddy bank, puffing through exertion as he fought the heavy tug of the planet's gravity. Finally, panting deeply, he reached the Fighter. The biomatter recombinator was fully charged and ready to be loaded with organic material. He could simply fill the various canisters with water from the lake and run them through the machine, but it would be highly inefficient. Once the water was removed from each sample, there would be little in the way of organic material left in each canister; each cycle of the recombinator might not even possess enough biomass to yield a single nutrition bar. The Nomad needed some way of concentrating the algae in each canister before he ran it through the machine. If he could effectively remove the water from each sample, he could load the recombinator with a far greater volume of algae and produce far more food each cycle; perhaps enough to last several months of spaceflight. Provided his idea worked, the Nomad reckoned he had figured out how to do exactly just such.

The Nomad returned to the cargo pod and gathered up the various canisters for the recombinator, clipping them to his EVA rig. Sliding various cases along the internal rails of the cargo pod, he uncovered a box buried at the bottom of the stowage container. Pulling it out, the Nomad sat the crate down in the sodden ashen soil. Unfastening the clasps, he lifted the lid and peered inside to find a long-neglected water filtration pump.

Designed for water purification, the pump filtered out toxins and organic materials to produce safe drinking water. The Nomad no longer used the device; his subsurface microwave ice mining technique had rendered the rather archaic pump and filter almost redundant. Furthermore, the filters were at the very end of their lifespan, and throughout his journey, the Nomad had never come across anything that could suitably replace them. The filters were in fact so degraded, the Nomad suspected they probably were past producing potable water altogether; but in this instance, it was unimportant. The Nomad was not interested in the water; he wanted the waste products. That the filters were near their end did not matter, they might not filter the algae from the water, but they would certainly do a good job at separating water from the algae.

In the strong gravity, the pump was heavy and cumbersome; a relatively low-tech piece of equipment, the filtration system had clearly never been designed with portability in mind. Lugging it towards the water, the Nomad grunted and strained as he reached the slope. Descending the bank, he dug in his heels as the scree gave way underfoot, the hillside growing quickly treacherous in the downpour. Finally reaching the water's edge, the Nomad lowered the weighty machine onto the mud. Glancing back up the slope in the direction of the Fighter, he quickly realised there was no way he would be able to drag the pump back uphill under his own steam. He would need to use the capstan winch.

The Nomad set up the pump, connecting the float and intake tubing, but forgoing the collection tank; it would only need to be emptied every minute or so once the pump was running; better to let the water flood straight onto the ground and run back into the lake. The pump lacked its own power source, and so the Nomad turned to make his way back up the slope to retrieve a junction cable. Halfway up the bank, the mud and shingle beneath the Nomad's feet gave way in the downpour and he was swept back down the hillside to the beach.

Stopping just short of the gelatinous residue caking the shoreline, the Nomad heaved himself to his feet. Wading through the runlets of rainwater flowing down the hillside, he scrambled back up the slope, this time on hands and knees. Large clods of sloppy shingle and sludge collapsed beneath him as he fought his way uphill, the cyclone raging ever more powerfully overhead. He reached the top of the slope coated in a layer of black muck, but in the deluge the sludge was quickly rinsed from his EVA suit.

The Nomad rummaged through the various cases of his cargo pod, the stowage compartment steadily filling with rainwater, and retrieved the power couplings. Sealing the pod, the Nomad stooped under the Fighter and opened a port on the undercarriage. Exposing a power socket, he plugged in one end of the cable, steadily unreeling the rest of the lead as he trudged back towards the slope. This time, he had barely set foot beyond the verge when the ashen shingle slid out from under his boot. He slipped, landing hard on his side. Still clutching the cable in one hand, he tumbled and slid down the entire height of the slope, grinding to a halt beside the pump.

His visor was caked black with grime, and as he fumbled at the helmet with his gloved hand, he only succeeded in smearing the mud. Waiting for the rain to clear his vision, he climbed to his knees beside the pump and felt for the power inlet on its side. Plugging in the other end of the cable, the Nomad listened for the faint beeping of the pump over the cannonade of rain drumming against his helmet. As his vision cleared, he grabbed the intake pipe and cautiously made his way over to the water's edge. Casting the float out into the sloshing emerald water, the Nomad watched it bob about violently in the storm.

Returning to the pump, the Nomad primed it and powered up the motor. A loud drone hummed over the howling winds as litres of thick, murky, algae-infested water were sucked into the intake and fed through the array of filters. Water soon began to spout from the outlet pipe, spewing onto the shore. The filtrate was far from pure, still tinged green as it gushed down the bank and drained into the lake, but unlike the viscous slime being swallowed at the opposite end of the pump, the end product was transparent and watery.

The machine had barely run for five minutes when the electric motor cut out. Fearing that the waterproofing seals for the electrics might have perished, causing the pump to short circuit in the storm, the Nomad was filled with a sudden sense of dread. To his relief however, the whirring of the pump was quickly replaced with a buzzing alert. Reading the display, the Nomad realised the device was instructing the user to clean its filters.

Powering down the pump, the Nomad detached the cover panel and removed one of the filters to inspect it. To his delight, and to what might have been the horror of anyone using the filtration device for its original intended purpose, the filter was heavily plastered in green algal gunk. Readying a canister hooked about his waist, the Nomad used a tool from his EVA rig to scrape the residue from the filter. The deposited algae was almost enough to completely fill the entire canister. Reinserting the cleaned filter, the Nomad quickly got to work harvesting the residue from the rest of them, easily filling all of the recombinator capsules. With the filters cleaned and the containers filled, the Nomad started the pump up again.

With the motor whirring away, he fought his way back up the treacherous incline, slipping several times during the ascent. Reaching the top, the Nomad slotted the canisters into the biomatter recombinator, and once the device had completed its analysis, he started the machine's first cycle. As the recombinator began to disassemble the algal colonies into their molecular constituents, the Nomad went in search of the capstan winch stowed somewhere inside the portside cargo pod. Hefting the winch to the top of the slope, the Nomad connected it to a secondary power outlet on the undercarriage of the Fighter. Using a mallet, he drove a series of pickets into the ground to anchor the winch atop the slope and unreeled the cable.

Taking shelter beneath the Fighter, the Nomad waited for the recombinator to do its job. Settling down for some rest, he was almost immediately roused as the recombinator started beeping. The Nomad moved closer to inspect it, only to discover, to his confusion, that the cycle was already complete.

The convoluted and longwinded procedure of molecular disassembly and reassembly, that normally took hours to process, had run to completion in just over half an hour. Not quite believing it, the Nomad checked the dispenser tray to find it filled with vacuum packed nutrition bars. Still refusing to accept his luck, the Nomad opened the excreta tray to find it lined with a small dusting of grey waste product rapidly rehydrating in the rainfall. Checking the display for a final time to confirm that the process had finished without any complications, the Nomad smiled broadly beneath his visor and began stuffing the nutrition bars into the pouches of his EVA suit.

Even with the most optimistic estimates based on the scans the Nomad had taken of the algae, he would never have predicted such a bountiful yield from the recombinator. The algae's biology must by sheer coincidence have had a very similar chemical structure and composition to the Nomad's own biology. He could scarcely believe his luck. This singular lake seemed the only one within a thousand kilometres to even harbour life. It could well have been the only site on the entire planet with this specific algae growing in it. And the Nomad had just stumbled upon it. The odds seemed somehow insurmountable. For once, the randomness of the universe had played out in his favour.

SEVEN

Abseiling down the ever more treacherous slope via the winch cable, the Nomad waded through the ankle-deep flow of murky water streaming from the hillsides. Lightning continued to crackle and flash across the sky and the wind picked up momentum, slanting the rain into diagonal streaks. The Nomad gazed about, wondering if he should wait for the storm to pass before continuing. His equipment was already set up and ready for a third cycle, but the weather seemed only to be worsening. He could bear to wait. He certainly had the time to do so. But was it necessary? His suit protected him from the elements, and his equipment was weather resistant. The hillside was rapidly turning into a river in and of itself, the ground regularly giving way in mudslides, but the winch now meant that if the Nomad slipped, he would no longer tumble to the bottom of the slope. Either way, he was at the shore of the lake again. If he was going to wait for the storm to pass, he would need to make his way back uphill to the Fighter; he might as well take up the next harvest of algae with him in the process.

The Nomad nudged the beached float of the intake back out into the turbulent green waters and started the pump, the whirring of the motor now inaudible over the raging storm. The pump soon cut out again and the notification instructing the Nomad to clean the filters flashed up across the device's display. Working swiftly, he ejected and cleaned the filters one by one, scooping the algal slime into the recombinator capsules. Powering down the pump, he secured the canisters about his person, and fighting against the tearing winds, the Nomad clipped the winch cable carabiner to his EVA harness.

Activating the capstan remotely via his suit, the Nomad felt the reassuring tug on his waist as the cable was reeled up the slope. Planting his feet into the thick mud of the bank, the Nomad ascended steadily, great swathes of clay and scree tumbling away beneath him. With the gale force winds whipping up the rain into a dense pall of mist and spray, the Nomad could no longer see the top of the slope; as he looked back downhill, he could barely make out the edge of the water receding behind him.

The Nomad felt the ground level out with his feet before he saw the winch ahead of him. He deactivated the turning capstan and plodded over to the biomatter recombinator. The stronger gravity was beginning to take its toll. The Nomad was weary. He could feel it especially now as he attempted to insert the canisters into their respective slots on the machine. What was once an easy task, requiring little thought, was now tiresome and clumsy; his arms felt heavy and uncoordinated, a sensation made all the worse by his failing vision behind a rain-soaked visor. When the task was finally complete, the Nomad set the recombinator to carry out the next cycle of biomolecular reorganisation.

Trudging back through the mire, the Nomad huddled himself against a rear leg of the Fighter's landing gear, beneath the shelter of a wing. Breathing heavily from exertion, he allowed his eyelids to lull shut. Before he knew it, he had plunged into sleep. When he next opened his eyes, the world around him had calmed. The chirping of the recombinator sounded through the stillness. The rains had ceased, the winds quelled, and the sky had brightened to a faint silver.

The Nomad crawled out from beneath the ship into the quagmire the landing zone had become. The skies were still hazy. The Nomad could make out the distant tolling of thunder as he peered through the veil of stratus obscuring the black cumulonimbus that had passed over. The volcanic landscape had been transformed into an extensive marshland, and as the Nomad glanced down the slopes still gushing with rills, he could tell the water levels had risen noticeably. Whereas before the pump was erected several metres set back from the shoreline, now the feet of the device were being lapped at by the green waters.

The Nomad waded over to the recombinator, the device now sat in a deep puddle of slowly draining rainwater. Collecting the nutrient bars and discarding the contents of the excreta tray, he stashed the dispensed rations and carried out a quick stock calculation. He now had enough food to last him for the next two months. The Nomad couldn't remember a time when his supplies had been so plentiful. But his food store was at far from full capacity; there was room enough for another two harvests. Now that the weather had cleared, he would be remiss if he did not seize the opportunity to fully stock his supplies.

The Nomad gathered up the containers and hooked the carabiner back onto his harness. Activating the winch to turn in reverse, he rappelled down the loose mud and shingle of the slope until he reached the shore of the lake. Kicking the float back out across the water, he powered up the pump, just as a fat globule of water splattered against his visor. The mechanical whirl of the filtration pump hummed to life, the weather deteriorating quickly into a sudden squall. The downpour intensified, and the pump guzzled up more water. The filters soon clogged with the algal growth and the pump cut out. The Nomad cleaned the filters and filled the recombinator canisters.

Gazing up at the darkening heavens, the Nomad realised his mistake; the storm had not passed over at all, he had merely been in the eye. Now, the eyewall was breaking, and the tempest would soon surge back to its fiercest intensity. The

Nomad reinserted the filters and began the pump on its final cycle. He clipped his harness back onto the winch cable and began the assisted climb back to the top of the slope. The flood of water had started to swell again. The Nomad's boots sank into the thick sludge as it slowly drifted downhill. He lost his balance near the top, and the tide of flowing mud swept his feet out from under him. His helmet planted into the black slurry as he was dragged by the winch up the final few metres on his side.

Killing the rotation of the capstan, the Nomad unhooked his harness and stumbled wearily over to the recombinator. Loading the canisters, the Nomad initiated the device. The skies went suddenly dark. Fighting against the wrath of the cyclone, the Nomad staggered back towards the winch. He leapt in terror as a bolt of lightning surged from the clouds and struck the ground barely twenty metres away. Suddenly, the Nomad became all too aware of the peril he was in. He needed to take refuge inside the cockpit. The Fighter itself was insulated against lightning strikes, but his equipment was not.

The Nomad glanced down the slope to the pump, then back behind him to the recombinator. The recombinator took priority. That it had not finished its cycle was unimportant. It could be resumed later on, in safer conditions. The Nomad turned and waded back over to the device. Interrupting the cycle, he powered down the machine. The solar cells folded away as another nearby arc of lightning impacted the hilltop. The Nomad hoisted the machine out of the puddle, exerting himself as he lowered it back into the cargo pod. He sealed the storage unit and reattached it to the clamps beneath the starboard wing, suspending it with the hydraulics to the relative safety of the undercarriage.

Lightning struck again, closer than ever, and the Nomad glanced back down the slope in a long moment of consideration. It was growing more dangerous every moment he spent out in the storm, but could he afford to leave the pump unprotected? This was the first time that the Nomad had used the device in a long while, but it had proven invaluable in this instance. Even if the filters were incapable of performing their intended task, the other components of the device were too important to forsake. Off the top of his head, the Nomad could think of a dozen parts that could be utilised in future repairs to the Fighter; if struck by lightning they would become altogether worthless.

The Nomad sighed in frustration as he marched back over to the winch and clipped the carabiner to his EVA harness. He descended the perilous hillside, slipping several times on the way down. Reaching the foot of the slope, the Nomad trudged over to the pump and began pulling in the intake pipe. When the machine was collapsed down, the Nomad attached it to the winch, hooking a second carabiner from his harness onto the cable. Readying himself for what the Nomad knew would be a gruelling ascent, he hesitantly activated the capstan winch, and began the exhausting fight uphill.

The cable tensioned under additional weight, as together, the Nomad and the filtration pump were heaved steadily uphill. The bank had turned to slop, and the Nomads boots sank into the gunge past the ankle. The suction of the mud ensnared his feet, making every step he took harder than the last. Battling with waning energy, the Nomad continued the slow unrelenting uphill climb as the downpour intensified and the winds hounded him from all sides. But despite the strain, slowly and surely, metre by metre, the Nomad ascended.

The verge up ahead loomed into sight through the swirling gloom and the Nomad could make out the rotating capstan. But in the blink of an eye, a gnarled fork of lightning shot down from the hurricane, exploding in a blinding flash in front of the Nomad. He felt the winch cable about his waste suddenly slacken. Before he had time to react, his weight shifted and the muddy slope gave way underfoot. He fell, tumbling in the mudslide, swamped off his feet as the entire face of the slope sloughed away around him. Scrambling with outstretched hands, the Nomad flailed helplessly, grasping for anything to hold onto, but his arms thrashed in futility as the wave of ashen sludge swept over him. Down he plunged, head over heels, blinded as the shale washed over his visor.

Somehow his fingers managed to snag hold of a fixed rock, but as he tried to stop himself from being swept further downhill, a carabiner snapped taught around his waist. The pump was still attached to his harness. The weight of the machine was too much. The Nomad's grip gave out. Acting as an anchor, swept up in the landslip, the pump continued to careen downhill, dragging the Nomad with it. Pummelled and battered by the avalanche of scree, the Nomad cascaded down after the pump, briefly slowing as he reached the shoreline.

Clawing at the bank of the lake, the Nomad felt the carabiner about his waist tension again. Upon striking the shore, the filtration pump bounced, arcing through the air in a moment of dreaded silence before splashing into the lake. Rent from the shore, tethered by the waist, the Nomad was dragged after it, plunging into the gungy waters of the algal lake. The viscous body of water swallowed the Nomad whole and he was enveloped suddenly by darkness. The thick layer of scum coating the water's surface sealed shut, blocking out any remnants of the sullen daylight above.

The Nomad was sinking fast, weighed down by the cumbersome pump still attached to his harness. Instinctually, he fought against the anchor, swimming with all the force he could muster in a desperate attempt to break the surface again, but even without the pump, the weight of his EVA suit alone would have made swimming difficult. He continued to sink through the murky waters, the algae soaking away all but the faintest light from the surface. He was panicking, rasping for air, sweating profusely. His heart drummed between his ears at what seemed a thousand beats per minute.

The Nomad swallowed several lungfuls of air and pressed his eyes tightly closed as he took a moment to calm himself. He reached for his harness and fumbled for the carabiner, but it was a triple lock system, and with the current tension applied to it he couldn't unfasten it... not until he reached the lakebed.

Sucking in several more deliberate breaths, the Nomad waited as he continued to sink. After what seemed an eternity, the filter pump came to rest on the lake floor and the Nomad beside it. The tension released and the Nomad fumbled once again at the carabiner. This time, through great difficulty, he was able to unclip himself from the cable. He was neutrally buoyant, and though the EVA suit was constricting, the Nomad was able to kick with his boots and pull with his gloved hands, beginning the climb through the murky lake back towards the surface.

He barely made it ten metres upwards before he was snagged once again. The winch cable had managed to coil itself around the Nomad whilst he was sliding down the hillside. Now it was knotted tightly around his ankle. He was still anchored to the lakebed, unable to ascend any further. The Nomad panicked again, scrabbling at his heel in an attempt to free his foot from the coils, but the wire had choked itself tightly around his ankle, and he lacked the dexterity whilst wearing his EVA gloves to untangle himself.

Anxiety continued to overwhelm him. His heart spasmed violently in his chest and his lungs constricted in terror. A buzzer sounded inside his helmet and a dreaded alert flashed up across his visor:

Warning! Oxygen Levels Low!

All his panicking and gasping in fear had squandered the air in his tanks. If he continued to hyperventilate, he would have barely two minutes of breathable air left.

Fighting the innate drive to swallow as much air as he could, the Nomad exhaled for as long as possible before inhaling deeply. For the next minute this was all he did. He inhaled and exhaled. Inhale. Exhale. Inhale. Exhale. His throbbing pulse steadied and his mind was brought back into clarity. Without physically checking, he sifted through his mind to recall all of the tools currently stowed in his EVA harness. Out of everything he took with him whilst carrying out EVAs he knew that there must be one that could help him now. His plasma cutter! That could save him.

Remembering exactly where the tool was

holstered, the Nomad calmly reached for the rear loop on his belt and drew the cutter. Flicking off the safety with his thumb, the Nomad primed the device and pulled the trigger. A white-hot glow illuminated in the murky depths and a sudden jet of bubbles frothed upwards. Calmly allowing himself to sink for a moment, the Nomad released the tension from the wire and lowered the flame down towards the line. The torch melted through the wire in a matter of seconds, and suddenly, the Nomad was free of his anchor. Switching off the plasma cutter, the Nomad stowed it back in his belt, and once again began to swim upwards.

He kicked and pulled with all his might through the viscous water, all the while watching the counter tick down on his remaining oxygen supply. Suddenly, he broke through the grimy surface. Thrashing about helplessly in the waves, he swivelled to get his bearings. He wasn't far from the shore, and in a few strokes, he had fought his way over to shallower waters. He managed to stand, despite his exhaustion, and waded out the last few metres before collapsing on the bank.

Rain clattered loudly against his helmet as the Nomad wheezed in exertion. His muscles were screaming, his head throbbing dazedly. The alarm on the inside of his helmet wailed with ever greater urgency, his final air reserves dwindling. He could barely move; but he had no choice. If he did not make it back up the slope in the next minute, he would suffocate there in the mud, on this lonely and sullen world.

EIGHT

The Nomad struggled to his feet. Water and mud continued to gush past. He planted a foot clumsily before him, and then another, and another, stumbling through dazed weariness towards the foot of the slope. He rasped heavily, straining to take the shortest and smallest gasps he could, fighting the rhythmic spasms in his lungs ordering him to inhale deeply. Reaching the foot of the bank, the Nomad dug his boots into the sopping mud and began to scramble upwards on hands and knees. It was slow going, too slow, but the ground had turned to slurry, and each time he extended his reach, he clawed away loose clumps of sludge.

He fumbled at his belt and drew out a small hand pick. The Nomad swung over his head and dug it into the slope. Heaving with all his might, he shuffled up the sliding muck and replanted his footing. He reached upwards again, driving the pick through the soft layer of shingle and silt, into the firmer ground beneath. Once again, he wriggled against the tide of drifting mud. Up he scrambled, as quick and steady as was possible, using the very last wisps of air left in his tank as he did so. Finally, he heaved himself up over the verge. The alert flashing in his helmet warned that his oxygen supply was entirely depleted.

The Nomad's lungs burned as he fought to his feet. His head buzzed and his fingers and toes tingled. He stumbled forwards. The Fighter was barely within reach. His knees buckled and his visor plunged into a puddle. Piercing agony throbbed across his scalp as the rain continued to batter him into the ground. He strained his arms, lifting himself out of the mire, but now his elbows faltered. He reached ahead, groping at the soft mud with his fingers and dragged himself towards his ship. His sight was fading white around the periphery whilst inky black spots formed in the centre of his vision.

He gasped and sputtered, choking on nothing more than nitrogen and carbon dioxide. He was not yet dead, but he knew that in a matter of seconds he would lose consciousness. If that happened, his fate would be sealed. He would never wake up again. Everything up until this point would have been for nothing. All he had endured and suffered, all the pain, all the loss, all the emptiness, despair, and hopelessness, the days, the months, the years, every cycle of every routine, every jump, every system, every planet, all of it would have been for nothing. And so, the Nomad stood up. How it was possible, and with what strength he did so, he would never know, but he rose to his feet and staggered the last few steps towards the Fighter. He heaved himself up the rungs of the ladder and opened the canopy, toppling headfirst into the cockpit.

Rolling over on the seat, the Nomad turned to face the control panel. Reaching with a benumbed hand, he raised the canopy lever and sealed the cockpit. Rotating a safety valve, he initiated an atmospheric purge. All fell silent as the Nomad was deafened by vacuum. Flicking a final switch in his last vestiges of consciousness, the Nomad repressurised the cockpit and began awkwardly fumbling at his helmet. In his oxygen deprived clumsiness, the collar bearing seemed an impossible puzzled to solve. His vision faded fully to dark as the Nomad felt his pulse weaken. By sheer luck, in his death throes, the Nomad somehow managed to flick the seal on the lock. His head lulled forwards as he lost consciousness. The helmet rolled from his pate, clattering to the cockpit floor.

NINE

When the Nomad finally reopened his eyes, night had fallen across the primordial world. A thin scattering of cloud wisped overhead, drifting beneath the dusting of infinite stars. The Nomad leant forward in his seat, groggily rubbing his brow. For a brief instant, he had forgotten what had transpired, awaking in his cockpit on an unfamiliar world as he'd done countless times before. But as he gazed down, he saw the green tinge of algal residue caked across his EVA suit. Traumatic memories of lightning, of being dragged underwater, of suffocating, of fighting for his life, all came flooding suddenly back. His pulse quickened. He gasped for air. He thrashed in panic about the cockpit. After a moment of relived terror, he realised he had made it. Somehow, against all odds, he had managed to reach the refuge of the cockpit. The storm had passed. It was over.

He was weary, his body fatigued, his mind depleted. Almost drunkenly, he searched the cockpit for his helmet, finally recovering it from the floor. Locking it onto his EVA suit's collar bearing, he depressurised the Fighter and opened the canopy.

Exhaustedly, the Nomad climbed out of the cockpit, down the ladder, and set foot on the sodden ground. With his head lowered in dread, he stumbled over towards the capstan winch to begin assessing the damage. It was as he had both feared and suspected. Lightning had struck the winch, splaying the machine into a scorched and molten mess. The capstan itself had been rent from the device. As the Nomad glanced around for it, he came to suspect it was now at the bottom of the lake, beside the filtration pump.

He'd been fortunate not to have a hand on the cable the moment the lightning struck. The loops on his harness where the carabiner attached were scorched, the partially molten fabric having just insulated the Nomad against the current surging through the metal. Were the harness not manufactured to its specifications, he may well have been killed outright by the lightning strike. But the fibres of the loop had held out, protecting the Nomad against the millions of volts conducted down the cable, driven by a current measuring into the tens of thousands of amperes.

The winch had not been so fortuitous. The thousand gigawatts of power, delivered in a miniscule fraction of a second, had ripped open the reinforced steel alloy housing the winch, frying the motor inside. The Nomad peered through the gouge in the casing; the majority of the internal components were charred and warped beyond recognition.

The winch was unsalvageable.

The Nomad dropped to his knees, frustration compounding his lassitude. He felt something beneath his shins, partially buried in the mud: the power coupling. Slowly tracing the cable with his eyes as it meandered through the sludge, his heart sank in sickening horror. A terrible realisation cut through the stupor of the Nomad's exhaustion. He had been so concerned by the loss of the winch, a relatively unsophisticated and potentially replaceable piece of equipment, that he had neglected to consider the vastly greater concern. The harness had indeed protected the Nomad from electrocution; had the current grounded through him, he would likely be dead. With the winch double insulated, the Nomad had until this point foolishly assumed that the majority of energy from the lightning bolt had grounded through the pump at the end of the winch cable. But now he realised, that simply couldn't have been the case.

Electricity always took the path of least resistance. True, the metal winch cable was relatively conductive. But what was even more so, was the length of power cabling specifically designed to carry a current, connecting the winch directly to the Fighter; more specifically, to the Fighter's power cells. That was what had happened to the energy of the lightning strike. It hadn't been earthed at all! It had been conducted away, directly into the Fighter: tens of thousands of amperes in a mere fraction of a second. And the Nomad knew all too well what happened to batteries subjected to too great an incoming charge.

For a long moment, the Nomad dared not move. He dared not turn his head to look towards the Fighter out of fear of what he would see. He didn't need to. He already knew what had happened. He was stranded on this planet. The Fighter's power supply had been obliterated by the lightning strike. The Fighter was dead. And so too would he die here, marooned on this isolated primordial world.

But it couldn't be true! He had opened and closed the canopy. He had depressurised and repressurised the cockpit. The Fighter was still somewhat operational, and therefore the damage could not be absolute. The ship still had some life in it. It wasn't dead yet. Even still, it might not ever take off again. He could still be marooned.

Terrified of what he was about to see, the Nomad steadily rose to his feet and began the arduous walk back towards the Fighter. He kept his eyeline low, following the snaking cable along the ground until it finally rose out of the mud, tracing upwards to the sockets on the undercarriage of the craft. Already, the Nomad could see the power cell access panel was hanging open on its hinges. The metal was bowed and scorched, confirming that at least one of the cells had exploded.

Crawling beneath the wing, the Nomad rolled

supine to inspect the compartment. Every fuse protecting the batteries had blown. Though irritating, this in itself was not too much of an issue; over the years, the Nomad had salvaged enough fuses to replace all of them and still have enough spare for future repairs. The fuses had undoubtedly protected the cells somewhat, but it was clear from the damage that electricity had arced across the broken circuit. Of the twenty power cells outfitted to the Fighter, seven had exploded outright. Of the thirteen remaining, an additional two had inflated and cracked their casings. Some of the circuitry was burnt out completely, but other portions of the battery housing were merely singed. The damage was extensive, but far from a worst-case-scenario.

The Nomad could not guess what portion of the seemingly undamaged eleven remaining cells would still be operational. They were already degraded, nearing the end of their operational lifespan. There was no saying from the visual inspection whether or not they would hold enough charge to get the Fighter airborne, let alone make an FTL jump.

The Nomad slammed his fist against the ground repeatedly in frustration, splattering mud across his visor. He had been careless. He had been foolish. He had been reckless. He should never have attempted to harvest the algae with a storm brewing on the horizon, and he definitely should not have continued heedlessly once it had struck. He had been greedy and complacent, too arrogant and obsessive in his routine to consider the dangers the hostile world posed.

This complacency had cost him dearly. He could only vaguely guess at the consequences. At worst he was stranded, doomed to die the moment his supplies ran out, which would be sooner rather than later now that his filtration pump was irrevocably sunk at the bottom of the lake. At best, his effective FTL jump range would be halved, meaning that his already unfathomably long journey across the stars was now doubly long, extended beyond the far reaches of his potential lifespan. He would never arrive. He would die along the way. It was almost assured, whether he accepted it or not. But what was done was done. There was no changing it now. And so, the Nomad continued.

Throughout the night he systematically stripped and cleaned down the Fighter's power core. He replaced the fried circuitry and rewired the entire system. As the alien dawn arrived, the Nomad welded the cracked bracketing and hammered the warped casing back into shape. By noon, he had replaced every fuse, testing each in turn to ensure they would blow in the event of a power surge. Finally, he cleaned and reinserted all eleven of the salvageable power cells. With a few hammer blows, the Nomad knocked the bow out of the cover panel. Resealing the compartment, he crawled out from beneath the Fighter.

Carrying out another full inspection of the ship's exterior to ensure the Fighter had sustained no other damage during the storm that had escaped his notice, the Nomad was relieved to discover that everything else was in order. He coiled up the power cabling and stowed it in the starboard cargo pod, before returning to the winch for a final assessment. With a heavy sigh, he quickly concluded that there was not a single component worth salvaging from the device.

Dusk was once again drawing in across the primordial planet. The Nomad could hear the distant rumble of thunder as black anvils spouted on the horizon. Taking several minutes to scrub the algal residue and mud from the exterior of his EVA suit, he finally climbed back into the cockpit and sealed the canopy. Safely within the ship, the Nomad powered up the system diagnostics and began a full assessment of the Fighter. The computer whirred away for several long minutes as it thoroughly analysed the state of the ship's countless components, before finally publishing the results on the holographic interface.

Beyond the damage to the power cells, the Fighter had escaped unscathed. Some erratic software behaviours had arisen during the power surge, and the scientific instruments on the undercarriage had powered up and gone haywire, recording and logging a string of absurd and nonsensical readings. But each of the delicate scanners and analytical tools had now been rebooted and were functioning normally. Finally, the Nomad turned his attention to the information he had avoided until last.

The ship's power cells were operating at just above half the capacity of their previous levels, congruent with what would be expected given the number of surviving cells. This was good. It meant that the undamaged cells had been unaffected by the lightning strike. Perhaps unsurprisingly, each cell was fully charged.

The Fighter retained the ability to carry out all of the tasks and scans expected of it on a day-to-day basis, though it would require more frequent charging. However, the FTL range had dropped from a maximum of ninety lightyears down to forty-nine; in safe practice, this translated to a range of forty lightyears per jump from a full charge. In the cosmic scheme, this range was barely further than skipping between adjacent grains of sand on an infinitely long beach. True, he was able to jump between nearby star systems with range to spare, but the issue arose from the fact that stars were not homogenously dispersed across the galaxy; they were clustered together in groups, with great expanses of empty space often stretching between them. If the Fighter's range were half again, the Nomad would have great difficulty navigating across these stellar voids; halved once more and it would be near impossible. If only a few more power cells had been damaged by the power surge, then the Nomad would have found himself in these dire circumstances.

It took a pessimistic kind of optimism, one that the unforgiving, unrelenting nature of the universe had endowed the Nomad with, for him to consider himself lucky. But fortune was what the Nomad did indeed feel. As devastating and cruel as this setback was, the Nomad knew all too well that it could have been worse—far worse. The Nomad had paid a steep price, but he had not come away with nothing. It had cost him his winch, his filtration pump, a number of spare parts, and a one hundred percent increase to his life sentence, but the Nomad had come away with several months' worth of food. That food was even more valuable now that his range had been slashed, since he could no longer be afforded the freedom to choose his destinations as he had once done.

No longer would a plethora of solar systems be available at any one time. He would now only ever have a handful of potential destinations within reach. He had lost an element of choice. Rarely now could he ever opt to be selective. This meant he would be travelling to less favourable stars. Fewer would accommodate life. Resources would be scarcer. Unable to span the distances between white main sequence stars, he would have to jump to far more red dwarfs. These smaller, cooler stellar systems rarely possessed the necessary starting conditions for life. He would need to ration his supplies, scrutinise each potential destination with greater care. But he was not doomed. The already arduous journey had been made all the harder; but it was not impossible, and so long as it was not impossible, the Nomad stood a chance, no matter how remote.

TEN

The Nomad dropped out of FTL and began his decelerating approach to a class M4 red dwarf. The long burn of his pulsejets gradually slowed him to orbital speeds on the periphery of the system. The dim glow of the small crimson star shone in the remote distance, barely distinguishable against the constellations in the galactic backdrop.

A low power warning flashed across the Fighter's display. The Nomad pivoted the ship, using a short burn to navigate into a closer orbit, where the light intensity was great enough to charge the cells. Optimally angling the craft for photon capture, the Nomad unfolded the photovoltaic cells and waited for the ship to recharge. Awaking a while later to find the incomplete array of cells at full capacity, he retracted the panels and powered up the ship's scientific equipment. After a time, the scan results pinged across the holographic display. The Nomad redeployed the photovoltaic cells to top up on power reserves and began sifting through the data projected before him.

The system was somewhat unremarkable. The star was twinned with a brown dwarf companion orbiting roughly twenty astronomical units out; in possession of a large magnetosphere, the failed star would be ideal for antimatter harvesting. Two small terrestrial worlds in close synchronous orbit were tidally locked to the star, and a belt of comets and asteroids encircled the outer reaches of the ecliptic. It was a barren and unpromising ancient solar system, akin to the vast majority to which the Nomad had journeyed in the years since the catastrophic loss of half his power cells. But as ever, the Nomad made do.

Scrolling through the last pieces of data, he was readying to close the results of the scans, when something leapt out at him: an anomaly. Something inconsistent with the rest of the solar system drifted out in the far reaches of the asteroid field. The Nomad quickly studied the readout, checking and double checking to ensure it wasn't a mere artefact in the scans. It was conclusive. An abnormality of significant size was floating on the fringes of the forsaken solar system. If the Nomad was correct in his guess, it was a wreck, and a large one at that.

There was nothing the Nomad could feasibly conceive of that he would ever find a drift in the endless void more valuable than a shipwreck. True, the carcass might already have been picked clean by scavengers, but equally, wreckage in such an inconsequential system as this one might have gone unnoticed for millennia. It could contain anything: valuable elements and resources, fuel tanks brimming with unsyphoned antimatter, oxygen, hydrogen, water, perhaps even useful equipment. But the Nomad knew above all what he hoped to find: power cells. Summoning his sense of cynicism that prevented disappointment, he suppressed his excitement and adjusted the Fighter's orbit to carry him out into the asteroid field.

The Fighter coasted in a wide swinging orbit towards the outer reaches of the ecliptic. The dim red star receded to a pinprick of light as the Nomad approached the cloud of residual rock and ice left over from the formation of the solar system. Upon approach to the expansive asteroid belt, the Nomad swivelled the Fighter rearward and slowed the craft with a series of short bursts from the pulsejets. Rotating the ship back around, the Nomad powered up the Fighter's radar array and flight computer, allowing the ship to begin mapping the location and distances of the vast sea of rock adrift in the void.

In their thousands, the asteroids were plotted into the flight computer, their locations highlighted across the Fighter's HUD, revealing countless floating islands hidden in the inky blackness. Using the RCS for a translational manoeuvre, the Nomad dipped clear of a stone goliath as it loomed dimly from out of the darkness. Another lateral shift moved the Fighter's flight path clear of the next rapidly approaching iceberg, the gargantuan mass of frozen volatiles tumbling slowly on its axis. The Nomad powered up the ship's compositional scanners, hoping to identify the wreckage by its differing makeup to the surrounding asteroids. On a whim, he likewise transferred power to the Fighter's communication scanners. The Nomad never expected to detect any form of signal, he had long ago accepted that he was alone in the crippling infinitude of space, yet within moments of toggling the scanner, his instruments lit up with a returning ping that sounded at regular intervals.

It was no broadcast or SOS, but it was a signal nonetheless; a transponder had activated upon detection of the interrogating signals emitted from the Fighter's scanners. The Nomad was alone, that was unmistakable. The response was merely a faint blip echoing what once was. What was important, however, was that the blip existed. The ping informed the Nomad that the wreck afloat somewhere within the asteroid belt still had power. Power enough to send and receive basic signals. And where there was power there would likely be power cells.

The Nomad delved deeper into the asteroid field, negotiating the cloud of residual material left over from planetary formation. Carried by the tide of gravity, the islands of rock and ice were endlessly adrift, forever floating on parallel orbits, their paths never diverting, never crossing, the lonely planetoids eternally condemned to float in relative proximity to one another, but never to interact. It was easy to think of an asteroid field as a maelstrom of collisions and impacts, yet these remnants of the early solar system were imprisoned by time.

Rejected by chance, the asteroids were doomed never to aggregate more so than they had done already. They would never collate to form a planet or moon, and save for the occasional unlikely interaction with an elliptically orbiting comet or the like, these fragments of creation were fated to continue eternally on their predestined paths. Shackled in orbit, their only chance of escaping eternity was the death of the parent star to which they were anchored. Yet this red dwarf burned so dimly that it would likely continue to do so for several trillion more years. These asteroids were bound unceasingly to existence with no prospect of change or finality—much like the Nomad.

Pressing such thoughts from his mind, the Nomad restudied the readouts in front of him as he continued to navigate towards the signal. Finally, his scientific instruments began to detect higher ratios of heavy elements in the surrounding debris. The Nomad activated the Fighter's landing lights. Two broad incandescent beams shone from the nose of the craft. Immediately before the Fighter, several fragments of debris were suddenly illuminated. The flotsam were shards of spaceship hull, that much was apparent from the readouts in front of the Nomad, yet beyond this, they bore no hint as to what lurked deeper in the field. Negotiating his way between the scraps of metal, the Nomad continued to follow the constantly returning transponder, tracing the signal towards its source.

Larger and larger chunks of wreckage drifted passed the Nomad as he piloted deeper in, the scans of each section offering him new snippets of information. Steadily, he began to build up a picture of the carrion he was scavenging for; it was a large ship, that much was clear, of unknown alien origin. The radiation damage to the metal indicated the wreck had met its end several millennia ago, yet from the littering of flotsam spread over such a wide expanse, the craft appeared to have broken up almost entirely.

The mystery continued to unfold as the Nomad sailed past what appeared to be a section of an immense rocket thruster nozzle. An exhaust that large could only belong to a warship, or perhaps and interstellar ark. The next recognisable item of debris was a turret barrel from a main battery; the wreck was definitely a warship, likely a destroyer or dreadnought.

Perhaps then, this system had been the site of an ancient battle between two warring races. But the degree of annihilation seemed excessive, even for the bloodiest of wars. It was more probable that the extensive disintegration of the warship had been due instead to a collision, likely with the asteroid field, and perhaps at relativistic speeds. Yet in order for that to have happened, at least accidentally, the ship must have suffered a catastrophic failure in navigational systems prior to the collision.

Something didn't add up, and not knowing what exactly perturbed the Nomad. He felt ill at ease, as if he had forgotten something vital, or if some crucial piece of information had escaped his conscious observations. This chain of thought was abruptly ended by a proximity warning that flashed up across the Nomad's HUD. The largest section of flotsam so far loomed out of the dark as the pinging signal built to a crescendo. An intact portion of the dreadnought's hull floated lifelessly up ahead, silhouetted against the faint red haze of the dwarf star. The metal carcass revolved slowly around its centre of gravity, steadily revealing the ruptures and shears to the metal. The buckled and bowed hull section was but a fraction of the original ship, yet even still, its dimensions were several orders of magnitude greater than the miniscule Fighter approaching it. Even at his present range, the gargantuan hunk of debris brimmed the Fighter's canopy, but still a considerable distance away, his landing lights merely scattered into the void ahead, the spread of the beams too great to cast away any of the shadow bathing the wreckage.

The debris was more than likely the aft end of the warship. A thousand dimples and scrapes mottled the armoured surface from where the dreadnought had ploughed through the asteroid cloud, before finally coming to rest as a scattering of flotsam lost in the lonely void. The range of the debris field stretched several astronomical units, the majority of the wreckage contained within the densest region of the asteroid belt. The Nomad knew that scouring the field in the hopes of finding other large sections of debris was pointless. The chances of finding anything remotely salvageable within the sea of ice and stone by coincidence alone was incredibly remote. The only thing that had led him to this specific section was a signal transponder still active after all this time. He had been incredibly lucky. This alone was enough to set the Nomad on edge. Luck was something he no longer believed in. Something was not right. But he could not afford to pass up this opportunity. And so, the Nomad continued.

The wreckage loomed larger and larger until the Fighter drifted fully into the debris' shadow. The mess of scarred and twisted metal had been drastically distorted when the dreadnought came to its violent end, but the ship's internal structure was still vaguely discernible. Corridors jutted outwards, ending abruptly in jagged edges, whilst rooms hollowed out of the mass of alloy, tunnelling backwards into the shadows. Ventilation and service ducts trailed piping and fraying cables, whilst immense tensile and load-bearing struts extended from the wreckage like a gnarled and mangled skeleton.

The Nomad ran an array of scans on the floating shipwreck, pinpointing the exact location within the crumpled carcass that housed the transponder. It was several compartments deep, inaccessible by the Fighter. Fortunately, the data suggested that the transponder would have its own isolated power source, separate from the main energy cells of the dreadnought that could currently be floating anywhere else in the system.

Reaching beneath his seat, the Nomad pulled out his helmet and locked it over his head. His HUD booted up across the inside of his visor whilst he began shutting down a number of the Fighter's systems to conserve power. Piloting in as close as possible via the RCS arcjets, the Nomad stabilised his orbit in accordance with the debris, minimising his drift to within a fraction of a metre per hour. The Nomad rotated the cockpit's safety valve and pressed a series of buttons across the control panel. The gasses of the cockpit hissed as they were rapidly sucked away. The pressure dropped steadily and the beeping transponder faded to quietude as the Nomad was plunged into a vacuum.

The eerie stillness of empty space had always haunted the Nomad. As he retracted the canopy of the Fighter, he was gradually exposed to the raw dangerous void that constituted the majority of the universe. All that now laid between the Nomad and death was an EVA suit barely a few millimetres thick: a thin layer of compression fabric to protect against the effects of the vacuum, insulated against radiation heat loss, which was then coated in an equally thin reflective weave to ward off ionising cosmic radiation, topped finally by the thickest layer of the suit: an impact resistant material for guarding against micrometeorites.

The Nomad unbuckled himself from the harness of his pilot's seat, and easing upwards, drifted gently out of the cockpit. On his first spacewalk in recent memory, the Nomad took a moment to fully acclimatised himself with the sensation of weightlessness that was never truly experienced whilst strapped into the pilot's seat. Acquainted with the microgravity, he activated his EVA suit's mobility thrusters via the holographic interface on his wrist.

A stream of charged ions expelled from nozzles located on the undersides of his boots, elbows, and back, gently accelerating the Nomad forwards. The propulsion felt cumbersome at first, but the Nomad quickly refamiliarised himself with the thruster control scheme as he negotiated his way over towards a jagged shelf extending from the wreckage. Clasping hold of a warped rung, the Nomad heaved himself inwards and planted his boots down onto the metal ledge. The boots, sensing a ferromagnetic alloy beneath their soles, automatically magnetised, attaching firmly against the metal and locking the Nomad on his feet. This too was a strange sensation, as there was no sense of weight in his attachment to the floor. Even though he was stood upright, his sense of direction was still lacking an up or a down. Only the very souls of his feet were cemented to the floor, the rest of his body was still free floating.

The experience immediately conjured a traumatic memory of floating in the dark, anchored by his feet to the bottom of a lake, the last vestiges of air ticking away inside his helmet. The haunting flashback summoned a cold sweat across the Nomad's brow. He stood frozen for a long moment, before pushing the harrowing images back into the deep recesses of his mind from where they had awoken.

Lifting a heel inside his boot and pressing with his toes, the Nomad felt his right foot demagnetise, the suit detecting the shift in pressure beneath his sole, interpreting it as the wearer's desire to step forwards. His foot floated weightlessly once more and the Nomad clumsily swung it out in front of his body. Then, acting against the natural instinct of allowing gravity to guide his foot back towards the floor, the Nomad actively drove his leg downwards, planting it on the shelf. The boot remagnetised and clamped firm and flatly to the metal.

A single step was all the Nomad had taken. In his lifetime he had taken millions. He had been walking since before a time when he even had any memories. A step was the most natural and intuitive movement he could ever conceive of making; it required little effort and thought to carry out. And yet, when something as simple as the force of gravity was removed from the equation, it suddenly became complex. Disorientated, and numb from concentration, he focussed on moving forwards one step at a time. It grew easier, as most things do when practised, yet this method of locomotion seemed alien and obtuse.

After a time, the Nomad had travelled someway down the corridor, in towards the heart of the wreckage. He peered back down the tunnel of cold steel to see the Fighter floating motionlessly not too far away. The Nomad required that reassurance. Whenever the Fighter was left unmoored, he needed to at least be able to see it. Had the Nomad made some miscalculation in negating drift, the Fighter could float away without him noticing. It could sail clean out of sight in no time at all if he had made even the slightest mistake when parking alongside the flotsam. He could lose the Fighter altogether, or perhaps worse, have it within sight but just out of range. The mobility thrusters of his EVA suit were simple enough to operate once the Nomad was at ease with them, but their range was limited to a few minutes of usage. If the Fighter drifted too far and too fast, he would never be able to catch up to it. So, every few metres the Nomad trudged down the corridor, he would turn back to check that the Fighter was where he had left it. And sure enough, it was.

ELEVEN

The Nomad's gold-coated solar visor slid down over his helmet as he prepped his plasma cutter. Stood between the transponder and his current position was a thick bulkhead door. Though a residual energy source running the transponder lay somewhere deep within the ship's carcass, the rest of the wreck was a lifeless skeleton. The heavy steel door in front of him now was sealed shut with no operational means of opening it. Constituted of a reinforced steel alloy, designed to withstand all the stresses and strains of space warfare, the Nomad knew that attempting to cut through the bulkhead with his plasma cutter alone was futile. However, the same could not be said for the metal panelling that covered the door's maintenance port.

The white plasma torch fired up, flaring blindingly in the dark corridor. The solar visor reacted photochromically to the glare, protecting the Nomad's eyes as he raised the cutting torch to the access panel and began cutting neatly around its periphery. The port cover was designed to be removed; really there was no need for the Nomad to cut through it, only, this being an alien vessel, the panel was held in place by some bizarre proprietary form of bolt, and the Nomad did not have a tool that even vaguely matched the fittings.

Slowly carving a wide ellipse with the searing plasma cutter, the Nomad pondered what could lay inside the port. He might simply find the internal electrics for powering the door, probably the worst-case scenario, given that he would then need to somehow relay power from the Fighter, down the corridor, and patch it into the circuitry in order to get the bulkhead open. It would be time consuming and somewhat finicky, but not an unworkable situation. Alternatively, he might find some form of emergency generator on an isolated system that could allow the door to be charged and opened; if still functional after all this time, it would certainly be an easier means to get through than running out dozens of metres of cabling. The Nomad continued to speculate as he finished slicing his oval through the sheet metal. Glowing orange around its molten edges, the cut plate dislodged and floated free from the panel. Careful not to touch the searing circumference, the Nomad delivered a gentle tap to the centre of the plate, sending it drifting off down the corridor safely out of reach.

Peering through the port, the Nomad's helmet light spilled into the hollow. He smiled to himself. The door's redundancy system was perhaps the simplest of all; certainly the most elegant and reliable: a mechanical crank. One that allowed an engineer to manually hoist open the hefty bulkhead. The

Nomad reached in through the glowing opening and firmly gripped the crank. He strained in an attempt to rotate it, but despite his efforts, it remained firmly welded. This deep inside the wreck, shielded by the surrounding metal from radiation damage, and with no moisture in the vacuum of space to rust the mechanism, there was no obvious reason as to why the crank should have seized up.

It took a brief moment for the Nomad to realise that the answer might be far more obvious. In turning the crank, he had applied a sense of logic instilled into him by his own culture. That sense of intuition simply did not apply to alien technology. The laws of design were bound to differ across species separated by vast astronomical distances and great epochs of time. Returning his hand to the crank, the Nomad once again tried to turn it, only this time the other way. Sure enough, after a bit of pressure, the crank rotated for the first time in millennia.

Stiffly winding the mechanism, the door ratcheted upwards, lifting from the floor. The clarity of the vacuum around the Nomad suddenly fogged as a gust of gas and dust evacuated from behind the bulkhead, jettisoning into space. The flow lasted a mere few seconds, ceasing with the door hoisted barely from the floor. The Nomad continued to crank, the mechanism ratcheting silently in his hand, as centimetre by centimetre, the bulkhead continued to rise, retracting steadily into a cavity above.

The Nomad stepped back, withdrawing his arm from the access port, and peered into the dark room before him. It was some form of engineering hub, perhaps merely a single node from a vast nexus of computer systems that had once existed aboard the immense stellar warship. Several dead machines were fixed into the walls, wiring and coolant pipes coiling into engineering ducts above. The Nomad glanced over them in turn and disregarded them each respectively. They were servers, or something of the like: computers too alien and long deceased for the Nomad to make sense of. Perhaps disassembling them might reveal some components or resources that could potentially prove useful, but the Nomad knew he would more than likely just be wasting time and oxygen.

Retrofitting computer hardware created by his own race was difficult enough, especially if more than a few decades of innovation had transpired between the two pieces of technology. Attempting to integrate a piece of alien computing hardware into the Fighter would be nigh on impossible. Technology from two species completely removed in time and space was almost always fundamentally incompatible. Basic key devices were often universal; a power cell was a power cell regardless of where and by whom it was manufactured. Their dimensions and form varied drastically, as did their voltage, capacity, and amperage; their terminals were seldom similar, and the method of storing or producing electrical charge often differed drastically from cell to cell, but these were all mere hiccoughs that could be worked out.

Almost half of the fixings and housing units in the Fighter were bespoke, crafted and adjusted by the Nomad himself to fit the various cells he had salvaged over the years. The mechanical logistics of the terminals mattered little; so long as the Nomad was able to fix a wire to both the positive and the negative terminal, he could potentially jury rig it into the Fighter. The issues of voltage, and amperage were slightly more complex, but nothing a transformer or capacitor could not address. But the mere thought of attempting to integrate and alien processor unit or memory drive into the Fighter's computer systems was almost unfathomable.

Computing evolved at near breakneck speeds, such that archaic technology from a single culture in itself became alien after time. Different races of differing levels of intelligence, with drastically varying biological methods of achieving higher thought, exponentially diversifying the spectrum of psychologies, meant that there was no singular straightforward approach to the advance of computing. Every species developed their own unique system architectures and methods to constructing computational devices, each varying from one another as much as their creators.

The Nomad continued to peer about the server room, looking for any indication as to where the transponder might lie. A few seconds later, he spotted something promising. A single diode blinked on and off in prolonged intervals. The Nomad stepped closer to the flashing LED, immediately halting in his tracks when a holographic interface unfolded in the dark. The projecting images flickered and stuttered weakly in the vacuum, depicting and array of indecipherable runic symbols. What they meant did not matter. What mattered was that the holographic display was operational, and thereby receiving power.

The Nomad scrutinised the panelling around him, and using an intuition garnered from years of scavenging, he identified the spot where the power cell was most likely to be housed. Once again, he fired up the plasma cutter. The panelling sparked silently as the cutting torch made swift work of the metal; unlike the bulkhead, it wasn't reinforced, and was barely thicker than a sheet of paper. In less than a minute, the Nomad had cut away a large section of the device's housing, revealing the internal circuitry. The Nomad's guess had been off, though not by much. Amongst the fiberglass epoxy circuit boards glinting with millions of silicon chips and other various components, the Nomad made out the very edge of a cylindrical module fixed upwards and left of where he had cut. From its overall appearance, it was not immediately obvious that the device in question was the power source the Nomad was hunting for, but marked onto the rim in phosphorescent paint was a symbol resembling a lightning bolt, a fairly universal icon for electricity. He'd found it.

Save for a personally addressed message written in his own language, the Nomad could scarcely think of a clearer indication as to the component's purpose. A ubiquitous natural phenomenon, lightning struck across the universe wherever there existed an atmosphere with sufficient dynamics to produce the necessary build up of charge. For almost every race to have ever evolved throughout the history of the universe, their first experience of electricity would undoubtedly have been in the form of a lightning storm. No wonder then that wherever the power of electricity was harnessed through technology, the symbol chosen more often than not to depict it was the distinctive icon of a lightning bolt. The unintended consequence was that it created a labelling system that could be understood across species without the need for anything vaguely resembling a common language.

Knowing he'd found what he was looking for, the Nomad cut away a second section of panelling, this time exposing the power cell in full. The device was contained inside a thick metal sleeve, welded in place and wired directly into the circuitry. A second indecipherable alien symbol, much larger than the lightning bolt, glowed red across the casing. Unlike the universal symbol for electricity, this second icon was completely foreign; merely an invention of the race that had constructed the warship, it held no innate meaning to it, but even still, something about it set the Nomad on edge. There was nothing specific about the alien graphic that sounded alarm, but the sharpness of the lines, the slant of the angles, and the overall symmetry of the shape somehow appeared different from the holographic runes that had flickered to life when the Nomad had entered the room. Whatever the cause, the symbol elicited an uneasily niggling in the back of his subconscious, one that was hard to shake.

His instincts told him to leave it be, to not risk disturbing the power cell, and to simply walk away. But the rational portion of his mind argued otherwise; once more he was relying on intuition nurtured from experience from his own culture. These intuitions seldom translated. But the lightning bolt had, he reminded himself. What then? Should he heed a vague symbol that held no real meaning, merely because he did not like the look of it? No. He was desperate. He needed this cell, and it was presented perfectly before him. It was even a favourable size and shape; with a little modification to one of the Fighter's receptors, the Nomad could easily wire it in. All he needed to do was to cut away the metal sleeve and remove it.

The Nomad ignited his plasma cutter. Eager to prevent damaging the cell in any way, he cautiously began to cut into the housing. Sparks started to stream silently from the metal sheath as the torch carved through the alloy, but after barely a few seconds of cutting, a warning suddenly flared across the inside of the Nomad's visor, swiftly accompanied by an alarming buzzer. His suit's sensors had detected a sudden radiation spike. It was no coincidence. The Nomad killed the plasma torch and stepped warily back. He initiated a scan from the interface on his EVA suit and waited anxiously for the analysis to complete.

It only took a few seconds for the scan to run its course. The results pinged across the inside of the Nomad's helmet.

Americium-241 detected.

The Nomad realised his almost fatal mistake. The device was no battery; it was a radioisotope thermoelectric generator: an RTG. And he had begun to cut straight into it! Another few millimetres deeper and he could have exposed himself to fatal levels of radiation that his suit was unequipped to protect him against. His heart was pounding. He suddenly felt sick. What he'd mistaken for a simple power cell was in fact a generator designed to produce electricity via the heat created by radioactive decay. That was what the alien symbol had been: a warning sign. One for radioactivity. And the Nomad had ignored it, against his better judgement.

Once again, he had been foolhardy. He was embarrassed that it had taken a radiation alarm from his suit to realise. Even without the alien warning symbol, he should have recognised he was dealing with an RTG. The signs were there from the moment he had first detected the transponder signal. RTGs were ideal for running low power automated systems for thousands of years, provided they were supplied with a large enough quantity of their radioactive isotope. They didn't provide enough power to run anything substantial, but a signal transponder on an isolated system was an ideal candidate for such a power source. Even the most advanced batteries could barely hold charge for more than a few hundred years, discharging over time until they ran flat, even with no device drawing from them. An RTG however, was powered by radioactive decay, and with radioisotopes such as Americium-241 with a half-life of four hundred and thirty-two years, they could provide a low wattage for several millennia before their output fell below usable levels.

The Nomad could tell from the faint and failing holographic interface that this RTG was at the very end of its extended lifespan. It was probably for this reason that the Nomad had avoided exposing himself to a lethal dosage of radiation. After all this time, the vast majority of the Americium-241 had decayed to Neptunium-237, Thallium-207, and Silicon-34. Because of this, the ionising radiation now leaking through the protective sleeve the Nomad had compromised was not intense enough to kill him.

The sickening sense of dread from the near-death experience was subsiding. The Nomad collected his thoughts. Knowing now that he was safe so long as he did not attempt to cut any deeper into the radiation shield encapsulating the RTG, he came to the realisation that this salvage operation had been a waste of his time. Even a newly manufactured RTG would have had little value to the Nomad. He could potentially use one to power some low-level systems onboard the Fighter, but the output of such a device was not substantial enough to be of any real service. Now, in its decayed state, this RTG was utterly useless to him; it could barely power the transponder, let alone the Fighter.

The Nomad stomped a magnetic boot in silent frustration. He was not a single step closer to restoring the Fighter's power array, and he had come to within a few millimetres of death. In the process, he had wasted precious oxygen, and the Fighter's power had dwindled with the systems left idling whilst he performed the EVA. Defeatedly, the Nomad turned and began the long and clumsy walk back down the corridor in zero gravity.

Suddenly, a notification pinged from the Fighter to the Nomad's EVA suit. The ship's background scanners had detected a second signal. One completely different in nature from that of the transponder. The frequency detected by the Fighter was indicative of a long-range scanner emitted from somewhere else in the system; a scanner searching for something; a scanner that had found what it was looking for! It was drawing closer, and as the Nomad inspected the readouts on his HUD, he realised he recognised the signal.

TWELVE

The Nomad kicked off from the floor and his EVA boots demagnetised. Drifting down the corridor, he fired all of his suit's mobility thrusters on full burn. Jetting down the mangled tunnel of dead steel, the Nomad flew out of the warship carcass, sailing rapidly towards his ship. Reaching with outstretched fingertips, he groped at the spacecraft. Hooking his grip around the edge of a wing, he slammed into the fuselage and nearly bounced clear into empty space. The Fighter shifted, nudged into motion in the impact, and the Nomad felt his gloved fingers lose their grip. He slipped, rolling across the hull, scrambling with flailing limbs as he fought to regain purchase. Snagging hold of the rim of the cockpit, the Nomad finally halted his weightless tumbling, and aided by a sharp puff from his suit's jets, he swung himself into the cockpit, thumping forcefully into the pilot's seat.

Hooking his arms through the harness, the Nomad clipped himself in place. He forced down the canopy lever, immediately transitioning into powering up the Fighter. Before the canopy had even sealed shut, the Nomad had booted up the RCS, warmed the arc jets, and primed the antimatter pulse engines. The canopy dome locked into place and the Nomad rotated a safety valve, repressurising the cockpit, though his helmet remained locked on its collar bearing.

Seizing hold of the joystick, the Nomad swivelled the nose of the Fighter sharply away from the wreck, and delivering a subsequent nudge to the thruster, he fired a single pulse through the antimatter jets. The brief burn propelled the ship away from the wreckage, sending it drifting off, deeper into the asteroid field. The Nomad pivoted the Fighter back on its axis, granting him a view of the receding ship carcass as he sailed away. Nervously flicking a number of switches and buttons, the Nomad killed power to the landing lights and systematically powered down all but the lowest profile scanners. Commanding various systems to hibernate, he set the Fighter into a state of standby, emitting a low energy signature, but ready to reawaken at a second's notice.

Finally, the Nomad engaged the Fighter's stealth systems. The craft's heatsinks worked rapidly to cool the exhausts, whilst the armour plating across the hull was electromagnetically charged to disrupt radar detection. The Fighter's colouration faded from its normal white and red livery to a dark electromagnetic-absorbing-shade. The Nomad was far from invisible, but in its current state, the Fighter would only be detected by a direct scan aimed in its direction.

The Nomad pulled up the holographic interface and watched as the incoming scanning frequencies peaked and jittered across the display. The signal was drawing closer. It was looking for him. His only hope was to drift clear of the wreck, far enough away before it arrived. But as he watched the dreadnought flotsam recede slowly in the distance, his hopes were dashed.

He saw it first as a pinprick of light, sailing out beyond the most distantly visible asteroids. Flickering in and out of view as it glided through the field, it grew steadily nearer, growing from a dot to a sweeping beam of projected light. A cacophony of scanning signals fizzed and popped across the Fighter's instruments as it closed in on the warship wreckage, finally drawing near enough for visual recognition.

It was a Cerberus: a combat and reconnaissance drone of unknown alien origin, equipped with an array of advanced weaponry and spaceflight technology. Puppeteered by a sophisticated artificial intelligence, the machine was perhaps one of the most formidable threats in the universe: a perfect killing machine, that for reasons unknown, followed a singular directive to eliminate all traces of intelligent life.

The Nomad gazed on in horror as the Cerberus cast its light ray over the wreckage. It paused, stopping abruptly in space as its beam swept across the twisted flotsam. The Nomad watched on bated breath. The Cerberus continued to scan the wreck. The ghostly quietude of space was deafening. A red flash glared suddenly in the darkness. A laser beam, fired from the Cerberus, punched effortlessly through the steel carcass of the dreadnought, blazing clean out the other side. The glaring ray lasted for a mere fraction of a second, fading swiftly back to darkness. The Nomad looked down at the display in front of him; the transponder signal had gone dead, along with the Cerberus's scanning frequencies. Silence had fallen.

The Nomad watched as the white spherical drone remained unmoving in position. The incandescent white beam continued to project in a narrow arc out across the warship hull, now illuminating a molten rupture in the armour, seared away by the brief stroke of the Cerberus's laser. It remained motionless as the Nomad drifted quietly further and further away. He could feel his heart throbbing between his ears. He strained his eyes as he kept them trained on the ever-shrinking drone, praying that with the transponder signal neutralised, it would simply fly off.

He could escape the Cerberus with a jump to FTL, but not from within the asteroid belt. So long as the drone was as near as it was, it would likely detect any use of his RCS. He was dead in the water. Unable to manoeuvre the Fighter away from its current path, he had to stay the course. But a peek back over his shoulder through the canopy revealed a nearby asteroid looming ever closer. The Nomad was on a collision trajectory. Impact was imminent. If he didn't act soon, the Fighter would coast straight into the gargantuan boulder. At his current speed, he was unlikely to survive the crash.

Turning his attention back front, the Cerberus still hadn't moved. The Nomad could not so much as swallow. His mouth was dry. His brow perspired beneath his visor. What few breaths he took were short and sharp, and his heart drummed quicker and quicker with each passing moment.

Without warning, the Cerberus suddenly revolved on its axis. Its singular red glowing optic gazed out into the asteroid belt, the light glaring as it swept across the Fighter's canopy. The Nomad's heart skipped a beat. His whole body chilled. The drone was staring right at him. A long moment of tension passed before the Nomad realised that it had not yet seen him. He was far enough away that the Fighter was disguised amongst the backdrop of asteroids littering the dark heavens. But as the Cerberus began to glide towards him, the Nomad knew he wouldn't stay hidden for long.

Cautiously powering up the Fighter's RCS, he primed the antimatter engines. Warily booting up the tracking and targeting computers, the Nomad placed his hands firmly over the flightstick and thruster, not once averting his eyes from the encroaching Cerberus. At this distance, the Fighter's heat and visual signatures were still low enough to keep him concealed against the backdrop of space, but the Cerberus was ghosting ever closer.

The Nomad glanced up through the canopy at the shadow of a large asteroid drifting overhead. Gently influencing the flightstick, the Nomad triggered a gentle puff from the underside arc jets. Still drifting rearward, the nudge of thrust propelled the sailing Fighter upwards, ascending the craft up out of the Cerberus's path, out behind the rear of the overhead asteroid. As the ship floated further behind the small planetoid, the drone vanished, the line of sight between it and the Fighter broken. Seizing the opportunity now that he was momentarily concealed, the Nomad gently bumped the flightstick forwards, piloting the craft closer in towards the asteroid. Gliding down over the rock's cratered surface, the Fighter looped back around the planetoid, all the while the Cerberus continued to sail spectrally onwards somewhere out of sight below.

Suddenly the readouts across the Nomad's dashboard flared to life with a tumult of scanning frequencies. The use of his RCS had given him away. The Cerberus had passively detected the arc jet contrails and was now actively scanning the asteroid field for signs of life. But the Fighter's stealth systems were still engaged; so long as the Cerberus's line of sight with the craft was broken, it would be unlikely to detect the Nomad. Regardless, following the trail of ionised particles left suspended in the vacuum of space, the drone was hot on his trail.

Sliding the flightstick forwards, the RCS jolted the Fighter into a translational manoeuvre, the Nomad navigating in the direction of the next nearest asteroid. Pitching the Fighter back to grant himself a view of the Cerberus tracking him, the Nomad guided the ship behind the cover of the next island just as the drone emerged into view. He transposed the Fighter's parabola into a weaving trajectory, accelerating now rearwards, back along his original vector, swerving in behind another asteroid. Still facing aft, the Nomad watched as his pursuant continued to track his movements, following the thin wisps of vapour left behind by his arc jets.

The Cerberus was closing in. Without a burn from the pulsejets that would unavoidably spell his immediate detection, the Nomad feared there could be no escape. He flicked several switches across the control panel and brought up a timer set to 217.57 seconds. He thumbed a red protective switch cover upwards on the joystick and primed the Fighter's plasma railguns. Enabling aim assisted targeting, he then initiated the warfare suite. Across the canopy's HUD, a translucent holographic projection of the Fighter's rear-view hummed to life.

The Fighter was ready for battle, but the Nomad was hoping against all hope that it could be avoided. He continued to guide the ship backwards in a weaving trajectory, hopping from asteroid to asteroid as he tried desperately to keep the drone's line of sight broken. But the Cerberus was drawing closer. The nearer it grew, the stronger the scent of the Nomad's contrails became. The Cerberus would detect him any moment now. He only had seconds left. All the Nomad could do was choose the opportune moment. He had to strike first.

Swinging out from behind a revolving planetoid, the Cerberus emerged suddenly into view. This was it. The moment had come. He'd run out of places to hide. There was still perhaps enough distance between him and the drone to make a run for the asteroid belt's limit. If he reached it in time, he could plot an FTL jump. But the Cerberus was faster and more manoeuvrable than the Fighter. There was every chance he'd be caught before he cleared the field. His only other choice was to engage the Cerberus head on. He had the advantage of surprise, but the AI's reactions were almost instantaneous. The drone outgunned his Fighter significantly; a head on assault could be suicidal.

The Nomad pitched the Fighter frontwards, and in a decisive action, disengaged the stealth systems. He jolted the thruster forwards and the pulsejets ignited. Pinned back in his seat under a surge of acceleration, the Nomad watched the drone's scanners suddenly spike across the holographic display. Triggered by his detection, the timer on the HUD suddenly began to tick down in microsecond intervals. Two hundred and seventeen seconds. Two hundred and sixteen. Two hundred and fifteen.

The Cerberus was merely a reconnaissance

drone, designated the task of investigating potential life signs across the galaxy. Upon positive identification, its first directive was to exterminate any lifeform detected. But it was merely the vanguard of a much larger squadron of machines lurking somewhere else on the edge of the system. In the event that the drone was unable to neutralise a target, it sent out quantumly entangled signals to all other nearby Cerberus units, requesting reinforcements. The factor that determined the request for backup was time.

A Cerberus drone would engage and pursue a target for precisely two trillion radiation periods of a caesium-133 atom. This translated to 217.57 seconds: three minutes and thirty-seven seconds of time before the Cerberus would broadcast a signal to all other nearby machines. Three minutes and thirty-seven seconds before an entire squadron of Cerberus, all far more dangerous than the drone, were alerted to his presence. Three minutes and thirty-seven seconds until he was doomed. Three minutes and thirty-seven seconds to either escape or destroy the Cerberus.

The Nomad switched all flight controls into their combat settings. The flightstick sharpened, RCS responsiveness attuning to the slightest twitch. The thruster stiffened, the pulsejets priming themselves for rapid successive bursts of explosive acceleration. Inside the cockpit, the HUD became simplified, all nonessential information and readouts minimising to prevent any unnecessary distractions in the heat of battle.

Punching the throttle, the Nomad wheeled the Fighter's nose on its pitch and yaw axes. Tumbling in sharp curves, the craft streaked between the oncoming asteroids, careening in a controlled but chaotic manner. The RCS minimised drift, effectively allowing the Fighter to bank off the arcjets' thrust. Aft, the pulsejets were firing in rapid bursts from the tail, continuously realigning the ship's momentum with its orientation. The Nomad continued to flee, swerving and spiralling through the field. He had no visual on the drone, but his LIDAR confirmed what he knew to be true: he was being pursued.

Three minutes and ten seconds.

Suddenly, a faint translucent image of the white spherical Cerberus loomed across the AR overlay projecting throughout the cockpit. The alien drone had taken up position to the Fighter's rear. The red glowing singular eye ominously fixed its gaze on the Nomad. He was seeing merely a reflected image captured by the Fighter's rear-view cameras; the drone in reality could not see him, possessing only a view of the Fighter's tail, but even still, peering into the menacing red glare of the machine, he felt his blood chill.

Weaving through the assault course of floating rock and ice, the Cerberus dogged his every manoeuvre. The machine's unwavering red glaze flashed suddenly brighter. Reacting with pure instinct, the Nomad depressed the flightstick, firing a swift burst from his upper arcjets. The Fighter plummeted. A beam of red light blazed overhead, skimming narrowly above the canopy. A nearby asteroid was struck by the stray laser blast, a section of its surface instantly vaporising, leaving behind a crater flooded with larva.

Three minutes dead.

The Nomad banked left. He fired the underside arcjets. The Fighter swooped tightly around a frozen planetoid. The cratered surface blurred above the canopy. Accelerating around the far side, the Nomad hugged the tumbling rock even tighter as another ray of heat fired from the Cerberus's optics carved narrowly past, erupting a chain of geysers across the asteroid's surface as ice turned instantly to steam.

Two minutes and fifty-two seconds.

Slingshotting clear, the Nomad punched hard on the thruster, accelerating rapidly into open space. He lurched left, plunging the craft into a barrel roll. Simultaneously firing the lower arcjets, he transitioned into a spiralling helix, just in time to avoid another beam of laser fire. The Cerberus was hot on his tail, and though it had yet to land a hit, its tracking systems were constantly refining, learning from its target's movements, steadily honing its aim.

Two minutes and thirty seconds.

A continuous ray of crimson light sliced through the darkness, carving in ever-tightening circles, closing rapidly in on the Fighter's tail as it lanced for the Nomad. The beam cut out, the Cerberus's weapons momentarily needing to recharge. The Nomad broke from the corkscrew, veering for the next cluster of asteroids. He banked right, swerving in behind the cover of the closest tumbling planetoid, escaping immolation by a margin of nanoseconds as another beam melted across the rock.

Two minutes and fifteen seconds.

The key to winning a zero-gravity vacuum dogfight was unpredictable acceleration. Predictable flight was easy to track. Easy to track meant easy to target. Easy to target meant easy to hit. Any form of constancy increased predictability. Constant speed meant certain death, especially when being targeted by an AI. Constant acceleration fared no better. Likewise, maintaining a constant vector proved all too easy for any automated targeting system to achieve lock. Able to compute complex trajectories with pinpoint precision in mere picoseconds, a Cerberus drone was able to hit a trackable target infallibly.

The only means of survival in a dogfight against an AI was to fly so erratically that the machine's targeting system was unable to predict an exact trajectory. With every calculation of projectile motion, there was a margin of error; the greater the variables, the larger the possible inaccuracy. Chaotically varying acceleration was the key difference between survival and obliteration; it made you difficult to track, and by extension, difficult to hit.

But winning the dogfight wasn't simply a case of avoiding the Cerberus, the Nomad needed to outfly it. Erratic manoeuvres alone wouldn't be enough; he couldn't simply fly haphazardly, he also needed to be calculating. Ultimately, the goal was not to careen around wildly, but to merely appear to be doing so from the perspective of the enemy. If he was going to survive, the Nomad needed to know exactly what the Fighter was doing, where it was, and where he was going to be. That meant remaining in complete control at all times. A paradox thereby arose: the need to appear to be flying chaotically, whilst in reality remaining in constant control. The key: vast amounts of creativity. For all of the Cerberus's sophistication, for all its raw computational prowess, it was lacking in creativity. Creativity was the Nomad's singular advantage. It was his key weapon. But was it enough?

The Nomad pulled out of the turn and launched into a straight run. An alarm knelled throughout the cockpit, warning of an impending target lock. Holding his nerve for a second longer, the Nomad stayed the course. The Cerberus's eye surged with light and the Nomad fired all of the Fighter's starboard arcjets. The craft jinked sideways, narrowly dodging a spear of crimson light as it bore through the void. Slamming the throttle to maximum, the Nomad reeled back into his chair, the Fighter momentarily pulling away from the drone.

Two minutes.

With the gap between them opening up, the Nomad killed thrust and shoved forwards on the joystick. The Fighter tumbled end over end, flipping one eighty as it continued to careen through the void. Now sailing backwards, the Nomad stared death square in the eye as the red optics of the Cerberus rushed towards him. He wrenched at the flightstick, banking sideways as jets on the nose and portside wing fired on full burn.

One minute fifty-three.

Target sighted, a reticle suddenly projected onto the canopy HUD. Fighting against the g-force of his turn, the Nomad tweaked his pitch and yaw, steadily tracking the crosshairs towards the incoming drone. Piloting backwards, his attention half focussing on the rear-view holograms projecting across the canopy, the Nomad concentrated the remainder of his awareness on lining up a shot. Sweat beaded across his brow. Heart pounding, his hands twitched on the controls, making a rapid succession of fine adjustments.

Suddenly, aided by the Fighter's automated aim assist, the reticle traced briefly over the red eye of the Cerberus. The Nomad squeezed the flightstick trigger. A dull drumroll reverberated through the cockpit as the railgun fired in the silent vacuum of space. A fusillade of white-hot plasma toroids streaked into the blackness. Accelerated by electromagnetic conductors, the projectiles exploded from the front of the Fighter, hurtling towards the drone as it crossed over the Nomad's sights.

One minute forty-eight.

The burst of fire mostly missed its mark, the majority of toroids sailing off into the dark, but a couple of glancing shots clipped the Cerberus, scorching black gouges out of the machine's glossy armour plating. But the damage was only superficial. The Cerberus was unharmed, and ready to return fire.

One minute forty-six.

The intense crescendo of concentration had proven momentarily too much for the Nomad. Too focussed on achieving a target lock, he'd neglected his evasive manoeuvring. Now his foe had him in its sights. The red glow of the drone's optics intensified. The Cerberus's laser charged. A streak of light cut through the blackness. The Nomad closed his eyes.

One minute forty-five.

THIRTEEN

One minute forty-five.

The Nomad punched the thruster. Antimatter and matter flooded the combustion chamber, annihilating one another in an immense outpour of energy, detonating from the pulsejet exhausts. The eye of the Cerberus flared. A beam of light carved through the dark. The Fighter rocked forwards, surging under a wave of acceleration. The laser struck, glancing off the Fighter's tailfins, charring a black gouge through the ship's armour plating. The Nomad opened his eyes, his gaze locking onto the Cerberus as it swivelled to keep the Fighter trained in its sights. Arcing around in a scarlet blaze, the laser beam clove across the sea of empty space, slicing in pursuit of the Nomad as he rocketed away.

Despite his immense speed, the ray of energy was gaining. A red haze swelled from behind. The Nomad could almost feel the heat of the laser on the back of his neck as it bore down on him. He killed thrust. Pitched. Rolled. Accelerated. The pulsejets fired again. A jolt of thrust sent the craft tumbling clear as the ray cut narrowly past, seconds before the crimson light faded.

One minute forty-three.

The Nomad peered up through the canopy. The Cerberus zipped past overhead, accelerating from a near standstill to speeds exceeding the Fighter's in the mere blink of an eye. The Nomad spun, upending the Fighter, launching off at speed as the Cerberus swung back around to intercept him. The drone gave chase, dogging his every move as the Nomad pulled off a series of evasive manoeuvres in quick succession.

One minute forty.

The Nomad glimpsed back over his shoulder. The red glare of the drone's optics continued to draw in. The tailfins were still smouldering where they had taken fire, but the damage was mostly superficial. The Fighter's armour was designed to withstand such attacks, if only for a brief instant. But another hit like that and he might not be so lucky.

One minute thirty-eight.

Weaving rapidly in snaking arcs through the field of buoyant stone, the Fighter banked left and right on the complex vectors of thrust generated from its arc jets. The Nomad pulled out every trick in the book, drawing on a lifetime's worth of flight experience to keep his head above water. Each glance at the faint rear-view hologram projecting across the canopy revealed the Cerberus tight on his tail. Unimpeded by the limitations of a biological body, and almost unbeholden to the traditional laws of momentum, the drone could pull off seemingly impossible feats of flight; able to move translationally in any direction at full acceleration and stop in a near instant, swivelling on its axes without any form of RCS. The Cerberus had an unrivalled freedom of movement in the vacuum of space. How it generated its momentum, the Nomad could only guess at, but the sophistication of its flight technology was realms beyond the traditional thrusters outfitted to the Fighter, possibly employing some form of gravity manipulation to achieve its spectral flight.

One minute twenty-seven.

Another ray of crimson light sliced narrowly past, searing across the cratered surface of an asteroid as the Nomad swerved clear. Gazing back at the clock, he cursed in frustration. Time was dwindling. He had less than a minute and a half to escape, and he was no closer now than when he had first begun the countdown. He had to try something new. Something unexpected. Something that could give him an edge.

One minute twenty-two.

Up ahead, two closely paired planetoids tumbled slowly in tight affiliation. Separated by a mere score of metres, entangled in each other's gravitational embrace, the two bodies locked together in narrow orbit around one another. Aiming for the gap between them, the Nomad jerked the throttle forwards. A surge of acceleration drove him back into his seat. Suddenly killing thrust to the pulsejets, the Nomad spun the Fighter back on its heels. Rocky craters blurred overhead mere metres above the canopy, the Fighter hurtling narrowly passed the first of the two floating rocks.

One minute fifteen.

The Cerberus dipped into view, emerging below the asteroid's inverted horizon as it continued to give chase. The Nomad held off the controls as long as he dared. He watched the frozen terrain recede above him. The Cerberus's optics flared brighter. Pitching the Fighter back, his finger squeezed hard on the trigger. The dull drumming of the railguns sounded. Another hail of white plasma bolts drilled from the Fighter's guns. Toroids of plasma blitzed through the vacuum, thumping into the surface of the asteroid overhead. Dust and rock erupted outwards, ejecting as a cloud of debris directly in the drone's path.

One minute ten.

The Cerberus veered downwards, reacting instantaneously to the geyser of ice and stone jettisoned by the blast. Travelling too fast to fully avoid the ejection, the machine cleared the larger pieces of debris, clipping instead through the upper cloud of dust and shingle. The flying shrapnel pinged and clattered off the drone's armoured shell, scuffing away more of the machine's glossy white paint.

Shooting out the far side of the dust cloud, the Cerberus's optics refocussed. Its rapid course correction had saved it from ploughing into the barrage of rock and ice, but now it was hurtling on a direct path towards the second of the two asteroids.

One minute nine.

Careening on a collision course, the Cerberus was faced with no other option than to bail. Swooping downwards and accelerating hard, the machine abandoned its pursuit of the Nomad, swerving away from the gap between the two rocks, electing to clear the asteroid around the outside instead.

One minute eight.

Still hurtling rearwards, the Nomad watched as the Cerberus vanished behind the curvature of the asteroid below. Slamming the thruster to full throttle, the pulsejets fired, decelerating the Fighter rapidly on a hard burn, slowing it to a momentary standstill, before accelerating it back the way it had come.

One minute five.

Forced off course by the Nomad's ploy, the Cerberus was still circling around the asteroid pair in an attempt to head off the Nomad on the far side. But with visual contact broken, the machine could no longer track the Fighter's movements, and was therefore completely unaware that the Nomad had turned around and was speeding back the way he had just come. It would be a few more seconds before the Cerberus would emerge around the far side to realise it had been duped, and a further few before it would be able to catch back up to the Nomad. For the immediate moment, he had managed to give his foe the slip. He had not bought himself long, but with the clock continuing to tick ever closer to zero, every second mattered.

One-minute dead.

Dozens of asteroids ripped past as the Nomad raced towards the edge of the belt. Continuing to accelerate, every increment of speed garnered made course corrections ever harder. His hand twitched back and forth on the flightstick. The Fighter rolled and pitched, darting left, right, up, and down, narrowly streaking past the incoming meteoroids at breakneck speeds. The Nomad was pushing his reactions and piloting skills to their very limits in his attempt to outrun the Cerberus, but it was not enough.

Forty-seven seconds.

An incarnadine iris suddenly dilated across the canopy's rear-view projection. The Nomad's heart sank in horror. The Cerberus was back on his tail. The edge of the belt was closing in fast, but leaving the cover of the field with the Cerberus in tow would mean certain death. Out in the open, the drone would cut the Fighter to pieces in a matter of seconds.

Forty-two.

The Nomad plunged into a helix. A ray of fire cleft through the void after him. Upending the Fighter, the Nomad began corkscrewing backwards, the Cerberus diving after him as he spiralled away. Straining against the lateral forces acting on his body, the Nomad struggled to gain control over his targeting reticle as he span in a downward arc. Trailing rays of laser pivoted after him, each beam barely missing its mark as the Cerberus constantly refined its targeting algorithm. The Nomad waited, holding his nerve, jostling with the controls, watching as his crosshairs slowly drifted towards the drone.

Thirty-eight

A glancing stroke of laser scorched his wing tip. The Fighter shuddered. The reticle kicked out, but reacting fast, the Nomad reined it back in.

Thirty-five.

Bracing his head against his shoulder, he continued to lean his weight into the controls. Closing in millimetre by millimetre, the crosshairs homed in towards the glare of the Cerberus's singular red eye.

Thirty-four.

The sights momentarily aligned. He squeezed the trigger. A burst of plasma toroids drummed from the railgun. Miss.

Thirty-three.

The Cerberus veered. The crosshairs drifted. The Nomad adjusted. The reticle tracked back towards its target.

Thirty-two.

A ray of red skimmed narrowly passed the canopy. The crosshairs aligned. The Nomad squeezed the trigger. Another burst of fire. Another miss.

Thirty-one.

Another evasion. Another adjustment.

Thirty-seconds.

Another retaliation. Another trigger pull. Another hail. Another miss. Another second.

Twenty-nine.

The g-forces acting on the Nomad's body were taking their toll. His head was pinned to the side of his helmet. His helmet strained against its collar bearing. The forces only continued to increase as the Nomad pulled the Fighter's dive into a tighter and tighter helix. His vision darkened around the periphery. His face contorted under the pull. His arms strained against the tenfold increase in their weight. The red eye of the Cerberus was fading to grey.

Twenty-eight.

Crosshairs scudded over the drone. The Nomad pulled the trigger once again. Another miss.

Twenty-seven.

Sucking short sharp breaths into his collapsing lungs, the Nomad could feel his consciousness slipping away. He couldn't maintain the corkscrew any longer.

Twenty-six.

The reticle aligned again. He clamped down the trigger. A long rumble of the rail guns thundered. A barrage of plasma accelerated outwards. Toroids splattered across the white armour of the Cerberus, scorching black burns into its hull. The final shot from the burst struck the machine dead on. As if guided by divine providence, the bolt hit the crimson optics of the Cerberus just as the eyepiece glared ready for another laser beam.

Twenty-five.

Striking the singular weak point on the front of the Cerberus, the glare of impending laser fire cut out. The optics and the weaponry of the drone shorted, the red glow dimming to black. Blinded by the impact, the Cerberus veered off course, zooming clean past the Fighter as the Nomad broke from his corkscrew.

Twenty-four.

This was it. The Nomad had given himself the window he needed to escape. He swivelled the Fighter's nose back towards the edge of the asteroid belt and jammed the thrust lever forwards. The pulsejets flared. The Fighter shot off through the vacuum towards the outer fringes of the belt. His eyes darted to the readouts in front of him, towards the dwindling power levels of the Fighter's cells. They'd been severely drain by the demands of the dogfight. He barely had enough to make an FTL jump. The margins were too close. Even a jump to the nearest star system would be treading a fine line. He looked down at the timer and cursed in frustration.

Twenty-one seconds.

The Nomad maintained his vector. His mind screamed internally, at war with itself over what to do. Escape was ahead of him, but only an escape that would deliver him from one peril to the next. He couldn't recharge the cells. There was no time. He couldn't make the jump, or he would end up adrift in space. Sweat gushed down his brow. His eyes flitted between the instruments on his control panel. He gazed ahead to the star speckled blackness as the final peppering of asteroids hurtled past. He looked down at the charge readouts. He looked back to the clock.

Seventeen seconds.

The edge of the belt was upon him. He needed to begin plotting the jump. He might just make it. There might just be a star within range that he could jump to. All he needed was for the cells to hold out. But he knew they wouldn't. He wouldn't make it. There wasn't enough charge. There wasn't enough time. He looked down at his instruments. He looked at the clock.

Sixteen seconds.

The Nomad gritted his teeth in desperation. He pulled back on the thruster and jerked the flight-stick forwards. The Fighter tumbled over itself and the Nomad reengaged the pulsejets. The Nomad spotted the Cerberus beneath him. It was still careening on a straight course. Neither its optics nor weapons had rebooted yet. He was in with a chance.

Fifteen seconds.

The Nomad drove the thruster to maximum, sending the Fighter hurtling after the blinded Cerberus. He darted between the medley of asteroids in pursuit, rapidly closing the distance between him and the drone.

Thirteen seconds.

The Nomad eased his approach, aligning the Fighter in behind the Cerberus. He locked his cross-hairs over the drone, aiming for the lightly armoured rear of the machine where a singular exposed exhaust blazed white. The Nomad squeezed his trigger finger and a burst of plasma crackled from the Fighter's guns. But in that moment, the Cerberus's optics powered back up. No longer flying blind, the drone swerved away at the last moment. The string of shots fired wide into the darkness.

Twelve seconds.

Cheated by fate, the Nomad roared in anger. The drone began to weave and wind its way through the field of asteroids; its weapons were yet to come back online, but it had regained full flight capability. The Nomad darted after the drone, dogging the machine as it did its best to shake him. Focussing with every iota of concentration he could muster, the Nomad clung to the Cerberus's tail, lurching the flightstick in sharp jolts as he gave chase.

Eleven seconds.

Temporarily weaponless, the machine was in full flight, running from the Nomad, weaving in and out behind the cover of asteroids as it bought itself the time it needed for either its weapons to reboot or for reinforcements to arrive. It didn't need long.

Ten seconds.

The crosshairs of the reticle traced narrowly behind the Cerberus. The Nomad fought to keep the machine in his sights. He fired. A burst of plasma trailed after the target, pummelling the ice crusted surface of a nearby asteroid.

Nine seconds.

Swooping in closed to the next planetoid, the Cerberus dove into a canyon gouged from its surface. The Nomad pursued, diving the Fighter into the ravine. Swerving left and right, the Nomad hurtled down the twisting corridor of stone. He fired again, sending another rumble of plasma after the Cerberus. The drone rounded a turn in the way, evading the shots. The toroids pummelled into the canyon wall, spouting dust and rock outwards. The Fighter plunged into the cloud and the Nomad was blinded.

Eight seconds.

Yanking back on the joystick and thrusting hard on the throttle, the Nomad felt his stomach lurch. The Fighter exploded upward, rock and debris clattering against the hull and canopy of the craft. Soaring out of the canyon, the dust cleared.

Seven seconds.

The Nomad pitched the Fighter back down in time to see the Cerberus launch clear of the gorge. The horizon of the asteroid fell away beneath them and the Nomad accelerated after the drone, closing the distance he had lost and letting fly another cannonade of plasma.

Six seconds.

This time, the shots found their mark, peppering the panelling across the back of the drone. The white armour charred, melting under the barrage of superheated ionised particles, and as the Cerberus veered away, a plate shook loose from the drone. The armour section rattled free and was flung rearward by the Cerberus's thrusters. The plate whirled past the Fighter's canopy, the Nomad swerving narrowly to avoid it.

Five seconds.

The Nomad guided his crosshairs back over the fleeing drone. Across its rear, an array of blinking lights and unprotected machinery now lay exposed. It continued to swoop between the oncoming planetoids, evading its pursuer. The Nomad locked on. He pulled the trigger. A hail of white toroids blazed outward. The Cerberus veered away. The salvo missed.

Four seconds.

The Nomad eyed the clock. He aligned the crosshairs again. Squeezed. The railgun thundered. Plasma streaked into the dark. The Cerberus rolled. The shots flew passed.

Three.

The Fighter swivelled back into alignment. The Nomad fingered the trigger. Shots fired. Miss. He readjusted. Fired again. The drone dodged. The shots streaked past. He eyed the clock.

Two.

The Nomad gritted his teeth. He tweaked the flightstick. The reticle drifted. Crosshairs traced over the exposed point. He fired. He missed. He fired again. He missed again.

One.

Launching the thruster to maximum, the Nomad sent the Fighter hurtling at the Cerberus. The distance closed. The Cerberus neared. The weak point enlarged. The target narrowed. Crosshairs aligned. Trigger. Gas ionised. Toroids accelerated. Shots fired.

Zero.

FOURTEEN

The Fighter overtook the Cerberus as the timer hit zero. The Nomad killed thrust to the pulse-jets. A ghostly silence had fallen. He dared not look back. He hadn't seen what had happened in that last second. It had all been too quick. But he didn't need to look. He knew. He had failed.

Upon taking catastrophic damage, Cerberus drones self-destructed. The Nomad suspected this protocol was to prevent any lifeform from salvaging the remains of a Cerberus unit. Far more advanced than anything else the Nomad had ever come across in the universe, any technology salvaged from the husk of a Cerberus could potentially be reverse engineered. If reverse engineered, it could be used against them. Because of this, the machines ensured there was never anything left to salvage, protecting themselves by preventing their technology from ever falling into the hands of organic lifeforms.

The Nomad had seen no blinding flash of light. No glare had lit up behind the Fighter. Had the Cerberus self-destructed, the Nomad would have known. Instead, he was drifting in a quietude of inky blackness, awaiting the fate that was coming for him. He had gambled and come up short. At least if he had chosen to make a jump to FTL, he might have eventually coasted into orbit around the next nearest star. Instead, he had condemned himself to extermination by the inbound squadron of Cerberus interceptors and destroyers.

The moment the timer had hit zero, the drone would have sent out a request for backup. Inside the drone's communicator module, a series of quantumly entangled particles would have been excited, inducing a binary signal based on the direction of the particle's spin. Twinned particles, entangled with those inside the drone's communicator, would react, behaving in tandem with their linked partners. Every Cerberus possessed a communication module containing quantumly entangled particles linked with those located in other machines in the squadron. The result: instantaneous signalling.

Whereas more primitive means of communication, namely the broadcasting of radio signals, was limited by the speed of light, quantumly entangled signals circumvented the delay of signal travel. When one particle was excited, its twinned partner reacted instantly, regardless of the distance separating them. This method of cheating conventional communication limits imposed by the vast distances of the cosmos allowed for the Cerberus to communicate and relay information across the universe with absolute immediacy.

The only delay to the Cerberus squadron's arrival was the travel time between their point of origin and the Nomad's location. Assuming the squadron was lurking on the fringes of the solar system, it was a matter of mere minutes before the Nomad would meet his end. He was done for, and for once, he accepted it. He had been running for so long. At long last, he sought relief. He sought an end to his colossal and infinite journey. He sought an end to his hardship and suffering. He sought an end to the crushing loneliness that had consumed him entirely.

The Nomad sat peacefully in the cockpit. The moments drew out as he continued to drift towards the edge of the belt. Finally, he gazed outwards. Way below him, off to his flank, the tiny white speck of the Cerberus drone coasted silently through the dark, awaiting reinforcement. It stayed out of range, its weapons likely still disabled, keeping the Nomad within visual until its allies finally arrived.

Only, something wasn't right. The Cerberus wasn't following the Nomad at all. Its vector was misaligned. Every moment the Nomad continued to drift onwards, the Cerberus seemed to recede into the dark veil of stars. Soon it would be out of sight all together, and the Fighter would likewise fall beyond its visual range. It could potentially be tracking the Nomad's coordinates via other means, but as the Nomad turned his attention to his instruments, he realised the Fighter wasn't picking up a single scanning signal. Ahead of him, the radio readout had flatlined, detecting little more than the cosmic background radiation.

All was quiet. Eerily quiet. The Cerberus was silent. It was... dead?

Scarcely believing the possibility, the Nomad continued to sit in silence, watching the Cerberus steadily fade from view. Drifting clear of the asteroid field, he scanned his surroundings. No approaching points of light. No incoming Cerberus. He was alone.

He elected to investigate further, knowing that even if he was wrong, there would be little consequence. Pitching the Fighter downwards, he delivered a pulse of thrust to the antimatter engines. Redirected, the Fighter glided silently through the vacuum. Within moments, the glinting mote of light of the Cerberus drone re-emerged into view. It loomed steadily larger, drawing slowly into detail as the Fighter approached.

The Nomad spun the ship around and issued a decelerating burn from the pulsejets, slowing his approach to a crawl. Flipping the Fighter back, he was granted his best view of the machine yet. It was tumbling chaotically on its axes, spinning like a marble rolling across an impossibly smooth surface. A number of black plasma burns pockmarked the drone's glossy metal exterior. A long moment passed as the Cerberus continued to tumble. Finally, the machine's singular eye revolved gradually into view. It was dark. Lifeless. The ominous red glow extinguished.

The drone was dead, but for some reason it hadn't self-destructed. Somehow, it had been disabled whilst remaining almost wholly intact. The Nomad had never heard of such a thing. But as the machine steadily rolled over to reveal its rear, he understood. His final burst of fire had struck the exposed electronics beneath the dislodged armour plate. What he had hit exactly, the Nomad could not say. All he could figure was that he had inadvertently taken out a component that should have initiated the Cerberus's self-destruct sequence.

The Nomad continued to gaze at the spinning Cerberus husk in disbelief. The shot that had been required to disable the drone in such a way was likely one in a million, yet somehow, he had achieved it, literally without a second to spare. The Nomad thought briefly of the many people, all now long dead, that would have given anything to have in their possession an intact disabled Cerberus drone. What good it might have done them in the end, the Nomad couldn't say.

Regardless of how valuable this machine might have once been, it was practically useless now. The Nomad had no capacity to reverse engineer any of the technology inside it, and he suspected that the entire machine was sufficiently advanced that none of its internal components would be even comprehensible to him.

Almost ready to disregard the drone entirely, he suddenly realised how absent minded he was being. Mere minutes ago, he had been hunting for a component this machine was certain to have. The drone undoubtedly possessed some form of power supply, and irrespective of technological sophistication, a power cell was a power cell regardless of where and by whom it was manufactured!

The Cerberus was perhaps as technologically far removed from the Nomad as he was from a troglodyte. For all intents and purposes, it was beyond his technological comprehension, sufficiently advanced that it appeared almost arcane. But if the Nomad's rapidly formed hypothesis held up, certain components of technology were universal. The Cerberus had to operate off a system of power cells; power cells that like all others, he could theoretically adapt to the Fighter.

Checking the coast was clear a final time, the Nomad rotated a safety valve and depressurised the cockpit. Ensuring he still had the appropriate tools clipped to his suit from his recent EVA, the Nomad raised the canopy lever and unfastened his harness. Floating gently out of the cockpit, he glided cautiously over towards the revolving drone with his mobility thrusters. Positioning himself alongside the Cerberus at it continued to spin end over end, he timed the revolutions. As the back end swung back around, the Nomad reached out, seizing hold of the drone's armour plating.

The Nomad was yanked suddenly into motion as he grappled the spinning machine. Clinging to the outside of the tumbling drone, he swung his boots out and fired their thrusters on full burn. Straining against the force of the jets, he held himself in place, fighting to keep his grip. The expelled gasses acted steadily to counter the spin. After several long dizzying moments, the revolutions slowed, finally settling into a very slow and gradual rotation.

Shaking off a momentary spell of lightheadedness, the Nomad hooked a carabiner over a loop of metal that resembled an eyelet, most likely having once acted to affix the dislodged armour panel in place. Tethered to the drone, the Nomad began studying the mysterious alien technology before him.

Most of the machinery was scorched and melted, damaged by the very same plasma toroid that had disabled the drone. That which was left was so abstract in its construction and design that the Nomad could barely make sense of it. Not knowing how or where to begin in locating the internal power supply, he was momentary overwhelmed with a sense of helplessness. Finally, concluding it to be the only logical first step, he began stripping the damaged electronics away.

The first layer of components, those scorched by plasma fire, seemed to have been modularly installed. With the aid of several tools from his belt, the Nomad swiftly managed to prise them away, severing their connections, discarding them into the cold vacuum of space. The next layer of cryptic technology was more firmly fixed in place, soldered into a hexagonal hive-like lattice that appeared to serve as the main chassis of the drone. Examining the array of units attached to the framework, the Nomad systematically cut each free with his plasma cutter, disposing of them one by one into the void.

Beneath the next layer, the Nomad could make out a dim white glow shimmering between the seams of the electrical components. The Nomad began cutting away the hive-like chassis, running an array of scans from his suit as he did so. Only the cosmic background and the radiation signature from the red dwarf showed up in the results. The Cerberus was definitely dead, and there seemed to be no risk of radiation exposure as he neared the machine's core.

The Nomad peeled away a gold film covering the next layer of machinery and cautiously slid out a convex module from what the Nomad suspected was the Cerberus's internal processor. With the machine's brain removed, the white glow shone suddenly bright. The Nomad's photoreactive visor tinged dark in response, his irises likewise constricting beneath. As his eyes adjusted, he caught his first glimpse of what he was seeking: an array of cylindrical cells glowing white with pure energy.

The Nomad peered for a long moment at the

four shining cells packaged tightly together in the heart of the machine. He ran another scan: still no signs of radiation. Given the intensity of the light being given off, the Nomad suspected the units were less batteries, and more generators. So far, his disassembly of the drone hadn't uncovered any form of photovoltaic cells, nor had he discovered any kind of fuel tank or intake valve; the machine appeared completely energy self-sufficient, circumventing any requirements for recharging or energy input. It suggested that the glowing cells within the drone's core were not storing energy, but instead producing it.

They weren't RTGs, nor did any form of chemical reaction appear to be taking place within them. What then? Were they some form of advance miniaturised fission reactors? No; there was no apparent way of refuelling them once the fuel was depleted. Perhaps fusion then? But surely it was impossible to carry out fusion on such a small scale in such compact vessels? It was most likely some far-removed undiscovered technology; one his own race hadn't even come close to theorising. Whatever the case, the Nomad reminded himself that it ultimately didn't matter.

He was tampering with things he didn't understand. Early technology was often dangerous and unstable; as it advanced, it traditionally became more intuitive, better optimised, but above all safer, with ever greater focus dedicated to protecting the user. But perhaps this philosophy only applied to the technologies of organic races. A race of machines designed by machines would likely have little regard for the welfare of any organic lifeform attempting to tamper with their technology. If anything, they might even take precautions to safeguard against it.

Whilst removing the power cells from the Fighter or salvaged alien technology was a relatively straightforward process that could be carried out with limited risk, the same might not be the case with the Cerberus. There was always the chance of electrocution, that same hazard existed with every power source, but there could likewise be other more subtle dangers. His EVA suit still wasn't detecting any form of ionising radiation, but what if this advanced technology emitted something similar, some unknown deadly emission that his suit was unequipped to detect. Even now he could potentially be exposing himself to some deadly discharge radiating from the power cells to which he was none the wiser.

All this was mere speculation. What he did know for certain was that the Cerberus were designed and manufactured for the sole intent of eradicating organic life. They were war machines, hunter-destroyers, bent on eliminating all traces of intelligent life across the universe. Should it not therefore be expected that, for in the unlikely event of a drone's self-destruct malfunctioning, its internal components would be boobytrapped against any would-be-scavengers.

The Nomad realised then and there that he had been lucky to have made it this far into the drone without triggering any such defensive fail-safes. The power cells themselves were likely the very thing that detonated in the drone's self-destruct protocol; they could be rigged to explode the moment any attempt was made to remove them.

Attempting to scavenge parts from the Cerberus now seemed altogether imbecilic. Infuriated and embarrassed by his own foolhardiness, the Nomad scorned himself. Why had it taken him so long to realise? He was normally so cautious, so meticulous, calculating. These characteristics were tenets that he swore by. They were what had allowed him to survive for so long. Yet every now and then he became suddenly and inexplicably reckless. This same recklessness had less than an hour ago nearly exposed him to a lethal dose of radiation from decaying Americium-241. Years ago, it had seen the Nomad dragged into the depths of the algal lake and half the Fighter's power cells burnt out by a lightning strike. Every faux par, every gaffe, every blunder that set him back, all cause by recklessness. His own mistakes were forever moving the goal posts, forever lengthening his already endless journey.

But what made the difference between a blunder and a gambit? Success. Success was what determined whether a risk was taken in vain or in confidence. A risk that doesn't pay off is foolish, but one that does is quite the opposite. The Nomad remembered all the times he had taken dangerous risks which had ultimately paid off; had he not taken them, he would never have profited from their success. Arguably, he would have never made it this far in his journey without them, perhaps having perished long ago, like so much of the rest of the galaxy.

It was true that at times he could be more calculating in the risks he undertook. And admittedly, he sometimes suffered lapses of judgement, but he could not punish himself for taking risks. He was desperate. Any chance to better his dismal and inconsequential existence was worth it. The power cells could kill him the moment he touched them. Or, they could see the Nomad through to the end of his journey. An instant death brought about by his desire to fight on seemed far better than a slow deteriorating demise induced by surrendering to all but absolute certainty. And so, the Nomad continued.

FIFTEEN

The Nomad took several deep breaths, listening to the rasping of his inhalations echo throughout his helmet. His heart throbbed. A sickening nausea welled in his gut. Frozen in hesitation, he stared fixedly at the glowing Cerberus core in front of him. Gritting his teeth, he finally mustered the courage to raise his arm. Gently, he touched his gloved fingertips against the first of the shimmering cells. So far so good. He was still alive and the cells had not discharged so much as a single joule.

The Nomad closed his grip around the cylinder. His breathing quickened. His pulse drummed. A clamour of protest screamed through his mind. He tugged sharply. The cell dislodged from its housing and the Nomad pulled his arm clear. He lowered his gaze to his palm, there in his grasp was the power cell. He sighed loudly.

The Nomad took a moment to examine the device. It was elegant and simple in its design: perfectly rounded and seamless, the white glowing tubular face of the cell lacked any form of discernible detail. At one end, the power unit was capped with a silver metallic sleeve etched with a fine grill that looked to play some role in heat dispersion, though the Nomad could not detect any warmth being given off. At the other end, the cell was similarly capped, only, instead of a heat vent, the unit was pronged with a pair of flat golden pins, no doubt the positive and negative terminals.

The unit was an ideal size and weight. With little modification, the Nomad would happily be able to insert the cell into a housing unit in the undercarriage of the Fighter. That said, the Nomad had yet to check the amperage and voltage; he might need to retrofit a transformer or capacitor, but for now that did not matter, the immediate task was removing the rest of the cells. Sliding the glowing cylinder into a pouch on his belt, he turned his attention back to the heart of the drone. Reaching back into the core, he plucked the remaining three power units from their fittings in turn, stowing them about his person.

Staring for a prolonged moment into the dark cavity left in the machine, the Nomad finally felt assured that the Cerberus was now well and truly dead. Throughout the whole procedure, he had been plagued by the niggling thought that the drone might reawaken at any moment. With that reassurance, and the most difficult part of his scavenging operation at an end, the Nomad relaxed with momentary relief.

Unclipping from the drone, he used his EVA jets to gently nudge himself away from the slowly revolving Cerberus corpse. He had drifted a good hundred metres from the Fighter whilst tethered to the machine, but he was still well within his suit's range. Directing himself with a short pulse of his EVA thrusters, the Nomad floated steadily back towards his ship, gazing out at the great bands of the galaxy twinkling in the distance as he coasted. Nearing the craft, the Nomad slowed his approach with a series of light puffs, positioning himself directly beneath the undercarriage of the Fighter.

Pulling the first cell from the pouch in his harness, the Nomad produced the volt-ohm-milliammeter from his toolset and connected the device's leads across the two terminals. The Nomad felt a sudden twinge of anxiety as he watched the figures on the digital readouts tick over into the red, way beyond the measurable values his basic multimeter was capable of determining. The VOM was designed for measuring electrical ranges found in technology designed by his own race; on a number of occasions, whilst salvaging unusual alien equipment, the Nomad had approached the upper ranges of the VOM, but never had anything exceeded them.

The results made no sense. If the Cerberus power cell was exceeding the VOM's measuring limits it was producing a higher voltage than a lightning strike. What was perhaps even more surprising was that, whilst a lightning strike delivered its charge in an instant, the cell's output was seemingly continuous! Unless the VOM was for whatever reason malfunctioning, or giving off a false reading, the cell's capacity was incomprehensible. Near inexhaustible. Anything otherwise and the cell would completely discharge almost instantaneously.

The Nomad could scarcely fathom what type of technology could potentially yield such a vast energy output; perhaps some form of quantum syphon that drew energy directly from elsewhere in the universe? Maybe it was linked to a Dyson sphere capturing the entire energy output from a star? What if it wasn't even coming from this universe? Maybe the Cerberus had managed to directly tap energy from parallel dimensions? Or perhaps they had discovered some impossibly advanced method of converting dark matter or dark energy into a usable power source? All the Nomad could do was speculate. But he didn't need to understand how the cell worked, all he needed to understand was how to harness it.

Cautiously drawing the remaining cells from his rig, the Nomad let them float freely around him. He needed to be careful. Outputting such a high voltage, the Nomad suspected, were they not in a vacuum, that electricity would be arcing between the terminals of each cell. He suspected that even the insulation built into his gloves would offer no protection. Were he to accidently touch any of the terminals, the cell would discharge, the current arcing straight through the insulating membrane of his suit, killing him instantly.

What the Nomad couldn't quite figure, was why the Cerberus drone required such vast quantities of power to operate. The drone's weapons were undoubtedly energy intensive, and the Nomad suspected that the AI core of the machine was power-hungry as well; the advanced propulsion technology that allowed the drone to move so freely in space probably used a considerable amount too, but even with these three systems, and all the other technology that the drone had lumped into it, four power cells seemed excessive. What function could it possibly require such an immense power output to run? The only thing the Nomad could think of that would even come close was the machine's FTL core; if such were the case, then the drone would possess an incomprehensible range. It might be able to cross the entire galaxy in a single jump. Perhaps it could even jump to a different galaxy altogether!

The implications of all of this were that the Nomad could theoretically power his Fighter off a single cell. His FTL jump range would be drastically extended, though it would never approach the limits of the Cerberus. Whereas the drone somehow seemingly converted electrical energy into thrust, the Nomad was reliant on the antimatter stored in his fuel tanks. The ship's power cells ran the Fighter's warp core, shortening the distances between stars, but the Fighter's pulsejets were what accelerated it to relativistic speeds. His maximum velocity was restricted by the capacity of his antimatter tanks, serving as the new limiting factor for his interstellar jump range. That and the supplies he could carry with him during FTL travel.

Even with the mass reduction the Fighter experienced whilst the warp core was engaged, every additional gram onboard the Fighter mattered. He could only carry so much food, water, fuel, and equipment with him, before requiring significantly higher reserves of antimatter to achieve superluminal speeds. It was for this reason that the Nomad had modified the fuel tanks to increase their capacity in the first place; with all the equipment and supplies he carried from system to system in the cargo pods, the Fighter's original tank capacity was insufficient to propel him to higher jump velocities. His ship, in its current state, was optimised as best it could be to balance speed, cargo capacity, and range.

With a set of degraded power cells, the duration for which the warp core could be engaged had been severely stunted. With potentially limitless power reserves now at its disposal, that restriction had been lifted; from here on out the Fighter was only limited by its fuel reserves and supplies. In theory, jumps in excess of three hundred lightyears weren't outside the realms of possibility. All this of course was dependent on whether the Nomad could actually patch one of the cells into the Fighter.

The task of adapting a cell to meet the specifications of the Fighter was simple enough in theory, all it required was wiring an appropriate number of resistors in series to reduce the cell's potential difference. The Nomad had a plentiful supply of resistors stashed away with the rest of his spare electrical parts; the real issue came from the Nomad's inability to actually measure the numeric value of the cell's voltage. With the VOM maxed out he'd have to resort to trial and error. It seemed a little crude, especially given how sophisticated the power cell was, and perhaps that's because it was.

His VOM measured potential difference, the key being in the nomenclature. The multimeter had measured the *potential* difference, the *maximum* voltage the cell was capable of outputting. Maybe the cell was smart enough to determine the desired voltage and would automatically output a current at that? The only way to find out was to try it.

The Nomad opened the starboard cargo pod and sorted through the various containers until he located his supply of scavenged electronic spare parts. Carefully rifling through the crate, doing his best to prevent spilling its contents out into the weightless environment, the Nomad pulled out one of the most commonplace and insignificant components he had to hand: an LED. Closing the case, the Nomad guided himself carefully back towards the nearest floating cell. With the upmost care and delicacy, using a set of insulated plyers, the Nomad attached the light-emitting diode across the two terminals. To the Nomad's delight, the LED illuminated. It didn't explode, short, spark, or even burn out; all it did was light up, functioning perfectly as designed, thereby confirming the Nomad's hypothesis.

In theory, the Nomad could install the cell just as it was. Other than a jury-rigged adapter to fit the cell's terminals, it required no extra modification. As a safeguard, the Nomad decided he would wire several extra fuses into the circuitry to protect the Fighter against any potential power surges, but otherwise there shouldn't be any further safety measures required. He could even rig up all the cells to the Fighter to minimise the output from each individual one, sharing the load across the four of them. Whether that would make a difference or not the Nomad could not say for certain, but even if it didn't, having all four cells connected to the Fighter meant that he had three redundancies; if the Nomad had been taught anything during his lifetime travelling amongst the stars, it was that it never hurt to have backups.

Without further delay, the Nomad depressed the battered and warped access panel on the Fighter's undercarriage and watched as it swung open softly on its hinges. The power core illuminated, revealing a score of receptor sockets, half of them empty. The casing was bowed and welded in a number of locations, whilst many of the array of mismatched cells were wedged into place or housed in modified units. Wires threaded and looped between transformers, resistors, and fuses, all feeding into the main circuitry of the craft.

The Nomad reached for the circuit breaker and pulled the lever into the downward position, killing all power to the Fighter. The ship's systems went dark. The passive scanner readouts on the Nomad's EVA suit faded away. The only powered units remaining were the maintenance lights surrounding the access panel of the power core; operating off a supercapacitor, they would give the Nomad a suitable window of time in which to carry out the work before they too went out.

The Nomad worked methodically. Cautiously wiring each of the glowing Cerberus power cells up to an array of fuses, he connected them to the Fighter each in turn. Once they were all connected, the Nomad slowly inserted them one by one into the receptor sockets of the housing frame. Though shorter than the cells the Fighter was designed to run off, they matched near exactly in diameter, sliding snugly inside the sockets, almost as if they had been made to fit

Then came the moment of truth. The Nomad lifted the circuit breaker back into place, completing the connection. He felt a series of humming vibrations reverberate suddenly through the lever handle as the Fighter began to whir back to life. A few seconds later, the ship's systems came back online. The Nomad jetted away several metres in cautious anticipation, certain that something was bound to be wrong. He expected the cells to blow out at any moment, or the computers onboard to suddenly short or explode in a power surge, but after several dreaded moments, nothing of the sort had happened. The Fighter was operating normally.

It was possible that the cells weren't outputting power; perhaps they had detected incompatible technology, shutting down as a safety precaution; or, maybe as a defensive strategy. What if the cells were intelligent enough to understand when they were connected to non-Cerberus technology, refusing outright to function? It wasn't outside the realms of possibility. All the Nomad knew was that there was no way the cells could be operating as he had hoped; it couldn't possibly be that easy!

He floated quietly in the dark, waiting another long moment before he dared to drift over towards the cockpit. Deftly manoeuvring into position, the Nomad lowered himself into the pilot's seat and gazed around at the dissonance of instrument readouts surrounding him. Several programmes were still booting up, but all the essential systems were operating. The Nomad turned his attention to the most important readout of all: power reserves. The holographic icon indicated they were at one hundred percent capacity. Likewise, the needle in the physical dial that the Nomad had long ago installed as a fail-safe was maxed out at the far end of the meter.

The Nomad opened the holographic interface and expanded the power usage data, studying the various statistics and projected outcomes. The interface listed the array of systems drawing power across the Fighter and their predicted consumption, but an error code was flashing across the top of the readout as the ships power management failed to detect the rate at which the cells were draining. A graph displaying projected charge percentage over time had flatlined along the maximum, never dipping beneath the hundred mark.

Currently, the ship was operating in a low energy state. The majority of the most power intensive systems were inactive. Wary not to stress the Fighter, but eager to put the Cerberus cells to the test, the Nomad began flicking various switches. He closed the canopy, repressurised the cockpit, engaged the system scanners, and booted up all the scientific instruments on board the ship at once. He powered up the navigation and flight computers, expanding every holographic interface at his disposal. He gazed back down to inspect the power management data to find that the charge was still holding at full capacity.

Loading up more and more systems, the Nomad continued to push the capabilities of his new power supply. He browsed through a list of stellar systems now available to him within his newly extended jump range, selecting from his options a G-type yellow main sequence star. Plotting the system into the flight computer, it began planning an FTL jump. The Nomad shook his head in disbelief. Even now, the cells were maintaining constant charge with no sign of faltering. It was as if he had discovered a perpetual motion device, or some other impossible piece of technology that defied the laws of physics.

The computers and systems onboard the Fighter continued to whir away, and to his relief the Nomad witnessed an almost imperceptible blip in the power levels. For a slight second, it deviated into the ninety-nine percent range before immediately leaping back up. It was a good sign; it meant the Fighter was accurately detecting the cells' outputs and the power management computer hadn't been damaged or overloaded during the dogfight. The Nomad began powering down various superfluous systems methodically; his energy supplies might now have been near endless, but the other components on his ship were still subject to wear. Leaving anything to run unnecessarily in the background would only shorten its lifespan.

An alarm suddenly knelled in the cockpit. The Nomad flicked his head around in panic. He had caused an overload of some sort; the Fighter was overheating, or the fuses had blown, or the power management was overtaxed and damaged. He looked frantically about the needles and lights, searching for any sign of what had gone wrong. He continued feverishly powering down systems, hoping against all hopes to quell any further damage or power surges. But then he realised.

The alarm was not warning of a fault onboard the Fighter. It was a detection alert. The long-range scanners had completed their cycle and had begun churning out their results. A cluster of objects travelling at FTL speeds were inbound to the Nomad's location. His heart sank. The signals were unmistakable. The Cerberus squadron was incoming. They had been alerted. Whether the drone had been disabled a fraction of a second too late, sending out its request for reinforcements when the timer hit zero, or whether it hadn't been as lifeless as it appeared, alerting the other Cerberus after it had been disabled into a low power state, the Nomad couldn't tell. Perhaps they were responding to the simple fact that the drone had gone silent, prompting the rest of the squadron to investigate. Whatever the reason, it didn't matter. They were mere seconds away.

The squadron was unlikely to consist merely of drones. There would be Cerberus interceptors, corvettes, and frigates, maybe even destroyers or dreadnoughts. Even a single interceptor was potentially more firepower than the Nomad was equipped to deal with. If caught, he would be doomed. Fortunately, the Nomad had already made his FTL jump calculations.

Frantically powering the navigation and flight computers back up, the Nomad primed the antimatter engines. He seized the flightstick and swivelled the Fighter around to face his intended destination. Aligning his craft along the holographic lines projecting across the Fighter's HUD, he aimed the nose of the Fighter at a distant yellow star nearly three hundred lightyears away. The Nomad punched forwards on the thruster and the pulsejets flared. White-hot plasma expelled from the exhausts. The Nomad sank heavily in his chair. The Fighter accelerated hard, driving him rapidly towards the outer reaches of the solar system.

An explosive flash of blue light erupted through the darkness to the Nomad's right. He strained to turn his head against the forces of acceleration to see the azure glare dissipate as the squadron of Cerberus dropped out of FTL. They were too far away for visual contact, but the Nomad knew they would be racing rapidly in his direction. His LIDAR confirmed it. Three Fighters were quickly closing in on him. In less than a second, they would be within range.

The Nomad raised the protective cover over the warp core controls and lifted the yellow and black striped lever. Inside the FTL core, the first array of lasers fired at the superfluid exotic matter, cooling it to absolute zero. The second array lit up, exciting the particles, reversing their spin. The core's weight plummeted, dipping into negative values, inverting the furrow of the ship's gravity well. The stars magnified and distorted in front of the Fighter as space and time shortened ahead.

The Nomad tightly gripped hold of the thruster, forcing it to maximum, waiting desperately for the faint blue haze that signified the light barrier breaking. A sudden thunder collided with the Fighter. Streaks of red laser blazed passed the Nomad, skimming over the canopy. The sapphire light of Cherenkov radiation illuminated ahead of the ship. The red dwarf vanished to the rear, along with the Cerberus interceptors. The Fighter shuddered, and suddenly, a blinding white flash detonated behind the Nomad.

SIXTEEN

A tumult of alarms, buzzers, and sirens roared throughout the cockpit. The entire craft juddered and rocked, steadily beginning to pitch and yaw. Fighting with the flightstick, the Nomad tried desperately to negate the rotation, but attempting to correct with the FTL core engaged was impossible. The Nomad yanked the warp core lever back upwards. The blue Cherenkov haze ahead of the Fighter dissipated. The stars refocussed, condensing back into their usual constellations. The Nomad killed thrust to the pulsejets, jostling with the joystick to regain control. The RCS jerked in a series of sharp movements, but the Nomad managed to skilfully realign the Fighter along its trajectory.

With the ship back under control, the Nomad gazed around as the discordance of warnings and error codes continued to blare. He silenced them one by one, powering down every system possible. Plunged suddenly into ghostly silence, he regathered his thoughts and began to piece together what had happened. It had all occurred in a fraction of a second, too quick for him to process in real time. But now, in the aftermath, as he replayed the images through his mind, it all gradually fell into place.

He'd been hit. A shot fired by one of the Cerberus interceptors had struck the craft just before it hit FTL and made its escape. The Fighter was damaged. Badly. But what exactly was wrong, the Nomad didn't know. He gazed out through the canopy across the wings to see the fresh lines of laser burns etched into the armour, but as he continued to study the fuselage, all he could make out was superficial damage.

There had been an explosion. The Nomad remembered that. A large one. It had been directly behind the Fighter. Even as he had hit superluminal speeds, he could feel the heat of it on the back of his neck. He had been facing the opposite direction to the blast, but even now there were ghostly afterimages still fading in the periphery of his vision from the glare of the explosion.

The Nomad gave a precursory glance across the array of dials on the control panel before him. Nothing seemed terribly awry. Temperatures and pressures across multiple systems were all stable. Power output from the Cerberus cells seemed constant. The only needle that was in the red was fuel. For some reason he was out of antimatter. The tanks were empty. Completely empty! Mere seconds ago they had been full. They had been breached. That was what the explosion had been. The antimatter and matter reserves had been expelled from the tank, mixing together and annihilating one another in an uncontrolled chain reaction with the detonation energy of several thousand hydrogen bombs. Had the Fighter not been travelling at FTL speeds, the Nomad would not have escaped the blast radius. He would have been obliterated.

The Nomad slumped wearily in his chair at the realisation that he'd just survived another near-death experience. This one had been closer than any in the past. Even now it seemed impossible that he'd escaped the explosion. How could he have been so lucky? The answer was simple: he hadn't.

The Nomad powered up the navigation computer. He was on the verge of panic once more as reality dawned on him. He studied the information, processing it slowly with muddled thoughts. He was still on route to the yellow sun, but in the few seconds of FTL travel before his tanks had emptied, he had made it less than a lightyear. He was still two hundred and seventy-six from his destination, and now that his antimatter tanks were depleted, he had no way of accelerating to normal interstellar travel speeds, nor any way of altering course to a nearer star. He was locked on an unalterable course by the first law of motion.

Realising he was doomed to continue on his current trajectory, he next needed to figure out how long it would take. The Nomad powered up the flight computer and ran an analysis of his current velocity. In attempting to escape the inbound Cerberus, he had engaged the ship's warp core earlier than normal. As such, he hadn't reached the

Fighter's subluminal top speed, continuing to build momentum once the FTL core was engaged. He'd shed a slight fraction of his velocity in RCS course corrections, but the effects had been minimal. All in all, he had made it to eighty-six percent of lightspeed: 257,821,513.88 metres per second. At this speed, it would take him over three hundred and twenty years to arrive at the yellow star. Taking into account the time dilation experienced at relativistic speeds, this would equate to one hundred and sixty-four years from his own perspective.

However, these equations were for slower-than-light velocities, not factoring in the contraction of distance achieved from the warp drive. When powered up, the FTL core contracted space ahead of the Fighter to roughly one six-hundredth of the undistorted distance. Therefore, with the warp drive engaged, the Nomad would be travelling at a relative speed of five hundred and sixteen times the speed of light, translating with time dilation to a proper speed of one thousand and twelve times lightspeed. All these figures rattled around in the Nomad's head, yet through his clouded mind he seemed unable to arrive at the one figure he actually needed. How long would his journey be?

One six-hundredth meant his distance to cover was point four six of a lightyear, or four hundred and thirty-six billion kilometres. At 0.86c that would take about 0.54 years. With a proper velocity of 1.66c, it would take roughly 0.27 years. 0.27 years was over three months. 0.27 years was one hundred days! One hundred days of travel to the yellow sun. The Nomad had enough water, but his food reserves only gave him enough for sixty days, and that was already taking into account rationing. His current rationing gave him one thousand five hundred calories per day; in order to extend his supplies to last him the duration of the journey, he would have to reduce his daily intake to a mere nine hundred. By the time he arrived he would be half starved to death. But the Nomad realised this might be the least of his troubles.

When he made the jump to FTL he had a squadron of Fighters on his tail. At a distance of less than a lightyear from the red dwarf, they could well be able to detect the Fighter and pursue it. He was near enough that they could be on him in a matter of seconds. They would drop out of FTL to find the Nomad dead in the water.

No. He was safe. The Nomad had escaped the blast only because he was travelling away from it with his warp drive engaged. The Cerberus were inbound towards it, travelling at subluminal speeds. There was no way, no matter how sophisticated and advanced their armour and shielding, that they could have survived the blast. They would have been annihilated, along with anything else within the blast radius.

But there was something else the Nomad had neglected to think about. He had given so much thought as to how long it would take him to arrive, that he had given no consideration as to what he would do once he did. How was he going to slow the Fighter to approach velocities? He would be travelling so fast that he would hurtle straight through the system and out the other side. He needed to reduce his speed to allow the star's gravity to capture him in orbit. In order to decelerate that much, the Nomad would require the same amount of energy that had accelerated him to his current velocity in the first place. He needed to somehow replenish his antimatter reserves. Not for acceleration to shorten his journey, but in order to decelerate to the speeds required for orbital insertion once he got there. Otherwise, arrival at the yellow star would mean nothing whatsoever.

He usually carried out refuelling within the magnetospheres of gas giants. Magnetic fields, particularly strong ones, captured and retained positrons and antiprotons. It was for this reason that the Nomad chose to refuel from orbit around the gargantuan celestial bodies. Because, over the millennia, antimatter accumulated and concentrated around these massive planets. The antimatter itself was produced elsewhere however, coming into existence in a variety of ways. It was produced in cosmic rays and thunderstorms, through the interaction of gamma rays and matter particles, and through pair production from photons anywhere in the universe where temperatures were sufficiently high enough.

Antimatter was concentrated in planetary magnetic fields, yet it existed ubiquitously at low levels throughout the vacuum of space. Theoretically, the Nomad could deploy his collection coils anywhere in the void and begin refuelling. It would take significantly longer to fill the tanks, but given enough time, it was inevitable. Normally it took several hours to refuel. The Nomad had one hundred days. He could not even begin to guess at the levels of antimatter that would be present along the journey, but he reminded himself that he required only a fraction of a tank to decelerate to orbital insertion velocities. After all, he was only travelling at a fraction of his usual speed.

Regardless of whether or not he could collect enough antimatter in time, one thing was certain: so long as his antimatter tanks were breached, he could not even begin refuelling. He needed to carry out repairs to the Fighter as soon as possible to give him the best chance. But before he could start the repairs, he needed to assess the damage.

SEVENTEEN

The Nomad rotated the Fighter's atmospheric safety valve. He listened to the warning buzzer grow steadily faint as the cockpit depressurised. Raising a lever on the control panel, he drew back the canopy, exposing himself to the vast emptiness of interstellar space. Unclipping his harness, he pushed gently upwards from the pilot seat, floating slowly out of the cockpit.

Adrift in the void, the Nomad gazed about in the haunting stillness. This far out from the red dwarf, the universe seemed impossibly dark, such that, paradoxically, every pinprick of starlight seemed to blaze with incredible vigour. Strange, he thought, that he should seem to be static. The stars were stagnant, set firm and unmoving against the backdrop of infinity, and yet the Nomad was careening through the interstellar abyss at a mind-bending velocity. The fact that even at eighty-six percent of lightspeed, the stars still drifted imperceptibly slowly through the inky blackness, spoke volumes to the true unfathomable scale of the universe. It was as if the Nomad and his Fighter were not moving at all, and yet, in truth he was hurtling so fast that the flow of time warped around him.

After a prolonged period of reverie, the Nomad gazed back down at his receding Fighter. Navigating his way towards the aft of the ship via a few subtle puffs from his suit's thrusters, he approached in dread. Nearing the damaged hull, he switched his helmet torches on and ran his gaze along the scorch marks carved out of the armour. A singular sweeping burn traced from over the portside wing, cleaving down towards the undercarriage at the tail end of the Fighter.

The Nomad sank lower, terrified of what he would see in the seconds to come. He descended below the wing, still following the laser scorch as it cut around the contours of the armour, down towards the welded plating encasing the extended antimatter tanks. It was bad. But not as bad as he had feared. A rupture stretched the full length of the expanded fuel tank, the breach measuring several centimetres in width. The Cerberus interceptor's laser beam had cut clean through.

The walls of the tanks themselves actually played no role in containing the antimatter; instead, they housed and protected the superconducting magnets responsible for trapping the fuel in place. In order for the antimatter to have been ejected from the tanks, one or more of the eight superconductor electromagnets that upkept the octupole magnetic field would have had to fail. The failure would have resulted in a distortion in the field. In this case, the Nomad could tell that a single superconductor had failed. With that failure, the magnetic field lines had splayed out of shape, channelling the antimatter out of the tank. By some miracle, the antimatter had been accelerated along the deformed field on an exact trajectory aligned with the rupture in the tank wall. For this reason, and this reason alone, the Nomad had survived.

Had the spout of antimatter ejection been channelled at any other angle, it would have sprayed into the tank walls, annihilating the ordinary matter from which they were constructed. The resulting detonation would have obliterated the Fighter in an instantaneous blast of energy. Instead, the explosion that had taken place had been caused by the annihilation of something else altogether. The Nomad could only speculate, but he suspected that the antimatter spewed from his tanks had formed a contrail; one which his pursuers had unwittingly ploughed clean through. It was poetic justice. In their belligerent attempt to annihilate the Nomad, the Cerberus interceptors had instead annihilated themselves. That explained how the Nomad had survived: the explosion had taken place some distance behind him; that was how he had gotten clear of the blast radius. Given the amount of fuel stored in the Fighter's tanks at the time, the explosion may well have exceeded a magnitude of two exajoules.

With this new information, the Nomad had trouble reconciling whether he had been favoured or slighted by fate. On the one hand, he was still alive, something that seemed impossible given what had just happened. But on the other, the fact that he had even found himself in such ill-fated circumstances seemed as equally unlikely.

There was an arising pattern to events. Whenever the Nomad seemed to make some fortuitous discovery, one that would make his life and journey all the easier, he would almost immediately suffer a devastating set back, one that outweighed all the rewards. Discovering a long-term power source for the Fighter had left him stranded in interstellar space. Discovering a rich and abundant food supply had crippled the Fighter's power supply. And these events were not isolated occurrences; similar incidents had happened time and time again. The only difference was that the severity of the setback always seemed to be greater than the last. With every step he took further along his journey, he would soon come up against some obstacle or complication that made the next seem unsurmountable. It was as if he were destined to fail; fated always to journey, but never to arrive.

The Nomad hovered staring at the ruptured tank for an unknowable period of time. It was fixable; it would be time consuming, but in theory, the repairs were relatively simple. But the Nomad could not muster the motivation to make a start. He floated without moving, weary, bruised, and defeated. What use was it all? Why did he bother fighting to continue? Why did he strive so hard to keep suffering? He could fix the Fighter. But why should he? So he could slowly starve over the next three months steadily going insane from sensory deprivation? It was all useless. It was all futile. But it was all necessary.

EIGHTEEN

The plasma cutter's white glare faded. The Nomad's sight readjusted, his irises flaring to swallow the faint light of a billion remote specks flickering in the blackness. He switched his helmet lights back on, guiding the torch beams across the Fighter's hull. The fresh welds across the fuel tanks were far from his neatest work, but they were fit for purpose, strong enough to hold against the stresses and strains of spaceflight.

The Nomad was coming to the end of a sixteen-hour spacewalk. He had stripped down the antimatter tanks, systematically testing and checking every component of the seven remaining superconducting magnets responsible for the containment field. Afterwards, he had turned his attention to the eighth. It had been torched by the Cerberus laser. It was beyond salvaging, and the Nomad didn't have a replacement. He had needed to fabricate a new one from scratch.

Assessing the vast collection of scavenged materials and components assorted throughout the containers of the Fighter's cargo pods, the Nomad got to work. Making a start by coiling over a thousand metres worth of niobium-tin wire, the Nomad next turned his attention to constructing a housing unit out of an old iron casing. Lacking any supply of liquid helium or nitrogen, the Nomad had instead elected to use hydrogen as a coolant for the coil, tapping the plentiful supply stored in the Fighter's chemical propellant fuel tanks. With limited trouble, the Nomad managed to reduce the temperature of the niobium-tin coil to below ten degrees kelvin.

Finally, he charged the coil, hooking it up to the Fighter's newly boundless energy reserves, successfully generating a powerful electromagnetic field. Short-circuiting the superconducting loop, the Nomad disconnected the energised electromagnet from the ship's power supply, the persistent current continuing to flow through the closed circuit of the coil due to its negligible resistance.

The task was done. He had managed to fabricate a perpetually magnetised device, capable of containing one of the most volatile and unstable substances in the known universe, from nothing more than scrap metal and a few spare parts. It was an achievement the Nomad would once have taken pride in. Nowadays, he often lost perspective of his own ingenuity. Driven by desperation and an inexplicably powerful survival instinct, the Nomad instead felt his actions were motivated solely by necessity. It was do or die.

When initially expanding the antimatter

tanks' capacity, there had been no requirement to fabricate any new components. What he had needed to do, was to disassemble, tune, and reassemble the pre-existing superconductors in order to carry out the modification. Because of this, the Nomad was already fairly familiar with their architecture and design; without this prior knowledge, it would have been unlikely that the Nomad could ever have repaired the tanks with the limited resources he had to hand. With the magnet hooked up and fixed in place, the final few hours had been spent sealing the tank with a new set of welds. The whole repair was a makeshift job, but it seemed like it would be up to the task.

With the lengthy repairs finally complete, all that was left was to run a series of diagnostics from within the cockpit. But for the moment, that could wait. The Nomad was exhausted. He manoeuvred carefully back into the cockpit and strapped himself into the pilot's chair. He sealed the canopy and repressurised. Lifting the safety cover, the Nomad reengaged the warp core. The stars ahead of the Fighter contorted, melting out of their constellations. A blue haze lit up in front of the ship's nose, signifying the break in the light barrier as he went superluminal. Removing his helmet and stowing it beneath his seat, the Nomad felt his eyes lull swiftly shut as he descended into a deep paralyzing sleep.

The next time the Nomad opened his eyes, a full eight hours had passed. Irrespective, he still felt exhausted. He knew he could probably do with an extra couple of hours, but he had been awoken by hunger gurgling in his stomach. It had been more than a day since he had last eaten. He felt starving, but he knew the hunger pangs plaguing him now were nothing compared to what was to come. This was his new baseline. In time, the sensation he was feeling now would become the new normal, nothing more than a dull niggling. But for now, at least, he needed to quell the pain.

Opening the cockpit footlocker, he retrieved a nutrition bar from his food hold. He unwrapped the mass of protein and carbohydrates, depriving himself a short while longer as he examined it in thought. Normally one bar constituted a meal. On a full diet, the Nomad would expect to eat three per day. With standard rationing, that dropped to two: one in the morning and one in the evening. Now, in order to stretch his supplies to the full term of his voyage to the yellow sun, under a regime of extreme calorie restriction, he was limited to little more than one bar per day.

The Nomad felt another groan in his stomach. He broke off roughly two thirds of the bar and rewrapped the remaining portion, stowing it in a pouch on his suit. He took a gulp of water from his canteen and gnawed slowly at his nutrition bar. In an attempt to fool his body into satiation, he stretched out the meagre meal as long as he could. Nibbling tiny bites at a time, he over-chewed every mouthful, taking long swigs of water in-between. Regardless, the morsel of food barely lasted him a few minutes. Unsatisfied and still hungry, he at least took comfort in the fact that the pains in his gut had subdued.

The Nomad sat gazing out through the canopy at the all-encompassing night sky, procrastinating a while longer. Finally, he booted up the systems diagnostics and selected a series of tests and simulations for the antimatter tanks. The computer ticked over as the tests unfolded across the holographic interface. The lines of the octupole field were mapped and measured through various energy intensities by the analytical tools. Even the slightest variations in field flux could result in a devastating fuel tank malfunction. The last thing the Nomad needed was another breach; he had barely survived the first. He wouldn't be so lucky next time around.

The diagnostic tools pushed the new superconductor magnet to the limit, testing it to withstand the pressures of twice the maximum tank capacity. To the Nomad's relief, it seemed to be functioning as well as any of the other seven. When the tests had run their course, the Nomad spent several minutes pouring over the data, scrutinising the results for any unusual fluctuations or red flags that the diagnostic software might have missed. He found nothing.

Powering down the analytical tools, he readied himself for the moment of truth. Tests were one thing, performance in the field was another. The Nomad felt his nerves tingle with anxiety as his fingers hovered over the switches on the control panel. After a minute of hesitation, he keyed in the sequence and deployed the Fighter's array of antimatter collection coils. The familiar groan of hydraulics extending from the fuselage sounded, fading thereafter to the faint clicking preceding the hum of electromagnets. The field lines from within the antimatter tanks elongated from the collection coils, extending into the space surrounding the Fighter, a net of invisible tendrils casting out through the vacuum, channelling the flow of antimatter inwards, trapping it inside the fuel tanks.

At first, nothing appeared to transpire. The humming of the coils faded into the background as the Nomad stared at the fuel gauge, the needle staying glued at zero. If the tanks were filling, they were doing so at an imperceptibly slow rate. The Nomad continued to stare fixedly at the dial, waiting for so much as a hairsbreadth flicker in the needle.

Sometime later, he opened his eyes. Having succumbed to his exhaustion, the Nomad had without realising drifted into sleep. Groggily rubbing his face, he felt the dreaded re-emergence of hunger pangs stirring in his gut. It was too early. His next meal was still some way off. Reaching under his seat, he grabbed his canteen and sipped at the tasteless water, his eyes returning to the fuel gauge. The needle still hadn't shifted.

The Nomad opened up the Fighter's holographic interface and pulled open a digital fuel readout. Offering a far greater degree of precision, the digital gauge recorded the tank levels to several decimal points greater than the physical dial. If the collection coils were capturing anything at all, the digital readout would give some indication. The capacity was climbing, but slowly: a rate of one millionth of a percent every few seconds.

The Nomad groaned, his head sinking into his hands. It was slow; incredibly slow. But it was enough. By the time of his arrival, the Nomad would have a quarter tank of antimatter; sufficient for the decelerating burn to put him into orbit around the yellow sun. But that was all. He had hoped his tanks might fill faster, allowing him to accrue enough antimatter for a burst of acceleration to shorten his journey, if only a little. His optimism seemed laughable now. Nothing had changed; he was still locked on a one-hundred-day voyage, with only sixty days' worth of rations. At least now he would be able to stop once he arrived.

NINETEEN

The Nomad awoke to the dark dawn of the second day. The significance of a solar period dictating the passage of time was a concept that had long ago grown abstract to the Nomad. He had travelled to countless stars and countless worlds, each with their own diurnal rhythm. Some span rapidly on their axes, granting quick sequential sunrises and sunsets separated by little more than a few hours. Others ticked slowly around in elongated rotations that drew out from weeks, to months, and in some cases, even years. Others were tidally locked to their stars, one side of the planet imprisoned to everlasting daylight, the opposite hemisphere trapped in eternal night. The Nomad had spent weeks at a time in non-stop daylight, and drawn-out periods in perpetual twilight, but he always seemed to spend the majority of his time in the dark.

Perhaps it was merely his own perception. Biologically diurnal, his internal clock was calibrated to daylight; perhaps it was merely that time appeared to pass more slowly in the dark. Alternatively, maybe it was due to the time he spent adrift in space. In the absence of an atmosphere, light did not scatter. In space, the sky was always one of night, even when bathed in the light of a star.

Whatever the case, be his nocturnal existence actual or merely perceived, it didn't matter; the Nomad had long ago lost any sense of his circadian rhythm. Dawn did not signify the start of a new day, just as dusk didn't signify the end. The Nomad kept his own time. Sometimes, he judged his diurnal cycle by the segmentation of twenty-four-hour intervals; he slept and arose as the atomic clock dictated. But perhaps more often, he followed no true rhythm at all, taking instead a more intuitive approach, sleeping when he was tired and rising when rested. Sometimes his day-night cycle stretched well beyond thirty hours. At other times it fell short of sixteen. He kept tabs on the passage of weeks, months, and years via a redundant calendar system, yet he often questioned why. Other than for garnering an overall perspective of how long he had been travelling, timekeeping seemed more or less meaningless this far into his journey. Aside from this, his perception of the passage of time was only relevant for his own reference frame. Elsewhere in the universe, time passed differently.

For a long stretch of his journey, the Nomad had attempted to keep track of time in the rest frame. This current stint was set to take him one hundred days, yet outside his observational frame of reference, the journey would take almost two hundred. This level of time contraction was not insignificant, but when compared to what he experienced under normal interstellar superluminal speeds, it was nothing. At near ninety-nine percent lightspeed, time from his own perspective shrank to a seventh of that outside his reference frame. He often spent a fortnight or longer in an FTL jump. Since his journey had begun, most of his life had been spent travelling at relativistic speeds. For each year he had spent travelling, seven years had passed elsewhere. He had long ago lost track of the actual figures, but he knew that his voyage thus far had exceeded several lifetimes. How much time might have passed if ever his journey came to an end?

The Nomad hated time. Time was a terrible thing. It was the one force, the one dimension, the one law of nature in existence that was deadlocked. It had always, and would always, continue to flow onwards. It could be twisted, stretched, squashed, and even folded, yet it could never be reversed. Time always marched on. It was unkind and unforgiving. It held no mercy. It showed no remorse. It merely was, is, and will always be. It had a beginning, but no end, forever trapped in the present. Time was the one true injustice of the universe.

The Nomad gazed out of the canopy at the black emptiness surrounding him. It stretched on forever. Perhaps somewhere, in some way his mind was incapable of understanding, it folded back on itself; maybe the universe was not truly infinite, but rather an infinite loop. But did it really matter? Did the simple fact that the Nomad perceived it to be endless make it in itself infinite? If something was so sufficiently vast that no one could ever possibly see where it ended, did that then equate to infinity?

There was an edge to the universe, at least, an observable one. The rate of expansion dictated that there must be. Space itself grew vaster with the passage of time. The expansion was driven not by the stars growing further apart, but instead, the swelling of nothingness in-between them. By this process, the more distant a speck of light, the faster the star receded away. The end result was a point where the rate of expansion, and therefore the velocity at which stars retreated, exceeded that of light-speed. Some stars were so far away that their light could never possibly reach the Nomad's eyes, even if he waited for eternity; their emitted photons swam against too strong a current, destined to forever be swept further away by the widening ocean of empty space.

It was because of this simple fact that darkness even existed. Were the universe not expanding, and were it infinite, then within time, the light from every star would arrive at every point in existence. An infinite number of stars would fill the skies, illuminating every patch of darkness. All that would exist would be an infinitude of light of infinite brightness and heat. Though no longer a singularity, the universe would in time resemble itself at the moment of its initial conception. The expansion was necessary for existence, the Nomad understood that; in some ways he was comforted by it. But a simple trait of it conjured disquiet: the expansion was accelerating.

Dark energy was propelling the expansion of space at an ever-increasing rate. That meant an inevitable end for the universe. In time, the galaxies on the periphery of the observable limit would be torn beyond the dark veil. Later, the next generation would also be ripped out of perception. Gradually, over time, the black pall dictating the edge of existence would constrict, choking its hold on the universe. Every galaxy, one by one, would accelerate away faster than its light could travel, until each was left alone in the universe. But the expansion would not end there. In time, the rate of growth would even exceed the forces of gravity binding the stars within their galaxies. The massive celestial aggregations would steadily evaporate, until, perhaps trillions of years in the future, each and every star would be stranded by itself, alone in a forever stretching infinity. But not even that would be the end.

Eventually the rate of expansion would prove too much for molecules and atoms. The forces binding together the very matter from which the universe was constituted would eventually be ripped apart. In the unfathomably distant future, all that would be left was an impossibly vast, impossibly cold, inconceivable expanse, where fundamental subatomic particles existed in absolute isolation. It was an end that juxtaposed the universe's beginning in every conceivable way, only it was not the end, merely the next stage of and endless infinity.

The Nomad hated infinity. Infinity was unkind and unforgiving. It held no mercy. It showed no remorse. It merely was, is, and will be. It could have a beginning, but it could have no end. Infinity was the one true injustice of the universe.

The truths of time and infinity were enough to drive any soul to despair, but on one as lonely and isolated as the Nomad, these concepts took a terrible toll. The Nomad could scarcely remember the last time he had spoken aloud; he often vocalised his thoughts, yet long ago he had lost the ability to distinguish between thoughts spoken aloud and those that existed solely inside his head. Did speaking one's mind hold any greater significance over silent thought if there was never anyone around to overhear the words? The Nomad knew that he spoke to himself from time to time, but he was seldom aware of when it was actually happening. It was reflex then? It wasn't necessarily responsive, more impulsive. Maybe it was instinctive.

The Nomad knew the psychological importance of hearing other voices. Even audio recordings from conversations held long ago could sometimes evoke the chemical responses in the brain normally stimulated during social interaction. They were often enough to convince a listener's subconscious into believing they were part of a discussion, even though it was one to which they could not contribute. Maybe then, the Nomad speaking aloud to himself was his mind's way of maintaining sanity. He was somehow convincing himself that he was not alone. Back in a time he could scarcely remember, before his journey had even begun, the Nomad recollected occasionally speaking to himself. Was it not something everybody did? If it was something everyone did, then surely talking to oneself did not make you insane?

In truth, the Nomad struggled to think why anyone would talk to themselves under normal circumstances. What is the purpose of expressing thoughts vocally if there is no one else to hear them? Speech is a relatively slow and inefficient method of conceptualising ideas and understanding emotion; certainly at least when compared to the speed of thought. Why then ever bother expending the energy to vocalise what would never be heard? Maybe it made sense for the Nomad to do so? To convince himself that the universe was not as crushingly empty as he knew it to be. But why under normal circumstances would anyone ever talk to themselves aloud? Perhaps it had some psychological significance insofar as determining self-identity; maybe hearing one's own voice is a control, a standard, or a baseline by which to judge and perceive others. Perhaps it was a mechanism that merely served to help understand one's own philosophies and feelings. The Nomad did not know. More than likely he never would. It mattered not.

Speech was for communication. That was its primary focus. In that respect, the Nomad certainly could not remember when he had last spoken for the intent of communicating. Not only could he not remember when, but why, or to whom. Who was the last person he had ever spoken to? And what was the conversation about? What were the last words he had ever said to another being? Did it matter that he could not remember? It more than likely meant the conversation was brief, or of little importance. Was that a good or a bad thing? Would it be more comforting to him if the last time he had ever spoken to another individual, it had been an exchange of meaningful significance? Would it have granted closure or reassurance knowing that his last uttered words held purpose? Or was it better that his transition into isolation was muddled and indistinct? Maybe it was better this way. Like falling steadily to sleep, never remembering your last moments of thought before drifting off. The Nomad did not know. More than likely he never would. It mattered not.

How long could an individual exist in isolation? The importance of social interaction was irrefutable. Without it, the mind slipped quickly into depression. But could depression alone kill you? It shortened your lifespan, the unhealthy stresses it exerted on the body slowly wearing down resilience. But it seemed unlikely that it could actually cause bodily deterioration to the point of death. It could drive you to suicide, the Nomad knew that. He had been close innumerable times. He kept a sidearm with him always. He assured himself it was for protection; he could encounter anything whilst exploring the infinite universe, and occasionally, those things proved hostile. But in reality, the Nomad could scarcely think of a half dozen times he had been required to fire the weapon. Whereas the times he had pressed the muzzle to his own forehead... that was far more frequent. He had never done it though; not yet anyway.

For a long time, the Nomad had considered suicide an act of cowardice. Fighting on, enduring, survival at all costs, that was bravery. Now however, he realised just how wrong he had been. It took bravery to pull that trigger. What he did now, what he was doing, that was the act of cowardice. He fought on to survive, because he could not face the alternative. No matter how many times he tried, he could never summon the courage to go through with it. He'd never managed to apply that small amount of pressure to his finger.

He had often thought about ridding himself of the temptation. The amount of times he had thought about casting aside the weapon, leaving it behind on some cold remote world so that the option was taken away from him. Once he had actually succeeded. He had cast the sidearm into the depths of a frozen ravine. He had trekked back to the Fighter. He had taken off. He had left the atmosphere. He had even reached escape velocity. But something had stopped him. He had turned back. He touched down, at the same landing site. Retraced his steps. He had climbed down into the ravine, nearly killing himself in the process in what would have been a cruel twist of fate. He had spent hours scouring that desiccated riverbed in search of it, finally finding the gun, half buried by the winds, the cold lifeless muzzle upturned in the dust, sights directed his way.

He knew what it was that had taken him back that day. It was cowardice. He knew he would never be able to take his life, but he was too afraid to admit it, even to himself. Having the sidearm strapped to his hip comforted him. If ever he found the courage, he would at least have the means to end it all. He told himself he carried it for other reasons, but deep down he knew the truth.

As if it were part of his routine, the Nomad unclipped the retention strap of his holster, and slowly drew the pistol. With a trembling hand, the Nomad switched off the safety and raised the gun. His whole arm shook as he pressed the cold deathly muzzle against his temple. Hot tears welled, burning behind his eyes as they blurred his vision, puddling chillingly around his cheeks. His finger wrapped itself around the hard and lifeless metal scythe forming the trigger. He sucked in several deep wafts of stale air. He gritted his teeth. He squeezed, pulling as hard as he could. He felt his finger tighten around the trigger. But the trigger resisted, his strength insufficient to overcome the threshold force. The Nomad remained locked in this struggle. What time passed might have been as brief as a few seconds, or as drawn out as several hours. Eventually, his eyes raw from tears, he surrendered. He did not have the strength to pull the trigger. He never would.

His hand dropped abruptly, the weight of the gun suddenly all too much to bear, even in zero gravity. His hand drifted limply into his lap and he began to sob. He wept tears that clung together in fat globules of salty water. Unable to fall in weightlessness, they pooled around his eyes, finally detaching once they grew too large, floating off throughout the cockpit. He wept until his eyes dried up, and all there was left to do was heave in spasmodic silent wails. Numbly, he flicked back the safety and stowed the sidearm in his holster, securing it in place once more with the retention strap.

Exhausted by despair, the Nomad sank back into the chair and allowed his eyes to lull shut. The Nomad hated loneliness. Loneliness was the one true injustice of the universe.

The Nomad slept.

TWENTY

What followed despair was often mania: a delirious high resulting from the imbalances in the Nomad's brain chemistry. It was the polar opposite of emotion to what the Nomad had endured before falling asleep. As he awoke from a deep and silent slumber, the memories of pressing a gun to his head came flooding back. He was ashamed. Embarrassed that he had been driven to such a desperate act. The thoughts that had been passing through his head at the time now seemed alien to him. Now, in the metaphorical light of day, he was a different person altogether. No longer plagued by crushing unfathomable loneliness, but instead filled with a subdued optimism. His situation was bad, but he found it strange to think that, only a few hours before, he had felt the need to end his life.

Yet, despite now being reinvigorated with a drive to fight on and survive, he knew that in time his mind would once more return to the dark place it had been. It could be in a few hours, or a few years, but it was inevitable. Sooner or later, he would find himself once again pressing the cold metal gun barrel against his temple. The Nomad accepted this. But what scared him was the idea that the next time he might finally succeed in pulling the trigger.

Today the Nomad no longer saw the dark futility of a limitless void; instead, he saw an infinitude of stars glittering across boundless heavens. Ahead, through the sapphire haze of Cherenkov radiation, a violet and cream nebula burned in a frozen maelstrom, flaring outwards from a crimson heart. That was where he was headed; the yellow sun lay just a couple lightyears from the supernova remnant. It was spectacular to behold, even at such a remote distance. Over the next ninety-eight days, the Nomad would watch the cloud of dust and ionised gas swell and brighten as he drew steadily nearer. What a sight it would be.

The Nomad gazed further afield, out past the cremated remains of the spent red supergiant, deeper into the ceaseless horizons of space. The galactic core shimmered beyond, a dense mega cluster of juvenile white and amber stars, the twinkling pinpricks packed so tightly that their individual lights melded together in a diffuse hazy glow. Twisting plumes of silver and copper dust wove in and out of endless constellations, tangled and intertwined with the gravity of the stars, an unseen mass of dark matter gluing the entire galactic structure together. It was unfathomably vast. It was as close to infinity as the Nomad's mind could understand. It was beautiful, and terrible, incredible, and frightening. It was everything and nothing. It was full, and it was empty. And at its heart lay an object even more impossibly inconceivable.

Deep in the galactic core turned a supermassive blackhole. An object whose very nature defied understanding. A cavity ripped from time and space by a mass so great and dense, that even the subatomic particles constituting its mass had been crushed into oblivion. At its heart lay a singularity, the true antithesis of the universe; whereas the universe was infinitely vast, a singularity was infinitely tiny. It held no dimensions, and yet it was supermassive. Infinitely dense, it caused spacetime to warp into endless curvature. Not even light could escape a black hole beyond the event horizon, the point of no return. This dark veil that shrouded the singularity was the reason why the secrets of a blackhole were forever locked away. Not only was a blackhole paradoxical in its nature, but due to that very nature, it was unobservable, and therefore incomprehensible.

Around and around this rupture in the universe, revolved a fiery vortex of matter, twisted and flattened into an accretion disk that framed the impossibly black orb of the event horizon. Further afield still, the stars nearest the centre of the galaxy were arrested in violent orbits, ensnared by the inescapable pull of the blackhole. Flung in sharp and vicious ellipses around the dark heart, forever skimming a brink that would see them drop out of existence, these death-defying celestial bodies survived on the velocity of their orbits alone. At safer distances, the stars settled into gentler circumambulations, until eventually, away from the chaotic turbulence of the inner disc, the influence of the supermassive blackhole was only slightly perceived. The heart of darkness formed the absolute centre of the galaxy and the axis around which every star orbited, steadily circling on the galactic plane, in rotations that transpired over hundreds of millions of years. The galactic core, and the blackhole within, lay dead ahead, directly in the Nomad's path, just as it had done so on the day he first set out on his endless journey across the stars.

The Nomad reached into the pouch on his EVA suit, retrieving a partially eaten nutrient bar. Peeling back the packaging, he took several small mouthfuls, washing it down with repeated swigs from his canteen. The meagre ration did not so much as dent the gnawing hunger eating away at his gut. For a moment, he considered finishing the bar entirely, decreasing the portion of his next meal in order to compensate. He quickly decided against it; all he would be doing was cheating his future self out of a meal, simply because at present he was too greedy to endure the hunger. In an attempt to further satiate his starvation, he took another long gulp of fluid and reclined in his chair to watch the universe unfold around him.

He glimpsed at the fuel gauge. The needle had definitely risen now, yet it was still sat firmly in the red. It would continue to be for several more weeks.

A quarter of a tank; that was what he would end up with at the end of this extended FTL jump: just enough to decelerate the Fighter down from its current speeds and place the Nomad in orbit around the yellow sun. Once he arrived, those reserves would be almost utterly spent, leaving only a few dregs with which to make course adjustments inside the bounds of the solar system. He would need every atom of antimatter at his disposal, that much was assured. The margins were incredibly tight, but assuming the yellow sun parented a gas giant, he should have just enough to bring him within range of gravitational capture around the planet. That was all he needed. Then he would be able to refuel.

But that was far from all he needed. The truth was, even if the Nomad managed to refuel his antimatter tanks when he arrived at the yellow sun, his survival hinged upon there being an available food source within the system. The Nomad normally tried to ensure he had enough food reserves for several FTL jumps. Fewer than half of all solar systems had any source of life, be it simple or complex. He normally maintained a supply that could last until he discovered not just the next available food source, but also the one after that. Often, he found himself rationing, and on occasion, he had gotten close to running out. But he had so far always found some form of organic matter from which he could produce food in time. Often it was near inaccessible and difficult to harvest, but he had always found a way.

His survival so far was not the product of luck, but robust and cautious planning. He always plotted FTL jumps with the next subsequent few in mind, selecting systems that held the best chance of harbouring life; in those instances where he didn't, he always ensured there was one close at hand for the one thereafter.

Red dwarves only occasionally had life bearing worlds, usually limited to microbial colonies. Hotter, larger stars meanwhile, were often sterile. The best conditions for life almost exclusively arose around main sequence stars; they produced the best levels of radiation and remained in a stable part of their lifecycle long enough for life to evolve. The Nomad was heading to one of these very stars. The yellow sun was among the most likely in the universe to yield life, but even still, the odds were only fifty-fifty. Under normal circumstances, the Nomad would have enough rations left for another jump or two, even when heading to a main sequence star in the prime of its life, just in case fate had been unkind to the star in question. But this time, the Nomad had no back up reserves. He had no plan for what to do if he arrived at the yellow sun only to find it a sterile wasteland. He could try to jump to another system, but he knew that there was little chance of him making it. He would be near starved to death when he arrived; another FTL jump would finish him.

Everything was riding on life existing around the yellow sun. His entire journey hinged upon this one chance. If there was nothing to be found, then the Nomad would die. He would continue on though, he decided, even if it meant starving to death, cold and alone in the emptiness of eternity. He would not give up. He would fight to survive, right up until the bitter end!

Or would he? Would he condemn himself to such a terrible prolonged fate? Would it not be better to end it all quickly? If his death was assured then what difference did it make? If he did, it wouldn't be cowardice, but mercy. Perhaps it would even be bravery. Was it braver to go on enduring suffering, or to have the courage to determine your own end?

The Nomad slept.

TWENTY-ONE

Twenty-one days later, the Nomad opened his eyes. His self-enforced malnourishment continued. His body had begun to whither. Today the pain was not so bad. Yesterday it had been torturous. Two days earlier, lost in hunger-induced delirium, the Nomad had forgotten that he had already eaten his full day's rations. It was easy to do. He was hungry all the time, and the few measly mouthfuls he allowed himself each day could never sate the constant pangs groaning through his abdomen. His brain was continually starved of nutrients. In a moment of confusion, he had eaten an extra two portions of rations. It was only as his head cleared, fuelled by the extra sustenance, that he realised he had eaten double his daily allowance. It was an honest mistake, but not one that could go unpunished. It had cost him. Because of this one slip he was now a day short of supplies.

It might only be a day's worth of rations, but with his calorie intake already stretched to the limit, it would make all the difference. He could spread the hit across multiple days, but the question remained of when to schedule them? The temptation was to cut his food intake over the final stretch the journey, but the Nomad knew better. When arriving at the yellow sun, he would need every ounce of strength he could muster; he would need to locate and harvest a food source before he could replenish his supplies and eat again. If he was too frail, he wouldn't be able to carry out even basic tasks. He needed every gram of food he could spare for the days leading up to his arrival; even then, it might still not be enough.

Realising the best solution was probably not to delay, he decided to take the hit immediately, electing to fast for the following twenty-four hours. Better to suffer the damage straight up than to drag it out over multiple days. Short and sharp. Tough but brief. Then, when the period of misery was at an end, he could return to rationing. He had known it would be hard; what he didn't realise, was that he would barely make it through.

He came close to breaking on multiple occasions, unable to tolerate the cramping in his stomach. But through sheer will and stubbornness, he had endured. A simple notion steeled his resolve: were he to cave, surrendering to the pain, that would be it. Sure, there was the option for him to try again. He still had another seventy-seven days left; he could fast on any one of them to make up the difference. But he knew if he failed now, he would never succeed. His hunger was due to only worsen. The further into the future he pushed the ordeal, the more difficult it would be. By this reasoning, he knew he couldn't afford to give in to temptation.

That alone carried him through to the end, even if only just.

A short while ago he had finally broken his fast. Now, in the wake of his first meal in twenty-four hours, he was neither gratified or satiated. The hunger was still there, dulled for a time, but omnipresent. But compared to the hollow anguish he had been suffering through the night before, he felt the best he had in weeks.

Now, to conserve energy, he was sitting as still as he could, staring ahead at the unchanging skies. The nebula was closer today, creeping up from above the periphery of the blue shimmer in front of the Fighter's nose. Of the millions of stars visible to the Nomad, only a few had drifted from their initial positions at the start of his superluminal jump. Those that had, did so by only a few arcseconds.

The Nomad dozed off, or at least he believed he had. It had reached the point where his hallucinations were now indistinguishable from dreams. But the Nomad didn't dream. At least, he hadn't in the longest of times. Either he was awake and hallucinating, or he had finally regained the ability. Whichever the case, the Nomad was still sat in his Fighter. His eyes were closed, but somehow, he could still see the same starry blackness that he knew would be there the second he opened them. Something was different, however. The Fighter. It was a twin-seater. His co-pilot was sat to the rear. The Nomad could see neither him, nor the Fighter's additional chair. But he knew they were both there. He could feel them. He could feel the presence of another being. He could sense his weapon operator's gaze as if it were boring into the back of his head.

He was having trouble remembering his co-pilot's name. They knew each other well… or rather, the Nomad felt like they did. But he couldn't remember his name. Nor could he remember how they'd met. The two of them didn't speak. They just sat there in silence, staring out at the infinity surrounding them. How did they meet? Where were they going? Why was it suddenly so difficult to remember the details? Who was this man sat behind him? Why couldn't he remember his Fighter being a twin-seater before?

Everything went cold. The Nomad opened his eyes and gazed out of his single-seat Fighter. The canopy was open. He couldn't remember raising it, but he was glad he had done so. The stars seemed so much clearer without the glass to tarnish his view of the heavens. But what about his helmet? Surely the visor also blemished the view? No, of course it didn't. He wasn't even wearing his helmet! He must have forgotten to put it on when he raised the canopy. He was holding his breath instead. He had been holding it for several minutes now. But he felt no discomfort? No tense strain in his lungs. No dry heaves convulsing in his chest. For whatever reason, it felt as if this single lungful of air would last indefinitely.

He knew he ought not to hold his breath. Doing so in a vacuum could rupture your lungs; the pressure difference was enough to tear the soft tissue. But he had already been holding it for some time now. Why hadn't he felt his lungs rupture? Maybe they already had? Maybe he was dying?

It didn't feel like he was dying. He just felt cold. And hungry. He needed to exhale. If he exhaled slowly, he might avoid rupturing his lungs and stay conscious long enough to operate the canopy controls. Would he be awake long enough to repressurise the cockpit though?

The Nomad began to exhale. He lowered the lever on the control panel and the canopy slowly began to descend. It was taking too long. He was running out of breath. The canopy wasn't even halfway closed. He was so cold. Why was he so cold? The canopy lowered the last few centimetres. The Nomad leant forwards in his seat to operate the safety valve.

He opened his eyes. Why had his eyes been closed? He could swear he had been looking directly ahead of him. He moved to operate the safety valve only to see that it was already in the correct position. The cockpit was pressurised. Of course it was; it had never been depressurised in the first place! The canopy hadn't even been raised. All just another hallucination. But he was still hungry. And cold! Why was he so cold?

Sensory deprivation did terrible things. After twenty-three days of the same endless night, no other stimulation than the inside of the Fighter's overly familiar cockpit, the hallucinations were only getting worse.

The Nomad slept.

TWENTY-TWO

Licking the last crumbs from the packaging of another nutrient bar, the Nomad peered out of the canopy. The nebula had swollen significantly since last he had paid it any attention. Seeing how he seemed to do little else but stare at it, he thought it strange that he had not noticed it creep up on him. How long had it been? How far had he travelled? It was day fifty. Did that mean he was halfway there? Yes, it did. He was only halfway. Everything he had endured so far was only set to be repeated. Only, the second half would be worse… much worse. The first fifty days he had started fresh, his body well fed, his mind untortured. But heading into the second fifty, he was frail, vulnerable, deluded. He was so hungry. So hot!

Why was he hot? He was sweating! He had only just noticed it, but he suddenly felt trapped, the cockpit baking with an oppressive heat. Sweat was pouring from his brow. It stung his eyes. He wiped it away, but it continued to trickle torturously down his face. It dripped from his nose and lips. He could taste it: sour and saline. Why did it sting so much? It was unbearable.

He needed to get out of his EVA suit. He moved to unclip his harness, fingering clumsily at the buckle with numb hands. It was stuck. He tried again, clawing desperately at the release. Nothing. It was locked in place. He thrashed about in the chair. It was tightening. Why was the harness tightening? He needed to get out. It was so hot. Why was it so hot!? Why couldn't he take his harness off? He could see the temperature gauge on his control panel climbing steadily. Something was wrong. Something was overheating. The power cells! It had to be the power cells! They were producing too much energy. They were overheating and causing the cockpit to boil. If he didn't escape, he would be cooked alive!

He could smell smoke. He could *see* smoke! It was streaming upwards in wisps from beneath the switches on the control panel. He was in an oxygen-rich environment; if there was smoke then in seconds there would be… Fire spouted suddenly out of the dashboard. The amber and blue flames licked upwards from the controls, thrashing against the glass of the canopy. The Nomad shielded himself from the heat of the fire with his hands. Black smoke flooded the cockpit. He sputtered and coughed. It was so thick! He couldn't breathe! His eyes stung. He couldn't see! He was blind! He needed to get out! There was only one means of escape. He reached forwards, flailing his hands under the seat, clawing for the lever he had hoped never to pull. Eject! He needed to Eject! But where was the lever!?

He leant further forwards, straining against his ever-tightening harness. In his attempts to fight free, he cracked his forehead on the control panel. He recoiled in agony. He was bleeding. He could feel the hot blood pooling across his freezing brow. He was so cold. Why was he so cold? He gazed around the cockpit. Where had the smoke gone? Where was the fire? There was none. There never had been! No fire, just another hallucination; the most lucid so far.

The Nomad reclined back into his chair. He dabbed his brow and inspected the blood coagulating between his fingers. It might have just been another hallucination, but this time it had seemed so real. Until now, somewhere in the back of his mind, he had always been able to distinguish between the sensory illusions and reality. The visions, sounds, and sensations had always had an ethereal quality to them. But not this time. This time it had been so vivid… so lifelike. And to think: he had been fumbling around for the eject lever beneath his seat! What would have happened if he had found it!? He didn't even have his helmet on!

The Nomad reclined in his seat. He rummaged through the pockets of his suit and produced a dressing for the split across his brow. Dabbing away the excess blood, the Nomad pressed the adhesive pad over his forehead and sat defeatedly watching the endless expanse before him.

The Nomad slept.

TWENTY-THREE

The Nomad could hear music. It was faint. It was distant. But it was unmistakably music. It had been eerie at first, so quiet that it lay on the very edge of perception. But it had built in a crescendo as the hours went by, until the Nomad could hear a full orchestra of wind, string, and percussion instruments. The noise did not come from any particular direction, instead reverberating throughout the cockpit as a whole. But the Nomad knew too well that there was no music emanating from the Fighter; the source of the melody was his own insane mind.

At first, the auditory illusion was soothing; beautiful even. It had been so long since the Nomad had heard music. It had almost immediately reduced him to tears. He had wept for nearly an hour as he listened to the haunting symphony. Now however, the unending melody had grown tormenting. It had risen so loud that the Nomad could not hear himself speak.

Drums thundered. Cymbals crashed. Strings whined. Wind howled. The music was no longer a beautifully executed composition; it had soured into a discordant clamour. The Nomad clasped his hands over his ears as acidic tears burnt in globules around his eyes, but nothing helped muffled the pandemonium. He rapped his knuckles against his temple, frantically trying to silence the squealing tumult. He slammed his pate against the headrest in desperation, yet still the music blared on, growing in volume with each passing moment.

He slumped in defeated sobs, listening to the ear-splitting shrill that could scarcely any longer be called music. Hours passed. Days passed. Still the music continued to whine. At times it quietened, but never by much. There was no escape. There was no reprieve. The Nomad could barely keep his eyes open. But no matter how exhausted he grew, he couldn't sleep. It was impossible. The music shrieked louder every time he drew close to drifting off, dragging him suddenly back to full consciousness with a dramatic crescendo of cymbals and strings.

The very inside of his skull felt bruised. He longed for nothing but a moment of quiet. Never in his life had he yearned so badly for silence. It was excruciating. It was unbearable. It had been going on for so long. The Nomad just wanted it to stop. He screamed as loud as he could. His throat tightened and burned under the strain. His own roaring cries inaudible, lost amidst the din of drums and horns.

He slammed his fists against the glass of the canopy. He sank his head into his lap, clawing at the tufts of hair rooted weakly in his scalp. He stomped his feet. He beat his chest. Pinched his arms. Slapped his face. Drizzled water over his brow. Nothing could silence the music.

He couldn't bear it any longer. He needed it to end. He needed *an* end. He unclipped the retention strap from his holster. Clicking off the pistol's safety, he raised the barrel and pressed the cold metal to the side of his head. He closed his eyes. He curled his finger around the trigger. He squeezed.

Silence.

The Nomad opened his eyes. His finger was still wrapped tightly around the trigger. The slightest increase in pressure would be enough. But the need had passed. Silence had fallen.

He released the tension in his finger and flicked the safety back into its rightful position. Holstering the weapon, the Nomad refastened the retention strap. He exhaled in a lengthy sigh that failed in the eerie silence. The canopy was impossibly quiet. The Nomad could hear nothing whatsoever. He was deaf. He had gone deaf!

The Nomad suddenly panicked. He had wished so hard for silence. And silence had come. He had not thought for a moment how much worse the silence could be. Perhaps he was just not used to the quiet. He spoke a few words softly, hoping to hear the familiar sound of his own voice, but his ears failed. There was nothing to be heard. Not even a muffled whisper broke the deafening quietude. He spoke again, hoping it might be only temporary. Nothing. He screamed at the top of his lungs. Silence.

The overwhelming quietude endured. He leant back as tears streamed once again from his raw eyes. Pressing his face into his palms, he shuddered in despair, heaving and balling. Yet not a soul in the universe could hear him. Eventually his tantrum dissolved into pathetic whimpering. Time continued to tick forwards, each second of his sentence bringing him closer to his eventual release. He sank deeper into depression and self-loathing as the painful silence stretched out over the accumulating hours. Eventually, he managed to find some comfort in the unwavering quietude. It was peaceful in a way.

The hours elongated into days as the Nomad sat unmoving in his haunted tranquillity. He sipped water. Occasionally he ate. Mostly he stargazed. Somehow, even after all this time, the Nomad still found the stars beautiful. He had seen more of them then anyone had any right to. Most sentient creatures throughout the universe only ever observed them from a limited perspective. Imprisoned to their planet of origin, lacking the means of escape, few were ever capable of seeing the infinite complexity of the universe from outside the confines of a singular planetary orbit. But the Nomad had seen the heavens from innumerable perspectives. Not only did the arrangements of the constellations change around him, but so did the stars themselves. With the passing lightyears, new stars grew visible on the distant horizon, igniting from out of the black veil as they drew into view, whilst those he left behind faded to the rear, blinking out of existence, never to be seen again.

Constellations were meaningless. Over the Nomad's journey, even the most remote and distant astral bodies shifted their positions across the sky. He never lingered in one part of the galaxy long enough to ever take note of particular stellar configurations. Only other galaxies ever retained their fixed points in the sky. The nearest appeared as little more than milky smudges, whilst those furthest away were miniscule pinpricks of light, hardly distinguishable from singular stars. Yet each and every one of these immense super clusters was incomprehensibly far away. Further away than the Nomad could ever hope to travel in a thousand lifetimes. They were unreachable. Observable through billions of years of light sailing across the infinite reaches of intergalactic space. But unreachable. They served only as a reminder of the true scale of infinity.

The Nomad Slept.

TWENTY-FOUR

The Nomad sat and watched as a Cerberus drone ghosted high overhead. Drifting several hundred metres above the canopy, it remained unmoving in the Nomad's line of sight, on the limits of his vision. But the drone's singular eye glowed unmistakably, piercing crimson against the canvas of black. It didn't approach. It didn't retreat. It didn't attack. It merely hung suspended in the darkness, haunting the Nomad as he sped across the interstellar chasm. No matter how often or how little the Nomad stared at the drone, it never changed position. From the day it had first appeared, shortly after the Nomad's hearing had returned, it had not once shifted, its ominous gaze unceasingly bearing down on the Nomad as he coasted steadily across the gulf of space.

He couldn't pinpoint the exact moment his deafness had subsided; all he could remember was the shock at hearing a subtle alert tone blipping inside the cockpit. The return of his hearing might have been a gradual process over the course of several days, or it could possibly have been an instantaneous event. All the Nomad knew was that it had been some time before he had realised. For a longed period, he had been listening to the background droning of the Fighter without even realising it; so accustomed to the subtle noises his ship made, he had long ago become deaf to them, irrespective of his sanity. Even now, with his hearing restored, the humming of the FTL drive, the faint hissing of the air filtration module, the occasional whir of a processor momentarily awaking out of a power saving mode, all faded into a background of silence that the Nomad had to concentrate to break through.

The truth was, even though it often felt the opposite, the Nomad was never in total silence. Absolute quietude was impossible for organic beings, even inside a vacuum or and anechoic chamber. There were always sounds that could not be done away with. The majority of background noise the Nomad was subject to came from machinery. The Fighter was always alive with the sound of a mechanism clicking away or a computer whirring to life. But once the white noise was stripped back, such as when on EVAs in the vacuum of space, it was soon replaced by subtler sounds that proved far more inescapable. The first thing the Nomad always noticed when adrift outside the Fighter's cockpit, was his own breathing. Inside his helmet, his inhalations and exhalations rasped and echoed loudly. Breathing was something the Nomad never ceased, yet only when plunged into quietude did he ever even register that he was doing it.

The Nomad could always hold his breath, and

at times he had done just such whilst floating in the stillness of space. But even with the sound of his rasping lungs removed from the equation, other subtler noises quickly arose to take its place. His EVA suit creaked and rustled with even the slightest movement, but even when he remained absolutely motionless, silence was unachievable. Once all external noises had been eliminated, the quiet was filled with the sound of his own internal biology.

At minimal volumes, the gentle throb of the Nomad's heartbeat filled the void, the organ's valves snapping shut after each contraction to prevent the backflow of blood. Likewise, the movement of viscous fluids through the stomach and intestines as smooth muscle contracted and churned his digestive juices became audible. Even something as seemingly noiseless as swallowing grew amplified in the absence of all other sound. Only in death would the Nomad ever be truly silenced. Death, and madness. It was for this reason perhaps that the unbreakable quietude the Nomad had endured for near a week had been so unnatural, so torturous.

Multiple times during that period, he had felt the cold metal of a gun barrel pressed to his temple. By some miracle, the Nomad had never summoned enough strength to finally pull the trigger. He had made it to the seventy-fifth day. For the first time since he had set out for the yellow sun, it seemed as if there might actually be an end point to the journey. The needle on the antimatter fuel gauge was approaching the twenty percent mark; within the upcoming fortnight, he'd eventually have collected enough antimatter to carry out the deceleration burn on approach to the yellow sun.

His body had wasted away over the past two and a half months of spaceflight. In a substantial calorie deficit, and in the absence of physical stimulation, all his musculature had atrophied significantly. He still felt the painful gnaw of hunger at every waking moment, but thus far, he had managed to avoid complete starvation. Even the hallucinations induced by sensory deprivation had seemed to diminish recently; for several days now, his only delusion seemed to be the singular Cerberus drone hovering high above the Fighter. Perhaps the worst was behind him.

The Nomad opened the footlocker beneath his seat and drew out a nutrient bar. He peeled back the wrapper and nibbled at it slowly. It would be worth carrying out a stock check to guarantee he had enough rations to see him through to the yellow sun. For the remaining twenty-five days, the Nomad needed a total of thirty bars: one and a fifth every twenty-four hours, the quantity he had been consuming since day one of the jump.

Pulling out several handfuls, the Nomad dispensed the bars in a free-floating pile above his lap, continuing to retrieve any remaining from within the locker until finally his fingers merely groped at the sides of the empty foothold. Then, counting them as he did so, the Nomad deposited them a few at a time back into the footlocker. With the foothold refilled, the tally topped out at twenty. But that wasn't right. He must not have been concentrating. He was too hungry, too distracted for basic arithmetic.

Sighing in frustration, he pulled the bars back out of the food locker. Double checking he had not missed any left inside, he started the tally again. Carefully plucking the bars out of the air, this time counting them one by one, he stowed them away, ensuring he paid greater attention the second time around. Final count: twenty. Plus the bar he was currently chewing on: twenty-one. Still not right.

He must have lost count again. He had to have made an error. It was possible, he conceded, that he might be a bar or two short; it had been difficult to keep track throughout his delirium, but he couldn't be nine down. There was no way he had lost a whole week's worth of food. He emptied the hold again, this time searching the entire cockpit for any free-floating bars he might have lost track of during the previous two counts, or at any other point during the voyage. He searched under and around his seat, beneath the dashboard, inside the pockets of his suit, behind the headrest, and even in all the storage compartments throughout the Fighter's interior. To his despair, no extra bars turned up.

The Nomad began to panic. He started over, this time, counting out loud, straining his weary brain to concentrate through the mind-numbing hunger. Twenty-one. No! This wasn't right. Once more. Twenty-one!?

Stirred into focus by frenetic desperation, the Nomad redid the calculations he'd made at the start of his journey. He checked and double checked the maths. He'd made no error. Where were the other nine bars!?

Maybe he had the day wrong. More time must have past than he'd realised. He'd just misread the digital countdown. He relaxed slightly, figuring he'd solved the dilemma. He checked the countdown: Twenty-four days, eighteen hours, and forty-two minutes remaining until his arrival at the yellow sun. No. Something wasn't right! What was happening!? Where were the other nine bars!?

It had to be the clock. A system must have been powered down too long, the timer reset by a power surge from the Cerberus cells? It was simple enough to verify; he just needed to check the navigation computer, recalculate his arrival time, and reset the countdown. The Nomad booted up the navigation system and waited anxiously as it whirred through its start-up procedure. He checked his current location and set the computer to calculate proper speed arrival times. Twenty-four days, eighteen hours, and thirty-nine minutes. Something was horribly wrong.

Nothing he could think of could reconcile the

shortfall in his rations. He was down nine bars, with no way to change that fact. As to how it had happened, there were two possibilities. The first was that the Nomad had erred in some calculation made at the start of the FTL jump. The error could have been in his initial stock taking, or in calculating his daily rations. If either were the case, then he had unwittingly been eating more per day than he should have done, thereby short-changing himself now.

Alternatively, and seemingly more probable, was that, at several points along the journey, the Nomad had unwittingly eaten more than his daily allowance of calories. There could have been innumerable causes, the most likely: delirium. Irrespective, the reason did not matter. He was now short of a week's food for what was more than a three-week journey. Already down to his critical fat reserves, the Nomad's body had long ago turned to eating away at his muscle mass; so close to starvation, he had little else left to give before he'd be nothing more than skin and bones. A week's shortage of food at this stage was now seriously life-endangering. Starving to death was all of a sudden a very serious possibility.

What had happened!? Where had he gone wrong!? What had put him in this newfound predicament? There was a simple way to find out. The Nomad produced a tool from his belt and unscrewed a panel inside the cockpit that housed the waste disposal unit. Opening the compactor, he removed a crushed cube of plastic from inside. It consisted almost exclusively of nutrient bar packaging. Pulling apart the compacted mass of rubbish, the Nomad began sorting through it.

The process proved a lot slower than counting the nutrition bars. Much of the packaging was clumped tightly together and it took time distinguishing individual wrappers from one another. Finally, with a cockpit now littered with free-floating rubbish, the Nomad started his count. Inserting the recovered packets one by one back into the compactor, the Nomad tallied the number of bars he'd consumed throughout the journey. He had ditched his waste back in the red dwarf system, therefore he'd started the jump to the yellow sun with an empty compactor. The final count would reveal all: the exact number of nutrient bars he had eaten throughout the voyage.

Final tally: ninety-nine. It was conclusive. It was damning. There had been no errors in his calculations. Only errors in his judgement.

Over the course of the entire jump, he had eaten a total of nine nutrition bars too many. Now, for the rest of his journey, he had nine bars too few. He was going to starve. He just had to hope that the extra nutrition he had taken on to date would be enough to help him survive what was to come. He needed to think carefully. He couldn't merely ration out what was left, otherwise he would be far too weak to search for food once he arrived at the yellow sun. Nor could he fast for seven and a half days. In his current state, it would almost certainly kill him. He could perhaps intermittently go a day at a time without eating; maybe two at a stretch. Alternatively, perhaps he could endure a fortnight on half rations. If he managed fifteen, that would give him a final week on full rations in order to recover his strength. But he reminded himself that what he was considering now to be full rations were in fact just a third of a healthy daily intake. It wouldn't be enough. Nine hundred calories a day was not as extreme a deficit as four fifty, but it was still a deficit nonetheless, and an extreme one at that. It would not rebuild his strength; only a surplus could do that. All he could hope for was to stave off the worst rate of bodily degradation.

No matter which way he looked at it, the situation seemed hopeless. No matter how he rationed his food, he would still starve. No matter how he tried to conserve his strength, he would still be too weak when the time came to search for a food source. He would be dead on arrival.

The Nomad sat still, eyes closed, turning the numbers over and over in his head in an attempt to determine the best strategy for survival. It took him near enough an hour to reach a conclusion. He had already eaten his full amount for today. That was done. Tomorrow he would fast. Every other day from then on, he would eat three quarters of a bar, fasting intermittently in between. This would amount to a meagre five hundred calories per day, or an average of two hundred and fifty when fast days were taken into account. He would continue starving himself in this way until the final six days of the voyage. On day ninety-four he would eat a full nutrition bar, prepping his body for what was upcoming, hopefully preventing bodily shock and refeeding syndrome.

The next four days, the Nomad would eat his standard rationing amount, upping his intake to a full two bars a day. Sat motionless in the cockpit with no physical exertion, this amounted to a slight calorie surplus. Finally, on the last day of the journey, to boost his energy reserves, and to ensure he had the best chance of finding and harvesting a new food source upon arrival at the yellow sun, he would eat a full three bars: two thousand two hundred and fifty calories. A healthy surplus that might just be enough to give him the strength to move around, if not with great difficulty, in a gravity environment.

It was far from a sound strategy. It was as likely to kill him as it was to keep him alive. But the Nomad reckoned it was the best chance he had. There was no margin for error. He needed to find a decent source of organic material within hours of arriving at the yellow sun. He also needed to first refuel, otherwise he would not have the antimatter to reach any potentially life-bearing planets; this reduced his time window severely. Every hour he did not find food, his chances of dying would drastically increase. He stood a good chance of collapsing from exhaustion the moment he set foot outside the Fighter, or perhaps worse, falling unconscious whilst still at the controls. On top of all of this, there was probably only a fifty-fifty chance the system would even be home to life. Without life there would be no source of harvestable organic matter. No organic matter, no food. Everything was against him. But he had to succeed. The alternative was unthinkable.

The Nomad gazed up at the Cerberus drone. It peered back at him with its ominous crimson stare. Mumbling several curses in frustration, he lowered his head, closing his eyes to conserve energy.

The Nomad slept.

TWENTY-FIVE

Total darkness enveloped the Nomad. The stars had gone out. The glare from the Cherenkov radiation extinguished. He existed in a state of semiconsciousness from which there seemed no release. He could not awaken, nor could he fully suffocate beneath the pall of lassitude hanging over him. It was torment. His mind lacked any form of clarity, inhibiting his every thought from taking shape. But the visions around him were as lucid as they had ever been. It was difficult to tell whether he truly existed, or whether his mind was merely an echoing remnant of someone that once had.

The all-seeing eye loomed overhead. Unrelentingly, it glowered down at the Nomad with its red, lidless gaze. He could feel it boring into him. He murmured a series of half-conceived words, almost oblivious to the fact that he was doing so. His head throbbed, the din of silence stifling his mind. He needed to wake up. He murmured once again, fighting to regain some semblance of self. The sound of his own indiscernible ramblings roused him. His eyes crept open to the blurred interior of the cockpit.

Slowly and painfully, the Nomad's surroundings faded back into focus. Raising a gaunt arm from his lap, he reached strenuously for the water canteen hovering beside his chair. Clutching the container in his feeble grip, he heaved the weightless canister upwards and sipped. A portion of the haze clouding his mind momentarily lifted and the Nomad was able to collect his thoughts.

It was day ninety-three. The final day of fasting. Tomorrow he would eat. The day after he would double his intake. From then on, it was two square meals a day, until finally, one hundred days after setting out, the last in a brutally long voyage, the Nomad would finish off the three bars he had saved for the end.

But the ninety-third day was far from over. Figuratively, it had only just dawned. The Nomad had wasted away. He was but a mere skeleton of what he had been a hundred days prior. Like a spectre, he haunted his once hale body, waiting for his final vestiges of life to waft away. His every thought, both waking and dreamt, was of food. The pangs were unbearable, but much of the torture was of his own creation.

Plagued by the fear of once again losing track of his food reserves, he no longer stored the bars in his footlocker. Instead, they floated in front of him, suspended in the zero-gravity environment of the cockpit, slowly revolving in place as they hung in the air. At times, the Nomad found himself staring for hours on end at his next meal. Denying himself the food hovering just within reach was an excruciating torment, but it was the only way to be certain that he had enough for his plan. He couldn't trust himself otherwise. It would be all too easy to slip up now in his barely cognisant state. But the tantalisation was double-edged; it took every modicum of strength the Nomad had left to resist, but it also reminded him of the reward awaiting him at the end of his suffering. Just one more day and he could eat.

The Nomad raised a thin finger and gently tapped the closest nutrient bar. It tumbled end over end, drifting slowly away until it bumped gently into the glass of the canopy. Bouncing in slow motion, it floated down towards the control panel, off of which it softly rebounded. Gradually revolving, the bar bobbed back towards the Nomad. He steadied it with an outstretched hand, setting it back in place amongst the others. Every hour or so, the bars would need to be regathered after they steadily drifted apart to the various corners of the cockpit. The Nomad tried his best to position them motionlessly in front of him, but even the slightest amount of drift caused them to migrate over time.

Calories had become the most precious thing to the Nomad. His entire existence seemed utterly devoted to them. He was consumed by them. They ate away at him. Every crumb of food held immense value. A single morsel squandered could spell the end for the Nomad. Even now, as the vacuum-packed bars slowly revolved in space before him, his mouth salivated over a meal that was nearly a whole day away.

A growl twanged suddenly across his innards. His entire stomach contracted and twisted emptily on itself in agonising convulsions. The Nomad crumpled under the pain, cradling his taught belly as he waited for the cramping to pass. When the pain had finally subsided, he fished his water flask out of the air, taking another meagre gulp to dull the ache. The water offered nothing in the way of nourishment, but it did blunt his suffering. It filled his stomach for a short while, fooling it and his body into thinking that he had ingested something of nutritional value. Without the plentiful supply of recycled water that the Nomad had at his disposal, he figured that he would have probably died long ago. For a while, the water took the edge off his suffering.

The hours dwindled by as the spasming fits of hunger grew more and more frequent. Each attack was more paralysing than the last. But the Nomad did not surrender to his body's commands. He resisted, sipping regularly at his canteen, watching the countdown tick slowly away. There was still a long while left, but when the clock reached zero, his pain would be quelled.

In truth, it was self-deception. When the timer zeroed out, his final period of fasting would be done, but the meal awaiting him was a mere seven hundred and fifty calories. It would likely see him through until the next day, but even then, his rations only increased to one thousand five hundred calories, a mere two thirds of what he would usually be ingesting on a daily basis. The damage was likely already done. He would never regain the weight he had lost, and certainly not in the final days of his journey. Doing so would take weeks of a stable hearty diet. Assuming there was even a source of organic material on one of the planets circling the yellow sun, the Nomad realised it was unlikely to be nutritious enough to help rebuild his frail body.

What had begun was the beginning of the end. Feeble and fragile, the Nomad was unlikely to possess the strength or stamina he needed to carry out the taxing tasks critical for his survival. The full two thousand two hundred and fifty calories he was due to eat on the final day of his voyage might prolong his existence for another few days, but in all likelihood, he would already be too far gone. He suspected that by now, his immune system had begun to fail. It was only a matter of time before several species of bacteria in his body's natural flora would turn opportunistic, preying on his attenuated immunity, spreading beyond their natural habitat to wreak havoc throughout the rest of his body. With his natural defences all but wiped out, the bacteria would bloom unabated, killing him through infection as his body was eaten from the inside out.

The other issue that the Nomad had considered time and time again, was whether his body would even be able to cope with the upcoming increase in calorific intake. Starvation could not be treated with a sudden ingestion of sustenance. If he attempted to eat a full day's worth of rations in his current condition, he would more than likely vomit most of the food back up. Even worse, he could suffer refeeding syndrome, his body going into shock as it struggled to reconcile the sudden influx of nutrients, causing his potassium, magnesium, and phosphate blood concentrations to plummet. If severe enough, that alone could kill him.

He needed to gradually acclimatise himself to a steady food intake once again. He hoped that the gradual increase in calories, from nothing, to seven hundred fifty, to one thousand five hundred, over the course of seventy-two hours, might just be enough to accomplish this. He planned on ingesting his meals over the course of hours, not daring to eat more than a small nibble at a time. But even this could prove too much for the Nomad's vanquished constitution.

At this stage, the Nomad reckoned his odds of survival to be near zero. There was too much stacked against him for any meaningful hope of continued existence. He was a ghoul. He was a shadow of what he had once been. He was a skeleton in almost every sense of the word. There was such little left of his body that he dared not peel back his EVA suit in fear of what he might see. Even through the few thin layers of high-tech fabric, the Nomad could feel his protruding ribs and knobbly joints. He was a ghost; he certainly looked it. He could see it in his reflection across the inside of the Fighter's canopy. His eyes were hollow and sunken. His complexion pale and sickly. His hair was thin and malting. His skin leathery, pinched taught over his skull. Even his teeth felt loose in his sore gums. He wasn't dying, he was already dead; his body just hadn't fully realised it yet. But it was close to doing so.

TWENTY-SIX

The Nomad peered through the pressing darkness at an eye wreathed in flame. The crimson optics had drawn nearer. For twenty-two days, the Cerberus had remained perfectly stationary. For twenty-two days, it had remained at a distance of several hundred metres. Yet now, on the twenty-third day, the ninety-third of the Nomad's voyage between suns, the drone had begun to move. It was happening slowly, almost imperceptibly so, yet the all-seeing eye was steadily nearing. At first, the Nomad had thought he was merely imagining the drone's approach; after all, he was imagining the Cerberus. But after several hours, it became apparent that the machine was closing inwards.

He knew what it meant. Deep down he had always known. Fitting that the Cerberus should signify it. It had been hanging over him for weeks, lingering always on the periphery of his thoughts, and now, it was finally coming for him. Centimetre by centimetre, it was drawing inwards, and in a few hours' time, it would be upon him. Death was coming for the Nomad. In a slow unceasing march, death was bearing down on him, and his deluded mind had chosen the most apt metaphor to serve as its harbinger. It almost seemed poetic.

Six hours left on the countdown. Six hours until he could break open the seal on the nutrition bar clutched feebly in his hand.

The Nomad winced as another wave of pangs knotted through his stomach. He could feel his heart tugging pathetically beneath his ribs. There was such little of him left that he was surprised he could not see his spasmodic pulse throbbing through his EVA suit. Even his heart, like so much of his anatomy, had grown weak. Each breath he took was but a shallow wisp of air flowing in and out of two deflated lungs. Every muscle in his body, even the involuntary ones, had wasted away. Many of his organs had swollen and enlarged, whilst others had shrank and withered. In a concerted effort to conserve every joule of energy possible, the Nomad's body had suppressed every metabolic process it normally underwent into near suspended animation. He was a dead man walking; only, he was not walking. He doubted he'd even be able to sit upright were he not in a zero-gravity environment.

Time passed and the burning stare of the Cerberus continued to descend. The end was drawing near. Time continued to tick down. The Nomad lost the strength to keep his eyes open. They drooped shut, condemning him once more to utter darkness.

A while later, the Nomad's sight returned. The incarnadine eye of death was now only a few metres above the canopy. The Cerberus's glowing optics sparked and revolved in a mechanical maelstrom of fire and metal. It was beautiful. It was terrifying. The blood-curdling glare swelled around the cockpit, bathing the Nomad in a bloody light, the deathly iris threatening to swallow him whole.

The Nomad could feel the heat of the machine's death ray building. At any moment it would let forth a beam of light, snuffing the Nomad out of existence. But it wouldn't be that easy. He knew his death could be neither sudden or abrupt. It would be drawn out. Long and enduring. He had to suffer first, more so than he had done already. Fate was not so kind as to take his life peacefully, and the Nomad was not brave enough to end it on his own terms. There was still time left on the clock. The end hadn't arrived just yet.

Two hours left on the countdown.

By now, the eye had swollen so large that nothing else was visible beyond the canopy. The Nomad's body was shutting down. He was in the final stages of starvation. He could feel his organs beginning to fail. He knew he needed to eat his next meal early, otherwise he would not survive. But not yet. He needed to stave off death a little while longer.

His vision began to fade around the periphery. Wave after wave of hunger pangs rolled into one another.

One hour left.

He couldn't hold on any longer.

Using every morsel of strength left in his body, the Nomad lifted his hand clasping the nutrient bar. But too weak to maintain his grip, it slipped through his fingers. He swiped his hand to try and catch it as it spiralled away, but to his dismay, as he groped clumsily at empty air, he batted the remaining stash of bars floating in front of him. Bouncing off the glass of the canopy and across the dashboard, they scattered throughout the cockpit, tumbling out of sight as they dispersed into every recess and corner of the ship beyond his reach.

The Nomad felt the iris of the Cerberus suddenly widen above him. It was about to swallow him whole. It accelerated, sinking towards the glass with terrifying intent. The Nomad gasped, squirming forwards in his seat. His benumbed fingers groped around the footwell, desperately searching for one of the wayward nutrient bars, but he could barely feel a thing as he fumbled clumsily about. Then he saw one, settled on the floor in front of him. He strained, flailing his scrawny arms in desperation, but he couldn't reach it, not with his harness on.

The fiery pupil of the drone gaped overhead. In seconds, it would ignite.

The Nomad could feel his heart quivering with its final few beats. His frail fingers fumbled at his harness, probing ineptly at the cold metal buckle, but they lacked the strength to flick the release.

The Nomad's nape burned. He continued to clasp in futility at his restraints. He outstretched his other arm, straining as he reached with all the might he could muster.

Time was running out. The eye was upon him.

Whether he managed to finally flick the release, or it had simply come unstuck on its own, the Nomad would never know, but with a sudden jolt, the buckle unclasped and the Nomad was freed from his fetters. He toppled headfirst into the footwell, striking his brow with dizzying force. Rolling over onto his back, his neck crimped painfully at a jaunty angle. His fading sight swivelled back and forth as the darkness pressed in, searching desperately for anything that might save him.

Then, he spotted it, rolling across the underside of the control console. Flailing an arm above him, the Nomad tried desperately to catch it. A series of awkward gropes only managed to bat it further away, but just before it tumbled beyond his reach, the Nomad curled several frail fingers around it.

He gazed overhead, up through the canopy. All he could see was a churning tempest of crimson flames. The Nomad attempted to peel away the wrapper, but devoid of all strength and dexterity, the task proved impossible for his quivering fingers.

Finally, the Nomad bit down on the packaging, trapping it between his loose teeth. Thrashing his head back, he successfully tore it open.

Stripping back the wrapper, the Nomad grimaced and forced a nauseating mouthful past his lips. He puffed and gasped through exhausting mastication, retching as he finally forced himself to swallow. In the moments that followed, heaving and gagging in the Fighter's footwell, he slipped into unconsciousness.

The Nomad regained awareness gradually over the next hour. He awoke groggy and confused. His head pounded, a lump swelling across his brow where he'd struck it. He felt as weak as ever. The partially eaten nutrient bar was floating beside him. Plucking it out of the air, the Nomad awkwardly pulled himself up out of the footwell. He retook his seat in the pilot's chair. Fastening his harness, he gazed overhead.

The Cerberus was gone. It was nowhere to be seen. Now, all the Nomad could make out above him, was an infinite sea of stars.

Raising the nutrient bar to his lips, the Nomad took another small bite, washing the mouthful down with a swig of water. Over the course of the next few hours, he nibbled away at it until it was finished. He felt sick several times throughout the drawn-out meal, but he managed to stomach the bar in its entirety. It was the largest meal he had eaten for weeks, and his portion size was only due to increase over the following days.

For the first time on his journey between the red dwarf and the yellow sun, the Nomad felt satiated. He knew it would not last. In a few hours' time his body would once again be crying out for sustenance; but he was convinced that the worst was over. He had survived the ordeal. What was to come was still dangerously uncertain, but for now at least, he was alive.

TWENTY-SEVEN

Over the days that followed, the Nomad's strength steadily returned. At first, eating was laborious. His jaw ached. His gums throbbed. The smooth muscle of his gullet felt so underworked that to begin with, he almost choked swallowing even the smallest morsels. Every meal seemed to curdle in his stomach. He felt constantly nauseous and bloated, often suffering from stomach cramps as his metabolism steadily reset from the period of extreme starvation. Yet with each calorie ingested, his body began to recover, until before long, he began to enjoy his meals, often eagerly awaiting the next as time ticked away through his perpetual boredom.

But it was more than a recuperation. The Nomad had been resurrected. Rescued from the brink of death by something so simple as a few regular meals. The weight seemed to pile on. He still resembled a gaunt skeleton, but compared to where he'd been mere days prior, he felt almost healthy.

Though still confined to the cockpit, his energy seemed boundless. Even suspended in weightlessness, in the final days of his fasting, his limbs had felt heavy, his neck so weak it struggled to stabilise his head on his shoulders; now, well-fed and on the road to recovery, he moved about with a renewed vigour. Before, he'd struggled to remain fully awake for more than an hour at a time. Now, he remained alert and cognisant for several, in spite of the mind-numbing monotony.

The mist of semiconscious delirium had finally dissolved. Sensory deprivation still acted as the puppeteer of his senses, but the haunting images and nightmares that had plagued him earlier in the voyage, had for now at least, vanished. He was still hallucinating, of that he had little doubt, but presently, the tricks of his mind were uplifting sights and sounds. Occasionally, he heard whisperings of loved ones long passed. Other times, he would catch fleeting glimpses of wildlife both within and outside of the cockpit. But all of these were fleeting mirages, rarely enduring for more than a few seconds. Only one figment remained with him as he continued to drift across the chasm of interstellar space.

It had come about gradually, and though he knew the images were merely an illusion conjured by his stimulant-starved mind, he found their presence comforting all the same. No longer alone, the Fighter was now part of a fifteen-ship squadron gliding across the endless heavens. The Nomad was at the head of his flight, taking point in the Vic formation. To his left and right, his two wingmen sat tucked just rear of the Fighter. Further out, and both above and below, the Nomad discerned the additional four flights of the squadron.

Peering either side, he could make out the other two pilots of his flight through their canopies. Faces obscured by visors, the two pilots sat motionless in their cockpits, their gaze never wavering from the approaching yellow sun ahead. Their ships hung suspended in the empty vacuum, hovering little more than a few metres off the Fighter's wings, locked in formation with the Nomad as he flew out at the head of the squadron.

They followed him, silent and unmoving, across the endless gulf of space, escorting him through the void on the final leg of his journey. It did not matter to the Nomad that they no longer really existed; they had done once, even if too long ago to be remembered. But they were with him now, guiding and protecting the Nomad, watching over him as he coasted across the final expanse to the yellow sun. So long as they were there, he knew he was safe.

The final day eventually came. Day one hundred of one hundred. The end was near. It began with the first of three nutrition bars, followed by another six hours later. With his second meal finished, the Nomad began preparations for dropping out of warp. He powered up a wide array of systems across the Fighter that had been mostly dormant throughout the jump, rigorously testing them for hardware malfunctions and software errors. It had been the longest jump of the Nomad's life by nearly a factor of five. It had also been the longest period throughout the Nomad's entire vast journey that so much of the Fighter's technology had remained inactive. With such a lengthy period of dormancy, any number of issues could have arisen. The last thing he needed when arriving on the edge of the yellow sun's solar system was for a sudden malfunction to occur. If he was going to arrive safely and without incident, his checks would need to be thorough.

The hours ticked by as the Nomad ran analysis after analysis. To both his relief and amazement, everything seemed fully operational. A number of systems had suffered a delayed start up procedure, but with them having spent so long in hibernation, it was to be expected. Like all machines, the Fighter performed better with regular use; long bouts of inactivity were often the cause of bugs and gremlins.

Finally, the Nomad retracted the antimatter collection coils. The needle on the fuel dial was exactly where he'd predicted it would be. He had a quarter tank. Just enough to decelerate him from eighty-six percent lightspeed for safe approach to the yellow sun with a tiny surplus left over. The margin of extra fuel afforded him several short pulsejet burns within the solar system. With a little luck, he should just be able to navigate to the nearest gas giant and decelerate for orbital insertion.

With everything ready, nothing left to prepare before the moment of truth, the Nomad tucked into his last nutrient bar, gazing out ahead as the final hours slowly ticked down. The yellow sun was swelling with the closing distance, making the transition from a distant star to a sun as it began to outshine the rest of the galaxy. Overhead, the supernova remnant had finally risen fully above the veil of Cherenkov radiation pluming from the Fighter's nose. This close, it was more magnificent than the Nomad could ever have imagined. Pillars of bronze dust churned inside the milky heart of the immense stellar cloud, ringed by a burning crimson vortex that flared outwards into violet fringes, fading in mauve whispers against the backdrop of stars.

The whole cloud was an explosion frozen in time. No doubt it was still expanding outwards, yet the immense distances over which it had spread meant it did so seemingly outside the passage of time. It was a wonder of the universe, so profoundly beautiful that only nature itself could have sculpted it. Mesmerised by the marvel, the Nomad found himself suddenly overwhelmed with emotion. Fat tears welled around his eyes, finally detaching in droplets as he blinked, glinting in the dim light as they drifted throughout the cockpit.

The universe was not unkind, it was indifferent. It was both harsh and beautiful in equal measures. It held no regard for the Nomad, but that did not mean it was out to get him. He was but a speck of dust adrift in an infinite expanse, imprisoned to a fleeting moment of endless time. His existence bore no significance in the grand scheme of things. But all the suffering he had endured was worth it; he was lucky to be alive to bear witness to the wonders of existence.

TWENTY-EIGHT

The Nomad gazed over the flight data and navigational readouts. His approach was good. He glanced up over the nose of the Fighter through the veil of blue haze. The yellow sun was enlarging by the minute. He watched the countdown. A while back it had transitioned from days to hours; then, not long ago, it had made the transition from hours to minutes. Very shortly it would tick down into seconds. He raised his scrawny arm and lifted the clear safety casing covering the warp drive lever. Gently tightening his fingers around the Fighter's controls, he eyed the timer. The one-minute mark was approaching.

This was it. One hundred days of superluminal travel were imminently coming to a close. Everything he had endured, all the tribulations he had suffered over the last three months, had led up to this specific moment. Once he dropped out of FTL, he would need to act fast; there was a lot to do, and he had only a limited amount of strength with which to accomplish it. But for now, for this one final moment, all he could do was wait.

The timer ticked into double digits. Less than

a minute left.

It would be a long burn, one that would subject him to several g's, even with the warp drive acting to lower his mass. In his weakened state he was in danger of losing consciousness. If that happened, the consequences would be disastrous. Unable to kill thrust to the pulsejets, he'd decelerate too much, burning through the surplus of fuel he was supposed to save for manoeuvres. It wouldn't take long for the tanks to run dry, only a few extra seconds under thrust, but in that time the Nomad would lose his only means of salvation. With the tanks empty, the pulsejets would cut out. No longer subject to any forces, the Nomad would awaken soon after, stranded on the outer limits of the solar system, unable to navigate towards a gas giant to refuel, doomed to live out his final days once more starving to death as he slowly orbited around the distant reaches of the yellow sun. He couldn't let that happen. Not after making it so far. Not after making it so close. He couldn't black out. He had to fight it. No matter what.

He gazed at the clock. Forty-five seconds.

Had he not salvaged the Cerberus power cells, he would never have made it here. Equipped with only his old, degraded ones, he would have run out of charge months ago. Unlike refuelling his antimatter tanks, in interstellar space he would have been utterly incapable of recharging the cells. Even now, after one hundred days of sustained FTL flight, the warp core heavily drawing power the entire time, the cells were still maintaining a constant output. How they were producing their power, or where they were drawing it from, the Nomad could not begin to fathom. Truly, Cerberus technology was advanced well beyond his comprehension. The race of sentient machines were every bit as formidable as he had ever given them credit for. More so even.

Twenty-five seconds remaining.

It was the end of a lengthy ordeal. A prolonged arduous chapter in the Nomad's life was finally closing. But it was not really the end of anything. It was merely the resumption of his journey. This was just one FTL jump in countless. He was about to arrive at the yellow sun, but that was not his true destination. Just one stop along the journey. The real end of his voyage was still unfathomably far away, both in time and distance. Even now, having travelled so far for so long, the Nomad struggled to comprehend the possibility of ever reaching it.

Ten seconds.

None of that mattered right now.

Nine seconds.

Survival was not accomplished over months or years.

Eight.

It was accomplished day to day.

Seven.

Eventually those days tallied up.

Six.

In time becoming years.

Five.

The long-term future didn't matter.

Four.

What mattered was the here and now.

Three.

That was how the battle for survival was won.

Two.

By fighting for every second.

One.

The Nomad pulled back on the flightstick. The Fighter somersaulted. Dropping down to subluminal speeds, the blue radiation haze dissipated. Flipped over, the Fighter hurtled rearward, the warp drive still functioning, only now acting in reverse, the effects inverted, elongating space along the way ahead and contracting it the way back.

The Nomad punched the thruster to maximum. The pulsejets roared with vibration throughout the cockpit, flaring silently outside in the vacuum of space. Antimatter and matter collided, annihilating in a massive outpouring of energy. Then it came. Even weighing next to nothing, the Nomad felt the hard crush of acceleration slam down across his chest. It was every bit as terrible as he had feared.

The Nomad lurched back in his seat. His neck whipped against the headrest, the air in his lungs ejecting as a tremendous pressure squeezed down on his chest. The strain was too much, his feeble malnourished body unable to tolerate the forces being exerted on it. His vision began to tunnel, fading black around the periphery.

He needed to hold on!

How much longer? He still had three quarters of his fuel reserves left. He couldn't ease up. If he did, he would miss his approach vector. With limited fuel he had limited options. His orbital entry calculations had given him a very tight margin for error; if he missed the window by even a little, the Fighter would either skim the gravity well of the yellow sun, hurtling back out into interstellar space with no means of return, or alternatively, it would plunge into an uncontrolled dive, straight into the heart of the yellow main sequence star. Everything had to be timed to perfection. Anything less and the Nomad would be dead.

His sight continued to narrow. He was halfway through the burn. It was still far too early to let up, but if he didn't, he would surely pass out. He tensed the muscles in his frail legs, then his buttocks and abdomen. The tension in his body raised his blood pressure enough to momentarily halt the tunnelling of his vision. He rasped in short rapid bursts, inhaling and exhaling every few seconds, holding his breath in between. The strain was immense. The skin across his face drew taught. His arms grew impossibly heavy. Clamping his fingers ever tighter, he fought to keep his grip on the controls.

Colour began to fade, greying out as the dark edges on the periphery of his vision resumed their advance towards the centre of his eyes. He glimpsed at the fuel dial through pinpoints sight. He was nearly there. The flight computer was confirming it. The ticking counter on the HUD was the last image to grace his vision before the Nomad went blind completely.

He was out, swallowed by blackness, slipping rapidly into oblivion. But he had not lost everything yet. He still had his hearing. The faint buzzer of the flight computer wailed throughout the distant cockpit. He had completed the burn. He needed to kill thrust. But the pulsejets were still firing. Already he was eating into the very last of his fuel reserves. He tightened his grip around the thruster and let the immense weight of his arm wrench back on the controls. The pulsejets cut out. The forces collapsed. Flung abruptly back into weightlessness, the Nomad slipped into unconsciousness.

TWENTY-NINE

The Nomad awoke. He inhaled. He was dizzy. Disorientated. His mouth dry. His head was pounding. He attempted to move his hand to his face, but his arm refused to listen to his brain's commands. A sudden tingling spread through his body in waves, washing from his fingertips over his skin to his limbs and torso. He tried to move again. To his relief, this time his body followed the instructions.

Rubbing his blurry eyes, the Nomad tilted back his head and gazed upwards. He had arrived. The yellow sun shone high above, glaring against the dark backdrop of the galaxy. But the star's light was distorted, bent out of shape. The warp core was still engaged. Dazedly glancing around the canopy, the Nomad clasped hold of the lever with tingling fingers and disengaged the superluminal drive. The lens effect in front of the Fighter's nose condensed back into focus and all fell ghostly still.

Glancing aside, the Nomad caught sight of the immense nebula, allowing him to regain his bearings. Groggily, he peered down at the control panel, his eyes darting to find the fuel gauge. He sighed with relief. The needle hovered just above zero, a few dregs of antimatter still in the tanks. It was enough. No surplus beyond what was required for a few short burns, but it was enough. He had made it. Now came the real challenge.

Knowing there was not a moment to lose, the Nomad hastily flicked several switches along the control panel and powered up the Fighter's vast array of scientific equipment and scanners. He watched as the sensors began their detailed analysis of the yellow sun's solar system. The Nomad sat back anxiously in his chair, drumming his fingers as he awaited the findings of his primary scans. In a matter of seconds, the first results began to trickle in.

The Nomad spread open the holographic displays in front of him and watched as figures, diagrams, and charts started to load across the interface. Eight planets; four terrestrial, two gas giants, two ice. That was all he needed. He immediately turned his attention to the larger of the two gas giants, the fifth planet from the sun, and fed the data into the flight computer. The microcircuits clicked and whirred as the complex course calculations were run through the software. A few moments later, the computer churned out an array of possible trajectories for orbital insertion. Of the five options available, the Nomad had fuel only enough for two of them. One took him too low into orbit for antimatter collection. The one remaining option was right on target.

The margins were laughably tight, but with

some skilled piloting, the Nomad would theoretically be able to slip the Fighter right inside the gas giant's radiation belt. If he pulled it off, that would be it, his fuel reserves depleted without a single antiproton to spare. But the Fighter would be positioned right in the midst of the richest antimatter reservoir for lightyears around. He'd finally be able to refuel. He just had to make sure he didn't undershoot the mark.

The Nomad keyed in the flightpath and locked the coordinates. A curving parabola projected holographically across the inside of the canopy. Tugging gently on the flightstick, he fired several puffs from the arcjets, rotating the Fighter back around, aiming it along the projected path. Readying the pulsejets for one final run, the Nomad made several fine adjustments with the RCS, perfectly aligning the Fighter for what might have been the most critical flight of its existence. Without any hesitation, the Nomad punched forwards on the thrusters.

He sank back into the pilot seat as fierce torrents of white plasma exploded from the exhausts. An instant later, the Nomad jerked the thruster back to zero. The burn was brief, but it was enough to catapult him into motion. The intended trajectory was a gravity slingshot past the smaller gas giant. The manoeuvre would shed enough velocity for the Fighter to become ensnared inside the immense gravity well of the planet's larger sibling. In the interest of both efficiency and expediency, the flight path took him on a close approach to the sun. Coasting now silently in towards the heart of the solar system, the Nomad rechecked the flight data. The margins were tight, but he still had enough antimatter for the final decelerating burn. So far so good.

The hours whittled away as the Nomad sailed on towards the yellow sun. As he coasted towards the heart of the system, more detailed results from the scientific equipment began to ping in. The incoming data cast across the holographic interface and the Nomad studied the feeds. The gas giant set as his intended destination was a whole system in itself; with four large moons tied in close orbit, and dozens of smaller satellites encircling further out, it parented more orbiting bodies than some stars. Of the four terrestrial worlds circumambulating the inner solar system, two were utterly inhospitable, boiled and scorched by their proximity to the yellow sun. But slightly further afield, the third and fourth worlds lay within the habitable region.

Studying the data closer as it steadily trickled in, the Nomad disregarded the fourth terrestrial planet. On the very outer reaches of the habitable zone, it was too old and small to realistically sustain any complex life. It might once have been a luscious ocean world, but now, its core dead and solidified, incapable of producing a magnetosphere, its atmosphere had been stripped away over the millennia, leaving little more behind than an arid planetwide desert. It was not outside the realms of possibility that it could harbour some form of microbial life, but searching the moons of the solar system's gas giants would probably prove more fruitful.

The third planet from the sun was the place to search. The largest of the four terrestrial worlds, it was in a prime position to harbour life, and with the initial figures that were appearing across the Nomad's display, the potential seemed promising.

The Nomad gazed up to see the star rapidly approaching. The photochromatic glass of the canopy was promptly polarising against the blinding glare of the yellow sun. Soon, the main sequence star had dimmed to a fiery amber, the canopy blackened to almost opaque. From this perspective, approaching the perihelion of his slingshot around the astral body, he could make out details on the surface of the sun. Burning tendrils arced across the searing corona, whilst planet-sized black pits pocked the raging sea of plasma.

A quadrillion watts of energy radiated out from the nuclear furnace every second, fired into the dark expanse in an unceasing deluge of photons. Temperature dials and readouts throughout the Fighter spiked as the spacecraft skimmed the fringes of safe proximity. Close enough that the Nomad felt he could almost touch the sun above him, the Fighter quickly grazed past. The approach was intense but brief. In a matter of mere seconds, the Nomad's ship had slung past, the sun receding behind it.

The Fighter's temperature needles plummeted back down, the glass of the canopy fading to greater translucency. With the flyby complete, the Nomad turned his attention back to the results of the system scans, but directly ahead, something bizarrely inexplicable caught his gaze.

At first, it seemed a trick of the eye. Perhaps he was still hallucinating; if so, he had truly been driven mad in his time adrift between stars. Peering ahead, it almost vanished from sight, lost amidst the backdrop of space, but as the Fighter's trajectory curved away, the visual spectacle began to creep across the periphery of the nebula. In seconds, the phenomenon blossomed suddenly into full visibility. It was immense. As it passed in front, it eclipsed the supernova remnant, but instead of masking the nebula, it distorted and magnified the spectrum of vivid ionised gasses. Warped out of shape, the interstellar cloud now appeared as if it were being viewed out of focus through a colossal convex lens. Likewise, the light from the surrounding stars elongated and swirled about the dark circumference of the phenomenon.

Despite its strange appearance, the artefact was eerily familiar. The Nomad had seen it before. He had just spent the better part of one hundred day staring at little else. The phenomenon he was seeing now was the same effect he witnessed every time the Fighter's warp drive engaged. The similarity was no mere resemblance; it was a replication.

The Nomad was staring at a fold in spacetime. It was a wormhole.

There was no other explanation. That was what it had to be. But how!? It was unprecedented. It was incredible! How had it come into existence? How did it remain open? Was it natural, or the product of some vastly technologically advanced race?

Through the three-dimensional hole in the universe, the Nomad peered at a remote point of existence, immensely far removed from the yellow sun both in distance and time. The Nomad could make out bright clusters of stars bundled tightly into unrecognisable constellations drifting gradually across the centre, their light shining outwards from the other side of the wormhole. It was a gateway. A tunnel. A shortcut through the fabric of reality.

It was not an impossibility. No laws of physics prohibited its existence. But nonetheless, its very presence seemed to contradict countless notions of time and space. It wasn't impossible, but it was unnatural.

Countless questions rattled through the Nomad's head, but amongst them all, one reigned supreme: where did it lead?

He peered down at the results streaming off his sensors. Previously concealed behind the yellow sun, the scientific equipment was only now picking up the anomaly. A reel of incomprehensible data slewed across the holographic interface. Graphs spiked, charts exceeded their maximum readings, and hundreds of error messages echoed across the data feed. It was as if the warped spacetime, and whatever powerful force of nature that was holding the wormhole open, was scrambling every ray and detection field expelled from the Fighter's sensory equipment. It was unreadable. It was incomprehensible. It was unfathomable. But it was magnificent.

The Nomad peered back up at the enormous passageway through the heavens, watching as the colours of the nebula continued to melt around its circumference. The stars within swelled and blossomed, fading and vanishing as they drifted across the visual window to the tethered point in the distant universe. The Nomad lost himself as he stared in disbelief over the passing hours. Never in all his time travelling through the endlessness of space had he ever witnessed anything quite like it.

THIRTY

The Nomad was pulled from his trance as the first of the two gas giants began to approach. Shimmering in the light of the sun, the planet glinted ever brighter against the starlit heavens. Swelling quickly from a pinprick of light, the spherical orb began to slowly oblate, stretching across the equator as the Fighter hurtled towards it. The Nomad double took, wondering for a moment if the distortion was perhaps the product of another as of yet unseen wormhole; but as the world grew in size, he soon realised that the apparent deformation was merely the result of his changing perspective.

The gaseous planet racing towards him was surrounded by a vast network of planetary rings. Constituted of trillions of particles of ice and dust scattered in orbit around the gas giant's equator, their span dwarfed the very world they encircled. Glimmering as a succession of countless copper halos, the rings crowned the gilded orb at their heart, casting curving bands of shadow across the clouded milky heavens below.

The Nomad's heart momentarily palpitated. His decelerating slingshot trajectory took him straight through the orbit of the planetary rings. Careening straight towards them, with no fuel to spare for course corrections, the Nomad was about to tear clean through the gas giant's halo.

He was locked on course. He couldn't slow down. He couldn't stop. If he changed trajectory, he would miss his slingshot window and be cast back into the outer solar system, overshooting his parabola set to carry him on towards the planet's larger sibling. He didn't have enough fuel to slow down enough for orbital insertion around the ringed world; he was reliant on the retrograde flyby to syphon off enough speed for ensnarement by the larger, more gravitationally powerful of the two gas giants. This was it. He was on a fixed path. He'd already committed. It was too late to change his mind.

The rings were composed largely of dust, but with chunks of rock and ice as large as ten metres across suspended in the planetary crown, the Nomad feared the worst. He was travelling at such a speed that even colliding with a particle larger than a few millimetres across could be enough to rip through the Fighter. If the Nomad barrelled straight into the rings, his ship would be ripped to shreds.

Frantically pulling up the flight path across the Fighter's displays, the Nomad zoomed in on his trajectory, staring at the point of interception. To his disbelief, the course he was locked on threaded a needle. Hurtling narrowly through a twenty-metre gap, the Fighter would skim between the planetary rings, hopefully emerging out the other side unscathed. It was tight. Very tight. There was no guarantee the gap would be clear of debris; there was still every chance he could be about to meet his end. But slipping between the rings, the Nomad would avoid the certain threat of annihilation that battering clean through them would bring about.

The rings rushed ever closer. The Nomad watched the distance tick down. Hundreds of kilometres became tens, then thousands of metres, before, with the shimmering veil of ice careening his way, hundreds. A curving band of black furrowed out of the silver trails ahead. The gap swelled. The Nomad's pulse drummed. He held his breath. The chasm expanded. He closed his eyes.

The Fighter vibrated. The glass canopy crackled, a million microscopic meteorites peppering the outside of the ship as it bulleted through the void, sailing clean out the other side. The Nomad opened his eyes. Ahead he saw the far curving horizon of the gas giant. He'd made it. He was clear. The milky heavens dropped out of sight, the Fighter travelling too fast to become ensnared by the planet's gravitational pull, but sailing away, the world fought to keep hold of the Nomad, draining the ship's momentum. The Nomad jerked back on the flightstick, upending the Fighter, lurching the throttle sharply forwards. The pulsejets lit up, blasting another short burst from the craft's exhaust, working in tandem with the ringed gas giant to shed as much speed as possible from the Fighter.

The Nomad killed thrust. The jets cooled. Out in front of him, the haloed world was coasting away, retreating into the night. His eyes flicked to the flight data. He'd done it. The Fighter had slowed and would continue to do so as he sailed away, just enough so that, with his final decelerating burn, he would dip beneath the escape velocity for the next planet in his path: his destination, the largest of the eight worlds around the yellow sun.

Several hours passed before the Nomad finally caught sight of it. Steadily, ahead of the Fighter, it emerged into view, enlarging from a mote of reflected sunlight into a globe dotted with two glimmering speck suspended either side of its equator. Even at this distance, the four icy moons of the behemoth world were visible, perfectly aligned along the gas giant's orbital plane. Drawing nearer still unveiled an atmosphere of bronze and cream bands encircling the upper heavens of the world, twisting into immense hurricanes and tempests that ripped through the dense soupy skies.

The Fighter continued to sail along the holographic vector lines projected across the inside of the canopy. Approaching the gargantuan world ahead, dropping swiftly into its gravity well, he was beginning to pick up speed. He checked the fuel gauge; lacking the precision to measure the dregs left in the tanks, the physical dial was reading nil.

The Nomad checked the digital readout on the holographic interface to see he did in fact have some fuel left, however little. This was it. He had enough antimatter for one final burn. It would be close, but it should be enough to slow him down below the gas giant's escape velocity.

The Nomad swivelled the Fighter rearwards. Thrusting forward on the throttle to maximum, the Nomad braced against the deceleration as the pulsejets flared for their final burn. The Fighter juddered. The engines sputtered. Seconds later they stalled. The thrust cut out. The pulsejets died. A buzzer sounded throughout the cockpit to warn that the tanks had run dry.

Gazing down with dread, the Nomad inspected his flight data. He swallowed. He checked his velocity. Speed: good. Approach vector... his approach vector was out!

Swivelling his head on his shoulders, the Nomad gazed behind him out the canopy towards the gas giant's approaching horizon. The burn had shed the speed he needed, but his trajectory was misaligned. He needed to correct, and fast. If he failed to, the Fighter would drop into the upper atmosphere; from there, there would be no escape. The resistance of the gasses would rapidly slow down the Fighter. It would plunge deeper, in towards the heart of the world. The immense pressure and temperatures would soon melt it, crushing it thereafter into oblivion; the Nomad along with it.

He was completely out of antimatter. His arcjets would have to do the job. Inverting the Fighter back around, the Nomad yanked up on the flight-stick, firing all of the RCS jets across the underside of the ship. Spouting a torrent of electrical discharge from the undercarriage, the craft slowly began to rise above the encroaching curvature of the planet. The arcjets continued to gush ionised gas for several minutes, and steadily, the Fighter climbed.

Peering back down at the flight data, the Nomad finally issued a sigh of relief. The orbital projections had stabilised. The Fighter was perpetually soaring with minimal decay towards the rolling horizon. He had done it. He was in orbit.

Flicking the half dozen switches across the control panel, the Nomad deployed the Fighter's array of antimatter collection coils. The hydraulics groaned and the electromagnets hummed. Their magnetic fields extended outwards into the magnetosphere of the gas giant, attracting and channelling the antimatter that had accumulated over the millennia into the Fighter's fuel tanks.

The Nomad sank back in his chair as the Fighter whipped steadily around the gas giant in orbit after orbit. The needle on the fuel gauge was steadily rising at a rate that would have made him smile if he had taken the time to glimpse down at the control panel. But he never did. Instead, his gaze fixed unwaveringly on the wormhole. Each time it vanished behind the stormy horizon, the Nomad's eyes would look ahead, anticipating the moment it would re-emerge.

Soon enough, the fuel needle maxed out on the dial and the diode indicating the tank was full illuminated. But mesmerised by the unnatural phenomenon above, the Nomad failed to notice, only peering downwards finally with a resurgence of hunger. The first pang twinged through his body, alerting him that it was once again time to eat. But he had no food. Not yet anyway.

The Nomad punched the coordinates of the third planet from the sun into the flight computer and awaited his options. He hadn't glimpsed at the scientific data since the initial results had pinged in. A closer inspection of the newer, more detailed scans would give him a decent indication of what to expect, but the Nomad didn't dare. If there was no life to be found there, he was as good as dead. He was delaying the inevitable, but not knowing meant he could hold on to hope for just a few hours longer. He didn't want to learn his fate studying data on a chart. He wanted to find out for himself.

The computations came in. Three optimal orbital insertions, each showing little variance. Fuel was no longer a limiting resource; the only factor that now mattered was time. He selected the most direct route and locked it in. With the course charted, a set of parabolic trajectory lines depicting his escape vector from the gas giant projected across the inside of the canopy.

Pitching the Fighter back, the Nomad aimed the ship along the flightpath and primed the pulsejets. Coasting in orbit, the Nomad waited as the Fighter drifted towards the ignition point. When the ship's trajectory aligned, he took a deep breath and lunged forwards on the thruster. The engines exploded with power. The Fighter surged forwards, driving the Nomad back into his seat. The craft raced faster and faster towards the oncoming horizon. The nightside of the gas giant fell away below as the glare of dawn erupted. The escape vector straightened as the Fighter cut across the penumbra, rapidly ascending into daylight. The gas world receded, falling beneath the craft as the Nomad broke free from its gravitational grasp. Shooting clear, escaping from orbit, the Nomad eased gently off the thruster and the engines began to cool.

Skimming past an icy moon crisscrossed with rusty fissures, the Fighter picked up one final gravity assist to send it on its way towards the inner solar system. The bump in velocity the Fighter gained was subtle, as was the induced curvature of its flight path, but it was enough to direct it perfectly on target towards the mysterious rocky world that held the secret to the Nomad's fate.

THIRTY-ONE

Hours later, the Nomad sat gazing at a perfect solar eclipse. The Fighter was steadily approaching the nightside of the third planet from the sun. At this distance, the world exactly masked its parent star, concealing the astral body with only the yellow sun's corona shimmering around the planet's circumference. Celestial alignments such as this one were not rare in spacefaring. The Nomad had witnessed thousands of eclipses throughout his journey across the universe. Yet of all of them, this one somehow seemed the most magical.

Perhaps it was his recent ordeal that had driven him both to the edge of sanity and the verge of death. Perhaps it was his still unknown impending fate. Or perhaps it was the aura of mystery shrouding it.

The Nomad had given no other consideration than haste when he had selected his approach trajectory. He had simply selected the fastest, most direct route. What he hadn't realised at the time, was that the flightpath took him on a direct approach from the nightside of the world for the entire duration. Cloaked in darkness, the planet kept its secrets hidden. Only upon the Nomad's arrival would he swing around towards the daylit hemisphere. Only upon his arrival would he see the world bathed in light. Only upon his arrival would he learn his fate. It seemed almost poetic.

The Nomad sat anxiously in waiting. The planet drifted across the ecliptic plane, breaking totality as a diamond of light erupted from over the horizon. Flaring outwards in a dazzling glare, the dawn broke from behind the mysterious world. This was it. The Nomad was on final approach. In mere moments he would discover his fate.

The Fighter sailed ever closer. The Nomad's heart pounded. His grip on the controls tightened in nervous anticipation. He held his breath. The sunlight began to refract through the planet's atmosphere, scattering in a thin veil of amber that cooled rapidly to blue. A crescent of light glimmered across the horizon, the daylit surface of the alien world turning agonisingly slowly into view.

The canopy polarised against the reflected glare. The Nomad's irises constricted and he was momentarily blinded. As his pupils adjusted, his vision returned and he finally caught sight of what was reflecting so much of the yellow sun's light back up at him: water. Water! There was so much of it. An entire ocean's worth! An ocean that seemed to stretch endlessly from pole to pole. More water than the Nomad had ever seen in his life. And where there was water there was bound to be... life!

The Nomad shook his head in disbelief. Emerging over the horizon was the coastline of a vast continent. The first crinkled edges of the landmass had only just revolved into view, but already the Nomad could see green. There was so much green! It was everywhere: a dense carpet of vegetation encompassing the land.

The Fighter sailed into the light, erupting from the darkness of night, emerging into a golden dawn. More of the world drifted into view. The verdant flora transitioned into shades of red and purple. The dark navy seas melded and swirled into warm turquoise shallows, whilst out at sea, immense blooms of yellow and green streaked through the ocean currents. A band of gold and silver deserts dusted the equator, bordered at the tropics by thick swathes of dense jungle, whilst white snowcaps blanketed the poles. It was an Eden. An oasis of life of incredible rarity that so seldom existed in the cold unforgiving wastes of the infinite void. It defied expectation. It defied belief. Yet here it was, as if it had awaited the Nomad all this time. It was a gift. A gesture of good will. An apology addressed from the universe to him for all the hardship he had endured to arrive here. It was a reward. His prize for fighting so hard to survive. He had found water. He had found life. He had found salvation.

THIRTY-TWO

The Nomad sat gazing down at the vibrant marble beneath him. He had all the data his scientific equipment could gather from orbit. It was truly a golden world; one tailored specifically to him. The atmosphere was roughly three quarters nitrogen, a fifth oxygen, with the final few percent composed of several noble gasses and a small trace of carbon dioxide. It was almost entirely devoid of chemicals toxic to the Nomad's biology, and at sea level, the pressure clocked in at almost one atmosphere exactly. The air was breathable.

The planet's average temperature was a tepid two hundred and eighty-seven kelvin. The equatorial deserts reached a balmy three hundred and thirty, whilst the polar tundras dropped as low as two hundred. But at the tropics and across the temperate zones, the temperatures were perfect: warm and mild enough for the Nomad to comfortably survive without any form of environmental suit.

It was a paradise. The perfect conditions for life to thrive. The perfect conditions for *him* to thrive. He had little inkling as to the biological makeup of the indigenous flora and fauna, but if the climate was so akin to that from which he had evolved, he saw no reason as to why the ecosystems wouldn't be.

A twang of hunger grumbled in the Nomad's gut, urging him to hurry. But the Nomad needed no encouragement; he was giddy, trembling with excitement. He was about to set foot on a garden world, something he thought would never happen again, not with the universe in its current state of decay.

He pushed forwards on the flightstick. The arcjets pivoted the Fighter upside-down and rear facing. The Nomad delivered a short burn to the pulsejets, bracing against his seat as his velocity decreased. The burn shed enough speed to set the Fighter's orbit into rapid decay. Pushing back on the flightstick, the Nomad re-righted his craft, aligning the nose with the oncoming horizon.

The planet continued to turn below as the Fighter started its descent into the upper atmosphere. The tranquillity of space faded. The curved horizon rose up across the canopy and the Fighter began to skim the thin veil of thermosphere. Vibrations began to tremble throughout the craft, slight at first, but as the Fighter plunged deeper into thicker and thicker air, they grew, until the ship jostled and shuddered with violent intensity. The Nomad pitched the Fighter's angle of attack upwards as the craft collided with the mesosphere, punching a fiery bow wave of immense pressure as it bore through the sky. The orange haze of glowing plasma washed upwards from the undercarriage, splashing over the Fighter's heat shielding and flickering around the edges of the canopy.

The Nomad rolled the Fighter left, canting the nose further back. The craft banked, carving against the currents of air, veering in a decelerating arc. The Fighter rolled back to the right, shedding more speed as the Nomad serpentined through the air. Continuing to slow, the Fighter dove through the stratosphere, plunging into white plumes of fluffy cloud. The bow wave of air beneath the ship cooled, the amber blaze dying away into crystalline air.

The Nomad switched the thrusters over to chemical propellants and engaged the ships air brake as he steered out of the final bend of the Fighter's meandering descent path. Pitching the ship's angle of attack back down, he felt the airflow steady over the craft's fixed wings as he swooped into the troposphere, transitioning out of his hectic atmospheric entry into a smooth and soaring glide.

White smoky mist frothed around the canopy as the Nomad continued his descent, the occasional air pocket buffeting the craft as it cut cleanly through the lower atmosphere. The surface of the world was inbound, but aloft in the cloud cover, the Nomad had still yet to see it. It was little more than a few thousand metres beneath him, growing closer with every passing second.

Suddenly, the heavens cleared and the Nomad sailed into open sky. He gazed down, peering through the glass of the canopy, and looked out in wonder across the surface of the golden world.

THIRTY-THREE

Foamy waves rolled inward across the sapphire seas, lapping gently into turquoise shallows as they approached the shoreline. The briny froth washed gently over yellow beaches of pebbles and sand, crashing in spray against the cliffsides and headlands as the waves broke against rock. Swirling in sheltered coves, the amplified swell erupted upwards against the bluffs, fountaining in steamy geysers that took to the winds as vapour. The crinkled coast yielded to smooth, rolling hinterlands swathed in green and crimson grasses, whilst violet shrubbery and purple scrub speckled the hillsides. The grassy knolls quickly gave way to thick jungles of tangled trees, their lofty canopies bathed in smoky mist that streamed in pluming wisps across the wind.

The Nomad startled in his seat as shadows raced overhead. He gazed suddenly upwards to see silhouettes against the amber sunrise. Feathery birds of vibrant plumage were flocking in the skies, gliding swiftly on costal breezes mere metres above the Fighter. The magnificent creatures swooped and soared in their hundreds, riding updrafts and helical air currents. They paid the Fighter little regard, but as the broad and angular wings of a reptilian predator emerged from the clouds above, they scattered on the winds, diving groundward towards the refuge of the rainforest below.

The Nomad croaked, emitting something between a chuckle and a sob as he felt the hot burn of tears welling behind his eyes. Unable to comprehend exactly what he was feeling, he began to weep, his eyes streaming uncontrollably as he both laughed and cried.

Wiping his eyes, the Nomad peered back down at the continent beneath him. The jungle canopies thinned and the trees surrendered to the expansive grasslands of a great savannah. Ahead, dark specks dotted the bronze and mauve pastures. The Nomad felt his lips curve into an involuntary smile as he watched the vast herds of roaming animals navigating the plains in their thousands. The colossal gathering of beasts cantered in rank through winding muddy rivers, persevering onwards over dry and barren brush on an immense continental migration that never ceased.

The Nomad pitched upwards as snow-capped mountains rose jaggedly from behind the oncoming horizon. Rocky spines toothed out from the rugged foothills, carving out great valleys streaked with bubbling rivers of white water. Upstream, the gushing torrents spewed from crushing glaciers, the immense frozen rivers grinding down from the snowy drifts of the mountain summits above. Tufts of pink woody trees sprouted from the white slopes, thinning as the Fighter climbed above the treeline, soaring up towards the peaks shrouded in cloud ahead.

Gaining more altitude, the Fighter cleared the range, vanishing momentarily into the blanket of cloud. Re-emerging back below the cloud ceiling, the Nomad soared out across an expansive beige dust plain. Sandstorms boiled from the desert winds, streaking in murky bands across the wastes, yet even throughout this barren region of the planet, the Nomad could distinguish hardy flora and fauna clinging to life in the nooks and crannies of the bitter badlands.

The Nomad continued to glide out across the desert, the brown dusts transitioning gradually into flowing dunes of silver and gold, before finally, hues of green and orange blossomed in the distance. A colossal winding river several kilometres in berth wove its way gently through the otherwise arid plains, cultivating verdant flora along its banks as it meandered slowly beyond the horizon. Ribbons of algae smeared through the grey waters, whilst bubbling shoals of creatures writhed beneath the surface, feeding on the aquatic plant life.

The Nomad crossed over the river, soaring onwards into more desert. Soon the sands solidified and blackened into craggy lava fields that crawled downwards from smoking volcanos continuously spewing fire across their ashen slopes. The Nomad engaged the Fighter's rockets and streams of exhaust condensed behind the ship in white contrails. The thrust provided enough lift to climb above the great pillars of black fumes rising from the volcanic ridge.

The Fighter darted back into the clouds. Lightning crackled and flashed from within the heart of a dark storm, stirred up by the torrents of hot air rising from the volcanoes meeting cool costal winds. Rain beaded and streaked across the glass of the canopy as the storm began to buffet the Fighter about. The Nomad pitched downwards, dropping out the bottom of the tempest. Rain lashed downwards across raging ocean waves and waterspouts connected the sea and sky in helical columns of brine. Thunder tolled and lightning flared, crooked bolts glaring over the violent black waters below.

The storm attenuated with the passing kilometres, fading steadily until the Nomad cleared the cyclone periphery entirely, gliding out above sunlit waters. Up ahead, the dark blues of the deep brightened to hues of clear teal, through which vivid spectrums of maroon, magenta, amber, emerald, and cobalt blossomed in gargantuan coral structures just below the surface. Sandy islands swept out of the waters, birthing chained archipelagos matted in tropical forest before yielding once more to endless ocean.

The Nomad peered out across the wide expanse of sea, marvelling as plumes of water jetted upwards from beneath the waves. Smooth fins cleft through the swell as massive marine animals rolled over the foam in great schools. The giant aquatic beasts frolicked and splashed playfully, leaping above the water before diving back down into the hidden depths below.

The Nomad soon left the great aquatic herds behind, arriving swiftly at a coastline of marshy wetland. The Fighter soared ahead as the crimson fens gurgled beneath the craft, the water coalescing into a broad and muddy estuary that gradually narrowed to a weaving river. The land either side grew rugged and steep, copper and tawny vegetation clinging to the windswept hills.

Flakes of snow began to flutter gently on the winds, settling across the highlands as feathery blue trees sprouted into woods too dense for the Nomad to peer through. The snow covering thickened, blanketing the hills and caking the trees. Soon, the forests thinned into flat frozen tundra, but even here in this frigid clime, the Nomad watched great herds of megafauna trudging across the frozen wastes.

The snow became more ubiquitous as the Nomad flew closer to the pole. The sun sank low to the horizon before descending into a seasonal night. Suddenly, the heavens were ablaze with vibrant auroras glimmering in an entire spectrum of colours above a sea of snow.

Not long passed before the Nomad's flight carried him back out into the dawn. Skirting over the polar continent's coast, he watched as the ice cap fragmented into colossal icebergs that drifted offshore, splintering gradually as they melted in warmer waters.

Sailing out across another vast ocean, the Nomad eventually arrived back where he had started. As the serrated shoreline approached for a second time, the Nomad gently reduced thrust to the engines and allowed the Fighter to steadily descend. The coast glided beneath him as he adjusted the Fighter's yaw, steering towards a prospective landing site.

The Nomad pitched upwards and steadily engaged thrust to the VTOL jets, using the cushion of air it created to brake and slow his approach. Drifting steadily above a region of flat open grassland close to the boarder of a forest, the Nomad reached for the landing gear lever and steadily deployed the Fighter's tripod of skids. Easing his lift gradually, the Nomad cautiously guided the Fighter downwards towards the ground. He watched the numbers slowly tick down as he floated closer and closer towards the grass. Suddenly, the skids made contact. The Fighter dipped subtly on the landing gear's suspension as the ship touched down.

Powering down the engines, the Nomad paused, peering around in disbelief. He had made it. This was exactly where he needed to be. Somehow, against all odds, he was alive to see all he had just witnessed. Unable to process the whirlwind of emotions surging through him, the Nomad broke down and cried.

THIRTY-FOUR

The Nomad breathed laboriously. In his diminished state, his first time within a sustained gravity field for several months, every piece of his anatomy felt heavy. His arms hung from his shoulders as if they were leaden. His lungs strained under the pressing weight of his chest. Even his lips and cheeks felt so heavy it seemed like they were contorting his face.

Summoning all the strength he could muster, fighting the golden world's unrelenting pull, he reached beneath his seat and opened his footlocker. Rummaging around through his various medical supplies, he came across an array of autoinjectors. Tensioning his arm, he managed to strainingly raise one of the syringes to his neck.

Pressing it to his vein, the Nomad pulled the trigger. A spring-loaded needle stabbed through his skin, pumping a cocktail of broad-spectrum bacteriostatic and fungistatic antibiotics straight into his bloodstream. The one-off dose was a crude but effective method of preventing infection. With the microbiome of the golden world a complete unknown, there was no way to predict how pathogenic the indigenous microbial life would be. If unprotected, any exposure to an opportunistic bacteria or fungi could prove deadly to the Nomad. The injection would slow down and potentially halt the rapid proliferation of any infectious microorganisms that managed to enter his body, buying the Nomad time for his more sophisticated immunological countermeasures to kick in.

Wincing as the needle retracted, the Nomad let the autoinjector slip from his grip, dropping it heavily into the first aid box before retrieving a second. Pressing the next syringe to the same spot, the Nomad jabbed himself with a dose of immunoboosters and stabilisers. The complex concoction of organic compounds and programmed stem cells would aid his compromised immune system in developing a natural response to invading alien pathogens.

Retrieving a third and final spring-loaded syringe from the medical box, the Nomad inoculated himself with the most advanced of the three injections: an adaptive vaccinator. As the last needle pierced his skin, millions of nanorobots swarmed into his blood. Designed and programmed to seek out and destroy alien pathogens, the nanobots broke down foreign microorganisms, neutralising them into harmless compounds before presenting them as antigens to the host's own immune system.

Functioning in much the way the Nomad's own white blood cells did, but with vastly greater speed and flexibility, and at an efficiency near a thousand-fold higher, the nanobots helped develop a powerful immunological response to any alien pathogens encountered. The end result was a potent lasting immunity to a multitude of indigenous diseases. The protection endured long after the nanobots were excreted from the host's system and was acquired in the fraction of the time compared to conventional vaccines.

The concoction of drugs and nanorobotics were not fool proof; the occasional resourceful microorganism sometimes manage to develop ways to circumvent the defensive measures, but such cases were extremely rare. The adaptive vaccinator was one of the few miracles of modern science that had been key in facilitating interstellar exploration. Without it, explorers would never have been able to remove their helmets in breathable foreign atmospheres without succumbing shortly thereafter to a host of opportunistic diseases.

For the first time in longer than the Nomad could remember, he was about to take a breath of fresh, unrecycled air.

Pressing a small dressing over the trickle of blood oozing from the injection site, the Nomad dropped the final autoinjector back into his medical supplies and kicked shut the footlocker. His pulse rising, and his energy and strength waning, the Nomad prepared to open the canopy.

This could still be it; there was every chance he was about to meet his end. Even after making it all this way, surviving the journey, finding a world rich with life, and successfully touching down, the Nomad could still be about to fail. He had endured a large degree of muscle and bone atrophy, and he was so severely weakened by his long stint in zero gravity, that there was no guarantee that he'd even have the strength to climb out of the cockpit. The whole process of inoculating himself had been strenuous. Even now, doing little more than sitting upright in his chair was proving taxing. His limbs were heavy and limp, his head felt like it was swaying on his neck. Even if he managed to clamber out of the Fighter, he wouldn't make it very far. Then, there was the matter of harvesting a food source, and setting up the biomolecular recombinator.

But he had to try. Every second he stayed still he was burning up precious calories. He needed to act. He needed to move. This was it. It was do or die.

THIRTY-FIVE

Heaving a lever upwards on the control console, the Nomad opened the canopy. The airtight seal breached, and as the glass steadily retracted, the golden world's atmosphere flooded the cockpit. The Nomad sat still, eyes closed, and took in a long draught of air.

His senses were suddenly swimming, his mind overwhelmed by stimuli. Since the day he had first set out on his voyage across the stars, he had subsisted on nothing but the cold sterile air recycled from his onboard supplies, topped up with oxygen extracted from asteroid ice. He had forgotten just how sweet natural air tasted.

The flowing ocean of fragrances and flavours was overpowering at first. He could smell earth and soil, salt and sea. He could smell rain. He could smell grass. He could smell pollen, nectar, and blossom. Those were only the odours he recognised. Intermingled amidst the blended aromas, a plethora of new scents whispered on the breeze. Sweet and dewy perfumes melded with other rich, heady base fragrances, all laced with sharp fresh notes that occasionally cut through the background aromas.

The Nomad felt like a blind man whose sight had suddenly been restored. He had never thought of his sense of smell as integral to who he was, but having suffered anosmia for longer than he could remember, he had developed a newfound appreciation for the richness scent brought to life.

Time was of the essence, but even still, the Nomad could not help but take a few moments longer to relish the world around him. He felt the warmth of the yellow sun against his bare skin, the cool breeze washing gently through his wispy hair. The world itself was rife with sounds, some ghostly familiar, others eerily bizarre. The wind soughed through the grass and trees, whilst the faint rolling of ocean waves breaking against the shore carried over the air.

He was surrounded by a hubbub of animal calls: chirrups, tweets, quails, and quacks, barks, growls, grumbles, and howls, braying, bleating, nickering, and neighing, buzzing, chirping, croaking, and hissing. Calls emanated from the surrounding grassland and echoed from the forest ahead; some droned continuously as a background chorus, whilst others pitched over the rest of the orchestra, sounding in melodic staccatos. Each was alien and yet somehow reminiscent. Each just a single part in a great unending symphony of life.

After several long minutes spent allowing his senses to digest the vast cacophony of new sounds and smells, the Nomad finally opened his eyes. Depressing a button on the control panel, he extended the Fighter's ladder. Taking a succession of deep breaths in preparation, the Nomad grabbed the rim of the cockpit, and with a prodigious effort, heaved himself out of the pilot's seat. His arms trembled, his shoulders burned, and his knees threatened to buckle, but somehow, against all odds, in spite of all the muscle wastage and time spent in zero-gravity, through a feat of heroic willpower, the Nomad manage to stand.

His head was spinning, his body swaying side to side as his core muscles struggled to stabilise him, but as he fought to keep upright, he steadily began to acclimatise to the downward pull of the golden world's moderate gravity. Finally regaining his lost sense of balance, the Nomad summoned another tremendous effort, and swung his leg up over the rim of the cockpit. Astride the fuselage, the Nomad clumsily dangled his foot back and forth as he ineptly attempted to gain purchase on the top rung. Eventually, his boot made contact, the magnetic sole affixing to the metal.

Awkwardly straddling the rim, the Nomad attempted to swing his second leg over. Easing his weight steadily onto the ladder, to his own astonishment, he managed it without too much difficulty. Finding himself perched uncomfortably atop the steps, the Nomad mentally prepared himself for what would undoubtedly be the most arduous phase of exiting the Fighter: the descent. Lifting a foot from the top rung, the Nomad felt his boot demagnetise. His thighs and arms strained under tension as he lowered his feeble body, reaching with outstretched toes for the next rung down.

One thing was in his favour: having lost so much muscle, his body was the lightest it had been in his entire adult life. He was lacking in strength and power, but his gaunt and scrawny frame made up some of the difference. Had he weighed much more, he doubted he would have ever managed to stand, let alone climb down the ladder.

The descent took far longer than the Nomad would have liked. By the time he planted his feet on the bottom rung, his arms and legs were screaming with fatigue. He was sweating. Panting. His knees seemed jellified, his whole body trembling through exertion. But the very moment his first boot pressed into the spongy vegetation of the planet's surface, he felt the burden suddenly lift. Planting his second foot beside the other, the Nomad released his hold of the ladder and shakily took his first steps out onto the Eden world.

Peering down, he shimmied his feet about in the crimson grass, chuckling aloud with glee as it rustled beneath his boots. Broad-bladed, lengthy, and crinkled along its edges, the grass sprouted flowery buds, each exhaling puffs of golden spores as they wafted in the warm breeze. Curly shrubs with bulbous foliage scattered the hilltop, and strange knobbly cacti growths bulged with tall prickling stigmata. Elsewhere, fungal nodules swelled and contracted in slow pulsating rhythms, their wrinkled surfaces shuddering each time the wind picked up.

Both baffling yet beautiful in equal measure, the Nomad studied each passively. After near a lifetime spent harvesting algal sludge and fungal mould from dried-up river basins on barren desert worlds, the Nomad felt like he was staring at a bursting cornucopia of organic matter. Any and all of it was no doubt harvestable; he could feed any of the surrounding vegetation straight into the biomolecular recombinator and no doubt produce food of some nutritional value, but his body hadn't evolved to digest fibrous grass or shrubbery, and the closer to edibility the organic matter fed into the recombinator was to begin with, the better the yield produced. And right now, though the Nomad felt he could scarcely afford to be picky, he knew he needed the most nutritionally dense food he could find.

Amongst all the nearby plant life, one specimen in particular caught his eye: a leathery tree with long drooping boughs, each draped with verdant conical leaves and pink blossom, but more importantly, laden with swollen teardrop fruit. The engorged berries were in various stages of ripeness, transitioning from purple to amber in colouration. Judging from a few littering the surrounding grass, the Nomad discerned that they were golden when ripe.

Staggering up the gentle slope, chest heaving and brow glistening, the Nomad approached the tree. A gentle tug was all that was needed to pluck one of the low hanging fruits from its spiralled stem. Roughly double the diameter of the Nomad's fist, he was surprised by its weight. The smooth flesh was supple in his grip, and turning it over in his cupped palms, he breathed in the perfumy scent given off in the warmth of the sun.

The Nomad powered up his suit's short burst scanners and allowed the simple scientific equipment to run an analysis on the potential food source. With his helmet doffed, the data instead displayed as a holographic projection from his wrist. The results pinged in. Barely believing his luck, the Nomad laughed nervously. Of the twenty amino acids from which the Nomad's biology was constituted, the fruit shared sixteen. Likewise, its flesh contained large stores of a six-carbon sugar, the molecule differing only subtly from one his body had enzymes to digest. It was laced with a few minor organic toxins, compounds arising mostly due to chirality, however overall, the fruit was nearly edible even before processing.

Despite the temptation, the Nomad resisted the urge to bite into the fruit there and then. Though unlikely to kill him outright, even a single mouthful could cause him to be violently ill; but then, even foods from his natural diet often require cooking before they could be digested. Regardless, the Nomad was still dependant on the biomolecular recombinator to produce a viable food source; little had changed in that respect. What was significant however, was that, firstly, he could expect a high yield, and secondly, with limited processing required, the end product would likely retain some of the nuanced flavours and textures of the original fruit, something that was sorely lacking from the ultra-processed meals he was accustomed to.

Using both hands, the Nomad tossed the fruit underarm in the direction of the Fighter. It flew pathetically far, but propelled by gravity, it rolled nearly the rest of the way down the slope, coming to rest in the grass close to the landing skids. Picking a second fruit from the tree, and then a third, the Nomad tossed them in a similar fashion, continuing to bowl the swollen pods down the hill, until, scattered around the foot of the Fighter were near a dozen of the teardrop berries.

Trudging back down the slope, the Nomad made his way to the Fighter's starboard wing and operated the hydraulics to lower the cargo pod. Shuffling up alongside it, the Nomad knelt over the access panel, depressing it to open the storage container. Air whistled through the port as it slid open, filling the vacuum-sealed cylinder. Locating the collection canisters and tossing them out onto the grass, the Nomad uncovered the dodecahedral-shaped biomatter recombinator and slid it along the pod's rails into position beneath the port.

The Nomad took several deep breaths in preparation for the lift. Even in low gravity whilst at full strength, the device was cumbersome. In his current state and in a full g of gravity, the Nomad had serious doubts as to whether or not he would be able to lift the recombinator out of the pod. If he couldn't get it out, it wouldn't be able to unfold. If it couldn't unfold, it was all but useless.

Grappling both handles atop the device, the Nomad nudged his boots right up against the pod. Pivoting his hips, he crouched down, keeping his back straight. With one long final exhale, the Nomad locked out his shoulders, planted his feet, and heaved. Every muscle down his posterior tightened. He grunted and gasped as he felt his blood pressure spike. His arms drew taught, his legs juddering as they pressed into the grass with all the might the Nomad could muster. He gritted his teeth as specks of light danced about the periphery of his vision.

Slowly but surely, the recombinator began to levitate. Fearing it would slip from his hands, the Nomad clamped his grip tighter as he strained and heaved. Emitting an involuntary scream, he swivelled his hips as the device rose above his knees. It cleared the rim of the port. Leaning backwards, the Nomad eased the weight down the side of the cargo pod, until finally, it thumped into the soil.

Collapsing beside it, panting and sick with exertion, the Nomad retched, almost vomiting from the strain of the lift, but after several moments spent wheezing to catch his breath, his nausea subsided.

Ignoring the spasms shooting through his lower back, the Nomad clambered dazedly back upright. His task wasn't over yet. In order for the voltaic cells to unfold, the device needed space. He had to drag it clear. Readopting his grip on the handles, the Nomad dug his heels in and yanked sharply with all his remaining strength. The tug shifted the recombinator a few centimetres. A second jolt dragged it a little further. He kept at it, lugging the bulky device incrementally through the grass, until eventually, spent entirely of energy, the Nomad had pulled it clear of the Fighter's undercarriage.

Another bout of hyperventilation recovered enough of the Nomad's wits to allow him to press the button on the top panel. A small diode flashed in response as the Nomad staggered clear, giving it a wide enough berth to unfurl. Whilst the device began to charge, the Nomad shuffled over towards the scattering of fruit he had gathered and collapsed in the grass.

Drawing a knife from a scabbard on his EVA harness, the Nomad cut the first of the pods into wedges. The skin was fairly tough, yet the inner amber flesh was supple and tender. Juice flowed steadily from the pulp as the Nomad continued to cut away sections, stuffing the pieces into the first biomatter collection canister, discarding the stone from the fruit's core.

One by one, he dissected the alien berries, filling the array of canisters, finishing just as the biomatter recombinator reached full charge. Hoisting himself back upright, he laboriously loaded the cylinders into their receptor sockets. The device powered up out of standby and began a detailed analysis of the biological material housed within the canisters. Once ready, the Nomad initiated the recombination and reclined in the grass.

He was just beginning to drift off, when, little more than fifteen minutes after the processing had begun, the recombinator began to bleep. Excitedly roused from his doze, the Nomad dragged himself back to the recombinator.

Anxiously pausing in a moment of dread, he finally summoned the courage to open the dispenser draw. It was full. He'd never seen so much food produced by a single harvest. A pang of hunger tore through the Nomad's gut. Without hesitation, he snatched a bar straight out of the tray, ripping open the packaging with aching teeth, and scoffed nearly the entire thing in a matter of seconds. It was sweet, moist, and rich. The same perfumy fragrance he'd smelt when he had first picked the fruit carried through in the flavour, melding with an unusual, but not unpleasant, caramelised herbaceous taste. It was the best meal he'd eaten in months. It was the best meal he'd eaten in years. As far as he could tell, it might have been the best meal of his life.

Mere moments after swallowing the last

mouthful, the Nomad tore open a second bar, devouring it just as quickly as the first. Temptation urged him to gobble down another, but fearing he'd make himself sick, the Nomad held back. Instead, he reclined, closing his eyes as he rested his head in the crimson sedge, bathing in the warmth of the yellow sun. The breeze swished gently through the vegetation whilst the surrounding choir of wildlife continued to sing. Comfortable, full, and warm, the Nomad let the moment wash over him. For the first time in perhaps his entire existence, he drifted off into a carefree slumber.

THIRTY-SIX

In the days that followed, the Nomad rested. He sat by the Fighter, scarcely moving for hours at a time, eating, drinking, and sleeping. He lay listening to the music of the world, watching the rich ecosystem around him as the great theatre of life performed in earnest. Tusked herbivores clad in fuzzy white and brown coats patrolled the steppes, their lips crawling unceasingly across the grass as they grazed. Occasionally, one would stray nearer to the Nomad, curiously rearing an oblong head to study the extra-terrestrial oddity in momentary contemplation, before always inevitably returning to the more pressing matter of chewing at the pastures.

For a time, a four-winged bird of paradise perched on the Fighter's nose, its protracted tail feathers drooping across the ship's hull. It clucked, cocking its beaked head sideways as it likewise inquisitively peered at the weary traveller, leaving after a time to take back to the wind. As dusk approached and the yellow sun's light scattered in mountains of flame boiling off the sea, phosphorescent beetles crawled out of burrows in the soil, scaling crimpled blades of grass before finally taking flight, hovering up from the grasslands in droves, coalescing to perform a hypnotic lightshow that put even the heavens to shame.

Shrill chirps sounded through the dark, the echolocation sense of a spectral nocturnal predator piercing the gloom as it scudded across the skies, swooping low above the steppe, stealthily plucking unsuspecting beetles from the air. Every now and then, the Nomad caught glimpse of a blur of dark wings ghosting through the swarm, but wreathed in shadows, the creatures were at one with the night.

As the evening wore on, the nebula rose from beyond the hills, soaring higher and higher until it loomed above the golden world to illuminate the heavens. Appearing shortly thereafter, though far more inconspicuously, the wormhole crept across the backdrop of constellations, distorting and blurring the starlight as it arced over the horizon.

Standing to better study the heavenly phenomena, the Nomad revolved on the spot, lowering his gaze as he caught his first glimpse of the forest since nightfall. The trees were ablaze with a cold sapphire incandescence, their shimmering leaves quivering with each chilly gust that swept inward off the sea. Then, aloft in the air currents, the Nomad sighted one: a leaf fluttering in the wind high overhead, drifting his way as it steadily floated downwards. Tumbling in slow motion, it settled between the blades of grass only a short distance away.

Mesmerised by the beauty of it, the Nomad

found himself moving closer. Suddenly he was stooping, his fingers brushing through the sedge as he gently picked the leaf out of the grass and studied it in his hands. The underside glimmered a soft azure as delicate veins of light branched in intricate patterns throughout the leaf. The Nomad turned it over to find the other side dark, the faint glow unable to penetrate through the waxy upper surface. Because of this, as the distant forest foliage danced in the breeze, millions of leaves fluttering back and forth, the woodlands flickered as if they were alight with blue fire.

The temperature dropped steadily as the evening wore on, and feeling the chill, the Nomad clambered back into the cockpit, sealing it shut as he turned in for the night. He awoke to the first light of dawn glistening through the morning dew beaded across the canopy. Opening the cockpit, he was greeted by the fresh ocean of aromas the golden world exhaled.

He spent the second day much the same as the first, sitting and spectating the unfolding wonders of nature around him, eating whenever he felt like doing so, relaxing in the sun, and recovering his strength. Time passed leisurely, yet before long, the night was drawing inwards again. The Nomad slept once more inside the shelter of the Fighter, awaking to another glorious sunrise as the first light of day streamed in hazy rays across the jungle canopy.

The Nomad relaxed for much of the third

morning, deciding around noon that it was time for him to harvest more food. His strength was returning, but even after several days in a calorie surplus, he was still little more than bone and sinew. His teeth were setting firmer in his gums and his hair no longer pulled out in handfuls. His skin was growing steadily tanned from his time spent sunbathing, a far cry from the sickly pallid complexion it had been several days earlier. But the most notable difference was his abundance of energy. Though still severely underweight, he was now well fed, and after a few days spent acclimatising, his body was growing used to the pull of the golden world's gravity

Gathering another crop of fruit from the nearby tree, the Nomad ran the biomatter recombinator through its cycle and sorted and stowed the produce. The task was still draining enough to tire him out, and so, after lunch, he spent a few hours dozing. Awaking in the late afternoon, the Nomad felt recharged and full of vigour. For nearly three full days he had sat watching the wildlife in his immediate surroundings from atop his perch on the hillside; now he was eager to see more.

He didn't stray far to begin with, venturing little further than the hilltop. From his vantage, he peered out towards the horizon, where the sky met the sea in the west. Revolving to glance north, he looked out across the unending swathes of grassland. Southward he traced his eyes along the crooked coastline, and finally surveying the fourth point of the compass, he stared over the treetops, out across the jungle to the east. The world was a paradise, one that perhaps no one else had ever seen. It could well have been the last remaining untouched oasis in the otherwise desolate wastes of existence.

For several more days, the Nomad stayed confined to the hillside, each morning watching the world go by as he sat near the Fighter, and every afternoon daring to venture a little further as his strength slowly returned. He was an explorer; that was all he knew, all he could remember. Remaining in one place for any length of time seemed unnatural to the Nomad. As beautiful as his immediate surroundings were, he yearned to discover more, to see what else was out there.

On the tenth day, the Nomad mounted the first in a series of short excursions. The early trips were little more than short walks. The first took him down the hillside into a meadow of tall emerald grass. He spotted new creatures during his half hour jaunt: small mammalian animals with snaking tales that scurried in and out of warrens with surprising swiftness, leaping from the ground to snatch buzzing insects clean out of the air. An armoured reptile sauntered through the long grass, nearly waltzing obliviously into the Nomad's leg; the moment it spotted him, it hissed and scuttled away in terror, vanishing back into the tussocks from where it had emerged.

Each day the Nomad returned only once his recovering body had grown tired, setting out again the following morning on fresh legs with the hopes of making it that little bit further. Soon his excursions took him out passed the meadows, into the vale beyond. Silver bracken carpeted the valley; their fronds recoiled as the Nomad brushed through them, the feathery leaves curling up for several minutes after they were touched, finally unfurling if left undisturbed.

One morning he spotted a six-pawed predator give chase to a lone bovine grazer in a highspeed pursuit. It lasted little more than a few seconds, the ambush hunter pouncing out of the ferns to tackle its prey to the ground, its jaws clamping shut around the herbivore's throat. Warily keeping his distance, the Nomad locked eyes with the predator as it tentatively dragged its kill back into its hide somewhere in the undergrowth.

Days later, the Nomad made it out onto the violet plains that stretched the final few kilometres towards the coast. Here in the lowlands, gushing rills flowed between rocks, soaking into peaty soil as they drained towards the sea. Scanning the fast-flowing water revealed it was free from toxins. Cupping his hands, the Nomad scooped the crystal water to his lips and sipped a long invigorating draught. Rich in ions and minerals, it was like a fine vintage when compared to the sterile, tasteless water extracted from asteroid regolith that the

Nomad had grown accustomed to over the years. The water from the stream he could drink for pleasure, not just survival. Splashing his face from the refreshing flow, the Nomad continued on his way, returning to the stream each day thereafter to fill his canteen.

The Nomad pressed further afield in the following weeks, finally making it to the clifftops. From there, the Nomad explored the bluffs, soon discovering a sloping animal trail that led down to a sandy beach tucked away in a sheltered cove. Twenty-limbed crustaceans wrestled one another for territory in tiny rockpools, whilst winged eels thrashed around the shallows, every so often spearing out the water to glide above the waves for short stretches, before plopping back into the brine.

Having reached the coast, the Nomad changed bearing, devoting the following weeks to exploring the jungle to the east. First, he explored the fringes, but as he grew both bolder and more inquisitive, he delved deeper. The undergrowth was dense and tough to navigate, but as the days went by, he mapped the quickest paths and routes of least resistance, allowing him to press further in each time.

The jungle held a diversity of life greater than the Nomad could ever have imagined. Wherever he looked, he spotted a new colourful reptile or bird of paradise. There were long armed creatures that howled as they swung amongst the canopies, and singing serpents that wove between the branches.

Strange flowers and fungi sprouted from every nook and cranny whilst ferns and vines tangled the undergrowth. Hives of insects buzzed in the air and marched in great ranks across the leaf litter as they patrolled the forest in droves.

The Nomad discovered countless new varieties of fruit, some pink and waxy, others sprouting hundreds of hairy appendages, each more alien than the last. The Nomad scanned every new find, harvesting the most promising and returning them to the Fighter, where in the evening he experimented with the biomatter recombinator to produce new sources of food. The Nomad even began blending different fruits together, producing new and exciting flavours as the recombinator preserved the essence of each food source fed into the machine. Very soon, the Nomad had a larder stocked with a broad variety of nutrition bars, each unique in flavour and texture. He labelled them, ensuring he recorded the recipes so that he was able to reproduce his favourites.

The Nomad was living in a utopia. Something he had never have imagined possible. Everywhere he looked there was some new unfound wonder. Every place he explored was as astoundingly beautiful as the last. Wherever he ventured, there was always something new to discover. Occasionally he got lost, getting turned around without realising, or losing his bearings altogether, but it seldom caused him any distress; no matter how labyrinthine the terrain, his EVA suit was always able to eventually guide him back towards the Fighter's homing beacon.

For months the Nomad explored unabated, venturing out each day without fail, often setting out at dawn and returning long after dusk. Only when the monsoon arrived were his adventures finally halted.

The storms swept inwards from across the sea, pelting the land with an unrelenting deluge that lasted for near a week. At first the Nomad was determined not to be deterred. He set out into the jungle with his helmet on to shelter him from the downpour. But as the rain hammered across his visor, coagulating into a blurry film, he struggled to see the way ahead. The familiar trails he'd carved through the undergrowth over the recent months grew marshy, flooding in sections and turning into rivulets in others. Each time the Nomad slipped or lost his footing, his mind traumatically flashed back to the haunting memories of being dragged into the depths of the algal lake.

His resolve shaken, the Nomad retreated, returning to the Fighter to wait out the monsoon. Over the days that followed, he sat watching the storms rage on from the shelter of the cockpit. The weather was seasonal, that much was obvious. In time it would pass. Though the Nomad cursed it, he knew the rain was what made the paradise he had found so rich and fertile. But having been spoilt by nothing but sunshine with only the occasional summer shower for months now, thousands upon thousands of square kilometres of pristine wilderness there for him to explore at his whim, the Nomad could not help but resent being confined once again to the Fighter. He yearned to stretch his legs, to throw caution to the wind and to set off out into the wild again, but a lifetime of caution was something he could not so easily overcome.

He had ignored the power of the weather once before and it had nearly cost him everything. Back then, when existence seemed so bleak, he had little to lose. But now—now the Nomad had everything to live for. He was no longer imprisoned on an endless voyage. He had found a paradise in which he could see himself living the rest of his life. He finally had a home. It was not where he had been heading, but did that ultimately matter? What sense was there in voyaging out once more into the endless void to spend a lifetime travelling, the whole time struggling to survive? He was comfortable here on the golden world. For the first time he could remember, he was happy; and that was all that seemed to matter in the end. He had found paradise.

THIRTY-SEVEN

The Nomad awoke to a roar of thunder overhead. A great fork of lightning streaked above the sea and rain pelted the glass of the Fighter's canopy. Suddenly alert, the Nomad swivelled around in his seat, his heartrate spiking before he began to relax. Realising it had been nothing more than the storm that had roused him, he rolled over and tried to fall back asleep. His eyes sank shut, but as he began to drift off again, he was pulled back into waking by a repeating ping sounding from the console. Groggily sitting upright, the Nomad rubbed his eyes and studied the pulsing notification. Still half asleep, he pulled open the holographic display and stared blankly at the information in front of him.

Yawning and taking a swig from his canteen, the Nomad's concentration finally clarified and he suddenly understood what was wrong. It was a scanning frequency. One that he had seen before. One that he dreaded. One that he had hoped never to see again. Cerberus. The frequency picked up, the scanning waves dancing frenetically across the holographic readout. The Nomad sat frozen, watching it in disbelief. They had come for him!

But that was impossible. How could they possibly know where he was? Perhaps they had charted his FTL jump vector? Tracked him to the yellow sun? But if he had been followed, the Cerberus would have gotten there months ago. Overtaking the Nomad in FTL, they would have arrived long before he ever did. Surely, they would have abandoned their search when they found no trace of him? Even if they had spent weeks scouring the system, they should have been long gone before the Nomad ever arrived.

How then, and why, were his instruments detecting an inbound Cerberus unit? It was in the system, and relatively nearby. Judging from the strength of the signal, it could even be in orbit around the golden world. But it shouldn't know where the Nomad was, nor that he was even there. The Fighter was completely powered down, save for a few basic systems. It was only detecting the Cerberus' scanning frequencies passively, sending out no signals of its own. But the Cerberus was growing nearer. It was heading straight his way. It had to be a coincidence. It couldn't be anything else.

He was faced with a choice. Another impossible choice. He could sit and wait, keeping the Fighter powered down, hoping that the Cerberus's approach was merely a chance encounter. Maybe it would pass him by without discovering his presence. Hopefully it would exit the system none the wiser, leaving the Nomad safe and undiscovered in his utopia.

But if the Cerberus already knew he was there, he was in trouble. He'd scarcely managed to disable the last drone that had detected him; he doubted he'd be so lucky again. He'd have to run. He had a decent head start, and he had almost a full tank of antimatter to make a jump. If he left now, he'd be safe, but the moment he powered up the Fighter and launched to orbit, he'd be discovered for sure.

They'd know he was there. The Cerberus would know he'd been on the golden world. He wouldn't be able to return. Not for a long time. It would be too dangerous.

The Nomad continued to watch the readouts as the Cerberus signal spiked higher and higher. It was inbound, and moving fast. It was heading straight for his coordinates. It had to be! But that couldn't be true! How could it!? The Nomad's stomach knotted. He cringed, feeling the weight of the alien machine bearing down on him. Judging from the signal intensity, it had to be within a hundred kilometres. Every second he delayed he was losing precious time to escape. But he couldn't run. He couldn't leave! Where now was there left to run to? The Nomad cursed loudly, slamming his fists against the glass of the canopy. The signals frenzied into even sharper peaks and troughs. It was coming for him.

The Nomad roared in fury. He flicked several switches on the control console, hurrying through only the most necessary prefight checks. It had been months since the Fighter had been airborne. If anything was wrong, it could spell disaster. He readied to power up the VTOL thrusters. Then he saw it.

A blur of white and red carved out of the lightning. A searching ray of light scattered through the dense storm clouds in the heavens above. Lightning flashed again, illuminating a spherical silhouette in the heart of the tempest as it sped closer. He was too late. It was already on him. He'd run out of time to get the Fighter off the ground. He'd delayed too long. His months of easy living had killed his survival instinct, and now, it would cost him his life. This was it. This was the end. But at least he had lived out his final days in paradise.

The Nomad wanted to close his eyes. He wanted it to be over fast. He wanted it to be quick and painless. He didn't want to wait out the last few seconds of his life. He just wanted it over and done with. But he couldn't close his eyes. Terror was gripping him. He was frozen in his seat, eyes locked dead ahead at the hazy searchlight racing through the storm. He couldn't look away. No matter how hard he tried.

The harrowing shriek of the Cerberus's thrusters operating in atmosphere roared over the storm. It was a sound the Nomad had long forgotten. Hearing it again brought back a torrent of haunted memories. In less than a second it would be on him.

The Cerberus's lights streaked overhead. The drone hurtled past, never dropping below the cloud ceiling. It was moving at such a colossal speed, that by the time the Nomad had comprehended that it had passed him, it was already several kilometres away, racing into the distance. It didn't know he was there. It never had. It wasn't looking for him, nor did it have any reason to. It was a coincidence. A narrow one, but a chance encounter all the same.

The Nomad's heart was racing. Cold sweat clung to his brow as he watched the signal waves mellow out, fading slowly towards a flat line. After nearly half an hour, the Nomad grew certain it was gone. The signal readings were nothing more than a dead streak across the holographic interface. The drone had probably left the system all together. It had been close, but the Nomad had made the right call.

Next time he might not be so lucky. Had he chosen to run, even if he had jumped to safety, then it would have all been over. The biomatter recombinator, along with the rest of the entire starboard cargo pod were on the ground, detached from the Fighter. He would have left them behind.

He had been foolish to think that he could live out the rest of his days on the golden world. At some point, something would happen that would mean he would have to run. It could come in minutes, or in decades, but eventually, the Nomad would be forced to leave. When that time came, he would have to be prepared. Everything needed to be ready to go at a moment's notice. Otherwise, he was already dead.

THIRTY-EIGHT

The Nomad didn't sleep for the remainder of the night. When morning came, the rains had finally abated. Opening the canopy to a grey sky issuing little more than a misty drizzle, the Nomad climbed down to the sodden hillside and began his preparations. He gathered up and took stock of all the nutrient bars he had accrued over the past months. He had nearly half a year's worth of supplies; far more than he ever remembered having before.

Packing his footlocker to bursting, the Nomad stowed the remainder of his supplies inside the cargo pod. He left a fortnight's worth of food out of storage, stacked neatly in mess tins beside the Fighter's front skid. Afterwards, the Nomad collapsed down the biomatter recombinator, along with every other piece of equipment he had pulled out of the cargo pods since his arrival, packing them methodically in their respective places.

Lowering the recombinator back into the storage pod with ease, the Nomad smiled to himself. Months ago, when his body had withered to near decay, it had been almost impossible to lift. Now, having eaten heartily every day since, not only had he regained the muscle lost during the three-month stint travelling to the yellow sun, but his prolonged time spent in the gravity well of the golden world had also allowed him to build muscle he had lost decades ago. He was the strongest and healthiest he ever remembered being, able to trek scores of kilometres over rough terrain with ease, always raring to explore further.

The Nomad sealed the cargo pod and aligned it with the Fighter's hydraulic clamps. Locking the cylindrical storage container in place, the Nomad raised the cargo pod into position beneath the wing. When the next two weeks' supplies were finished with, he would once again unpack the recombinator and produce a new batch of nutrient bars. Those stowed onboard the Fighter were not to be touched; they were his emergency supplies, stored in preparation for the inevitable day when he would be forced to flee.

From now on, whenever he was finished using the recombinator, or any other piece of equipment for that matter, he would re-stow it. Everything not in immediate use, from this point forth, belonged inside the cargo pods, which themselves should remain affixed beneath the Fighter as much as possible. This way, he wouldn't be caught unprepared; he was ready to go at a second's notice. The precious minutes it might save him could be the difference between life and death. This was his new routine. It was routine that had kept him alive to date. It was routine that would keep him alive hereafter.

The Nomad clambered back up the ladder and seated himself in the cockpit. Powering up nearly every system onboard, he spent the rest of the morning carrying out a comprehensive array of checks and procedures, ensuring the Fighter was ready for take-off and space flight. Moving forward, every week he would run through the same checklist. If something was wrong, he'd carry out the necessary diagnostics and repairs. Just like his equipment and supplies, his ship needed to be ready to go at any moment.

For years the Nomad had lived for nothing but routine; now, finally, after decades journeying across the stars, he had discovered something else worth living for. He had found wonder. He had found beauty. He had found purpose. His life was no longer devoted to routine, but that did not mean he could forsake it. It still was as important as it had ever been. Without it he would die. Of that he had no doubt.

By the time all the checks were done, it was mid-afternoon. It was too late to set out on an expedition into the forest, and if he made for the cliffs to the west, it would be nightfall long before he arrived back. Instead, he decided to chart a new course, setting out northward for the first time, out across the steppe.

In the coming years, the Nomad figured he would take to the skies again, leaving his current landing site behind to explore other regions of the globe. There were whole other continents to explore; any or all of them could be drastically different from where he was now. On foot, the distances he could navigate were minute compared to the range of his ship. What took hours when walking could be covered in a mere fraction of a second by the Fighter. But that did not limit his exploration in any way. Distance had little to do with discovery. The exploration merely took place on a different scale.

The Nomad had spent a lifetime exploring the macro. Now he took great pleasure in being able to explore the micro. His gaze no longer fixed on distant starlight, he could finally focus on what was right in front of him. The world around him was what mattered now. What laid beyond the horizon was a mystery, but the greater mystery was what lied closer at hand. The Nomad could spend his entire lifetime exploring and wandering the wilderness of this world and still not see all there was to see.

He pondered for a moment the notion of finding a perfect place; somewhere more beautiful than anywhere he had found thus far. Somewhere he'd want to settle down and build himself a home. But he quickly dismissed the notion; the Fighter was his home. It always would be, and nothing could ever change that. It had become a part of him. It had carried him across the heavens for a time; now its job was to carry him across the planet. Once it had been a prison, but now, it was the ultimate expression of freedom.

THIRTY-NINE

Two years later, out in the wilderness, the Nomad was scampering up a scree slope. Reaching the rockface at the top, he hooked his fingers over a crimp in the bluff and began to scale the vertical cliffside. Inserting a spring-loaded cam into a crack, the Nomad threaded his climbing line through a carabiner and agilely scrambled up the next series of handholds dotting the bluff. Slotting his fingers into another pocket in the stone, the Nomad steadied himself, his feet perched on a narrow lip. He slipped another cam into a fissure, establishing a new top anchor, and nimbly darted up the last few metres. Hauling his lithe athletic frame up over the ledge, the Nomad summited the butte.

Catching his breath, he slowly revolved atop the vantage to survey the surrounding sweeping vistas. He peered out across the badlands to the south, the region he intended to explore in the weeks to come, before gazing back north, towards the mountainous woodlands he had spent the last few months scouting. Peering through a gap in the luscious canopies, the Nomad could make out the red tail of the Fighter a few kilometres away.

High overhead, four-winged raptors soared on updraft vortices, scouring the silver grasslands out west, whilst to the east, the rising mists from an immense waterfall steamed above the canyons. Flooding through the craggy gorges and gullies, the river swarmed with pink fish leaping through the rapids, using underdeveloped forelimbs in the early stages of evolution to scamper across the rocky shallows in between.

From atop the butte, the Nomad could distinguish an endless dune sea of beige desert sand out past the badlands. But even there, in the arid wastes battered by wind and sandstorms, the Nomad knew life would still flourish. There wasn't a corner of the globe where both flora and fauna had not carved out an ecological niche. On the golden world, life was seemingly inescapable.

The Nomad sat, dangling his feet over the ledge, soaking up the breath-taking views, watching the world go by. He took a sip from his flask as the hot wind blew across the butte, tussling his thick hair, humming in his ears. As the breeze died, the Nomad's ears pricked up at the sound of pebbles tumbling across rock. He leapt to his feet, spinning towards the noise.

His eyes locked suddenly with those of a hulking, scaly predator. Stalking the Nomad, it had stealthily scaled the ridge, following his scent, until finally it had cornered its prey atop the butte. A set of spines quivered and erected down the animal's neck. Its throat gurgled with a deep rasping growl. Six yellow eyes fixed unwaveringly on the Nomad, the predator's rectangular pupils narrowing as it barred a maw of polished razors. It padded closer, squatting on its haunches as it prepared to pounce.

With less than a second to react, the Nomad's hand darted for his holster. The retention strap popped open, and in a blur of instinct, the Nomad had drawn his pistol. Thunder clapped as he squeezed the trigger. A slug erupted from the sidearm. Avian creatures flocked to the air, abandoning their roosts for miles around as the gunshot continued to echo through the rocky hills. The predator floundered out of a half-cocked pounce, turned, and bolted, unharmed. The warning shot had been enough to scare the beast off. There had been no need to wound it.

Even still, it had been a close call. The Nomad had been caught unawares. Had the predator not been betrayed by a few tumbling pebbles, he suspected the beast would likely now be dragging his corpse back to its lair. Heart still throbbing, the Nomad sat back down to once again drink in the natural splendour, this time ensuring he looked over his shoulder every now and then.

A short time later, he was pulled back out of his reverie by a pinging notification relayed to his suit from the Fighter. It was the passive scanners. They had detected something: another inbound Cerberus. The Nomad cursed. It couldn't possibly have come at a worse time. He was hours away from the Fighter. If it was heading for his location, he couldn't possibly make it back in time. He had to wait it out. He had to get to cover and hope he wouldn't be sighted.

The Nomad clipped back onto his climbing line, ready to abseil back down the ledge, when a flash of crimson flared across the sky. Raising a hand to his brow, he squinted against the sun. He made something out: a dark shape scudding across the upper atmosphere. It quickly smeared into a black streak angled downwards towards the ground. Smoke and fire. A meteor?

Blazing white hot at the head of a slanting torrent of ash, it flashed blindingly as it carved a line across the daytime sky. The Nomad shielded his eyes from the glare, watching the fire steadily extinguish as the object slowed in the lower atmosphere, still trailing great billows of black smoke as it careened towards the ground. Suddenly it vanished behind a hilltop to the north, and seconds later, the Nomad heard the dull thunder of an impact.

Checking the Fighter's readouts on his suit, the Nomad watched the Cerberus scanning signals slowly fade. Moments later, they were gone. In the air above, the smoke trail was dissipating in the wind, but a few kilometres north, it was now rising from the crash site above the treetops.

It had been no meteor.

It was a ship.

FORTY

It had been shot down from orbit. A ship had been shot down from orbit by the Cerberus! But that couldn't be true!? There were no ships! The Nomad was alone; it was an inescapable fact of reality. There couldn't be another ship.

Kicking off from the ledge, the Nomad abseiled rapidly down the cliffside. The moment his feet touched down on the scree at the bottom, he unclipped and took off on foot across the shale, abandoning his climbing line in place. Charging up the ravine, splashing through streams, scrambling over crags and tors, and tearing through the brush, the Nomad hastened towards the woodlands, following the fading trail of smoke scorched across the sky.

He ran, heart belting in his chest, lungs panting as he pushed himself faster and faster across the rugged terrain. Nearing the crash site, he caught sight of black smoke wafting above the forest. Following the smell, he closed in on the impact zone. The Nomad paused, spinning to gather his bearings. High above, the canopies were torn asunder, the treetops ripped to splinters in a great swathe carved dead north. Following the trail of destruction, the

Nomad crested a brow, halting at the top to peer down into the dell beyond.

A wide furrow of scorched earth had been ploughed across the basin, bifurcating a brook that minutes earlier had babbled serenely through the undisturbed woods. Ash and embers fluttered about in the air, billowing out from a column of smoke rising from a steep-sided crater up ahead. That was where the wreckage of the ship would be... if there was anything left of it.

It wasn't a crash; it was a crash landing. The angle of descent was too shallow for anything otherwise. An unpilotable flaming wreck would have struck the ground much harder, much faster. There would have been an explosion. A shockwave. A tremor. The surrounding trees would have been flattened; the whole wood might even have caught fire in the aftermath of the explosion. Whatever had come down had done so with some level of control. It had come in dangerously quick; far too quick to touch down safely, but it had been guided down, of that the Nomad was almost certain.

Jogging anxiously down the slope, the Nomad slowed to a trepid trot as he approached the final resting place of the ship. Peering down over the crater rim, he sighted scraps of blackened buckled metal littering the banks. The brook was bubbling up over the lip of the impact site, washing down into the crater, hissing as it turned to steam against the red-hot glowing fuselage of a crashed ship.

It was a fighter; much like the Nomad's, and yet somehow, different in every way. It was alien. Obtuse. Strangely angled in its formfactor. Yet, in principle, it appeared to be designed for war. It remained surprisingly intact, given the speed of the collision. Much of its hull was ripped away, and what remained had been charred by its atmospheric entry. Flames and smoke billowed from the aft end, the engines, whilst arcs of discharging electricity shorted and sparked from exposed and frayed wiring at the fore. Both wings had been torn clean off, obliterated during the impact. The ship was a total wreck. There was little chance that anything could have survived.

Cautiously, the Nomad lowered himself down from the rim. Sliding across the scarred shingle, he came to a halt in the ankle-deep wash puddling at the bottom of the basin. Shielding his face from the heat radiating from the flames and glowing metal, he tentatively moved closer to investigate.

The Nomad had barely made it a half dozen steps when he leapt back in astonishment. A blackened dome over the front of the craft started groaning mechanically as it struggled to retract on warped hydraulics and molten electrics. Jarringly, the opaque and scorched canopy lifted back, unveiling a cockpit brimming with smoke. Inside the fumes, the Nomad sighted a pilot slumped forward on the controls.

Scarcely aware of what was happening, he dashed forwards. Acrid smoke burned his eyes and flooded his lungs, sending the Nomad into a fit of sputtering coughs. The heat was unbearable; the Nomad could feel his skin blistering. But he pushed closer, heedless of the danger, planting his boots onto the simmering fuselage. His chest spasmed. He choked and retched, shielding his eyes as he tried to peer into the cockpit. The pilot was larger in morphology than the Nomad, and no doubt heavier. Without pausing to think whether he'd even be strong enough to lift him, the Nomad grappled the hefty pilot by the shoulders and attempted to heave him out of the cockpit. It was no use; he was tethered in, attached to his chair via some form of harness.

The Nomad shifted the alien aside, granting a view of the chain-like tether fettering the pilot into his seat. Hooked onto the back of the pilot's flight suit, and feeding into a reciprocating socket in his seat, the Nomad knew he stood little chance of breaking the restraint. He needed to find the release. His vision now blurring through a stream of stinging tears, the Nomad searched frantically around the alien cockpit, finally sighting a metal clasp on the arm of the chair.

The release was almost too hot to touch, even through the gloves of his EVA suit, but prising back the warped lever mechanism, the Nomad activated the quick release and the pilot's harness suddenly detached, reeling back into the chair.

Reaching under the pilot's armpits, the Nomad heaved again, hoisting the alien's limp body up out of the cockpit. Dragging the pilot through the water and ash, the Nomad fought his way clear of the ship. Smoke and embers swirled about the crater as the Nomad clawed his way up towards the rim with the alien in tow. Finally heaving him up over the lip, the Nomad released his hold of the pilot and slumped to the ground exhaustedly beside him.

He wheezed, coughing and sputtering as his lungs belched out the toxic fumes he'd inhaled. Acidic tears continued to roll down his scalded cheeks, whilst the sickly smell of burnt hair hung around his scalp. Reaching for his canteen he gulped down several swigs of cold water, soothing his burning throat, before splashing the remainder on his face.

Capping the bottle, the Nomad rolled onto his side, scrambling away suddenly in alarm as he looked back at the body beside him.

It was moving. The pilot had stirred from death. Now he was beginning to sit up right. Consumed by terror, the Nomad's hand moved without thinking. Before he knew it, he had unholstered his gun and was aiming it squarely at the pilot.

The pilot wavered back and forth as he steadily took stock of his surroundings. Finally, the being's darkened visor turned the Nomad's way. His gaze lowered to the pistol aimed at his chest. The pilot panicked, scuttling away on hands and knees in terror. Slipping and falling supine in the upturned soil, the helmeted creature stopped and cowered, surrendering to the Nomad with upraised palms

Finally regathering his senses, the Nomad ashamedly holstered his sidearm. Returning the same gesture of submission, he raised his own hands.

"It's okay," the Nomad said. "I mean you no harm…"

FORTY-ONE

For several moments, both the Nomad and the Traveller sat frozen looking at each other. Slowly, the Traveller lowered his palms before raising them again to his helmet. His meaty gauntleted hands fumbled at a clasp, and with a sudden hiss, the Traveller released it. The sweeping pyramidal helm lifted away, revealing the being underneath.

The Traveller peered back at the Nomad with two expressive beady eyes. Sunken into an angular leathery face, they stared out from beneath an ossified brow that extended down to just above the alien's wrinkled lips, protruding outwards into a singular horn. Scaly plates linked in series from atop the being's skull, down the creature's broad muscular neck, vanishing beneath the thick material of his flight suit.

A pair of two-fingered hands, each equipped with a padded opposable thumb, tentatively clutched the Traveller's helmet. A broad doming chest tapered down into a narrow abdomen, whilst huge muscular haunches extended from the Traveller's broad pelvis, angling into a set of rear-jointed calves that seemed to end abruptly as wide cloven hooves.

The Traveller's anatomy was tough and thickset. Every feature of the alien seemed hardened and aggressive, yet somehow, this demeanour was entirely offset by the creature's amiable gaze. Even now, as the being cowed from the Nomad with trepidation, he seemed almost outwardly friendly. Visible in the alien's little eyes was a gentle intelligence; one that appeared to behold the Nomad with an inexplicable sense of empathy.

The Nomad sat watching the Traveller in stunned silence. The alien pilot gazed back at him with the same sense of anxious fascination. This was the first intelligent being the Nomad had seen in too long to comprehend. And he had the distinct impression that the case was much the same for the Traveller.

A long moment passed between them, before slowly, in realisation, the Traveller's head craned to look back at the lashing flames and black smoke rising from the crater. The Traveller emitted a guttural cry of alarm. He struggled to fight to his feet, but too weak to stand, his body crumpled under the heft of its own weight. The traveller winced, gargling something in an undiscernible language, his meaty hands clutching at his right thigh.

Viscous green blood was oozing from a laceration through the alien's suit. Attempting to stem the bleed with one hand, the Traveller began dragging himself across the soil with the other, fighting towards the crater rim and his ship beyond.

"Wait..." stuttered the Nomad in a moment of disorientation. "Wait!" he repeated more commandingly. "You can't go down there! It's not safe!"

The Traveller continued to crawl clumsily towards the ship, not comprehending a word the Nomad said.

"Wait!" the Nomad cried. "You are injured—let me help you!" he urged, rising to his feet to stumble after the Traveller.

The Traveller momentarily glanced back at the Nomad before dragging himself the last metre up towards the rim. The alien pilot's eyes widened suddenly in horror as he saw for the first time what had become of his ship. Desperate to save what was left, he began to lower himself down over the ledge.

"Stop!" the Nomad urged. "You are badly hurt!"

The Traveller continued to ignore him.

Reaching the edge of the crater himself, the Nomad heard a hiss steadily growing over the crackle of flames. Rapidly rising in volume, it transitioned quickly into a shrill whine. The Nomad peered down at the wreckage; a jet of gas was spewing from a ruptured tank. In seconds it ignited into a gout of flame, the piercing tone building in crescendo as the pressure continued to rise.

"Get back!" warned the Nomad. "It's going to explode!"

Understanding the Nomad despite the language barrier, the Traveller froze in place, watching in despair as he straddled the rim of the crater. Seizing hold of a set of tubing on the Traveller's flight suit, the Nomad wrenched the creature back from the brink.

The tank exploded with a deafening boom. A shockwave slammed into the Nomad, knocking him dizzyingly to the ground as a ball of fire and smoke mushroomed out of the crater. The Nomad rolled prone, sheltering his head as flaming debris rained down, peppering the soil around him. His ears were ringing, his vision spinning. Rolling over, dazed and shell-shocked, the Nomad gawked around with blurred vision, searching for any sign of the Traveller. He was beside the Nomad, likewise protecting his head from the raining wreckage

When the final fragments of metal and ash had dropped out of the air, the Nomad climbed shakily back to his feet. Seizing hold of a strap on the Traveller's flight suit, he began dragging him across the singed ground. A second explosion blew out from the crater, sending up another deluge of fiery wreckage. A jagged chunk of smouldering metal speared into the soil less than a metre away, whilst ash and shrapnel pelted the grass. Finally, clear of the blast radius, the Nomad collapsed, the Traveller slumping down beside him.

"Are you okay?" he puffed exhaustedly.

The Traveller was clutching his leg, wincing in pain as he gazed distraughtly back towards the crater.

"Stay still," he instructed the alien, rummaging through the first aid kit strapped to his hip. He momentarily studied the Traveller's weeping wound, quickly realising he knew absolutely nothing of his biology. There was no guarantee that anything he attempted would actually help the alien; by administering any form of first aid it was possible he could do more harm than good. But if convergent evolution counted for anything, then the Traveller was almost certain to have a few basic anatomical similarities to the Nomad.

He would undoubtedly have a circulatory system of sorts that would supply his organs with nutrients, and judging from the Traveller's lack of a helmet, oxygen too. The green fluid weeping from the Traveller's wound was almost certainly the medium through which oxygen and nutrients were distributed throughout his body, similar in principle to blood. The Traveller himself was applying pressure to the wound, and so it wasn't much of a leap to assume that the best course of action would be to try and seal the laceration.

The Nomad produced a spray canister from his first aid kit and knelt over the Traveller. "I need you to lift your hand away," he explained, gesturing to the Traveller's leg.

The Traveller looked back at him and responded with a deep gurgling noise that vaguely resembled a sentence. Tentatively, the creature then lifted its palm from the dripping gash to reveal a fibrous flesh bathed in green fluid.

Issuing the Traveller a reassuring nod, the Nomad pinched the gash shut, spraying a layer of thick gel over the wound to seal it. The Traveller thrashed in pain as the gel coated the cut, but despite the agony it caused him, he fought to keep his leg as still as possible to allow the Nomad to work on it. Within moments, the gel had congealed, forming a second skin over the laceration, sealing it shut. The Traveller slumped back into the grass, issuing something that resembled a laboured sigh as he gazed up at the smoke column rising from the crash site.

"Come on," urged the Nomad, rising to his feet. "I've stopped the bleeding, but you'll need sutures. We'll have to go to my ship in order to get them."

The Traveller looked blankly back at the Nomad, finally uttering a few words of his own in his strange native language.

The Nomad put a hand under his shoulder to help the alien to his feet.

"It's not that far," explained the Nomad. "Only a few klicks north from here."

The Traveller struggled to his feet, leaning heavily on the Nomad for support. His horned head revolved slowly on a set of square shoulders to gaze back at the smoking crater. The Traveller spoke again, motioning with his hand towards the wreckage.

"There's nothing left of it," the Nomad shook his head.

The traveller vocalised the same set of chesty vowels and consonants, once more gesturing towards the crash.

"Okay," the Nomad sighed reluctantly, understanding that if the tables were turned, he would want to inspect what was left of the Fighter. Every single piece of technology was worth salvaging.

Shouldering the weight of the limping alien, the Nomad aided the Traveller back towards the rim. Together, they peered down over the verge into the impact crater. There was little more than a scorched husk crushed into the teardrop hollow. Anything that had survived the initial crash had been obliterated in the subsequent explosions. There was nothing left.

The Nomad felt the Traveller slump heavier over him in defeat.

"I'm sorry," apologised the Nomad.

The Traveller responded with a set of indecipherable murmurings.

“Come on,” he sighed, “let’s get out of here.”

FORTY-TWO

Over the next few hours, the Nomad aided the Traveller across the brutal craggy terrain, back up the slopes towards the Fighter's landing site. The Traveller grunted and groaned continually, each jolt to his leg making the alien wince in discomfort. As they made their way along the final spiny ridge, the light began to wane, the first stars piercing the purple dusk on the horizon. The Nomad shouldered the traveller's weight throughout most of the trek, but with the terrain so rude, there were times where the Nomad needed both his hands free to scramble up the boulder-strewn escarpments. With no way for the injured Traveller to make the ascents on his own, the Nomad was forced on multiple occasions to establish anchor points with his cams and carabiners, hoisting the weighty alien up the bluffs via his spare climbing line.

Finally, more than an hour after nightfall, the Nomad and the Traveller arrived at the Fighter's landing site, emerging into a moonlit glade of green and yellow trees. The Nomad collapsed exhaustedly into the crinkled red grass and stared up at the nebula above. When he'd finally caught his strength, he sat back up. The Traveller was upright beside him, staring in mesmerisation at the Fighter.

"That's mine!" the Nomad snapped sharply as his mind was suddenly haunted by an image of the Traveller flying away in his ship. "Don't get any ideas!"

The Traveller looked back at him and uttered a few melodic grunts.

The Nomad suddenly realised he may have made a fatal mistake in bringing the Traveller here. He eyed the creature's flight suit, immediately identifying a strangely shaped device that bore some resemblance to a pistol. Without realising he'd even drawn it from his holster, the Nomad found himself looking down the sights of his own sidearm, the weapon trained unhesitantly on the Traveller for a second time. The Traveller raised his palms again in confused submission as the Nomad marched over to him. Gun pointed to his head, he uttered a few appeasing vowels as he looked meekly up at the Nomad.

"Your gun..." the Nomad barked, fuelled by paranoia, pointing to the device holstered at the Traveller's side. "Give me your gun!"

The alien traced the Nomad's gaze to the device on his hip, and issuing a reassuring gesture with his palms extended in the Nomad's direction, he calmly unfastened it from its strapping and surrendered it to the Nomad. The Nomad quickly snatched the suspected weapon from the Traveller's hands, retreating several steps clear of the alien. Keeping his own pistol aimed at the Traveller, he inspected the device. Equipped with a trigger, muzzle, and a set of sights, there was little doubt as to its nature; but that did not mean the Traveller had held any intention of using it. It had been holstered at his waist when the Nomad pulled him from the wreckage. He more than likely carried it merely as a precaution; out of habit more than necessity, much as the Nomad did.

Pondering his actions, the Nomad momentarily considered returning it to the alien, but quickly deciding against it, he instead fastened the gun to his belt. The Traveller in all likelihood meant him no harm, but there was a chance he might be wrong. The Nomad had to be cautious. After a prolonged pause, he finally lowered his own weapon, stowing it safely in his holster.

The Traveller mumbled something softly, gesturing first to the Fighter, then to the Nomad, before pointing to both again quickly in succession once more. His words held no meaning to the Nomad whatsoever, but the alien's demeanour and tone went some way towards quelling his suspicions, putting his mind at ease.

It was a difficult situation, and both parties appreciated that. If the Traveller lived, as the Nomad suspected, a similar existence to himself, then he had no doubt at times been forced to make difficult decisions in his struggle to survive. The Traveller was the first sentient creature the Nomad had met since he first began his flight through infinity. He had no real reason to distrust him; but equally, he had no reason *to* trust him. Distrust was merely another form of precaution; precaution was merely another form of preparation. The Nomad was always vigilant. He was always prepared. If he offended or upset the Traveller as a result, then why should he care? Better to be feared and resented than to be betrayed.

The Traveller scrutinised the Nomad's face, no doubt trying to discern what was going through his mind. He repeated the same sequence of sounds, gesturing for a final time in the direction of the Fighter, then the Nomad, this time adding a new combination of humming gurgles as he gesticulated toward himself, finishing his communication with a queer inflection.

"Alright," nodded the Nomad reluctantly. "I get it: I can trust you."

FORTY-THREE

The Nomad rummaged through his medical box, constantly glancing out of the cockpit at the Traveller sat observing him from the grass. Once he'd pulled out everything he figured he'd need, he clambered back down the ladder and made his way over to the Traveller. The alien watched apprehensively as the Nomad laid out the various medical provisions across the ground.

"I need you to stay calm," the Nomad instructed as soothingly as he could.

The Traveller seemed to understand.

Powering up his suit's scanners, the Nomad ran an analysis of the Traveller's biology. The scans took several minutes, during which time, the two of them sat in uneasy silence. Finally, the results clocked in. It was not good.

The Traveller's biochemistry differed from the Nomad's on a fundamental level; like himself, the alien pilot was a carbon and water-based life-form, but that was where the similarities ended. Whilst the Nomad's proteins were constructed from twenty amino acids, the Traveller's constituted over forty, of which only six were shared between the two of them. The alien's genetic material was encoded in a set of unique seven-carbon sugar nucleotides, linked and wound into a complex triple-helix chain. The Traveller's circulatory system was open, forgoing enclosed blood vessels in favour of a compartmentalised thorax, limbs, and skull, with the transportation medium that the Nomad had mistook for blood being circulated via a number of pulsating heart muscles located throughout his body. The Traveller inhaled and exhaled through a set of organs more akin to gills than lungs, and though the majority of his brain and nervous tissue resided within his skull, its chemistry and architecture was completely alien to the Nomad's.

All this meant that, though the Nomad could potentially patch the Traveller's wound, he was unable to administer any form of sedative, painkiller, or antibiotic, and was likely limited to only the crudest of antiseptics. Anything else posed a serious risk of poisoning him. The Nomad cursed in frustration as he surveyed the supplies laid out on the grass in front of him. Selecting a bottle of povidone-iodine solution, he presented it to the Traveller.

"Iodine..." the Nomad uttered. "Can I use this to disinfect your wound?"

The Traveller gazed back at the Nomad with momentary confusion before grasping what he was being asked: *was the solution compatible with his biology?* He depressed several patches of fabric across the chest of his flight suit, and suddenly, a set of thin light beams fanned over the bottle of iodine solution. A series of bizarre hieroglyphs projected out from the Traveller's chest piece. The alien studied them. The moment the Traveller realised exactly what was in the solution, the Nomad immediately understood he couldn't use it. The Traveller recoiled, shuffling away, covering his mouth with one hand and his wound with the other.

The Nomad nodded, discarding it back into the grass. "What about this?" he questioned, offering up a sachet of ethanol.

The Traveller analysed the new liquid with his suit's inbuilt scanners, reacting once again in much the same manner. The two of them repeated the process several times over, the Nomad presenting a wide array of antiseptics from his supplies, from hydrogen peroxide solution to engineered antibiotics, whilst the Traveller scanned them each in turn, all without success. Every chemical garnered the same response. They were all toxic to his biology, though to what degree exactly, the Nomad could not say.

"I can't disinfect the wound then!" the Nomad sighed finally in defeat once he'd run out of options.

The Traveller gazed back at him blankly.

"I can only stitch you up."

The Traveller continued to stare at him without understanding, replying only with a couple of noises that the Nomad had no hope of comprehending. Were the situation reversed, the Nomad reckoned he would be panicking. Stranded on an alien world with an open wound and no means of sterilising it, the Nomad would likely be dead within a few days from infection. Yet the Traveller appeared to have an uneasy calm about him.

It was altogether possible that the Traveller was in fact exhibiting great distress, and that the Nomad was not so adept at reading the alien's body language as he believed. Alternatively, perhaps the Traveller simply did not fear death, as unnatural as that seemed to the Nomad. Or, maybe his biology was so incredibly alien that it was unsusceptible to pathogenic microorganisms in the way that the Nomad's was. Perhaps the Traveller's ancestors had won the evolutionary arms race against bacteria and viruses, long ago having developed the perfect immune system: one capable of repelling all manner of infection and disease, whether alien or not. Perhaps equally likely was some other explanation, one he couldn't yet think of. Either way, there was nothing he could do other than attempt to close the wound.

The Nomad produced a set of scissors. At first, the Traveller recoiled, yet as the Nomad issued a calming gesture, the alien relaxed slightly. The Nomad cut away a portion of the Traveller's flight suit surrounding the wound, before using a set of forceps to peel away the silicone layer of second skin he had applied back at the crash site. The Traveller winced as the Nomad exposed the injured flesh once again, shutting his eyes and averting his gaze from the gash as it began to profusely weep more green fluid. Using only distilled water, the Nomad washed and prepped the wound.

The Nomad pinched the gash closed with his forceps, and using a surgical stapler, he hastily clipped a run down the wound, crimping it shut. The Traveller gasped through puckered lips as the staples went in, finally daring to glance at his injury once the Nomad was done. The wound was closed, but with it still weeping, the Nomad applied a number of sutures before finally sealing it with a fresh application of second skin.

"There," mumbled the Nomad, washing his hands with an antiseptic solution. "I've done the best I could."

The Traveller looked up at him feebly, whispering a few syllables that the Nomad took for gratitude.

"You are welcome."

The Traveller spoke again, gesturing now to his lips.

"You want something to drink? Some water?"

More guttural noises.

"Okay. Wait here."

The Nomad gathered up the medical supplies scattered across the ground and returned them to the Fighter. Sterilising the surgical stapler and forceps, he stowed everything away and climbed back out of the cockpit. Grabbing an empty mess tin, the Nomad filled it from the Fighter's water tank and carried it over to the Traveller.

"Here," he offered, careful not to spill the contents as he handed it over.

The Traveller issued a few appreciative grunts before tipping the water down his gullet in a single swig. The creature let out a satisfied belching noise when he was finished, making the Nomad chuckle.

"You are welcome."

FORTY-FOUR

The Nomad fired a small jet of flame from his lighter at a clump of dried blue moss wedged in a stack of tinder. The moss quickly ignited, and within moments, the fire had spread over the knotted, resinous kindling, lilac and amber flames quivering up from the campfire centred in the clearing.

"There," shivered the Nomad as he pulled his log seat up closer to the fire and began warming his hands.

The shuddering Traveller did the same, taking another gulp of water from his mess tin.

"How's your leg?" asked the Nomad, pointing to the wound.

The Traveller replied with an untranslatable phrase, yet somehow, the two of them seemed to understand one another perfectly.

"That's good," the Nomad beamed, assuming from the alien's tone that he had been given a positive response.

"I don't think I can give you any food," sighed the Nomad after a time as he rose to his feet to fetch himself one of his nutrient bars. "We might be able to find something for you in the morning, but I don't like foraging after dark."

The Traveller remained quiet this time, watching as the Nomad peeled back the wrapper of his evening meal. Uncomfortable eating whilst the Traveller went hungry, the Nomad scoffed the bar down quickly, scrunching up the wrapper and tossing it into the flames when he was finished. Once the remains of the package had diminished to ash, he sat quietly observing the traveller. Every so often, he would take another swig from the mess tin as he continued to stare sedately into the flames.

A while later, he noticed the alien had reclined, his head upturned towards the heavens. The Traveller lowered his gaze to the Nomad and pointed upwards to the supernova remnant burning in the night sky. Uttering a few gentle murmurs, his lips flitted into something that was uncanny in its resemblance to a smile.

"Yeah," the Nomad agreed. "It's beautiful."

The Traveller met eyes with the Nomad again, speaking briefly. His arm arced across the heavens, this time falling over the distortions of starlight that traced the circumference of the wormhole.

"The wormhole...?" breathed the Nomad quizzically. "What do you know about it?"

The Traveller spoke again, this time stringing together several sentences.

The Nomad sat and listened to the sound of the alien's language. It was unlike anything he'd ever heard before; comprised of mostly abstract vocalisations and guttural utterances, the Nomad doubted his own throat and vocal chords were even capable of making half the sounds from which the language was comprised. Regardless, it had a pleasant rhythm and was full of sing-song intonations that were soothing to listen to.

Silence fell as the two of them sat gazing upwards at the galaxy overhead.

"Where are you from?" the Nomad asked after a time.

The Traveller responded by indicating to several points of light in the sky, tracing out some previously unseen constellation.

"A long way away then?" the Nomad chuckled. "Me too."

The two of them sat talking in this way deep into the night. Neither could understand a single remark spoken by the other, yet this seemed barely to impede their conversation. The gestures they made, the tones they spoke in, and the variety of inflections and intonations they used seemed to convey all the meaning they needed. Though the Nomad had no real way of knowing how much either he or the Traveller understood, he felt nonetheless that they were sharing a meaningful discussion.

Throughout the night, the Nomad spoke of

his past, remembering for the first time in the longest time, who and what he had been before his journey had begun. He spoke of the sights he had seen whilst travelling across the cosmos, he explained the trials and tribulations he had endured, the strife and struggles that had moulded him into who he had become. He spoke of loneliness. He spoke of isolation. He spoke of desperation. He spoke of despair. He recalled the luck he had encountered, and he spoke of the ill fates he had befallen. He recounted several near-death experiences, from narrowly surviving starvation on his journey to the yellow sun, to the encounter with a Cerberus drone back in the red dwarf system, and the time he had very nearly drowned at the bottom of an algae infested lake years earlier.

The Nomad spoke about himself at length, all the while, the Traveller sat quietly listening. Then, it was the Traveller's turn to speak whilst he listened. It did not matter that they could not really understand each other; understanding was perceived. For the first time ever in his journey, the Nomad was able to confide in someone. The conversation was cathartic, irrespective of the language: a means by which to unload the heavy burden from his soul forged from decades of solitude.

The Traveller was a kindred spirit: a being sentenced to the same fate of endless flight through the stretches of eternity. That the two of them had somehow ended up in the same small area of land, on the same continent, on the same planet, in the same star system, in the same galaxy, at the same time, seemed impossible. But the fact that it *had* happened meant that it was possible.

The night wore on, and as dawn approached, the Nomad felt his head begin to nod. He reclined in the grass, the Traveller doing the same as they continued to talk, their tired voices descending into soft whispers after hours of conversation, until finally they both drifted off.

FORTY-FIVE

The Nomad awoke abruptly. His heart was drumming loudly, the nightmare still racing through his mind. The Traveller had stolen the Fighter. He'd flown away, leaving the Nomad stranded and alone, marooned on the golden world. Cold sweat dripped from his brow. He was panting. Panicking. Leaping to his feet in dazed confusion, he span dizzily on the spot.

The Fighter was still there, parked in the centre of the glade. The Traveller was sprawled out on his front, dozing by the embers of the dying campfire.

The Nomad exhaled nauseously, his thumping pulse slowing as he began to relax. It had only been a dream, but even now, the blind panic made him feel physically sick. Uncapping his canteen, he guzzled down several chugs of fresh water and began to pace about the campsite, eyeing the Traveller as the alien respired peacefully in a growling snore. He checked his holster for his sidearm. Still there. He checked his belt for the Traveller's. Likewise.

It was hard to shake his paranoia. If he were

wrong in trusting the Traveller, he was as good as dead. The Traveller had every reason to be selfish. He had every reason to steal the Fighter: he was stranded, with no way off the golden world. He had shown no intention of betraying the Nomad, but he could merely be biding his time. The two of them bonded the night before, but that could all be a facade. The Nomad had to be careful. He had to be vigilant. One mistake could cost him his ship. One mistake could cost him his home. One mistake could cost him his life!

Gradually calming down, the Nomad took another sip of water and scoffed his breakfast whilst the Traveller slept. He tossed the wrapper into the embers and stood watching the Traveller. The Nomad had now eaten twice in the time that the Traveller had been fasting. The data uncovered by his scans the previous day indicated that the alien's metabolism burned slightly faster than his own. Though the Traveller was more than likely at no immediate risk of starvation, he would no doubt be hungry when he awoke.

If his journey across the stars was anything similar to the Nomad's, the Traveller would unquestioningly have gone hungry on many occasions before. He might even be accustomed to the feeling, numb to the dull pangs like once he himself had been. It had been years since the Nomad had been left wanting, but having come so close to death through starvation in the weeks leading up to his arrival at the yellow sun, he knew the true meaning of hunger. Staring at the sleeping Traveller, he felt wracked with guilt.

But the Nomad could not simply offer the Traveller one of his nutrition bars; they were chemically tailored specifically to his own biology. Eating one would in all probability poison the Traveller, in much the way eating any unprocessed alien flora would poison the Nomad.

The situation did not look good; but it was not without hope. It was possible that something on the golden world might be edible to the Traveller. The utopian world's ecosystem was so rich and diverse, if the Nomad gathered a broad range of samples, there was a chance, a slim one, that there might just be something out there compatible with his biology. It was unlikely, but it was not impossible, and if the Traveller's arrival had been a sign of anything, it was that the most unlikely of things could sometimes happen.

The Nomad leant over the Traveller, checking that he was most definitely still asleep. Satisfied the alien was deep in slumber, he gathered up a few basic supplies, and ventured off into the woodlands to forage.

The Nomad wandered through the trees, gathering samples of almost everything in sight. He plucked vibrant berries from the surrounding bushes and collected sprigs from the trees and undergrowth. He peeled off samples of flaking bark from swollen trunks and picked needles and leaves from low hanging boughs. He gathered bundles of purple sedge and crimson grass, and bouquets of colourfully petalled flowers and blossom. He harvested handfuls of spherical green fungi from the soil and scraped tufts of black and white moss from the rocks. Every nut, seed, or fruiting body the Nomad saw, he gathered up, hoping that something, anything, might just be the very thing he needed.

After a good few hours, the Nomad had stuffed every pouch and canister he was carrying with him to bursting, whilst his arms were laden with everything he could carry. Satisfied he was unlikely to find much else in the immediate vicinity, he set off back towards camp.

When the Nomad emerged back into the glade, his heart immediately sank. The Traveller was gone, no longer asleep by the fire. He glanced rapidly around in search for him. The Fighter was still in its usual place, but where was the Traveller? A few seconds later, the Nomad caught sight of the alien's hooved legs, visible behind the Fighter. The Traveller was doing something to his ship! He had been right to be suspicious; the alien *was* trying to steal the Fighter!

"Hey!" the Nomad screamed, dropping everything he was carrying. His hand snatched the pistol rapidly from his holster. "Get away from there!"

Gun drawn, the Nomad sprinted towards the Fighter. His finger squeezed the trigger and the muzzle clapped. The crack of the gunshot ripped through the glade. Hundreds of birds took to the air, fleeing their roosts in terror. The slug drilled into the soil beside one of the Traveller's hooves. A mess tin clanged against the Fighter's skids, water splashing from it as a gurgling flow began to douse the grass.

The voice of the Traveller cried out in distress and a set of two-fingered hands emerged from behind the tail of the Fighter in surrender.

"Move away!" the Nomad screamed, thrusting his gun forwards in anger.

Tentatively, the Traveller emerged in full from behind the ship, uttering a few apologetic vocalisations in an attempt to quell the Nomad's fury.

"Get away from there!" he repeated, flicking his gun sideways.

The Traveller understood and obeyed, limping timidly back over to the remnants of the campfire. Keeping his gun trained on the alien, the Nomad edged closer to inspect what the Traveller had been doing. The moment he stepped around the far side of the Fighter it became abundantly clear. Water was gushing from the faucet of the supply tank. The mess tin the Nomad had given the Traveller to drink from was lying on the ground beneath the flow.

The Traveller had awoken without anything to drink. The Nomad had been gone a while. The alien had watched the Nomad refill the mess tin several times the night before, and, thirsty, with no knowledge of where the Nomad was, or when he might return, he'd decided to refill the tin himself from the Fighter's reserves.

Feeling immediately ashamed, the Nomad stowed his weapon and snatched up the mess tin from the grass. He filled it from the flow and shut off the water. With his head lowered, he trudged over to the Traveller and offered him the water. The Traveller hesitated, studying the Nomad for a long moment before accepting it.

The Traveller uttered a few words in his alien tongue that seemed repentant in tone.

"No..." the Nomad shook his head. "I'm sorry. It was my fault. It was a misunderstanding... I shouldn't have shot at you... It's just... I came back and I saw you by my ship and I thought... I thought the worst, and I'm sorry. I'm just paranoid."

The Nomad returned a few gentle syllables and his lips curved once again into a facial expression that bore an uncanny resemblance to a smile.

"You forgive me?"

The Traveller responded with an up-tone noise and took a long sip of the water before belching in satisfaction.

"No hard feelings then?" the Nomad smiled. "I brought you some food..." the Nomad continued, changing the subject as he pointed back to the pile of foraged vegetation scattered across the ground at the edge of the glade.

The Traveller returned a quizzical glance.

“At least, I hope there is something there you can eat,” he added. “Come on,” he motioned for the Traveller to follow.

The two of them made their way slowly over to the array of plant samples scattered across the grass. The Nomad picked up a green and pink striped oblong fruit and mimicked taking a bite from it.

“What do you think?” he asked, offering the bulging berry to the Traveller.

The traveller took the plant in his leathery palm and scrutinised it for a long moment. Then, still studying it with intrigue, he depressed various regions on his chest. Thin rays of light flickered over the vegetable as the Traveller’s suit ran an analysis of the plant. A few moments later, the results displayed as strange alien script in a hologram projected from his chestpiece.

The Traveller issued a few gurgling noises before chucking the fruit to one side.

“No good then, I take it?” The Nomad picked up a brown cone he had pulled out of the earth. “What about this?”

The Traveller took the alien flora from the Nomad and scanned it. Once again, he discarded it to one side.

"No good either?"

The Traveller selected the next item from the pile and the process continued. One by one, the alien scanned and analysed each sample the Nomad had collected, and one by one each was rejected. At one point, the Nomad felt hopeful as the Traveller took a long while studying the results of a scan, but after a little deliberation, the cream tuber in question was discarded to one side. When the pile was exhausted, the Nomad began producing all the samples stuffed in his various pockets and canisters, but once again it all proved fruitless.

When everything was cast aside, the Nomad looked at the Traveller with pity in his eyes. "I don't know what to do..." he uttered.

The Traveller replied, defeatedly lowering his gaze to the pile of discarded flora.

"What about one of these?" asked the Nomad hopefully as he hurriedly fetched a handful of his own nutrition bars.

The Traveller reared his head and scanned the various rations on offer, but as the results flickered across the holographic display, the Traveller looked mournfully at the Nomad.

He didn't need to make a single sound.

"I understand."

FORTY-SIX

That night, the Nomad and the Traveller once again sat by the light of the fire, conversing in their incompatible languages. The Nomad recounted further tales from his journey, and events that had shaped him over the course of his life. The Traveller was equally talkative, and much like the previous night, they took turns speaking whilst the other simply listened. The Nomad knew his companion couldn't understand what he was saying, but he often felt the general meaning of what was being said seemed to be conveyed. They were divided in language, but united through experience; living a similar existence, they perhaps understood each other better than themselves. And ultimately, that was the purpose their one-way conversations served: a cathartic means to work through their own thoughts. Putting ideas and feelings into words helped the Nomad gain a better understanding of who he was.

Later on, they fell silent, reclining in the grass to gaze up at the night skies. A meteor shower criss-crossed the heavens, white streaks darting in and out of the dark, fading as they burnt up in the golden world's atmosphere. They took turns pointing them out as they fell from the sky, admiring the nebula during the lulls in the shower, occasionally passing remarks about the wormhole lurking subtly against the backdrop of fixed constellations.

The Nomad awoke the next day to find the Traveller already up. The alien was sat cradling his stomach, prodding the fire's last dying embers with a stick.

"Morning," the Nomad greeted him with a yawn as he rubbed his eyes.

The Traveller raised his head and responded chirpily, hunching back over to hug his gut again as soon as he thought the Nomad wasn't looking. A few minutes later, the Traveller picked up the mess tin the Nomad had given him to drink from, speaking a few grunts as he presented it; it was empty.

"Of course," the Nomad nodded. "Go ahead." He gestured to the Fighter.

The Traveller looked back at the Nomad apprehensively for a time, not quite sure he'd understood.

"It's okay," the Nomad insisted, pointing to the Traveller, the mess tin, and then the Fighter.

After the incident the previous day, the Traveller was still somewhat nervous. He slowly rose to his feet and limped toward the Fighter, continually glancing back at the Nomad along the way to ensure he wasn't being presumptuous.

"Don't worry," the Nomad assured him. "I'm not going to shoot you."

The Traveller flipped open the access panel and filled his tin from the water supply. Taking a long swig, he topped it back up a second time before closing the panel to make his way back over to the firepit. The Traveller was still hobbling awkwardly, favouring his uninjured leg, but he was moving about with much greater ease than he had done the previous day.

"You need to come foraging with me today," the Nomad explained as the Traveller sat on the grass beside him. "If you use your scanner, we might just find something for you to eat."

The Traveller looked at him blankly.

"If we don't go today, you might not have the strength later."

The Nomad peered down at the translucent layer of second skin sealing the wound on the Traveller's leg. There was no sign of bleeding, which suggested the gash was healing nicely, but more surprisingly, the Traveller seemed to show no signs of infection. It could simply be that the symptoms had not yet manifested, or that they were presenting in a way that the Nomad couldn't see, but besides the cradling of his gut, which the Nomad took for hunger, the Traveller showed little sign of sickness or malady. Perhaps the Nomad's guess had been right; maybe the Traveller possessed a sophisticated immune system far more capable than his own. Maybe disease was an abstract concept to his people, one which had not concerned them for millennia. Or maybe the golden world's pathogens were merely slow to act. Either way, he would likely find out in time.

The Nomad rose to his feet and marched off into the trees. It didn't take long to find what he was searching for. Using the serrated edge of his knife, the Nomad sawed through a sapling. Cleaning the branches from the main stem and snapping away the remaining ribbony leaves, the Nomad returned to the clearing and presented it to the Traveller.

The alien issued him a puzzled look.

"It's a walking stick," the Nomad explained, demonstrating how to use it. "So you can come with me."

A look of recognition flickered across the Traveller's face. Gurgling a few words of thanks, he accepted the cane, heaving himself to his feet to try it out, lumbering swiftly around as he used it to ease the weight off his bad leg.

"You've got it!" the Nomad beamed. "Now come on," he beckoned, heading back into the trees.

The Traveller followed a few steps behind. Once they were in the undergrowth, the Nomad gestured to his mouth to signify food, before waving his arms in wide arcs about their surroundings.

"You need to scan everything you can!" the Nomad urged, pointing to the Traveller's chest piece. "There has to be something here that won't kill you."

It took several moments for the Nomad's meaning to sink in, but after a few seconds of bafflement, hobbling forwards, the Traveller depressed the buttons hidden beneath the fabric of his flight suit and activated his scanner. Rays of light fanned over a red fern in front of him, and a minute later, more alien hieroglyphs projected holographically into the air.

The Traveller mumbled unenthusiastically and shambled over to another plant, running a new scan on a length of tangled vine. The two of them gradually made their way through the forest, the Traveller going from tree to tree, bush to bush, fungus to fungus, analysing each specimen in turn. Hours passed as they trudged slowly through the undergrowth, all without a single positive response. By noon, the Nomad and the Traveller had scoured several square kilometres of woodland, scanning everything they had seen. But it had become clear some time earlier that it was all in vain. They would not find anything edible.

It seamed a cruel twist of fate that, on a planet as rich and diverse as the golden world, there was not a single thing for the alien to eat. It was a matter of fundamental biochemistry. Though the basic building blocks that made up life on the golden world were incredibly similar to the Nomad's own biology, they could scarcely be more divergent from that of the Traveller's. On most planets, life evolved from a single genesis. On occasion, different forms of life could take shape in the primordial soup independently of one another, but in most cases, only one ever prevailed. As a result, the various organisms in complex and diverse ecosystems, like those of the golden world, were all the descendants of the first singular progenitor. Due to this, with few exceptions, all organisms in an ecosystem tended to have a similar biological makeup to their common ancestor.

Though evolution could produce wildly divergent biology, the fundamentals, the genetic blueprints, seldom underwent alteration in any major way, becoming enshrined in a singular biochemistry that linked every single organism together in a complex tree of heredity.

The Nomad was incredibly fortunate; the first cells to arise on the Eden world, by sheer chance, had adopted a similar genetic and structural make up to his own primordial ancestors. The match was not perfect, but he had the benefit of a biomatter recombinator to reshuffle the final pieces of the puzzle and make up the difference, producing food that was a near perfect nutritional match to his own biology.

The Traveller on the other hand was the descendent of a line of primordial organisms that adopted an entirely different structural language to life here on the golden world, and without a biomatter recombinator, there was no feasible way the Traveller could ingest anything grown here.

For the Nomad, the golden world was a utopia, one that seemed almost tailored to him by design. It was spectacular and novel, breath-taking and bizarre. It was where he belonged. For the Traveller however, it was a dystopia. To him the golden world was strange and alien, terrifying and inhospitable, where everything was toxic, and where survival was impossible. It was where he was going to die. It was just a matter of time.

"Come on," sighed the Nomad in defeat, "let's head back."

FORTY-SEVEN

That night, the Traveller watched the Nomad eat his evening meal, sipping regularly from his water tin as they sat by the fire. Wracked with guilt, the Nomad lost his appetite, sealing the wrapper to his unfinished nutrient bar, pocketing it for later when the Traveller wasn't watching. Every so often, the alien would keel over, curling up as a wave of hunger pangs audibly gurgled through his abdomen. Between the bouts of pain, they resumed their conversation, chatting late into the night as they lay stargazing in the grass.

The next morning, before the Traveller awoke, the Nomad disappeared into the trees to scoff down his morning meal in private. Emerging back into the glade, he found his companion still resting, his grumbling snores sounding more laboured than they had before.

Already the Traveller appeared thinner. He was losing weight fast, growing weaker day by day. At first it was difficult to notice. His wound healing, the Traveller had at first grown more mobile as the days went by. But the Nomad knew it wouldn't be long before the rate of decline would outpace his recovery. One saving grace at least, was that the risk of infection seemed to have passed; if ever the Traveller's wound had been contaminated by the local microflora, his body appeared to have fought it off with little trouble.

The next day, the Nomad lowered the Fighter's starboard cargo pod and set up the biomatter recombinator. Scrolling through the device's various settings, he pondered long and hard. In theory, the machine was fully capable of rearranging biological molecules into all manner of structures and compositions. It was calibrated to the Nomad's own physiology, but in principle, it had the capacity to produce food tailored for the Traveller.

The issues arose from a number of factors. Firstly, the recombinator was not merely calibrated to the Nomad's biology, but designed with only it in mind. There were no alternate settings or selectable programs to run the machine for an alien biology. In order for the machine to be calibrated to the Traveller, it would have to be reprogrammed from the ground up, and the Nomad had not the first inkling of where to begin.

The next major issue was that, even if the Nomad knew how to hack and reformat the biomatter recombinator to a different biochemistry, he would not know where to begin in attuning it to the Traveller. He possessed the raw bioanalysis data of the Traveller's physiological and biochemical makeup, but that did not mean he had any comprehension of the intricacies of the alien's metabolic processes, nor the required nutritional profile of viable food sources. He had scans of the Traveller's digestive system, but that did not mean he could work out the minutia and subtleties of how it functioned; that alone could take years of research to uncover.

The Traveller himself likely had a better understanding, but there was an impossible language barrier to overcome. Even if the Nomad could begin to translate his companion's strange guttural utterances, concepts as sophisticated as biochemistry were far too complex to convey without a deep fluency of the language. They had grown reasonably adept at communicating without the need for words, but their implied inferences derived from gestures and tone was worked out mostly through guesswork, limited only to the most basic concepts and notions.

And aside from everything else, the truth was that the intricate inner workings of the recombinator were beyond the Nomad's understanding, even when it was programmed for himself. He knew how to operate the device, but not how it operated. The details of how the recombinator went about reorganising complex biomolecules was something of a mystery to him; he understood a few of the basic principles, but the specifics were beyond him. He doubted, were he working from a blank canvas, that he'd even be able to programme it to his own biology; he knew the basic building blocks comprising his own nutritional profile, but he had no extensive knowledge of the sequences of amino acids in the proteins, let alone their secondary, tertiary, or quaternary structures, nor did he have a full grasp of the ratios of micronutrients he needed.

This alone led to the final matter: say he did somehow manage to calibrate the machine to the Traveller's biology, was there any guarantee he could revert it back to his own afterwards? Nutrition was a precarious thing; the slightest imbalance, the smallest contamination could result in deadly poisoning. Even nutrients with exactly the same structures and make up could prove deadly if their chirality was reversed to their mirror image. In all of this, only one thing was certain: tampering with the biomatter recombinator would be a sure-fire way to get himself killed.

The Traveller sat watching the Nomad in silence for several hours as he pondered the impossible problem. Eventually, overcome with frustration, the Nomad emitted a roar of dismay and petulantly packed the recombinator back away into the cargo pod. The Traveller gazed wearily at the Nomad as he joined him by the fire. He suspected the alien understood what he had been trying to do.

The Traveller was first to speak, offering a few broken noises that were somehow consoling, his demeanour incredibly tranquil. He had already accepted his fate.

"Doesn't it bother you!?" the Nomad erupted abruptly after a long time sat staring off into space.

The Traveller peered back at him silently with his amiable gaze.

"Look at you! You are starving! To death! You must know what's coming! Doesn't it worry you!? Aren't you scared!?"

The Traveller responded with a short melodic gargle.

"What does that even mean!?" he snapped in frustration.

The Traveller apologised with a soft grunt.

"You are going to die! You know that... don't you?"

Silence.

"I can't save you. I tried. I really did... but there is nothing I can do for you!"

His friend merely looked back at him with solemn eyes.

"I don't understand how you can just accept this!?"

No response.

The Nomad defeatedly rose to his feet and disappeared into the forest for his evening meal. Sick to his stomach, he could scarcely manage a single bite.

FORTY-EIGHT

The next day, the Nomad awoke in silence. Hours passed without either him or the Traveller speaking. Once again, he ate his breakfast in private, making his way back to the glade when he was done. Climbing the ladder to the Fighter's cockpit, he slumped into the pilot seat. Methodically working his way through his weekly tests and checks, he booted up various on-board systems and ran a number of simulations, all the while, the Traveller sat watching him curiously.

Even the Fighter was not a viable option for the Traveller. The Nomad peered around at the innumerable switches, dials, levers, and buttons clustered across the control consoles. The controls would be utterly undecipherable to anyone without training, even someone able to comprehend the language of all the displays and readouts.

The Nomad had briefly peered inside the cockpit of the Traveller's ship the day he had pulled him from the wreckage. The controls he'd seen were remarkably different to those of the Fighter. There'd been no discernible flightstick, nor anything recognisable as a thruster. He remembered seeing a series of mechanical levers and a number of spherical orbs set into a control console, but beyond that, there was little the Nomad could pull from the smoky images in his memory. The alien cockpit had been so unfamiliar, so abstract, that he had difficulty even recalling exactly what he'd seen. But he knew one thing for certain: he wouldn't have had the faintest idea of how to fly it. It was absurd to have thought that the Traveller might steal the Fighter; the alien wouldn't even be able to figure out how to take off without instruction, let alone fly anywhere. And with the impossible language barrier to overcome, the Nomad stood little hope in ever teaching the Traveller.

The Nomad gazed about the confines of the cockpit. Even for a single-manned Fighter it was relatively cramped. He had never really thought so thus far, but as he looked out at the Traveller, he realised just how tailored the ergonomics were to his own physiology. When upright, the Traveller stood a head taller than the Nomad, and even now, starved half to death, his shoulders were far too broad to fit comfortably inside the cockpit.

Aside from this, the controls, the flightstick, the thruster, even the pilot's chair, were all designed with a particular anatomy in mind. It might not be comfortable for the Traveller to hold the flight controls, but the Nomad suspected it was doable. Whereas sitting in the pilot's chair, with his hoofed feet and backward bending knees, the Nomad had real doubts as to whether it would even be possible for the Traveller.

As far as piloting the Fighter went, the Traveller seemed doomed before he even started, but his prospects as a passenger seemed even less hopeful. At a push, the Nomad could potentially fit another person of equal or smaller proportions to himself inside the cockpit with him; even then, it was something only really feasible for a very short journey. But with the Traveller's tall heavyset frame, it would be impossible, no matter how thin he became through malnourishment.

Even if the Nomad knew somewhere he could take the Traveller where they might find him a viable food source, there was no way to get him there.

The Nomad would have given the Traveller the Fighter if he could. It was his home. It meant everything to him. But he genuinely believed that, were it a feasible solution, he would give it to him. The Fighter was his home, but the Traveller was his friend; his only friend in the entire universe. The Nomad could not bear the thought of him dying. He would rather give up the Fighter and watch the Traveller fly away, never to return, so long as he knew his friend had a chance of survival.

But the Traveller had no chance. The Traveller's fate was already decided. The Traveller was going to die there on the golden world. Suddenly, it no longer felt like a paradise; it felt like a purgatory.

The Nomad wanted for nothing. He had everything he needed to survive. But what did it matter if he could not share it? It seemed a cruel irony: he had everything, and yet he could give nothing.

It was one final insult issued by an indifferent universe.

The Nomad wept.

FORTY-NINE

As the weeks slowly passed, the Traveller grew weaker. By night, they sat watching the stars, by day, they conversed, gazing at the wildlife around the glade. Once the Traveller's leg had healed enough, the Nomad took him on walks beyond the forest. They managed several kilometres at a time, granting the Traveller the opportunity to see more of the world which would in time become his final resting place. But with his diminishing strength, their excursions grew shorter by the day, until finally, not long after they'd first began exploring together, the Traveller was no longer strong enough to venture further than a few tens of metres beyond the border of their glade.

Things grew steadily worse from there on. The Traveller rapidly became frail and gaunt. His leathery skin pulled taught over his facial bones, green lesions of raw flesh flared up as welts across his body, and the spasms of hunger the Traveller suffered from often verged close to full blown seizures.

The Nomad could not bear to eat in front of his starving friend. Several times a day he disappeared into the concealment of the trees to eat, most often during the Traveller's long bouts of sleep. Sometimes, whether out of guilt or for the sake of solidarity, the Nomad forwent eating himself; he couldn't explain why he was skipping meals, he knew it would do nothing to ease the Traveller's own suffering, but it did something to ease his own sense of helplessness. Ultimately, he always broke his fast, realising it was all futile. Starving himself would do nothing to help his friend.

One morning, the Nomad returned to find the Traveller keeled over in the centre of the glade, vomiting up black steaming bile. At first the Nomad feared the Traveller might have succumbed to infection, but discovering a nutrition bar wrapper discarded on the fringes of the fire, he realised what had actually happened.

Driven by desperation, the Traveller had eaten it, despite knowing it was poisonous to his own digestive system. The Nomad spent the entire night by his companion's side as he continued to vomit and convulse. He burned hot to the touch, and sweat issued from pores on his scabby skin. The sickness lasted throughout the night, with the fever only subsiding come morning.

At one point, the Nomad drifted off to sleep and dreamt that his friend had died during the night. He awoke from the nightmare to hear the Traveller's rasping breath still beside him, but the sound did not bring any comfort. It might have been more peaceful for the Traveller if he had passed away that night. Instead, the illness merely lingered for a few days thereafter before the Traveller was returned to his enduring starvation.

A week later, the Nomad offered the Traveller his gun. The Nomad had never officially returned the Traveller's firearm after he'd confiscated it, but since the end of their first week together, it had been lying out in the open by the Nomad's supplies.

The Traveller raised a palm, offering a few feeble syllables of rejection.

The Nomad insisted.

The Traveller refused.

For a moment, the Nomad considered pulling the trigger himself. It would be a mercy. It would be murder, but it would be a mercy. The Traveller could clearly tell what he was thinking. So often now they knew exactly what thoughts were going through the other's head. But the Traveller did nothing to discourage the Nomad, he simply gazed up at his friend with amiable eyes, just as he always did. It was all he needed to do. The Nomad knew then and there that he would never be able to pull the trigger. He'd come closer trying when a gun was pointed to his own head.

The weeks turned steadily to months as the Traveller continued to waste away. By now, he spent most of the day sleeping. For a few hours they would speak beneath the starlight, but the Traveller was too feeble to string together much more than a few mumbles at a time. Instead, the Nomad spoke for both of them. He shared things with the Traveller he never believed he would be able to tell anyone. He confessed all the dark moments, when alone and lost, he had pressed a gun to his temple, hoping to bring an end to it all; he explained that he understood why the Traveller could not take his own life. Even still, the Nomad offered his friend a gun on several more occasions. But each time, the offer received the same polite gesture of refusal.

"Please!" the Nomad begged him with tears streaming down his eyes. "Please! If not for you, then do it for me!"

The Traveller gazed silently back at him.

"Please! I can't watch you die like this!"

But the Traveller did not take the weapon.

The Nomad knew in the week that followed that the Traveller was entering the final days of his life; but the Nomad refused to merely sit and wait for it to come. He gathered together his expeditionary gear and fashioned a stretcher from two sticks and a sheet of insulation fabric. The Traveller watched quietly from the grass, compliantly allowing his friend to lift his light and withered body onto the makeshift litter and strap him in place. Dragging the Traveller behind him, the Nomad ventured out into the forest.

It was hard going across the steep and rugged

terrain, but by late afternoon, the Nomad had arrived at the foot of the cliffs to the butte he been climbing on the day he'd first sighted the Traveller's ship. Almost too weak to talk, the Traveller simply watched as the Nomad readied his climbing gear and prepared for an ascent to the summit.

The climb was slow and gruelling. Following weeks of inactivity sat in the clearing with the Traveller, the Nomad had quickly grown unfit, but with the line still in place from the last time he'd ascended the butte, he already had a top anchor established. Eventually, he reached the top, and after a short rest, he made sure his secondary line was in place before beginning the arduous task of hoisting the Traveller up to him.

The whole process took several hours. Occasionally, the Traveller's stretcher would snag on outcrops and crags and the Nomad would need to lower him slightly before hauling him back up, but eventually, the Traveller reached the top and the Nomad heaved him up over the ledge. Unfastening the strappings holding the Traveller in place, he moved his friend over to the edge, propping him up on his own shoulder so that together, they sat with their legs dangling over the precipice, gazing out towards the very furthest reaches of the horizon.

The sun set soon thereafter and an endless sea of stars pierced through the veil. The nebula rose into the heavens, burning more brightly than it had ever done before, the wormhole beginning its seasonal traversal over the fiery star remnant, blurring the violet and cream nebula around its fringes. The Nomad and the Traveller shared a few last words as they looked out across their world. The Traveller fell asleep a short while later, slumping in the Nomad's arms, leaving his friend to gaze out at the haunting beauty of the universe alone.

The Traveller passed away a short while later.

FIFTY

The Nomad buried the Traveller atop the peak the next day. Piling rocks over his friend's body, he erected a cairn, one he knew would be visible for kilometres in all directions. At dusk he laid the final stone atop the memorial. He stepped back as an amber haze enveloped the skies, the fiery light blurred through stinging tears. He had hoped to speak, to say a few words at the Traveller's grave, but he couldn't muster the strength to do so. Instead, he merely stood weeping, head bowed. He stood there until the orange light faded to violet, dwindling then after to a deep blue. He stood there until the stars shimmered in the night. He stood there until the nebula and the wormhole rose overhead. He stood there until they had set once more, vanishing with the first light of dawn.

The warm desert winds brushed away the cold tears from his cheeks as the yellow sun's rays swept across the land. Knowing it was time to go, the Nomad raised his head and uttered a single word to his friend.

"Goodbye."

The Nomad climbed down the butte, leaving

his lines in place. Untethering his harness at the bottom, he began the long slow march back to the Fighter. He returned to the glade and sat by the cold ashes of the firepit, the place where he and the Traveller had spent so many nights staring up at the heavens. He screamed. He cried. He whimpered.

Days passed. The Nomad ate. The Nomad slept. The Nomad mourned.

Weeks passed. The Nomad ate. The Nomad slept. The Nomad mourned.

Months passed. The Nomad ate. The Nomad slept. The Nomad mourned.

After a time, the Nomad began to wander once more. Venturing out, he began exploring the world around him again. But after everything that had happened, he no longer took pleasure in it. No longer did he see life and vitality in a perfect Eden. Now his view of it was tainted. He saw the harsh fight for survival, the brutality of nature, the indifference of the universe. At times, he would simply stop walking. Sometimes he would stand gazing onward to the horizon for hours on end. Other times he would stand gazing at his feet.

One evening, he came across the Traveller's gun. It hadn't been hidden; for months it had been lying in the grass beside the Fighter, out in the open. But until now, the Nomad hadn't seen it. He picked the cold metallic alien weapon up from the ground and studied it. It was the only item he had to remember his friend by, but it was perhaps the item he wished least to see. Even still, his finger naturally found the trigger as he gripped it. And before he knew what he was doing, the barrel was pressed to his temple, hot tears streaking from his eyes. He never did pull the trigger. But of all the times he had tried, he came the closest that night.

Finally, one day in late autumn, when the alien leaves were fading to gold and brown, fluttering down from the deciduous trees each time the wind gusted, the Nomad ventured back towards the towering butte, where almost a year ago to the day, he had buried his friend. He ascended the rockface via the lines he had left in place, reaching the top just as the sun began to set. He stood before the cairn with his head bowed, tears burning behind his eyes.

"I'm sorry I didn't come sooner..." he began, knowing he was speaking to no one but himself.

A long silence endured before he spoke again.

"I was happy here... Before you arrived, I was happy. I was lonely. I know that I was lonely; but I had nothing to compare it to. I had been alone for so long that I had forgotten... I had forgotten what it was like to not be lonely."

The Nomad wiped his cheek and stood in eerie silence for a long time.

"I really was happy... and then... and then you came along... and... and!" his voice broke in frustration.

"Why did you have to die!?" the Nomad demanded. "Why did you come here!?"

He stood in the ghostly breeze, waiting for some response. None came.

"It's not fair what you did. I hate you for it!" he hissed. "It's not fair.

"I miss you," he issued apologetically after a time. "I wish things had been different... I wish we could have met at some other time... in some other place. I wish there was something I could have done to help you... That is the worst thing of all... that I couldn't help you. I tried! I promise I tried! I thought of everything. But there wasn't anything I could do!

"I still try to think of the things that I could have done... there had to be something."

The breeze swept over the peak and night fell.

"I'm leaving," the Nomad declared regretfully. "There is nothing left for me here. I can't stay on this world much longer.

"I don't want to leave you. But *you* left me.

"I'm sorry.

"I'll never forget you.

"I have to go."

Hours later, as twilight bloomed in the east, the Nomad descended the peak, recovering the cams and carabiners on the way down, and reeling in his climbing line at the bottom. He paused, looking up the sheer face of stone to the jutting peak, atop of which he could see the cairn of stone that formed the Traveller's grave.

"Goodbye my friend."

The Nomad was alone.

FIFTY-ONE

The next morning, the Nomad readied the Fighter to depart. Powering up each onboard system in turn, he ran every conceivable preflight check and simulation, ensuring the Fighter was space-worthy, ready after a three-year hiatus to resume its never-ending voyage across the stars. Igniting the chemical rockets, the Nomad climbed back out of the cockpit and allowed them to warm up, using his final few minutes on the golden world for one last stroll through the surrounding woodlands.

Wandering through the luscious flora, he listened as the orchestra of animal life performed the finale of its symphony. Climbing up the gentle slope of a nearby hillside, the Nomad broke through the forest canopy and gazed out across the treetops, basking in the light of the yellow sun. His vantage granted him sweeping vistas stretching to the far-flung horizon in every direction, and there, in the distance, standing in silhouette against the sun, was the cairn-topped butte.

It was time to go.

The Nomad turned away, preparing to descend back into the forest, when a familiar haunting alert chirped from his suit. The Nomad shook his head in disbelief and gazed down at the hologram on his forearm. A Cerberus was inbound.

Not now! Why did it have to be now!?

The Nomad broke into a sprint. The trees rushed up to meet him. He tore through the forest, racing back towards the glade. He peered back down at his wrist; the scanning signal was spiking. The Fighter had no stealth systems engaged. Its chemical jets were running; it was hot, no doubt glowing like a fiery beacon on any Cerberus thermal scan. And there was nothing the Nomad could do. Even if he were sat at the controls, able to power down the jets, they would never cool in time to avoid showing up on the Cerberus's scans. He had to run. It was his only option.

Ducking and weaving through the tangled undergrowth, the Nomad scampered over steep banks and splashed through fast-flowing rills as he raced back towards his ship. Bursting into the glade, he darted across the sward of crimson grass, leaping onto the rungs of the ladder, and clambered up into the cockpit. He pulled down a lever and fastened his harness. With the canopy steadily lowering, he reached under his seat, fumbling frenetically around for his helmet. Finally grasping hold of it, he pulled it out and forced it over his head, locking it swiftly into his collar bearing.

The canopy hermetically sealed and the

Nomad delivered a burst of thrust to the screeching VTOL jets. Hydrogen flared from the exhausts and a hot cushion of lift swelled beneath the Fighter. The skids lifted gently from the crimson sedge, and the Fighter rose out of the glade above the treetops. Retracting the landing gear, the Nomad pitched up and pulled open the holographic interface.

A jagged scanning signal cascaded in warning across the readout, but the Nomad did not need the wailing alerts blaring throughout the cockpit to know how close the Cerberus was; he could already hear it. Even over the roar of the Fighter's engines, the deafening howl of an inbound Cerberus interceptor cut through the atmosphere. As the Fighter canted back in preparation to launch, the Nomad saw the red glare of optics pierce through the clouds above. An instant later, white vee-shaped wings sliced out of the gloom. It had seen him. The Nomad had been made.

Cursing, the Nomad activated the Fighter's countdown and punched forwards on the thruster. 217.57 seconds began to tick downwards just as the rear rockets of the Fighter ignited. The ship surged forwards in a thunderous surge of thrust, pinning the Nomad back into his seat as a series of sonic booms ripped through the air surrounding the Fighter. In mere seconds, the Nomad was past Mach three and still accelerating hard towards hypersonic velocities.

Easing off the thruster, the Nomad powered

up the Fighter's combat suite, enabling aim assisted target tracking, and projecting a translucent rear-view overlay across the canopy. Immediately, he caught glimpse of the angular interceptor closing in, bearing down on him from out of the stratosphere. Larger, and far more heavily armed than a Cerberus drone, the interceptor was outfitted with thick armour plating and powerful shields. But all of that came at a price; whilst it matched a drone in straight-line speed, it sacrificed manoeuvrability. And in and in-atmosphere dogfight, manoeuvrability counted for everything.

The Nomad watched the pursuing interceptor as its faint image swelled larger across the canopy. Below, the forested mountains blurred quickly into beige desert, buttes and mesas rising above the rock-strewn sands a few hundred metres beneath the Fighter.

The interceptor's pupil dilated across the canopy, glaring suddenly brighter as the machine's weapons readied to fire. Snapping his wrist left, the Nomad twisted the flightstick sideways, lurching the Fighter into a sharp swerve. A column of laser carved narrowly passed as the Nomad banked on the desert wind, ploughing a black furrow as it scorched through the dunes below, turning the sands to glass.

Yawing right, the Nomad rolled out of his turn, swinging the Fighter back around just as another beam of fire seared close behind. Pinned into his seat by the g force, the Nomad gritted his teeth, ditching out of his turn just in time to avoid a third ray. The wayward beam of energy carved wide, decapitating a butte as the laser cut clean through the rock, sending thousands of tonnes of stone cascading down the bluffs into the sand below.

The Nomad pitched downwards, plunging rapidly towards the dune sea, pulling out of the dive mere seconds before impact. A torrent of dust ripped into the air, kicked up by the Fighter's jets as the ship skimmed above the dunes. The Nomad glanced up; the interceptor was overhead, its flaming optics lining up another shot.

Heaving back on the joystick, the Fighter's elevons cut against the airflow, and with a punch to the thrusters, the Nomad rocketed suddenly skyward. Narrowly clipping past the interceptor's nose, the Nomad felt the heat of the laser on the back of his neck as it blazed millimetres past his tailfins. The interceptor pitched back, pursuing the Fighter as the Nomad punched through the clouds, but unable to pull as tight a turn as the single-manned ship, the Cerberus curved wide, losing the Nomad from its sights.

Killing thrust, the Nomad yanked back on the thruster. The airbrake engaged, the Fighter's elevons and slats locking against the wind. Aided by the tug of gravity, the Fighter rapidly decelerated, pausing briefly at the top of its arc before gravity overtook inertia and the Fighter began to plummet back towards the ground.

Somersaulting the Fighter, the Nomad pitched his nose groundward and disengaged the airbrake as he hurtled back through the surrounding cumulus, propelled only by the draw of the golden world's gravity. As the clouds cleared, he caught sight of the interceptor scudding across the desert below. It had lost sight of him entirely, its scanners powering back up as it began to scour the vicinity for the Fighter's heat signature.

His rockets still cooling, the Nomad used the airflow over his wings to cock the Fighter's nose towards the interceptor. His targeting crosshairs aligned and adjusted for lead, pulling ahead of the Cerberus's prow. Locked on, he pulled the flightstick trigger and his railguns screamed as they unloaded into the golden world's atmosphere. A fusillade of shots rained down at the interceptor, streaking through the sky as a hail of white-hot plasma. The cannonade drummed into the interceptor, bouncing off its hull as the toroids were deflected by the Cerberus's shields. Peppered by the glancing shots, the interceptor reacted, swerving and accelerating, breaking the Nomad's target lock as it raced away.

Still gliding without engine thrust, the Nomad rolled, banking in pursuit as he readjusted his aim, realigning his reticle on the interceptor. Firing again, another salvo of plasma riddled the Cerberus. The toroids splattered against the invisible electromagnetic field encapsulating the machine, deflecting left and right as they were repelled. But just as the drumfire of the Fighter's guns died away, the final plasma bolt to strike the Cerberus sent a deluge of sparks cascading off the rear of the interceptor.

The Nomad had done it. Unable to hold out against the incoming barrage, the interceptor's shield capacitors had shorted. The invisible electromagnetic field encapsulating the Cerberus was down. The interceptor was vulnerable. It was still heavily armoured, but it was vulnerable. And better yet, still in the Nomad's sights.

The Nomad punched forwards on the thruster. The rockets reignited. A shockwave of vapour erupted around the Fighter as it lanced back through the sound barrier. Sinking back in his seat, the Nomad pulled level with the horizon and gave chase to the interceptor dead ahead.

The Cerberus banked erratically, attempting to shake the Nomad. But it was no use; the Fighter had a much tighter turning circle, and the Nomad was locked on the interceptor's tail. Sweat beaded across the Nomad's brow as he tweaked the flight-stick left and right, lining up the Cerberus for his next shot.

The machine scudded across his reticle and the Nomad squeezed the trigger. The Fighter shuddered as it launched another cannonade of toroids. The shots clattered across the nose of the Cerberus, on target, but glancing. The Nomad fired again.

Toroids peppered the machine's hull, scorching a track of black gouges across the interceptor's white glossy armour. A better hit, but still not enough to puncture the interceptor's plating. The armour was too thick; the Fighter's guns weren't powerful enough to pierce it. The Nomad had to do better. Only a direct strike to the interceptor's exhausts stood any chance of disabling it.

The deserts sands below blurred rapidly into an approaching coastline. In seconds, the shore had vanished, the sea of dunes replaced suddenly by one of raging waves. Storm clouds brewed across the oncoming horizon, pluming in black anvils streaked with lightning. The interceptor surged ahead, accelerating hard in an attempt to outrun the Nomad, but the Fighter kept pace, belligerently dogging the interceptor, remaining tight on its tail.

The Nomad fired again, dealing more superficial damage to the interceptor's fuselage. He peered at the clock. Fifty-eight seconds; less than a minute remaining. But he could do it. He knew he could. He fired again. Another glancing blow, but the black pockmarks scorched into the interceptor's wings were mere centimetres wide of their intended target.

The Nomad tightened his grip of the flightstick, narrowing in with each passing second as he continued to twitch left and right. Nudging the thruster forwards incrementally, he increased his airspeed, creeping ever closer to the interceptor's tail. He fired again. The shots went wide, evaporating geysers of steam from the waves below as they splashed into the sea.

Lightning forked all around them. Howling hurricane-strength gales buffeted both the Fighter and the interceptor as they cleft meanderingly through the tempest. Rain rattled against the Fighter's canopy, congealing as a thin film flowing across the glass. The Nomad squinted, peering through the screen of water blurring his view. His reticle traced over the dark silhouette of the interceptor, fleetingly aligning with the white glow of exhausts. The Nomad stayed his hand, the interceptor lurching out of alignment before he could get a shot off.

The Nomad closed in, coaxing the Fighter tighter in on the interceptor's tail as they hurtled through the hazy downpour. Fighting the wind, he pressed up, zeroing in on the interceptor's blind spot.

He glimpsed at the countdown: Thirty-two seconds.

He fired. Miss.

Twenty-nine seconds.

He just needed a break in the weather. He fired. Miss.

Twenty-five seconds.

The glaze of water whipped suddenly off the

canopy. The Fighter had pierced through the eyewall of the storm into a vortex of calm at the heart of the tempest. Target lock. He pulled the trigger, firing a long burst of plasma. The Fighter vibrated as the railguns thundered, a stream of toroids blasting from their muzzles.

Hit!

Striking the white blaze of the interceptor's thrusters, the salvo drilled into their target. A blinding glare flashed ahead of the Nomad, the Fighter's photochromatic glass darkening against the light of the explosion. An instant later, the glare died away. The canopy reclarified and the Nomad gazed ahead.

The interceptor was gliding silently through the eye of the storm, exhausts dark and lifeless. Seconds later, a torrent of black smoke issued from the machine's rear, its nose slowly dipping as it began to descend.

Pulling up to avoid being blinded in the smoke trail, the Nomad watched from above as the interceptor sank quickly into a nosedive. Suddenly, the Cerberus began to corkscrew, plummeting out of control, vanishing as it plunged into the waves in a mushroom of white water.

The Nomad had done it. He had shot down the interceptor.

Coasting on the wind, he issued a sigh of relief and watched the swell swallow the machine, when suddenly, a crimson glare carved down from above. The Fighter shuddered. Alarms knelled throughout the cockpit. The sea and sky inverted. Now it was the Fighter that was nose-diving towards the ocean. The Nomad pulled back on the flightstick, wrestling back control as he levelled out.

He'd been shot! The streak of laser had come from above. Impossible! He checked the timer. It ticked passed fifteen seconds. He hadn't run out of time. But it did not matter. Cerberus backup was inbound all the same.

FIFTY-TWO

Lightning glared through the typhoon as the Nomad scanned the skies for his assailant. Pitching up into an ascending corkscrew, he watched his instruments go haywire. A trio of red eyes illuminated through the murk, and as thunder clapped the Nomad sighted a vee of silhouettes outlined in the storm. An instant later, a second interceptor erupted through the eyewall, flanked by a pair of accompanying drones.

Swerving out of his turn, the Nomad hit the thruster and skewered through another collar of vapour, the air rupturing in successive sonic booms as the Fighter rocketed back into the hurricane with the vee of Cerberus in hot pursuit. Rain slicked back across the canopy as the winds picked up and buffeted the Fighter about in the storm. Dropping out of the cloud ceiling, the Nomad accelerated, eyeing the rear-view overlay across his canopy as three crimson eyes drifted into focus.

Hurtling above the waves, the Nomad continued to flee, the Cerberus giving chase. Red glared to the rear, and suddenly, the air was aflame with crisscrossing laser beams. Rolling and banking in the turbulent air currents, the Nomad avoided immolation time after time as the Cerberus rays continued to carve narrowly past.

The storm began to wane, and up ahead, sea cliffs rose above the horizon, the coastline of the next continent hurtling into view. Soaring over a blur of cliffsides, the Nomad sped towards an oncoming sierra of snow-capped mountains. Hugging the terrain as near to the ground as he dared, the Nomad pitched up with the topography, climbing rapidly up the snow-blanketed slopes towards the peaks ahead.

A ray of laser streaked passed the Nomad's wing as he spun into a roll, flipping the Fighter into a snaking valley below. Canting his head back, the Nomad glimpsed the interceptor cruising above, its crimson optics flashing with each beam of fire that burned the Nomad's way. Rearward, the drones had broken formation, dogging the Nomad as he tried to shake them from his tail.

Out in the open, outnumbered and outgunned, the Nomad stood little chance. His only hope was to use the terrain for cover. Shooting down all three of his pursuers was an impossible task. He had to run. He had to escape.

Summiting the peaks, the Nomad swooped downwards, diving over the mountain ridge just as two parallel rays blazed above the canopy. Careening downhill, the Nomad hugged the slopes even tighter, the occasional bristling treetop clipping the Fighter's undercarriage as it hurtled past.

Glancing either side, the Nomad sighted the drones pressing in on his flanks. Allowing them to close in tighter, he suddenly deployed the Fighter's airbrake. Elevons and slats locked out and the Nomad lurched forwards in his seat. The drones shot past down the mountainside and the Nomad kicked the thruster back up to full, accelerating hard after them to give chase. The tables had turned, the Nomad now becoming the hunter and the Cerberus the hunted.

Pitching back into a climb, the drones raced towards a saddle in the ridge, tearing between two peaks as they dove back down into the valley beyond. The Nomad sped after them, nearly clipping the mountaintop as he skimmed the ridge and gave chase through a meandering gorge. Wrestling with the flightstick as the drones wove side to side ahead of him, the Nomad traced his reticle towards the nearer of the pair.

Squeezing his trigger, he sent a salvo of plasma careening down the mountainside. The drone swerved, dodging the shots, but clipping the second machine in the process. The drone the Nomad had taken aim at pitched skyward as it rebounded in the collision, soaring back out of the ravine, but the second was knocked off course and sent swerving into the craggy wall of the gorge. Rebounding off the cliffside in a shower of dust and debris, the drone drifted suddenly into the Nomad's crosshairs.

Without hesitation, the Nomad took the shot. His railguns drummed, and a hail of plasma flew down the gorge ahead. Striking a bullseye, the fusillade drilled into the drone's glowing exhaust port. A detonation of white heat lit up the ravine, and as the flash died away, the drone plummeted out of the air, ricocheting off the walls of the chasm, before a secondary explosion vaporised the machine's husk when its self-destruct sequence triggered.

Pitching into a steep climb, the Nomad accelerated to try and get clear of the blast radius, racing back up to hypersonic speeds with a cascade of sonic booms at his rear. A mushroom cloud erupted behind, searing heat radiating throughout the Fighter's cockpit before suddenly, hit by an electromagnetic pulse emitted in the explosion, the Fighter went dark.

With a terrifying stutter, the Fighter's instruments cut out and the engines stalled. For a brief moment, the Nomad was coasting silently on the wind, but an instant later, the shockwave from the explosion struck the Fighter, swatting it clean out of the air, sending the Nomad plummeting towards the ground with no engines and no controls.

Spinning in a dizzying corkscrew, the Nomad gazed down in horror as the rugged mountainside raced up to meet him. The Nomad jostled the flightstick to no effect. Everything was dead. Panicking, he flicked dozens of switches across the control panel. Nothing! He didn't have much farther to fall. The ground was closing fast. Gritting his teeth, he braced for impact.

Suddenly, the holographic displays surrounding the Nomad flared with static and the Fighter began to reboot. The Nomad flicked the ignition. Nothing. He flicked it again. Still nothing. The ground was hurtling towards him in a revolving blur. He flicked the ignition again. The rockets flared to life. Jamming the thruster forwards, a jet of fire erupted from the Fighter's tail.

Launched back in his seat, the Nomad wrenched rearward on the controls, pulling up mere seconds before impact. Squashed into his chair by the immense g-force of the manoeuvre, the Nomad felt the muscles of his face contort and the blood flow to his head dwindle. His weight momentarily increased by a factor of ten as his vision greyed and tunnelled in a dizzying moment of sickening disorientation. The mountainside blurred past the Fighter's nose, suddenly replaced by open sky as the pressure of the turn eased off and the Nomad rocketed back into the heavens.

A vee shaped silhouette suddenly eclipsed the sun above as the interceptor soared directly overhead. Through some freak chance, the Nomad's death-defying nosedive and recovery had delivered the Cerberus directly into his crosshairs.

He squeezed the trigger. The Fighter's railgun howled, but in that same instant, red light glared across the canopy. The Fighter lurched violently. The ship's targeting reticle flung out wide and the guns fell quiet.

The Nomad had been hit again, this time by the drone he'd lost sight of. His attention focussed solely on the interceptor, he'd been taken by surprise. The drone hurtled passed, banking as it swerved back around for another attack run, but the Nomad was still climbing, and the interceptor was still directly above. He corrected his aim, realigning his sights back over the interceptor. He still had a few seconds before the drone would have a clear shot at him again. The Nomad pulled the trigger. Silence. He pulled the trigger again. Nothing. His guns weren't firing! He looked down to see a dozen error messages and warnings flashing across his displays. His weapons had been completely disabled.

He was disarmed. Defanged. Weaponless. Stuck facing down two of the most dangerous adversaries in the universe utterly unarmed. In seconds, he would be in the line of fire again. It had all been a trap. The interceptor had baited him, offering itself up as an easy target, knowing full well its armour could absorb the hit, all to lure the Nomad into an attack run, leaving himself exposed. It had worked. He *was* exposed. And now he was defenceless. All he could do was flee.

The Nomad jabbed the throttle to maximum.

The Fighter's rockets surged with flame as it shot upwards into a vertical climb. The drone fired. A beam of laser carved narrowly passed the Fighter's tail. The silhouette of the interceptor expanded as the Nomad charged towards its undercarriage. The drone pitched up after him in chase. The Nomad pulled back. The Fighter skimmed millimetres passed the interceptor's wing, shooting upwards as it raced into the stratosphere. Faced with a crash with the interceptor, the drone swerved away, momentarily abandoning its chase.

The Nomad had bought himself a few precious seconds. He continued to ascend, his rockets roaring at full thrust, carrying him higher and higher into the atmosphere. He had to get to orbit. He had to make the jump to FTL. It was his only chance.

The whole cockpit shuddered and vibrated as the Fighter fought its way into the mesosphere. The air began to thin and the vibrations quickly subsided. The Fighter accelerated harder, no longer hindered by the fluids of the atmosphere. The sky darkened and the horizon curved away on all sides. He was in orbit.

The Nomad killed thrust to the Fighter's chemical engines, feeling his weight suddenly vanish as he entered a microgravity environment for the first time in over three years. His fingers frenziedly moved across the controls, flicking countless buttons and switches as he toggled over to the

Fighter's arc and pulsejets.

A beam of crimson flashed silently over the Nomad's canopy. The drone and interceptor were inbound, now in orbit themselves above the golden world as they continued to pursue him. Controls switched over, the Nomad shoved forwards on the thruster. Matter and antimatter annihilated in the pulsejets and the Nomad was flung back into his chair again as the Fighter accelerated rapidly to escape velocity.

Crimson rays streaked narrowly passed as the Nomad booted up the navigation and flight computers. Pivoting the flightstick in erratic jerks back and forth, the Nomad took evasive manoeuvres, dodging the incoming fire as he blindly thumbed at the nearest star available to him, heedless of the data on display. Continuing to veer this way and that, his enemies closing in with every passing second, the Nomad anxiously awaited the incoming superluminal flight calculations. Finally, they pinged in, and the Nomad jabbed at the fastest flight path on offer. Head pounding and vision blurred by the shifting g-force, the Nomad straightened up, aligning with the parabolic flightpath projecting across the canopy.

Crimson light flared violently around the Fighter as the nebula swung into view, its vivid spectrum of colours smeared out of focus by the eclipsing wormhole dead in front of it. The Nomad forced the thrusters towards maximum and flung open the protective cover for the FTL controls. Clasping the black and yellow lever, he engaged the warp drive.

Out in front, the stars dilated and unfocussed, the Fighter's mass plummeting as it accelerated faster and faster up the energy exponential towards superluminal speeds. Red light blurred across the lens distortion. The Fighter shuddered. He'd been hit. The cockpit shook again. Another hit.

The Fighter rocked violently a third time, and the Nomad suddenly flopped forwards in his seat. The pulsejets had cut out. The stars ahead of the Fighter's nose condensed rapidly back into focus. The warp drive had disengaged. The nebula scudded across the canopy as the Fighter began to tumble.

A tumult of alarms and buzzers were roaring throughout the cockpit. Snapped suddenly back to his senses, the Nomad seized hold of the controls and tried to steady the Fighter. Nothing happened. He wiggled the flightstick in desperation, but it had gone limp. All of his controls were completely unresponsive. The Fighter continued to spin helplessly, tumbling end over end at a mere fraction of lightspeed.

Red optics revolved into view. The interceptor was closing in on him. He had only seconds left. His controls were dead. The Fighter was dead. And if he didn't eject in the next few seconds, he would be dead also.

Lunging for the handle beneath his seat, the Nomad seized hold of the ejector. Hesitating, he glanced up as a glaring crimson eye bore down on him from above. Yanking upwards, the Nomad pulled hard on the ejector lever. The canopy exploded away from the Fighter, plunging the Nomad into sudden silence as the vacuum of space collapsed inward around him. An instant later, an explosion detonated beneath him, shuddering up his spine as the rocket motor in his seat fired.

The pilot seat ejected, propelling the Nomad rapidly clear. Drifting silently through the vacuum, the Nomad watched the Fighter recede beneath him, shrinking into the backdrop of constellations. A red flash glared against the stars as the interceptor fired. A thin beam of crimson light carved distantly through the dark, followed immediately by a blinding glare of white.

The Fighter vanished, consumed in an antimatter detonation as the fuel in the breached tanks was annihilated. The blast flared into a white inferno, swallowing the interceptor as it grew, swallowing the drone soon after, and finally, swallowing the Nomad.

Everything went dark.

EPILOGUE

The Nomad was alone. He opened his eyes. He was drifting silently through space. Below him, the golden world receded as a tiny pinprick of light. The Fighter had been completely obliterated, taking the Cerberus drone and the interceptor along with it. The Nomad had just made it clear of the blast radius.

Gazing overhead, he watched the cream and violet clouds of the nebula swirl and blend together as they melted around the circumference of the wormhole. The tunnel through time and space was looming ever larger as the Nomad drifted gradually closer. He could make out constellations shining through from the other side, with more steadily drifting into his ever-widening field of view the nearer he floated. It was a window to the unknown. A gateway to an entirely different region of the universe.

The Fighter was gone. His home destroyed. And the golden world was drifting steadily away. Using the directional thrusters on the ejector seat, it would perhaps be possible for the Nomad to make his way back to it. But that would take weeks. He was too far out, moving away too fast to realistically return to the utopian world. And even if he could make it back to orbit, he would almost certainly burn up if he attempted an atmospheric re-entry. But even if his EVA suit could resist the temperatures and pressure, and the ejector seat's parachute managed to deploy, what then? He would be stranded on the world without a biomatter re-combinator, condemned to the same fate as the Traveller.

The Nomad knew what was behind him. Now, his only option was what lay ahead. His one chance at survival was to pass through the worm-hole. It would be dangerous. He had no way of know-ing what passing through the tunnel in spacetime would do to him. He didn't know where, or even when, the passage led. And there was no possible way of telling what awaited him on the other side. It could be a new system, ripe with rich and luscious worlds, or equally, it could lead nowhere but empty interstellar space. But someone or something must have created it. Something was powering it, keeping it open, so that the two points in the universe re-mained permanently linked.

The Nomad was drifting directly towards it, its aperture steadily widening. It was calling him; beckoning him to pass through. It was the ultimate leap into the unknown. He had no guarantees of survival. He had no guarantees anything would be awaiting him on the other side. But that did not mat-ter. The Nomad was an explorer. He had seen more of the universe than he had ever thought possible. The golden world was but one stop in his never-ending journey. It had never been his destination.

The wormhole continued to grow, swelling until it eclipsed the nebula entirely. But as his view of the universe on this side of the wormhole vanished, the Nomad was granted ever wider horizons from the far side. Countless stars and galaxies twinkled beyond in the endless void of eternity. He was on the precipice. Any minute now he would cross over the threshold to the other side and continue on to the final leg of his eternal journey. In mere seconds, he would be swallowed by the universe itself. For the first time, he felt he truly understood the boundlessness of time and space. This was it. This was the end. But it was also the beginning. It was just one part of a forever looping cycle. It was flight through infinity.

ACKNOWLEDGEMENT

Though science fiction has always been my greatest passion, this is my first venture into writing the genre. Physics was always my favourite subject at school , but for reasons even I don't understand, I opted to study biomedical science at university instead. Though I've long been acquainted with the basic ideas of special relativity, getting my head around Lorentz transformations and all manner of other mind-bending concepts required to write this book was something of a puzzle. I'd like to thank my A-level physics teacher, and pretty much my favourite teacher in general, Luke Waller, for looking over Flight Through Infinity back in its early raw stages, to make sure I hadn't made any embarrassingly blatant scientific errors. To my pleasant surprise, he was also a fan of the story!
Whilst I'm sure he'll never admit it, I was undoubtedly his favourite pupil. Plus, I did get that 'A' in the end, after all! I know he was disappointed I didn't go onto study Physics for my degree, but hopefully this book has gone some way towards making up for it.

BOOKS BY THIS AUTHOR

Rise Of The Apostate

Rhys North awakens to find that his village has fallen prey to a dark curse. All life and colour has been sapped from the land and every single inhabitant of Longford has perished during the night; all except Rhys.
Amidst the ruin, Rhys comes upon a mysterious stranger named Arlas, the leader of the Circle of Magi, an ancient order of magical warriors sworn to the protection of the continent of Cambria. Driven by the need to uncover the truth behind the fate of his village, Rhys embarks on a journey to join the Circle of Magi, yet in doing so, he becomes entangled in cataclysmic events that threaten peace across the continent.
Thrust to the forefront of a conflict that has been building for centuries, Rhys is forced to seek out long lost stone circles that reside in every forgotten corner of Cambria, in a desperate attempt to save the world from a fanatical mage of unspeakable power.

Dawn Of Tyranny

Rhys North and his companions find themselves in Orthios, the once capital of the Cambrian Empire, in search of another stone circle to restore the Nexus. But the so called 'City of the Gods,' is a dangerous place. Orthios is on the brink of revolt, and their presence has not gone unnoticed. In his attempts to seek retribution against the traitorous mage Indus Mark, Rhys finds himself caught at the heart of a long-brewing political struggle between the city's Council of High Lords, whilst targeted by a mysterious religious cult known as the Church of Ashes.
With war looming, and Indus's influence growing ever more powerful throughout the continent, Rhys once again finds himself at the heart of world changing events, unsure who to trust, yet determined to stand against the tyranny of his enemies.

Beyond The Brink

Rhys North's journey continues as he and his companions sail beyond the Brink of the World, into the heart of the perilous Wyrm's Triangle, to the mythical Stormy Isles.
Having narrowly escaped Indus and his followers in both Orthios and Westport, Rhys and the others set sail for Thule in search of the next conduit. Reaching the shores of the Stormy Isles seems an impossible task in and of itself, as past the Brink of the World, the laws of nature break down. But onboard the White Marlin, with the help of Captain Arne Anderssen and his sons, Rhys and the others stand

their best chance of making landfall in a part of the world lost to time.

An eternal tempest, a leviathan of the deep, and a spectral cavalcade roaming the skies all stand in the way of Rhys and his task, but with the aid of his friends and the ancient inhabitants of Thule, he will ascend the slopes of Sumeru in search of the lost stone circle.

Printed in Great Britain
by Amazon